WRONG TURN
Right Direction

ALSO BY ELLE CASEY

ROMANCE

The Bourbon Street Boys (4-book series)
By Degrees
Rebel Wheels (3-book series)
Just One Night (romantic serial)
Just One Week
Love in New York (3-book series)
Shine Not Burn (2-book series)
Desperate Measures
Mismatched

ROMANTIC SUSPENSE

All the Glory
Don't Make Me Beautiful
Wrecked (2-book series)

PARANORMAL

Duality (2-book series)
Pocket Full of Sunshine (short story & screenplay)

CONTEMPORARY URBAN FANTASY

War of the Fae (10-book series)
Ten Things You Should Know About Dragons
(short story in The Dragon Chronicles)
My Vampire Summer
Aces High

DYSTOPIAN

Apocalypsis (4-book series)

SCIENCE FICTION

Drifters' Alliance (3-book series)
Winner Takes All (short story prequel to Drifters' Alliance in Dark Beyond the Stars Anthology)

To keep up to date with Elle's latest releases, please visit www.ElleCasey.com

To get an email when Elle's next book is released, sign up here: http://www.ElleCasey.com/news

The Bourbon Street Boys, Book 4

WRONG TURN
Right Direction

ELLE CASEY

Montlake
Romance

Published by Montlake Romance Publishing, Seattle

www.apub.com

Amazon, the Amazon logo, and Montlake Romance Publishing are trademarks of Amazon.com, Inc., or its affiliates.

ISBN-13: 9781477848715
ISBN-10: 1477848711

Cover design by Lisa Horton

Printed in the United States of America

To Sidney
I'm not sure who rescued whom, really, but I sure am
glad we found each other.

CHAPTER ONE

"Where are you going?" Pavel asks me, looking up from the couch in his warehouse office. I've known this man for six years and worked as his employee for five, but does that stop me from being scared to death at the sound of his voice? *Hell, no.*

I hike my purse up higher on my shoulder. "Just going to see the doctor." I rub my hand over my massively bloated belly. My indigestion has been getting worse every day; I swear to God, sometimes it feels like I'm going to explode. The stress of living a double life is slowly killing me. Even my ankles are puffy.

"What doctor?"

"Uhhh . . ." I have no immediate answer for him because I'm lying through my teeth. I don't have a doctor's appointment, even though I could probably use one. I finished another bottle of Tums at my desk this morning. The empty container sits next to the computer, its large, antacid-dusted interior reminding me that I've ingested about five pounds of what I suspect to be merely flavored chalk in just the last week.

"The one over on . . . Oak Street?" I hope there's a medical office somewhere over there in case Pavel decides to check up on me.

"He is a good doctor?"

I can't tell with his crazy-ass Russian accent and that lazy smile he's got whether Pavel really gives a crap about the quality of my medical care or if he's baiting me. One can never tell for sure with him. He catches people unawares all the time, and when that happens, watch out—time to call in the blood-splatter expert. After several misjudgments on my part and more bruises than I care to remember, I've learned my lesson. Pavel will never blindside me again. Now I always assume the worst, and if I'm wrong, I celebrate with a good, stress-relieving cry. There are always tears with Pavel, but sometimes they're the good kind: the hell-yeah-I-didn't-die-today kind.

"We'll see." I hesitate at the door, ignoring my instinct to run like hell. It's never good to let him see fear, because he feeds on it. It excites him, not just mentally but sexually. "Do you need anything while I'm out?"

He purses his lips, staring at me for the longest time, slowly nodding. "Yeah. Get me a coffee. And get yourself something diet to drink. No sugar. You're getting fat."

My brain stops working for a second as I process this strange request tied up with an insult. Pavel doesn't drink coffee. He drinks only Vitaminwater and vodka, being the quintessential Russian metrosexual gangster that he is. And since when does he talk about my weight? Never. He's definitely baiting me. A chill runs through me. *Does he know what I've done?*

I have to play along and act dumb. I have no choice. He's right about the fact that I've gained a few pounds, but that's his fault for being a psychotic asshole who makes me stress-eat. My revenge is going to be so sweet. I'm going to eat a giant, jelly-glazed donut to celebrate it too, once I've put my plan into action. He's got a lot of nerve calling me fat when his head is so big it can barely fit through the door.

"Okaaaay . . . What kind of coffee?" I ask. "From anywhere in particular?"

"No special kind. No special place. You decide. And make sure it is a *good* one." His smile is sinister now.

My heart races. This is a test. He's going to find a way to mess me up over this because he's in one of his moods. What in the hell qualifies as a good coffee to an asshole like Pavel? I have no idea. And therein lies the trap.

"Yeah, sure, no problem. Can do." I give him my biggest smile, which is secret code for *One day I'm going to get you for this, you bastard.*

He laughs. "You are a good girl, Tamika. I can trust you to take good care of me, yes?"

I walk through the door as I answer, bitterness boiling inside me. "Always, Pavel. Always."

CHAPTER TWO

"Get me a coffee . . . You're getting fat . . . No sugar for you . . . Who in the hell does he think he is?" I'm mumbling in my car all the way back from the police station where nothing at all happened, since Detective Holloway wasn't in and didn't bother to tell anyone where he'd be. *Jerk.* His no-phone-call policy is a serious pain in the behind.

"Pavel can kiss my big butt. I'm not his slave. I'm not his servant. I keep his books, that's it. And I do a damn good job of it too, thank you very much. But does that mean anything to him? No. He's going to mess with my head just because he's bored or he's mad at someone else." I am so sick and tired of being everyone's whipping boy. Or whipping girl.

"Oh, shoot. *Jesus*, that hurts." I rub my belly, the acid indigestion kicking up big-time. I forgot to buy more Tums. I need to go do that after I get his stupid coffee. I can't believe I'm stressing so hard over a hot beverage. I'm a college graduate; buying coffee should not be such a challenge for someone like me.

"Okay, that's enough of that negativity." I grip the steering wheel as the latest intestinal cramp moves through my bowels, making me break out in the cold sweat of pain. "Time to be positive. Power of positive thinking, right? Hmm, what can I say that's positive?" I wait for the traffic light to turn green as I mine my brain for something happy going on in my life. "Oh, I know!" I hold up my finger as the lightbulb goes on. I think the rest of it in my head instead of talking out loud to myself because who knows . . . maybe Pavel has had my car bugged. *The one positive thing I have going on in my life right now is I got all of Pavel's financials backed up onto the cloud and put that software program in there to code everything and cover my ass, so when Detective Holloway finally gets his butt back in to work, I'll be getting the heck out of Pavel's hellhole and starting my new life.* Boom. Positivity engaged.

Once I work out my final deal with the police and get me some of that witness protection and a new identity, I will be outta here. Goodbye, New Orleans, and screw you for everything you never did for me. I'll be on the road to my new life, and Pavel will be off to prison for the rest of his.

Booyah. Screw with me and see what happens, Pavel. Ha! I feel so empowered right now. I'm also terrified. I will soon be divulging all the secrets and accounting records of a high-level Russian Bratva member, "The *Vor*" as his lackeys like to call him—The Thief—which seems innocuous enough, but it means a whole lot more than stealing *things*, in Russian; it means stealing *lives* too. I know for a fact that Pavel has stolen more than ten of them because he likes to brag. He also likes to remind me how much power he has over my life. That's what this stupid coffee is all about, probably.

The light turns green and my mind snaps back to my more immediate concern: Where am I going to get a "good" coffee, delicious enough to satisfy the Devil himself? I look left and right, and a flashing neon coffee mug catches my eye. I don't know this area of town well, but I know a coffee shop when I see one, and all the tables outside of it are full of people. "Jackpot."

I ignore the people honking behind me as I turn right. They're just jealous of my slick driving maneuvers. So what if my tire scraped the side of the curb a little; nobody can shift through the gears as smoothly as I can. My little Toyota might be old, but it's still a well-oiled machine. I've turned down Pavel's offer of a new car at least five times. I don't want to be beholden to him any more than I already am. Everything Pavel gives comes with strings. Besides, my car has almost zero electronics in it, which means Pavel can't hack into any navigation systems to find me. He has way too much technology at his disposal. That's also why I still use a flip phone.

A woman is waving at me from the sidewalk and frowning, yelling something rude, probably. Racial tensions have been high in the city lately, so maybe she's one of those redneck rabble-rousers who judges people by their skin color. I ignore her, not wanting to make things worse than they already are. I'll be leaving New Orleans soon, but it doesn't mean I want the place to fall apart behind me.

I need to keep a low profile now that I'm so close to being free. The last thing I need is to get into an altercation with some random woman and get arrested. Pavel would watch me like a hawk after I made bail, and he's already observant enough. Putting his data on the cloud was a life-threatening maneuver that had to have been touched by God himself to go as smoothly as it did. I don't want to press my luck and ask the Big Man for any more favors. Just the thought of Pavel questioning me about why I got arrested and what I might have said to the cops gives me another intestinal cramp.

I grip the steering wheel hard and focus on the Lotta Java sign coming up on my right. Everybody's looking at me, alerted by that woman who's still yelling. I can't hear a word she's saying with my window up and the air-conditioning on, but I'm sure I don't want to. *Haters gonna hate.* I'm going to ask some of those people sitting outside the coffee shop to recommend a good coffee drink for me to bring back to Pavel. Maybe I'll get lucky and he'll actually like it enough to forget to come after me about whatever's bugging him.

I frown as my stomach lurches again. Pain shoots through my entire bottom half. "Oh, shit," I say, grabbing my belly. I look down for a second and watch as it actually moves . . . It's like there's an alien in there. Although I've felt plenty of them, I've never seen an actual gas bubble move through my belly before. *Maybe it's a tumor.*

Suddenly there's a loud boom at the front of my car. I slam on my brakes without thinking and look up, my heart racing. I see nothing at first, and then there's this guy appearing out of nowhere from the street in front of my Toyota.

"What the hell!" he yells at me, his face beet red. He's leaning on the hood of my car, and that's when it hits me: *Oh, shit.* That man ran out in front of me! What kind of idiot does that?!

"Oh my god *damn!*" I pump my window down using its flywheel handle. "What're you thinking, walking out into the middle of the road like that?" I yell at him. "Are you drunk or what?" I glance over at the Lotta Java, wondering why they'd serve Irish coffees so early in the morning. There has to be a law against that.

The man is glaring at me, obviously not that hurt since he's standing there showing off his fine body. And he might be cute as all get-out with that face and those muscles of his, wearing those tight jeans, but that doesn't make it okay for him to act like he's got the right to be angry. He's the dummy who walked out into the road and hit my car with his big old muscly body. My car is bright green and impossible to miss. Even little kids know to look both ways before crossing the street. He's probably one of those insurance claim scammers, working the system to sue me and get a payday out of it.

"Lady, you just *hit* me!" He rests his hand on his thigh as he leans over, breathing hard and mumbling things that might be cuss words. And then a couple seconds later, he straightens and starts limping over to my window. He's totally faking, I know he is.

"You're crazy is what you are." I scramble for my purse, panicked because he looks angry and I'm stuck in this car with stomach cramps that are about to kill me. I'm fearing a loss of bladder control more than the man's temper at this point, though. The pressure down there is unbelievable. *Screw the coffee. I'm going to the doctor's office. Pavel can wait.*

I roll my window down the rest of the way. This guy doesn't scare me one bit. I eat breakfast, lunch, and dinner with Russian mobsters, so this muscle-bound gym rat with his tight T-shirt and pointy boots is nothing. "You better stay back," I warn, glaring at him.

He keeps limping my way.

"Don't you come over here thinking you're gonna manhandle me. I have Mace and I'm not afraid to use it." I hold up a can of mosquito spray at him, the only thing toxic I happen to be carrying today. Hopefully he won't know the difference.

He points at a black-and-white sign on the corner that I have to squint to see because it's so far away. "This is a one-way street, lady, and you're going the wrong direction on it. You hit me! Practically ran me right over!" He hops on one leg. "You messed up my knee bad."

Oh, damn. He's right; it is a one-way street and there're a bunch of cars coming toward me from the other direction. And he does look a little hurt. But damn, he just walked out in front of my car! I might've made a wrong turn, but he's the dummy who walked out into the road without looking. It's his fault he's hurt, not mine. If Pavel catches wind of this, he'll want to know what I was doing so close to the police station when I was supposed to be at the doctor's. I need to get the hell out of here.

I twist my lips as my plan comes together. I can sell this. I'm a seriously good actress when I need to be. "Who do you think you are, calling me *lady*? Claiming *I* hit *you*? Are you for real? I didn't hit you. *You* hit *my* car. Walked right into it. I've got witnesses, so don't even try to play that game with me." I glance at the crowd of people gathering on the curb. I believe I see supporters in there, some of them smiling. I raise my voice so everyone can hear me. My pulse pounds at my neck and my insides twist harder.

"You should be using a cane with a red tip on it if your eyesight's so bad you can't see a big old green car coming down the street right in front of you." I sit up straighter and look out over my steering wheel, inspecting the hood of my car. "You probably damaged my bumper. Scratched the paint too." I look at him with narrowed eyes. "But I'm going to let that slide today because I'm in a hurry."

I gesture with a sweeping motion, encouraging him to step back. "Move outta my way. I have somewhere to be, like *bystro* . . . like now." The stress is hitting me hard enough that I'm dropping Russian words, and I never do that if I can help it. Panic is taking over. I have to breathe in short bursts to control it: "Hah-hah-hee! Hah-hah-hee!"

He looks at me funny.

I open my mouth to say something else, but then stop immediately and wince, putting my hand on my stomach. The pain is . . . *holy hell . . . Am I dying?* I think I could possibly be dying. "Oh, Jesus, Mary, and Joseph . . ." I'm sweating like a pig all of a sudden. I smell something metallic coming from my body. I feel something warm between my legs. *Holy mother of all that is holy, I just wet myself.* "What in the hell is happening?!" I yell, looking down at my body and then at the man staring at me from outside my window.

My vision goes blurry with pain, my brain swimming with confusion and fear as my head drops back against the seat. Cars ahead of me are honking and people are videotaping us with their phones. The angry man is still in my window and acting like he's not going anywhere, and I don't know if my mosquito spray is going to work to drive him away. *Why is this happening?!* That's all I need . . . Pavel catching wind of this via some crazy video one of these Lotta Java freaks puts on the Internet.

"Where're you going in such a hurry?" the guy asks, moving closer to my window.

I have to grunt the words out past the pain. "None of your damn business is where I'm going." I glare up at him, beyond annoyed that he can't understand plain English. "Do you mind?" I move my stare to his hand that's resting on my window.

He opens his mouth to say something, but I can't focus on him anymore. Death is too near. "Ohhhh, Lord have mercy on my soul." My eyes roll up into my head, and I grip the steering wheel so hard my fingers go numb. My insides are exploding. I should have bought those Tums first thing instead of waiting. Now I'm going to lose my bowels in front of a complete stranger, who on any other day would have had me dreaming about going out on a date.

"What's going on?" he asks.

I look at him, desperation and pain bringing tears to my eyes. No words will come out, only the crazy breathing that's keeping the pain from totally taking over my brain. "Ha-ha-*hee*! Ha-ha-*hee*!"

He puts both hands on the windowsill and leans in, looking at me so closely, he'll surely be able to see the freckles I try to hide with my foundation. He opens his mouth and says the craziest, most ridiculous thing I've ever heard:

"I don't mean to be rude, ma'am, but are you having a baby right now?"

CHAPTER THREE

"No, no, no-no-no," I moan, shaking my head to clear it. This is not happening. This is NOT happening! I'm not pregnant! I can't be!

The man reaches into my window and puts his hand on my sweaty forehead.

I reach up instinctively and slap him away. "*Get* your paws off me!" I glare at him, almost wishing I had a gun to wave in his face. "Who said you could touch my person?"

He looks at me like I'm stupid. "Relax, I was just checking your temperature."

People are gathering on the sidewalk to gawk. I'm glad I have witnesses. I raise my voice again so they'll be sure to hear me.

"Relax? You're telling me to . . . No. Huh-uh. That's not happening. Not today. I'm going to call the cops on you. That's assault." I just want him to go away so I can leave. I'll drive up on the sidewalk to get around those damn cars in front of me if I have to. My body is failing, and I need to make sure it happens somewhere private because I'm certain it's not going to be pretty. My entire seat is soaked with something that smells too awful to contemplate.

"Actually, it's not assault, it's battery," he says, like a cocky jerk, "but you haven't answered my question yet, so why don't you hold off on my arrest." He glances up at the people who look like they're watching a sporting event, before focusing on me again. "Are you having a baby? Are you in labor, I mean?"

My voice comes out like an animal's growl. I can't help it. "No, I'm not in . . . lay . . . boooooor!" I scream the last part and then pant, trying to keep from passing out. "Ho, ho, hee! Ho, ho, hee! Dang, that hurts!" Pain slices through me and grips me like an iron band around my middle.

The stranger pulls my door open and leans over me, his face just inches away. "Ma'am, you might not be in labor, but it sure seems to me that you're experiencing a medical emergency of some kind."

"Oh, yeah?" I half-whisper, wanting to punch him in the nose so bad, but too wracked by pain to do anything but hang on to the steering wheel. "And what're you gonna do about it?" An abdominal cramp seizes me, tearing a scream from my lips. "Ahhhhhh! Noooo!"

Next thing I know, he's unbuckling my seat belt and sliding his arms under my legs and behind my back. Then he lifts me out of my car like I'm no heavier than a feather.

"Not in labor, my ass," he growls, swinging me around to face the back of my car. "Call an ambulance!" he yells at the people standing nearby. He starts to walk, his gait uneven.

Out of the corner of my eye, I see more traffic backing up in front of my car. And he's leaving my Toyota just sitting there in the middle of the street. It'll get towed and then I'll really be screwed. Pavel will find out everything. *Everything.* His interrogation methods are renowned in certain circles.

"Put me *down*, you Neanderthal!" I reach up to slap him, but have to stop in mid-swipe because of another slice of pain going through me. I grab his ear instead. "Oooooh, damn that hurts," I hiss. Warm liquid gushes out between my legs. The stranger's words come back to me. *Are you pregnant?* My heart stops beating for a few seconds.

Nooooooo . . . I can't be. Can I?

He tilts his head sideways. "The ear!" he yells. "Can I have it back?"

"Sorry." I let his ear go and grab his shirt, balling it into my fist as more pain hits me.

"She's having a baby!" a woman gasps.

"Shut up!" I yell. "I am not!" I squeeze his shirt again. "Ahhhhh! That hurts so bad!" I look up at the man carrying me, desperately needing him to hear and believe me. "It's just a bad bladder infection. Or indigestion. I had my gallbladder taken out . . . I have chronic indigestion. Seriously. All the time . . ." The pain comes again. "Hah, hah, hee!"

"Please step aside," he says to people in our way, limping up to the sidewalk.

"Where're you taking me?" I ask, barely able to get the words out. I feel wasted and weak. Scared and lost. In great danger and completely without control of my body or my life. This is not a place I can be in; I am truly fearing for my life, but I'm in so much pain, I can't do anything about it. I've never felt so vulnerable.

"Somewhere you can lie down."

"Not to be rude or anything," I pause to pant a few breaths in and out, "but I really need to find a restroom."

He shakes his head, saying nothing.

I open my mouth to yell at him for not listening to me, not doing what I want, which is to put me down and leave me alone, but the only thing that comes out of my mouth is a scream.

CHAPTER FOUR

The nail salon stinks of hazardous chemicals, an assault on my senses that instantly makes my nostrils flare, but all I care about is ending the pain. I'd let them pour that nail polish solvent down my throat if I thought it would take it away. My body feels like it's breaking in half at the waist.

"Hey! What you doing?" a tiny Asian woman yells with a heavy accent as she shuffles on flip-flops toward us.

"I need one of your massage chairs," the man carrying me says. When he swings me around, three come into view, lined up in the back corner of the room.

The salon owner is shaking her head. "No! No! Those for paying customers only!"

"I'll pay," he says, limping past her and stopping at the first chair. He slowly lowers me into it.

I grab the armrests, lifting myself as much as I can, grateful to be put down onto a non-moving surface. That limping around was killing me. My insides calm for a moment and I breathe a sigh of relief. "Thanks," I say, wincing as I try to adjust myself. Everything inside me is tender, and my clothing is soaked through with sweat and God knows what else.

Several people have followed us into the salon. The business owner starts yelling again. "Nobody in here without nail job! You want nail job, you come in! You don't want nail job, you go out!"

"I want a nail job," a woman says, rushing over to take one of the other massage chairs.

"Me, too," says a young guy peeling himself off from the crowd, filming the entire thing. He stumbles over a cart of supplies on his way to the last seat, making a horrible racket.

The owner of the salon is holding one of those collapsible, Victorian-style fans, threatening to beat people with it if they come any farther into the room.

"Call 9-1-1!" the man hovering over me yells at her. He puts his hand on my arm and says softly, "Don't worry. Help is on the way." It's the tone in his voice and the expression on his face that get me; he's not here to hurt me. He really wants to help. And damn, do I need it.

Clarity comes like a lightning bolt out of the sky delivered right to my brain, and with it comes a feeling of dread like I've never experienced before, not even when Pavel was standing over me with a gun pointed at my face. I reach down and put my hand on my giant, round belly. This isn't indigestion or an ulcer or a problem created by a long-gone gallbladder. It's not me stress-eating myself into an extra ten pounds. I've been fooling myself for months, ignoring all the signs and forcing myself to believe my own lies because the truth was too horrible to consider: *I'm pregnant.* I'm having a baby and I'm having it now. The pressure builds instantly between my legs, and even though I've never been a mother, I know what it means.

"An ambulance is coming," he says, patting my hand.

"It's not gonna get here in time." Fear takes over, and I find myself slipping into a persona I do not recognize: I'm weak and scared to death, no longer certain I can take care of myself. I reach for the man and grab his arm. "Help me."

He pauses for several long seconds, first a look of panic and then one of confusion coming over his face before he finally nods. "What can I do?" He rests his hand on my leg.

"Take my pants off," I order. Then when I realize how strange that sounds, I temper it with, "But don't be getting any funny ideas."

"Right. Take your pants off and no funny ideas." He nods at me with a slight smile. "I can do that."

He struggles to do as I asked. I try to help him with the task, but we're still having a hard time. I'm too out of it with pain to realize why, but when he puts his hands under my big, flannel shirt, I remember.

"You have something holding your pants together," he says, examining it like a puzzle. He reaches down and pulls a knife out of his pocket, coming at me with it.

In my panicked state, I imagine he's a friend of Pavel's and he's going to declare his fealty to the Brotherhood by getting rid of this little problem: me.

"Oh, God, he's gonna cut me!" I grab the arms of the chair, trying to lift myself up. I have to get away, but I can't. The pain is too great, my belly now too heavy; it's weighing me down in the chair like an anchor.

He frowns at me and backs away. "No, I'm not!" He lowers his voice. "I'd never do that. I'm here to help you, not hurt you."

I stare at him, panting through the pain as he lowers the blade slowly to my belt. I watch it go, every single inch, waiting for him to flick his wrist to the side and jab me with it. I trust no one, not even this guy who carried me out of my car to safety and let me nearly pull his ear off.

"I'm just going to cut the string you have holding your pants closed."

"Oh, yeah, okay." Convinced I was gaining weight from all the stress-eating I was doing, I started tying my pants together with string at the button. I didn't want to buy new clothes when I knew my stress would be gone soon and I'd quickly lose the weight I'd gained. My panic recedes when I realize I'm not going to be a victim of his knife . . . only of my own stupidity. "You can cut that. Just don't cut me."

"I promise, I'll be really careful."

I rest my hand on his thick, muscled arm. It's warm . . . steady, as he does the job of releasing the waistband of my pants. It's the strangest thing to be lying here and letting a stranger use a knife so close to me; for so long, knives held by men near me have meant only one thing: pain. But as soon as my pants open, I feel relief.

"Oh, thank God." I let out a long sigh.

He dances around a little on one leg to readjust his position, wincing as he slides his knife back into his pocket.

My body tenses up as I feel another wave of pain coming at me. "Oh, God, something's happening." I squeeze his arm again, my nails digging into his skin. I can't help it. It feels like something inside me is going to break me in two.

He yanks on my pants, making quick work of getting them down to my ankles and off my legs even though they're soaked through. Odors waft up that aren't familiar to me, metallic and sour. *Ick.* I'd be embarrassed about this man being in such an intimate place doing such intimate things if I weren't in such agony. I hiss out each breath as the pressure grows, gripping my entire abdomen.

"Get me some towels," he barks out.

The woman sitting in the chair next to us jumps up to help.

As soon as she and the owner return, he arranges several towels under me, using a couple to cover me at the waist as well. I appreciate his attempt to allow me some modesty. Being naked from the waist down and dripping God knows what all over this Asian lady's chair and floor doesn't leave me with much.

"What's your name?" he asks, coming back up to my shoulder.

"Tamika. Just call me Mika." I try to smile but feel the expression on my face sliding into a grimace. "Oh, Jesus, Lord. Please don't let me die." I grab the front of his shirt, holding on for dear life.

He reaches up and holds my hand there, the warmth of his fingers and strength of his grip giving me the momentary sensation of safety. Then the pain comes again, slicing me into shreds.

I grip my belly with my free hand. It's now shaped into a hard ball. It's freaking me out to see and feel my body doing this without my active intellectual participation. The whole process has gotten away from me, throwing me down a dark road I can't see the end of. *What if there's something wrong with the baby? With my body? Will we both die?*

The pain is telling me, *Yes. You are about to die. Say goodbye to your life.*

I start to cry. I've been fighting to survive my whole life, and the thought that I could be taken out by childbirth when I've survived the Russian mafia is too much to handle. I've been alone for so long . . . What if I die and my baby survives? Then she'll be alone and it'll be all my fault!

"Oh, Jesus, I'm dying!" I look up at him. Desperate. Dying . . .

"You're not going to die. You're having a baby. Is there someone I can call for you? A husband? Partner? Friend?"

"No," I groan out, sweat pouring down my face and back, "don't call anyone. There's no one. Just me." The pressure between my legs is unreal. I squeeze my fist against his chest involuntarily. "Something's happening!"

"Sweetie, you'd better get down there and play catcher," the woman next to us says to the man.

"Righteous," says the kid filming. "Dude, she's having a baby in the *nail* salon."

The man leans close to my face. His hazel eyes are rimmed with the darkest, thickest eyelashes I've ever seen. His expression is steady. Determined. Fearless. I start to fade out, imagining what he sees with those eyes of his when he looks at me, knowing it's nothing good. How could it be?

"Mika, I need to check out the situation . . . see what's going on down there. You okay with that?" He puts his hand on my cheek, his touch pulling me from the hazy place I was in.

I blink to bring him into better focus. "What?"

"I need to go down to your . . . private area. Okay? I'm just going to look. I promise I won't hurt you."

"Just do what you have to do." I let go of him and take the arms of the chair, squeezing my eyes shut as I arch my back in pain. "Oooooooh, shiiiizzle!" I move my feet partway up the semi-reclined massage chair when the spasm passes, readying myself for the inevitable. It's happening. *This* is happening. I'm about to have a baby in this Godforsaken nail salon.

He positions himself near my feet, leaning awkwardly against the chair. "Can you open your legs a little?" he asks.

I part my knees, no longer embarrassed by a stranger seeing whatever there is to see down there. I just need it to be over with, and if he wants to help me get there, good for him. He can see it all as far as I'm concerned—my lady-v, my behind, my body turning itself inside out . . .

He leans down and winces.

"What is it?" I ask, scared by his expression, worried for the baby, worried I might have pooed on the Asian lady's chair.

He looks up and then around the salon, his eyebrows drawn together in concentration or concern, it's hard to tell which. I pant through the pain, staring at him, hoping he'll say something I can hang on to, something hopeful.

"It's go time." He races over to the sink, barely limping, washes his hands furiously, and then grabs a nearby stool and drags it over. He rubs his palms together and claps them loudly once. "Okay. Let's do this." He sits down and looks up at me. "Mika, I hate to break this to you, but you're definitely having a baby. I can see its head. We're almost there." His attention shifts to the space between my legs.

I have to lie back in the chair because the pain is coming again, and the urge to push is too great to ignore. I grip the arms of the chair. "I'm dying! I'm dying!" is all I can say, my head shaking left and right as I try to rid my body of the agony I'm enduring. "I'm dying."

"No, you're not," the woman at my shoulder says with a smile in her voice. "You're becoming a mom. Are you already a mom? Or is this your first?"

I seriously want to slap this woman, even though I know she's just trying to be nice.

"Just hold her hand," the man says. I'm grateful for his interference. Did he know my slapping hand was getting itchy? He winks at me before looking down at the space between my legs again. "Okay, Mika. Here we go . . . You ready?"

I shake my head as tears course down my cheeks. "No!"

He smiles, a charm I know he was born with shining out of every pore on his face. "That's okay. I'm ready enough for both of us. Now *push.*"

I feel a wave coming, a contraction designed to force this little human out of me, and I grab the arms of the chair, giving it everything I've got.

CHAPTER FIVE

"One more push and we'll have the head out." The stranger touches my knee as his other hand hovers down below. I pray he's going to catch the baby before it slides down the massage chair and lands on the floor.

"Oh, boy, here comes another one!" The words fly from my mouth unbidden, followed by a series of unholy shrieks. The stretching, burning sensation between my legs is unlike anything I even imagined possible, and it lasts for what seems like way too long. My body is going to split in two, I know it is.

"Gotcha!" the man yells triumphantly. "Almost there!" His face is twisted in concentration as he stares at the space between my legs. Then he looks up at me, and his expression morphs into one of great excitement. I'm reminded of a high school volleyball coach I once had when he yells, "Push! Again! Come on! You got this, Mika!"

He inspires me to try harder, to get this impossible thing done, to triumph over the intense pain that feels as though it's destroying me. I never believed what women said about childbirth before. I thought they were exaggerating about the agony, but I get it now. Nothing I ever do will be as painful as this is.

"Go, Mika, go!" he yells, grabbing my knee and squeezing it. "Push! You're the woman!"

"I'm the womaaaaaaan!" I yell, bearing down and giving it my all.

The baby's tiny shoulders and then legs pop free, yanking a scream from my lungs. Holding the baby, the man folds his arms into himself, looking like a guy who just caught a touchdown pass in the end zone.

"It's a boy!" he shouts.

There's a gurgling sound from the baby and then a slight cry. The man stands, flipping the gooey baby over onto its belly so he can pat its back.

I cannot stop staring. *That thing . . . that baby . . . was inside me this whole time?* It's impossible to believe. *Impossible, impossible, impossible.* I've read stories about women not knowing they were pregnant, but I never thought it would happen to me.

"He's safe," the man says, his breath coming hard. He sounds like he just ran a 5k race and came in first place, and he's sweating like he did, too. "He's a boy. He's a boy and he's safe." He presses his lips closed, making his nostrils flare as he holds up each of the baby's hands and feet, checking them over. "Got all his fingers and toes." He bends over to look at the baby's face and pauses, frowning. "He's got three eyeballs, but hey, that's not such a bad thing; he'll be able to see better than all his friends, right?" He looks up and grins at me.

My eyes bulge. "Say *what*?" I sit up as far as I can, to see this horror he's describing.

He laughs. "I'm kidding. Just making sure you're still with me. He's got two eyeballs. Cute as can be."

Relief floods my body. I shake my head at him, not sure which I want to do more right now to this man: hug him or slap him. I hold my arms out. "Just give me that baby and hush up."

He extends his arms and places the tiny being on my belly as the woman walks over with a fresh towel, helping me wrap him up as best we can with the umbilical cord in the way. My son's face is tiny, his cheeks especially puffy, his eyelids swollen. He looks like a little prize-fighter. I can't believe he's mine or that he even exists.

"Somebody pinch me," I say in a daze. "This can't be real."

"Oh, it's real. I can vouch for you. And he's gorgeous," the woman says. "Congratulations." She smiles so warmly at me, it brings tears to my eyes.

"Thanks." I stroke his cheek where it's been dried by the towel; his skin is impossibly soft. "He is pretty cute, huh?" Emotions well up in me, and feelings awaken I didn't even know were possible for me to have: Intense love. Protectiveness. Fear. I imagine Pavel knowing about my baby, taking him from me. And I can just as clearly picture myself picking up a gun and shooting that evil man right between the eyes. Never will I ever let him hurt this boy or take him from me.

I make a silent pledge to my newborn son as I stare down into his dark-blue eyes: *No one will get in our way of making a new life together. No one. I promise you with all my heart and soul.*

"Absolutely, he's cute," the guy says. He reaches between my legs to move the towel out of the way so he can see the baby's face. "Cute little nose."

I can't stop smiling. I did make a cute baby, that's a fact. I can't believe how impossibly small he is. His thumb is no bigger than a Tic Tac.

The younger guy with the cell phone comes over, tripping over a pile of wet towels on the floor before righting himself. "He just caught your baby like he's Johnny Bench or something." He moves in closer, pointing the camera at the baby for a couple seconds and then at my face. "Do you have any words you want to share with your soon-to-be YouTube fans?"

I put my hand up and try to push his camera away. "No, get out of here. This is a private moment."

The man reaches over and takes the phone away from him. "She's right. Let's turn this off."

"Hey, man, that's mine." The kid reaches over to try to take his phone back, but the man stops him with a chop to the wrist that shuts the kid up instantly.

The man looks at me, holding up the phone. "Do you want to keep this video?"

I shake my head vigorously. "Heck, no. No, thank you."

"Where's the delete button?"

"Hey, you can't do that!" the kid yells, trying once more to get his phone from the man as he works to erase the file. The kid gets an elbow to the shoulder for his trouble. "That's my video! I took it! You have no right to erase it!"

"Too late."

The relief that floods through me feels as good as a warm bath on a frigid winter's night. Now I won't have to worry about Pavel seeing the video online. I entertain the idea for a few seconds that I'll be able to hide everything from him, including the baby's existence, until the moment I glance up and see no fewer than twenty phone cameras recording everything through the window of the nail salon. There's no way this isn't going to be on all the news channels for days. *I am so screwed.* Fear seizes my heart and makes me feel like I can't breathe.

The man gives the phone back to the kid with a warning: "No more filming unless you get permission first, got it?"

The younger guy snatches his cell away and mumbles something rude as he goes back to the other massage chair. He falls down into it and starts texting like crazy, ignoring us.

"I have to cut the cord," the man says. He pauses and looks at me funny. "You okay?"

I nod, brushing away my concerns about Pavel. I have bigger fish to fry right now, namely the fact that I have a baby in my arms and absolutely zero preparation for that. I watch as a large tow truck slowly drives by.

The man grabs a nearby towel to wipe his hands. It looks like he's participated in a slaughter; he's got blood and who knows what else up to his elbows. I wince, wondering if I should apologize, but I'm loath to bring up the subject of him being all up in my business. This is just surreal. A half hour ago I was trying to figure out what kind of coffee would make Pavel happy. Now I'm wondering how in the hell I'm going to pull off being a mother to a child I didn't even know existed until five minutes ago. My mind is officially blown.

"I need something to tie the cord with before I cut it," the man says, looking around.

The salon owner pulls open a drawer in a counter next to the massage chair and takes a ball of string from inside, holding it up. "This work?"

I eye it warily. That can't possibly be sterile. Does it need to be? I have no idea. I start to panic again, until the man speaks.

"Sure. Just wash it with soap and water and then soak it in alcohol for me, would you?"

It's so nice to have someone standing there by my side taking care of my concerns before I even have to express them. I'm so used to doing everything for myself, it feels like a luxury, and for this moment I can give in to it and not worry about someone taking advantage of me having my guard down. I rest my head on the chair and draw the baby up closer. He starts to twist his head into me.

"He wants to nurse," the woman says, as the owner of the salon takes the string toward a sink.

I look at the woman in a panic. "I have no idea how to do that."

"If you want to wait, the paramedics in the ambulance can help you," the man says. He glances toward the window. "I hear the sirens."

I nod, loving the idea of waiting until medical professionals are on hand. I've already made enough of a fool of myself for one day, and besides, my little baby has fallen asleep again. I'd worry about his super-short attention span, but he looks awfully content.

The stranger turns his attention to me. "Congratulations, Mika. He's beautiful." His expression is soft, stress free. It transforms him in a flash from a take-no-prisoners badass to a gentleman. I feel my heart warming toward him. He very possibly saved my baby's life. Maybe mine, too. Who knows what would have happened if I'd kept driving? I could have hit a car head-on or started having my baby while I was sitting on its head. Any number of things could have gone really wrong for me and my little one today, but this man showed up in the street, threw himself in front of my car, and made sure none of those things happened. I might have humiliated myself in front of fifty people, but at least my son is alive and breathing. I look down at his sleepy, innocent face and know what I have to do.

"What's your name?" I ask, my voice breathy, soft, full of wonder as I stare down at my boy.

The room goes silent.

I look up at my savior. "Well? You got a name or what?"

"Oh. Yeah. Sorry; I thought you were talking to the baby. I'm Thibault."

"How do you spell that?"

"T-h-i-b-a-u-l-t."

"Good," I say, going back to admiring my son. "I'm going to need to know that for the birth certificate." I can't stop smiling, and when I glance up at Thibault, I see that he looks happy too. He might even have a tear in his eye.

CHAPTER SIX

The ambulance ride to the hospital is no big deal. Being in the hospital, though, that's a different story. I'm put in the maternity ward and harassed by one nurse after another until I'm ready to scream at all of them to leave me the hell alone. Everyone wants to know what my pregnancy symptoms were, why I didn't know I was pregnant, whether I had any prenatal care, and if I realize how serious this is.

"Of course I know how serious this is," I say to the third person who's asked me in the last hour. "I'm holding a baby in my arms. You think I don't realize what that means?"

"But there must be someone we can call for you," the young girl says, smiling at me with a slightly strained expression showing around her eyes. "The father of the baby, maybe?"

I have a really hard time reining in my emotions and the reaction my heart and brain want to share with her. She's lucky there's nothing within reach that I can throw, because the hold I have over myself is very tenuous.

"As I already told you and your co-workers, there is no one you can call. And I'll thank you to stop asking me the same questions over and over again like I'm some kind of child who doesn't understand."

She holds up some papers. "It's just that we need you to fill out the birth certificate forms, and you really need to put the father's name on it."

I nod my head over at the table on wheels that still has my leftover lunch on it. "You can put your papers right there. I'll look at them later."

She walks over and places them down, spinning around to look at me again on her way out. "I'll be back within the hour to pick them up."

"You can come back whenever you want, but I'll fill them out when I'm ready."

She presses her lips together and stares at me for a little while before speaking again. "You know, we're all just trying to do our jobs here. You could be a little more helpful; it would make our lives easier."

I raise my eyebrows at her. "Is that a fact? Well, I'll try to keep that in mind while I'm sitting here dealing with a surprise baby and the new life I'm about to start *on my own*." I drop my gaze to my son, patting him on the bottom as he suckles. I can't look at the nurse anymore or I'm liable to say something ruder than I already have. I know they mean well, but they're pushing me and I don't like being pushed, especially when I have so much thinking to do. It stresses me out, and that's bad for me and the baby.

I hear footsteps moving across the room and assume that means I'm alone, so I'm startled when a man's voice comes from the doorway.

"Hey there, feisty lady."

I lift my head immediately, expecting to see the male nurse who's already been in here twice. They're nothing if not persistent. The scowl melts from my face as I see it's him, though. *Thibault.* I can't believe he came to visit me. I'm both happy and suspicious.

"Oh, hey, Thibault. What're you doing here?" I scan his body and take in the crutches. *Crutches?* He swings himself into the room, stopping at the foot of my bed.

"Oh, just recovering from a hit-and-run. Got a room down on the second floor for the night. Two-oh-four, just down from the nurses' station."

"Hit-and-run." I can't believe he just said that. Here I was all excited that he came to say hello, giving me a chance to thank him again, and instead he's here to try to scare me. And I thought my day couldn't get any worse.

He leans his armpits on his crutches. "Yeah. Some crazy lady hit me with her car and drove away. I didn't catch her plate number, unfortunately." He's smiling.

I can't figure out what's going on inside that head of his. His face is friendly but his words are anything but. "What're you playing at?" He probably wants a payoff. I have some money in savings, but I'm going to need that for me and Baby Thibault. Bribery and hiding those kinds of monetary exchanges are all a part of my job as Pavel's bookkeeper; I know very well how the darker edges of the world work. Maybe this conversation would have shocked me five years ago, but today it doesn't. Not one bit. I lift my chin, trying to show him I'm not easily intimidated.

He leans his crutches up against my bed and drags the chair over, easing himself down into it. "Just trying to keep things from getting too complicated."

"I have insurance," I say. I made sure I got health insurance as part of my deal with Pavel, although I never thought I'd be using the maternity benefits while I was working for him, and I have car insurance too, although I have to pay that out of pocket.

"Can you afford the premiums being doubled?" he asks. He sounds doubtful. Confident. Like we're playing cards and he's holding a trump in his hand. He must think I'm a welfare case. *How rude.*

My nostrils flare while I attempt to remain civil. "That's none of your business."

He frowns. "Well, I think it *is* my business, since you hit me with your car."

I shrug. He thinks he can manage me, acting like a schoolteacher or whatever authoritarian figure he's trying to channel, but it won't work. Measuring this guy against Pavel is like lining up a newborn kitten next to a lion. I nod my head toward the corner of the room. "My purse is over there. The ambulance driver was nice enough to get it from the tow truck driver before they hauled my car away. Bring it to me and I'll get you my insurance information."

His expression softens. "There's no need to get upset with me. I'm just here to see how you're doing. Really, I don't need the insurance stuff. I was just teasing. I'm just going to let my health insurance take care of it."

I shrug, not believing him. Everyone has an angle. "I'm not upset. You keep talking about my insurance and me hitting you with my car, even though everyone saw you walk out into the middle of the street without looking where you were going, so, whatever. Get my purse, I'll give you the information, and you can be on your way."

Thibault was a nice guy when everything was falling to pieces, which was really cool and I appreciate it, but now he wants to play games and intimidate me. That's fine. I can handle it. He's just one more person I can cross off my Christmas card list, which is convenient because now it can go back to having zero people on it. It's a lot less work at holiday time.

Holding Baby Tee tighter gives me comfort—a sense of strength, even, when I'm sitting here across from a man who is working at tying me up in knots. I'm not alone now, and I never will be again. I have a son. Warmth floods my heart as I look down to stare into his face. I'm feeding him, keeping him alive with something my body has created. It's a miracle . . . I'm literally holding a miracle in my arms.

Thibault's tone is supposed to be soothing, I think. "Tamika . . . three hours ago I was elbows deep in your business, helping you give birth to that gorgeous boy you're holding. Not to mention the fact that you nearly ran me over before I'd even had a sip of my mocha latte. Not that I'm filing a claim against you, but I think I'm at least *entitled* to ask you about your insurance. But you act like I'm trying to hurt you. Why would I do that?"

I look up at him, my face impassive. "I don't know you, Thibault. I appreciate all you did for me and Baby Tee here, and if you want some sort of payment for services rendered, I can probably swing you something. But I'd appreciate it if you'd leave now and come back later. I'm pretty tired." I lean back in the bed, letting my head rest on the pillow.

"I overheard you talking to the nurse," he says, moving his chair closer to my bed.

My mind races to remember what was said just before he came in. I don't think I said anything too revealing, but still . . . I lift my head. "You were standing outside my room and listening in on my private conversations? Have you never heard of patient privacy?"

"I didn't do it on purpose. I just came up to see you, and your door was open. I was going to knock but then I heard angry voices."

"There were no angry voices."

"It sounded like you were mad at the nurse for trying to force you to fill out some papers."

I shake my head. "You misunderstood. I'm fine with the papers." I glance over at them and then down at the baby.

He stands, but I ignore him, not wanting to encourage more conversation with eye contact. Then I hear papers shuffling and look up to find him at my table.

"What're you doing?"

"These are for the baby's birth certificate." He's frowning.

I sit up straight, raising my voice. "Put those down. Those aren't any of your business."

He leaves the forms and limps back over to the chair, sitting down again. "Can I ask you a personal question?"

He must be crazy. "No, you cannot."

"Please?"

I want to keep denying him the right to be in my business, but I'm finding it hard when he's being so polite and looking at me like he is now. He has such a handsome face, and if it weren't for him, I might not be sitting here with a healthy baby boy in my arms.

"Fine," I say, sighing heavily so he'll know he's being annoying, "what do you want to know?"

He reaches over and takes my hand gently. I let him, even though it makes me suspicious about his motives. Why is he being nice now? Why does he care about my paperwork?

"Do you have someone who can pick you up in a couple days and help take care of you and the baby?"

"Sure." I shrug, like it's no big deal, even though on the inside I'm panicking at the idea. I pull my hand away from his and adjust the baby's blanket.

Who am I going to call? Sonia is the only one I can think of. My roommate and I aren't really what I'd call friends, but maybe she could put aside her loyalties to Pavel just this once, help me out for a day or two until I can get my feet under me. I've been good to her. I helped her set up a savings account that Pavel doesn't know about. I know she dreams about getting away someday too.

"Who is it?" he asks.

"I said you could ask me one question. That's two." I hate to admit it to myself, but I enjoy sparring with him. He's determined, but not in the hateful way Pavel always is.

"Can I ask you another question?"

"Not until you answer one for me."

He shrugs. "Shoot. Ask as many as you want. I'm an open book."

"Who are you?"

He just sits there and blinks at me.

"Is that too difficult a question?" I can't help but smile. He looks like the cat's got his tongue, and I find I like bringing out that reaction in him.

"No, I'm just trying to figure out how to answer it."

"However you want."

He nods slowly. "Okay. Freestyle. I can handle it." He leans back in the chair before continuing. "My name is Thibault Delacroix. I've lived in N'Orleans all my life. I have one sister named Toni who's married to my best friend, Lucky. They have two kids—twins—and I'm their favorite uncle. I work at Bourbon Street Boys security . . ."

"I've heard of that company." The name tickles the back of my mind. "I can't remember where I heard it, though."

"That's kind of surprising," he says, his grin slipping.

"Why's that?"

"We do some private security work in the area, but most of it is with the police department. Not that it's a big secret, but our work is contracted, done behind the scenes. It never makes it into the newspapers."

Now I remember where I've heard it. Pavel said something about them once. I can't remember why or what it was about. "Oh. Maybe I'm confusing your job with another one that sounds similar. Bourbon Street Billiards or something."

"Yeah." He holds up his hands for a second before resting them on his thighs. "So that's me. Now do I get to ask a question?"

"Sure. As long as it's not too personal." I'm no longer in the mood to spar with Thibault. He seems like a nice enough guy, and now that I know he's in security, I can see why he might have been motivated to come to my aid when he saw me suffering. Most men who go into the law-upholding business, even on the private side, have a desire to help people, unlike men who work the other side of the law, who couldn't care less who they hurt, like Pavel. But even though I've lost some of my suspicions where Thibault's concerned, it doesn't mean I want to get cozy with him. My relationship as a confidential informant for the NOPD is dangerous enough that I don't need to invite more of Pavel's enemies into it.

"Not too personal . . . Let me see . . . What can I ask you . . . ?" Thibault narrows his eyes at me, nodding his head. He knows he's charming. Maybe he is a little. Maybe not. I no longer trust my instincts with men.

I can't help but line up the two men in my life right now—Thibault and Pavel—side by side in my mind. One man: compact and olive-skinned, dark-haired, muscular, handsome, confident, and kind . . . The other: tall, pale, blond, thin, not very handsome, overly confident, and unkind. Had I been given the choice years ago between one or the other, I know which direction I would have gone. It was never in my plan to work for a criminal; life just worked out that way for me. I wish I'd been able to find a job with an outfit like this Bourbon Street Boys place instead of where I ended up. I'd be willing to bet that Thibault is fun to work with. He probably jokes around a lot—he has laugh lines around his eyes. But there's no point in crying over how my life rolled out, since there's no way to change the past.

"What do you do for a living?" he finally asks.

"I'm a bookkeeper."

"Huh. Interesting. Where do you work?"

"I keep the books for a man who owns some laundry businesses. Wash-dry-fold places."

"Here in town?"

"Yes." I look down at the baby, worried how far this questioning is going to go. I don't want to be rude now that we've found an easy conversation between us, but if Thibault works with the police, he might know too much about some things I'd rather keep out of our relationship, even though it promises to be one that will end before this day does.

"Maybe we could call your boss. Do you think he'd be willing to help you out?"

A bitter laugh bursts out of me before I can stop it. "Uh, no. I'm not going to do that." I look up at him and try to smile. "Listen, I appreciate you worrying about me and all that, but you really don't need to. I'll be fine. I have a roommate."

He smiles. "A roommate. That's great. Want me to get your phone for you?" He moves to get up.

"No, it's fine. I'll talk to her later."

He stands at the side of my bed, staring down at me. "She might need some advance warning, you know. So she can get a car seat and some diapers and things you might need . . ."

I have to work to keep my temper in check. He's pushing again. Too far. "Thibault, you know what? I really, really appreciate you coming to visit and worrying about me, but right now I'm kind of tired and I'd like to take a nap. If you don't mind . . ."

His jaw pulses out a few times as he reaches over and takes his crutches from the side of my bed. "No, I don't mind at all. I'm sorry if I bothered you with my questions." He puts the crutches under his arms and turns sideways. "Can I get you anything before I go?" He looks over at the table. "Some water?"

It's on the tip of my tongue to say no, but my lips are practically stuck together. "Water sounds good. That would be nice."

He makes his way over to the table and brings my insulated mug back. He holds it out, smiling. "This cup is probably going to cost you five hundred bucks, you know. Make sure you stuff it in your purse before you leave."

I roll my eyes as I take it. "I know. Thank goodness I had Dr. Thibault Delacroix on call to help deliver my baby; otherwise I'd be paying about twenty grand for that."

He smiles, leaning over to pick up the baby's tiny fist. "I'll send you a bill."

"I hope it's not too expensive," I say, wondering if he's joking.

"Maybe when you're back on your feet you can take me to lunch to cover the cost."

I want to laugh and cry at the same time. In another place, another time, another life, I might really enjoy that. But it'll never happen. Not with Pavel in my life. I need to put New Orleans in my rearview mirror as soon as possible. "That would be nice," I say with a wistful sigh.

"Don't look so sad about it," he says. "I haven't been that mean, have I?"

"Why would you say that? When were you mean?"

"I was being pushy earlier. I'm sorry about that. My sister says I have a Superman complex and have a hard time taking no for an answer. When I see someone who needs help, I want to help." He shrugs. "It's a character flaw, I guess."

I have to smile at that. I could totally see him with a cape on, fighting crime, leaping tall buildings with a single bound. "Yeah, well, we all have our crosses to bear. My grandma used to say I'm as stubborn as a mule. Too independent for my own good."

"Who? You?" he says in a high voice. "Nooo . . ."

I push his hand away and gesture at the door. "Go. Be gone with you. I've had a long day and I need to sleep."

He swings away on his crutches, smiling. Stopping at the door, he turns around. "Would you mind if I visited you again before we check outta this joint? Just to see how you and the baby are doing? I promise I won't harass you about calling anyone or going to lunch with me."

I close my eyes and rest my head on the pillow, snuggling Baby Tee into my arms. I probably shouldn't encourage Thibault and these friendly gestures he's making, but the idea of never seeing him again, the man who was the first person to hold my son in his arms, is too sad to accept. I'm usually okay with being alone in the world even when surrounded by people, but something inside me has changed. Maybe it's motherhood already working its powerful and dangerous magic. "Sure. See you tomorrow."

"Yeah, okay. I'll come at breakfast. I'll bring you a donut."

"With sprinkles," I say when he's nearly through the door.

He chuckles. "You got it." The door clicks softly behind him.

CHAPTER SEVEN

I can't relax. Thibault's words keep echoing around in my head, how whoever is picking me up will need time to gather some things. The nurses have already said more than once that I can't leave without an approved car seat—hospital policy and all that. And I'm supposed to check out of here by noon tomorrow.

I've put off calling my roommate, Sonia, because every time I imagine the conversation we'll have, it never goes well. Pavel rewards loyalty and punishes people who keep secrets. I doubt it will even enter her mind that, without me, she wouldn't have that nice fat mutual fund account in a place Pavel will never find it, for the day she steps out and makes a life for herself outside his circle. Right now she's under his thumb, so her first loyalty will most likely be to him.

Somewhere in the back of my mind, I'm thinking that having another conversation with someone who doesn't want anything from me and is no threat to my personal safety might be good for my mental health. Maybe that's why I find myself two floors down from the maternity ward, looking for room 204, where Thibault is spending the night.

It's only seven o'clock in the evening. I won't even knock if I don't get a good vibe once I'm at his door. I'll just walk on by and go to the elevators on the other end of the wing. The nurses kept telling me I need to move around to help myself recover as quickly as possible. Leaving Baby Thibault in the nursery felt horrible at first, but now I'm happy I don't have him with me; I'm already exhausted. I have never been so sore in my life, not even as a kid after I did a two-hour trail ride on horseback at the one and only birthday party I ever attended. I didn't walk right for days after that, but I think it'll be at least a week before I'm past this pain and stiffness.

As I'm approaching Thibault's door, three women coming from the other direction stop in front of it. I pull my robe tighter around me and pretend to be interested in the room across the hall as they push in his door and enter, leaving it cracked open behind them.

I step to my right to be closer, my curiosity getting the better of me. Who are they? Is he married? Is one of them his wife or girlfriend? Co-workers? Friends? Relatives? One of the women was compact like him, with the same hair color and skin tone, too. Maybe she's his sister.

I should probably feel guilty about listening in, but he did it to me earlier. Turnabout is fair play, right? I lean as close to the door as I can without being too obvious about it, placing one hand on the wall and the other on my belly. I don't have to pretend to look wiped out. I sure wish they had a chair out here so I could eavesdrop in comfort.

"Thibault, oh my god, how *are* you?" The woman's voice is really animated.

"Hey, May, I'm good. Hey, Jenny. Hi, Toni. What're you guys doing here?"

"Where are all your bruises?" a girl—May—asks.

"What bruises?" he asks.

"You were in a car accident, right? Where are all the cuts and bruises and stuff?"

I snort quietly. *Car accident. Yeah, right.* More like he forgot one of the lessons he learned in kindergarten, like how you're supposed to look both ways before crossing the street.

"I wasn't really hit by a car. I was just tapped."

"Hey, bro," says someone with a more serious tone. His sister, I guess. I wonder if she's Toni or Jenny. "How does somebody *tap* you with their car, anyway?"

"That's what I'd like to know, Toni," says a voice similar to the first—Jenny, apparently. If I were a betting woman, I'd say she and May are sisters. They looked enough alike. That would make Toni the one who looks like Thibault—his sister.

"I was getting some coffee, and I stepped off the curb without looking where I was going."

Ha! I knew it; he was playing with me earlier, trying to pretend it was all my fault. Yeah, okay, so I took a wrong turn, but still . . . he should've been looking out for cars, and now at least he's admitting it.

"What were you thinking?" May asks. "You could've been killed. What if it had been a bus that *tapped* you?"

"He probably would've heard a bus coming," Jenny says. "What happened to your knee?"

"I'm waiting for the radiologist to read the x-rays. It could be just a bruise. The tech said something about my meniscus, but what does he know?"

"You're going to be off your feet for a while," Toni says. "Does Ozzie know about this yet? Does he know you're going to need time off work?"

Ozzie? That must be his boss. I feel guilty over the part I played in his injury. I hadn't realized until now how messed up his leg really is.

"I texted him. He said he's going to stop by later. And nobody's saying I need time off, okay?"

May speaks up. "Ozzie's talking about hiring that new guy, Jerry. He doesn't want to do it without talking to you about it first, though. Maybe this is going to be good timing with you off your feet for a while. Jerry could cover for you."

Toni sounds like she's mocking the guy when she adds her two cents. "Jerry? You mean *Jericho*?"

"Come on, Toni, he's a good guy," Thibault says. "I think he'll be a great addition to the team, especially with his Special Forces background. And he can't help it that his parents like their Bible stories; stop giving the guy a hard time about his name."

"If it were me, I'd go by Jericho," Jenny says. "I think it's a cool name."

May's voice is really squeaky. I can picture her jumping up and down. "Hey, Jenny! You could name your . . ." She stops herself abruptly and then stammers out the rest of her sentence. "Dog . . . or cat . . . or gerbil Jericho. If you want. Or not." She pauses. "What's that out the window? Is that a parrot? I think somebody lost their parrot."

"The blinds are closed, May," Toni says. "How are you seeing a parrot anywhere?"

"So," Jenny says brightly, "are they talking about sending you into surgery for this meniscus problem?" She's acting like May seeing an invisible parrot isn't completely bizarre. Maybe her sister's a mental case and she's used to it. Pavel has a cousin with issues, and we're all totally immune to his stuff now. *Alexei.* I brush the worry away. *One problem at a time . . .*

"Yeah, pretty much," Thibault says.

"Surgery?" May says. "Really? Wow. That must have been some tap."

Surgery? I had no idea Thibault would have to go under the knife to fix his leg. Now I feel seriously guilty. I thought he was experiencing man-pain, taking a simple bruise and turning it into a major event. I should have known better, though, when he said they were keeping him overnight. Nowadays they kick you out of the hospital as soon as they can. I bite my lip, wondering if I should apologize. I *was* going down the street the wrong way.

"No idea," he says. "I'm just supposed to rest my knee for now."

"I still don't understand how you walked off a curb right into a car." Toni sounds seriously annoyed. "I've never known you to be so careless."

I can hear Thibault's sigh through the door. "What I did wasn't careless. The car was going the wrong way down a one-way street, okay? It's not a big deal. She barely touched me."

The room goes silent for a few seconds and then May says, "Oh, I seeee. So it was a *she* driving the vehicle, eh? Now I'm starting to understand."

"Is she cute?" Jenny asks, a smile in her voice.

The heat rises in my cheeks. I should walk away now, but I'm dying to hear his answer.

"Please," Toni says, annoyed. "As if some chick driving the car is going to make a difference. Give me all her insurance info, and I'll start filling out the claim forms for you."

I narrow my eyes. Did she not hear him say that it was mostly his fault? I can see pushiness runs in their family.

"No need. It's all cool."

The room goes quiet. I turn away, just in case they're thinking about coming out. Thibault's voice stops me. "Listen, I'm kinda tired from the painkillers they gave me, so if you could give me a little bit of time to relax before I check myself out of here . . ."

"Sure, we can give you some time to rest," May says. "Get better real soon. We'll see you tomorrow."

Jenny is next to speak. "Heal quick. We'll see you tomorrow. Call me if you need anything at all, and I'll bring it over or Dev will bring it. He said to tell you hi, by the way. He's locked down with Jacob in therapy right now, but he should be done soon. I'm not sure if he'll visit, but he'll definitely call."

"Cool. Thanks."

Footsteps move toward the door, so I turn around and start walking in the opposite direction they came from when they arrived. After the door opens and closes and the sounds of their exit fade down the hall, I walk back over to Thibault's door so I can apologize for what I did to his knee. I feel terrible. But when I hear a female voice still inside, I freeze just outside, unable to move.

"Thought you got rid of me, didn't you?" a female voice says.

Toni. It must have been just Jenny and May who left.

"Uhhh, yeah." Thibault sounds disappointed.

"I don't chase away that easy." There's a creaking sound, like she just sat on her brother's bed. "Tell me what's going on."

"Nothing. I told you everything already. I'm in pain right now, do you mind?"

"Bullshit. That's not what's going on. What's up with the insurance?"

Damn, they sure do grow them stubborn over at the Delacroix house. I smile, knowing full well the frustration he's suffering. I'm enjoying listening to him getting a taste of his own medicine.

"What insurance? I'm covered," he says.

"I'm talking about the driver's insurance. Did you get the details or not?"

"I don't need to."

There he goes again. No matter what I say to him about being covered, he's not going to file that claim against me. He said something about my premiums doubling. Part of me is annoyed he's trying to protect me when I don't need his protection, but the other part of me sees that it's just his personality; he likes to help people. He's doing what he does best, maybe. I can respect that.

"Since when? You've probably got a torn meniscus, Tee. Somebody's got to pay for that surgery. You'll be lucky if you get out of here for less than fifty grand."

"Don't worry about it."

Her voice softens. "Brother, you know I love you. And you know I'd give you a kidney if you needed it. But if you think I'm going to let you walk away from an insurance claim because some chick showed you her tits, you're nuts."

My jaw drops open. This girl's got some nerve. She doesn't know me, but that still doesn't give her the right to assume I'd do something like that. So what if I showed him my lady-v? That was different; I wasn't trying to get his attention with it or anything, and even if I were, it wouldn't have worked. Talk about a train wreck. If anything, he should have charged me for making him look at it.

Thibault's voice drops to a soothing level. "Listen, I get what you're saying, okay? You're not wrong about the costs involved in my situation here, but you have to trust me when I tell you that there were no tits involved."

I have to smile at that. He's right. He might have seen everything I've got going on below the waist, but I never took my shirt off. Not until I got to the hospital, anyway.

There's a long pause and a sigh before Thibault speaks again. "Okay, she has tits, but I promise I wasn't looking. Not for more than two seconds, anyway. There was a lot more going on that had my attention."

I feel a little flush come over me at the idea that he *did* look, if only for a moment.

"Do tell."

"You won't believe me."

"Try me."

He sighs. "Don't tell May. She'll go bananas and harass me over it. I need to be in a lot less pain to deal with that."

"Fine. I won't say a thing. What happened?"

"She hit me because she was in labor. I helped her give birth to a baby in a nail salon."

"Get the fuck out."

"No, I'm serious."

"I heard that on the news on the way over here!" she yells. "That was you?"

"Yeah, shhh, May is probably standing out in the hall."

My entire body freezes, making me look like a statue, until Toni speaks and I can tell from her voice she's still across the room.

"Nah, she's at the car. She just texted me to hurry up."

I let out a long sigh of relief over not being busted.

"Fine, go. I'll tell you the rest later."

"No, now. May can wait."

"That's it, really. She had the baby, and we were brought here in two different ambulances. She's up in the maternity ward. Her car got towed away, and she doesn't even have any clothes to wear, since I had to cut hers off in the nail place." He sighs really loud. "She's a single mom, okay? She's tough, but she's on her own. And I've got good health insurance, so I'm not about to ruin her life over a small accident I could have avoided if I'd simply looked where I was going."

"Oh, so we're doing the Superman thing again, are we?"

"Give it a rest, Toni. It's not like that. You'd have done the same thing."

"Bullshit."

"Oh really? After raising twins for the last eighteen months and seeing everything that goes into that, all that it takes out of you, you wouldn't have a *little* soft spot in your heart for a girl who, until the moment she gave birth, didn't even know she was pregnant? Who doesn't have friends or family to help her out? Please. You're not that cold."

He's defending me so stridently, it stirs something inside me. I shouldn't care, but I do. I haven't had someone fight for me in years.

"How could she not know she was pregnant? And no family? What about the baby's father?"

"I don't know. I don't know any of that. She wouldn't tell me. I got the impression it wasn't a good situation, though."

Now my face is burning with shame. "Not a good situation" is *one* way to describe my life.

There's a long pause before she responds. "That sucks."

"Yeah. It sucks. So just let it go."

"I'm not sure that's a good idea, even though I get it . . . she's in a tough spot."

He groans. "Can we have this conversation another day? I really don't feel so hot."

"Fine. But you're going to tell me everything else that happened tomorrow when I come to pick you up."

"You're checking me outta here?"

"Hell, yeah, I am."

"What about the kids?"

"Lucky's got it covered. By the way, he's coming over later if he can get away. Ozzie has him on this case that's got him up to his eyeballs in financials, but he wants to see you. I have to get back before he starts texting me."

"Good." Thibault sounds really tired. "Tell him to bring my tooth-brush and razor."

"You got it."

Knowing she's about to leave, I start to walk away, but not so quickly that I don't hear her last words.

"I hope she's worth it."

I pause to listen to his response, but he speaks too low for me to catch it. I hurry down the hallway, not looking back, even when I hear the door opening behind me.

CHAPTER EIGHT

I'm dozing off after having put the baby in his bassinet. It's eight thirty in the morning, and I've gotten maybe three hours of sleep total all night. Baby Tee is a cute little bugger, but damn, he likes to eat. I look down at my chest, freaking out over how big it's getting. I think I have enough to feed three infants at this point, and I know I don't have a bra that's going to fit. I'm jealous of other women who have months to prepare for these things.

There's a knock at my door. Thibault and my donut have arrived. I thought about calling him on the hospital phone system to tell him not to bother, but then I thought about it some more and realized that would be rude. He did deliver my baby, after all.

"Come in." I smooth my hair down and make sure my breasts are covered by the annoying hospital gown I'm forced to wear since I don't have a change of clothing yet. Hopefully Sonia will remember to bring me the things I asked for; she wasn't happy about being woken up at seven thirty with the news that I was in the hospital and needed a ride to the tow yard.

A nurse pokes her head in the door. "You have a visitor," she says.

I smile. "Is it a man with a donut?"

She looks worried. "Um . . . no. It's a man. But he doesn't have a donut." She looks over her shoulder.

Her weird expression is giving me a bad feeling. My smile falls away. "Who is it?"

She slides into the room, holding the door closed with her hand. "He said his name is Pavole. Or Pavelli. I'm sorry, he had an accent."

My blood goes cold as sweat breaks out all over my body. "No. Don't let him in," I whisper.

She lowers her voice to match mine. "He's not in the ward yet. He hasn't been buzzed through." She pauses. "Normally, if someone says they're visiting a certain person and they know all the details about the patient and the baby, we don't bother double-checking, but he didn't . . . And he seemed . . . angry." She grimaces.

I sit up straighter, my voice rising. "Don't buzz him in. I don't want him in my room."

She holds out her hands. "I won't. Stay right there."

As soon as she's gone, I get out of bed, walking as fast as I can over to Baby Tee's bassinet. I gather him up in my arms and go into the bathroom, shutting the door and locking it behind me. I sit on the toilet and wait for my world to crash down around my ears.

Fucking Sonia. She sold me out. I knew I couldn't trust her. *Why did I call her?* My heart sinks as the answer buzzes through my brain: because she's the only person in the entire world who I thought I might have a chance with—someone who could keep my secret for just a few hours and give me enough time to get away. Now it's been confirmed: I have no one but my baby. It's just me and Tee . . . us against the world.

All the movement has wakened him and he starts to fuss. I help him latch on and then stare at the door, going over my plan in my mind: I will borrow clothing from one of the nurses. One of them has to have something in a gym bag or a locker somewhere around here. Or I'll just go in my hospital gown and robe. I don't care. I have to leave before Pavel finds a way to get in. Once I get clothing and shoes, or just some shoes, I'll catch a cab to the tow yard. I'll call first to make sure Pavel isn't there. Then I'll go empty my bank account, buy some provisions and a map, and hit the road. The social worker who came to my room yesterday told me they could loan me a car seat if I agreed to go to a parenting class. I'll sign up for that deal, take the seat, and drop it off after I buy a replacement. Screw the parenting classes, though; I have to get out of town as soon as possible.

A knock comes at the bathroom door, and I tense up. Baby Tee detaches and starts to fuss. I guide him back into place. "Yes?"

"Miss Cleary?" a woman's voice says.

"Yes?"

"Could you come out here, please?"

"Ummm, no. Sorry, I can't. I'm a little busy right now."

"I'm Joanna Readling, director of social services for the hospital."

"Now's not really a good time."

There's a long pause before she answers. "The man you didn't want to let in has been removed from the hospital by security, if that's what you're worried about."

Relief floods me. It's so strong it makes my ears ring. I have to take several long, calming breaths before I feel comfortable standing. Once I'm on my feet, I reach over to unlock the door. After checking my look in the mirror and fixing some errant strands of hair, I walk out of the bathroom, acting like it's the most natural thing in the world to take my baby with me to the toilet and lock us in.

There's a nurse and a lady with a clipboard standing in the middle of the room. I go over to the bed and climb in, mindful of Baby Tee. He doesn't miss a beat, drinking for all he's worth.

"Miss Cleary, hello." The woman with the clipboard walks over and extends her hand. "I'm Joanna Readling."

"Nice to meet you." I nod at her but keep my hands to myself. I read a pamphlet one of the nurses gave me about protecting my baby from germs. I figure that's all the excuse I need to keep these people at arm's length.

"It appears as if you might have a situation . . ." She looks at the nurse, who nods at her. ". . . With someone who was very insistent about seeing your baby." She pauses, looking uncomfortable. "He claims he's the baby's father."

I shrug. "He can claim it all he wants, but that doesn't matter, does it?" I also read the hospital's welcome brochure for new mothers, and it clearly states that I have complete authority over who can see my baby. Anyone who insists on their rights needs a court order to back them up.

"Technically no, it doesn't, but I've been informed that you don't have a car seat; nor have you made arrangements for anyone to check you out. There's a form you need to fill out with that information."

I shift Tee to my other breast as a way to grab more time to gather my thoughts. Once he's settled I look up. "Who told you I don't have someone to do that?"

The nurse standing next to her smiles at me, but the emotion doesn't reach her eyes.

"Who said it doesn't matter. The question is, was it correct? Do you have someone to take you home? And do you have somewhere to go? We'll need you to fill out the forms if you do." Joanna holds up a hand to stop me from speaking. "Just so you know, we have services available to you if you don't have other alternatives. We don't want you to think you're in some kind of trouble if your situation is . . . isn't ideal."

"My situation is just fine. I asked social services to loan me a car seat, but if that's a problem, I'll just have my friend bring one."

"What friend?" Joanna holds a pen above her clipboard. "I'll be happy to call her or him and confirm they will have what you need in order to check out."

I detach Baby Tee from my breast since he's fallen asleep and put him over my shoulder as I glare at the two pushy women in front of me. "Just what is your problem, exactly?" I ask.

"Pardon me?" the nurse asks.

"Why are you harassing me?" I look at one and then the other. "I can't believe you do this to all the new mothers who come through here. You'd have to hire ten extra people just to keep up."

"We're not harassing you; we're trying to help you," Joanna says.

"Bull. You're covering your asses so I don't sue you later for something."

Joanna clears her throat as she looks down at her clipboard. "That's not true. We have policies and procedures in place to ensure your safety and the well-being of your baby." She tucks a long curl behind her ear and shakes her head a little, still not looking at me. "We assume you want the same things we do."

I narrow my eyes at her. "Don't try to threaten me."

"Who's threatening?" the nurse asks. She looks at Joanna. "I told you she's being difficult. She still hasn't filled out the birth certificate."

"I'll fill it out when I'm ready!" I say a little too loudly. The baby startles, so I rub his back to soothe him. Lowering my voice, I try again to get them to understand. "I'll be ready to leave soon, so you don't need to worry about me overstaying my welcome. I thank you for your concern and your help, but I'm a little tired right now, and I'd like to be alone with my son so we can both rest."

Joanna purses her lips. "I'm sorry, but we need to approve the car seat . . ."

They just don't get it. No matter how nice I am or how politely I try to express myself, they keep pushing. *I give up.* "Leave."

They both freeze with their mouths open.

"You heard me." I gesture at the door. "Go on." I look at Baby Tee's face on my shoulder, puffy and scrunched up as he half-sleeps, milk-drunk from his meal.

"How about if we come back in a half hour?" Joanna says. "When the baby's sleeping and you can focus on the conversation better."

"Yeah. Do that." I don't even watch them as they go.

Time to move my plan into fast-forward. I have to get out of here *now*. Is it ideal? No. Not even close. But these busybody women aren't going to be happy with just examining my car seat. Now that Pavel's made an appearance that necessitated him being physically removed from the hospital, they're going to start squawking about how it's not safe for us to go, or not safe for the baby. The idea that somebody from social services might take my child away nearly gives me a heart attack. I have to get out of here, *pronto*.

CHAPTER NINE

Wandering the halls of the maternity ward and trying to find clothing gets me exactly nowhere. Well, not exactly nowhere; I did find a pair of scissors, which made it easier to remove my and Baby Tee's hospital bracelets. They have a warning system in place that alerts the nurses when a baby leaves the ward with one of those bracelets on. Just cutting it off doesn't work, though, because that's what any baby stealer would do; the system rings an alarm when the bracelet isn't removed properly.

But there is one benefit to working with criminals: they do tend to become experts in defeating locks and systems that act like locks, and they're not shy about sharing their skills. All it takes is a fork from my breakfast tray to create a bridge for the signal between the two cut ends, and the system stays in place while my baby goes free. I hide the rigged bracelet behind a dusty machine I know they haven't moved in ages by the layer of grime it has on it.

Lucky for me, once I make up my mind to go, two things happen that work in my favor: a couple of grandparents show up to see their grandchild and get buzzed in, and a woman down the hall starts yelling like crazy during her labor, pulling most of the nurses away from their station. I've got a wide-open door and no one to watch the cameras.

I'm ready in the hallway with my purse over my shoulder, stuffed with all the things for the baby they stocked my room with, so when the door swings open wide to let in the two old fogies, I walk right out with my head held high. The grandparents are too excited to see their new grandchild to pay me any attention. I get a couple strange looks when I walk through the lobby, but no one stops me . . . the crazy lady in the hospital robe carrying a newborn out the door.

When I get to the curb at the hospital's front entrance, there are two taxicabs parked there. I walk up to the first one and bend down to look at the driver from the passenger window. "Hey there."

The old man pulls himself from his newspaper and gives me a bored look. "Hello."

"I need a ride to the Right Way Tow yard."

"You have a car seat for that baby?" He goes back to his paper.

"Uh, no. But I'm going to buy one."

"You steal that baby?" He looks over at me, tipping his head down to see over his glasses.

I look down at myself, annoyed over having to explain my situation again. "Do I look like a baby stealer, or maybe like a girl who gave birth to the baby and wants to get the hell out of here because she's sick and tired of people treating her like a welfare case?"

He puts the paper down and gets out of his car. "Get in," he says, as he walks around to the trunk.

I bite my lip. *Is he playing a game? Will he lock me in while he calls over hospital security?*

His trunk goes up and the car jiggles as he moves something inside. Then the trunk goes down, and he walks around to the far side of his car with a baby seat in his hand. "You gettin' in or not?"

I move as fast as I can to the back seat and slide in. "Thank you so much. You have no idea how much this means to me." I feel nauseated over how scary this is all of a sudden. Any second someone from the ward could realize I'm not there and call down looking for me. My heart hammers in my chest as I wait for the driver to strap the seat in. I've been scared a lot of times in my life, but it was always just me I was afraid for. Now that Baby Tee is part of the mix, I'm finding it a lot more difficult to handle.

"Ready to go?" he asks.

I nod as I strap the baby in. I have no idea what I'm doing. The cabbie hesitates outside the car and then opens the door again, assisting me with the buckles. "He's got to ride facing the rear until he's bigger. When you buy a seat, read the directions carefully about that, you hear?"

"Yes. Thanks. I got it." I tuck the baby's blankets in around him, stroking his soft little face with my finger as the driver gets into the car.

He looks up into his rearview mirror at me. "We goin' to the tow yard or the baby store first?"

I hold Baby Tee's hand and think for a few seconds. The regular me would say tow yard. I need to get the hell out of town. The other me, the one who just gave birth, knows better. "Baby store."

"Good girl." He nods at me before starting up the car and driving out of the hospital's valet area.

I don't need this stranger's approval, but it sure does feel good to have it. I stare at Tee's face the entire way over to the store, plans and outcomes swimming through my head.

CHAPTER TEN

The cabbie drops me off at the tow yard's office. I try to pay him with the remaining cash in my wallet, but he won't take it. He says he has grandchildren, and he can't imagine his daughter having to manage them alone wearing a hospital gown. He moves me to tears, not only with his generosity but with the reminder of what a bad place I'm in right now.

As I'm sliding the car seat and pack of diapers I bought toward the tow yard's office door with Baby Tee in my arms, an SUV pulls up to the curb. It's one of those big ones like you see federal agents driving in the movies, with black-tinted windows. My heart skips a beat until I see the driver get out and come around to the curb. She's a couple inches shorter than me and about twenty pounds lighter.

I expect her to walk past me into the office, but she doesn't; she stops right in front of me, invading my personal space. That's when I recognize her. *Toni.* This is Thibault's sister, the woman I saw in the hospital yesterday. *What in the hell?*

"You're Tamika," she says. No preamble, no hello, no nothing. I recognize her voice now, too.

"So? What's that got to do with you?" I hold my baby tighter against me. If she even thinks about touching me, I'm going to make her wish she was never born.

"Thibault asked me to come over here and help you out."

I frown. "What? Why would he do that? And how did he know I was here?" I'm getting a creepy feeling over this.

"Because he thinks he's a superhero, and he can't resist a damsel in distress." She looks up at the sign above our heads. "It wasn't difficult to find you. You got your car towed and you left the hospital in a cab. A bunch of people saw you. It's not like wandering around in a robe and slippers is going to escape notice. So where else would you be going but here?"

I let that simmer in my mind for a little while before I respond. "I guess you're right. You can tell your brother that I don't need his help, but thanks for the offer."

"Will do." Toni salutes me and starts to walk away.

Her easy dismissal of the whole thing bothers me. It shouldn't, since she's giving me exactly what I asked for, but it does. "Is he going to be mad at you for leaving me here?"

"Probably," she says, opening her door.

"And you don't care?" I say loudly so she'll hear me over the car.

She rolls down the passenger window to talk to me. "I do care. But sometimes my brother does stupid shit because he's too busy fighting ghosts to realize what's actually going on, so as his sister, I have a duty to piss him off when necessary." She starts to roll the window up.

"I'm not a charity case, you know!"

The window closes and she starts to pull away.

I stand there watching her go, the car getting smaller in the distance. This is the last I'll hear of Thibault Delacroix, and there's a piece of me that's sad about that. He's a good guy. He sent his sister out here to look after me, and she did it, even though she didn't want to and she's completely rude. That says a lot about what kind of man he is, that people would have that kind of loyalty to him. It's not the same kind of loyalty Pavel gets, the type that's based on the fear of suffering a horribly painful death. The kind Thibault inspires comes from love. My heart aches a little, imagining what it might be like to be a part of that. I lean down and kiss Baby Tee's face, proud that he carries this man's name.

Down at the end of the street, the brake lights of the SUV go on. The car idles for a long time. I should go inside the tow place and get my car, but I'm too intrigued about what Toni is going to do next.

The reverse lights come on and the SUV comes racing back, faster than I imagined a car could go in reverse. It screeches to a halt next to me and rocks a few times before settling in. The stink of burned rubber assaults my nostrils.

I wait for the next crazy thing to happen, but I'm left disappointed. Toni stays in the vehicle and her windows remain rolled up. I shrug and turn around, taking the shopping bags, car seat, and the baby into the tow yard office. I don't have time for games right now.

The woman at the counter doesn't even glance at me. I stand in front of her and bounce the baby a little as he starts to whimper. Then I clear my throat.

"Can I help you?" she says in a voice that tells me she smokes a lot of cigarettes in a day. She doesn't look up; a pile of wrinkled pink forms has all of her attention. She's wearing reading glasses that have a chain on them made of a long string of tacky turquoise and yellow beads.

"Um, yeah." *That's why I'm standing here.* "I've come to bail my Toyota out."

She sighs. "What's the tag number?" She pulls a form out from under the counter, picks up a pen, licks the end of it, and waits for my answer, her hand poised and ready to write.

"I'm not sure. It's a nineteen eighty-nine? Corolla? Green?"

She looks up at me, drops her head down to see me over her reading glasses, and lets out another long sigh. She slides the form to the side and reaches over to drag the pile of pink papers to her. Licking her thumb, she looks at me expectantly. "When was it brought in?"

"Yesterday. Morning. It was facing the wrong direction in front of a coffee shop called Lotta Java."

She starts to page through the forms and then stops, putting down the paper she was holding. "Oh, yeah. I remember that one." She stands up straight and puffs out her chest a little. "Already released it." She backs away from the counter, like she's going to leave.

"Already released it? What does that mean?" Dread fills my heart. This can't be happening.

"It means what it means. It was already claimed."

I can feel my ears going hot as her meaning sinks in. My car is gone. I'm stranded. "By who? That's *my* car!"

She gets a funny look on her face. "I don't want any trouble."

As soon as she says that, I know what happened. *Pavel.*

"How could you?" Tears well up in my eyes. They're the angry kind. The I-want-to-kick-a-hole-in-the-wall kind.

"If you have a problem with it, you can talk to the owner: Andreas Polotnikov." She looks at me, nodding once. The man's name tells me everything I need to know about this place and how fruitless my pleas will be . . . how dangerous it would be to raise a fuss and get the attention of another Russian man who rules with an iron fist.

The door opens behind me, but I ignore it. "Yeah, okay. I get it." This woman's as stuck in the shit as I am. "Just so you know, you gave my car away to a criminal, and now I'm totally screwed."

"Need a lift?" someone behind me says.

I recognize her voice, so I don't bother turning around. "Nope. I'm fine."

The old woman looks over my shoulder at the woman standing behind me. *Toni.* "Yeah, I think she does."

I want to scream, but I can't because it'll wake the baby. I turn around slowly, nudging my packages out of the way so I can face Toni. "I don't need your help."

"You got a car?"

I grit my teeth, hating the answer I have to give. "No."

"You got a place to go?"

I imagine catching a cab to my apartment for about a half second before I nix that idea. That's exactly what Pavel will expect me to do, go home and gather my things. Either he'll be waiting or that traitor Sonia will, and they'll block me from leaving. Any dream I had of getting my freedom will be gone in an instant.

"No. But I can find a place."

"You know what happens to homeless mothers and their kids?" she asks, her hip cocked, her arms crossed over her chest.

"I can imagine." She's trying to push my buttons, but I won't let her.

"They split them up. Social services comes in and takes the kids away. You'll be lucky to get supervised visitation." She looks at me, from my feet to my head. "You look like an escaped mental patient. You think a hotel is going to give you a room? Don't even try to play that game. You're smart enough. You know they won't."

I open my mouth to tell her where she can get off talking to me this way, but I'm interrupted by the lady behind the desk.

"She's right, you know. Happened to my niece. She didn't get her kid back until he was two. Two years. That's a lot of time missed."

The thought makes me sick to my stomach. I look down at Tee's face and can't imagine some stranger taking him from me, feeding him formula with bottles, rocking him to sleep in their arms, and putting him to bed in their house. Not my house, *their* house.

I've only ever been this desperate once in my life, and that's what got me here, standing in this tow yard's office wearing a hospital robe and disposable slippers with a newborn baby in my arms. I need to make a better choice this time.

"What do you want from me?" I ask Toni. "Because I'm not in the mood for any games."

"No games. I'm just doing my brother a favor, that's it."

"And what's your brother got to do with anything? With any of this?" I gesture with my elbows at my stuff on the floor, the old woman, the mess that is my life.

"I already told you. Ghosts. He fights them every day."

I don't like her cryptic answer, but even more so, I don't like the idea of being so vulnerable. Maybe I can take some of the help they're offering without going all in. I have a baby to think of now; I can't be concerned with always being such a nice person. I have to be more selfish—do what needs to be done for myself and Baby Tee.

"Fine. You can give me a ride."

"A ride where?"

I sigh out in annoyance. She's so pushy. "I'll figure it out on the way."

Toni moves forward, and I jump back to avoid her. She leans down and grabs my shopping bags, glancing up at me with a funny look on her face. "Jumpy."

"Don't make such sudden moves and I won't have to be."

Toni shrugs and turns around. "I'll be in the truck waiting. Don't take too long." The door slams shut behind her, the bell on the handle banging sharply against the glass.

"Good luck, honey," the woman at the counter says, for the first time her voice sounding not so harsh.

"Yeah. Thanks a lot." I walk out the door, wondering what kind of trouble I'm getting myself into by accepting Toni and Thibault's offer of help, while at the same time knowing it can't possibly be anything worse than what I'd suffer at Pavel's hand.

CHAPTER ELEVEN

S o, where to?" she asks. We're still parked in front of the tow yard office. The longer we sit here, the more panicked I become. Pavel will send someone here to intercept me once he realizes I've left the hospital. I have to leave. I'm in the back seat with the baby, and it feels like I'm sitting in a fishbowl. The tinted windows offer me little security.

"Just drive."

"Yes, ma'am." She pulls away from the curb as someone in a restored Camino pulls up behind us. I look out the back window as a man exits his car. He's got a distinctive double-headed eagle tattoo on his upper arm that marks him as one of Pavel's friends. I break out in a cold sweat as I realize how close we came to meeting him face-to-face.

I look at my new friend from between the front seats, wondering if she noticed the guy. She's driving without flinching or looking in her rearview mirror.

"I need to pick Thibault up from the hospital," she says. "Mind if we swing by and get him on the way to your place?"

"Yeah, sure. No problem." *My place.* I don't have a place anymore. My mind is racing. I'm without a car now, too, so until I get some wheels and some clothing, I'm completely vulnerable. I want to cry angry, rage-filled tears, but I don't bother. There's nobody in this car who's going to give a hoot about my problems. Toni's made it clear she's not a fan.

Thibault's waiting just outside the glass doors of the hospital as we pull up in the valet area. He's on crutches, and he's got a white coffee mug with something sticking out of it hooked through a finger.

Toni rolls down the passenger window. "Hurry up."

"I'm going as fast as I can," he says. When he reaches the door, he opens it and maneuvers himself in, hissing when he bumps his knee. "Son of a . . ." Once he's settled, he twists in his seat and looks at me, a slight smile on his face. "Fancy meeting you here."

"Yeah." I have nothing to say to that. I'm embarrassed to be here, hating the feeling of being at the mercy of strangers. Practical strangers, anyway.

Thibault twists back around and taps the dashboard. "Let's roll."

"How's your leg?" I ask after a couple stoplights. The silence is too awkward.

"Fine."

"I heard different," Toni says.

"You don't need to worry about it," he says to her.

"I'm happy to give you my insurance information," I say, remembering how focused Toni was on that when she was visiting him in his room. I don't want her still thinking it's my boobs that inspired Thibault to be nice to me.

"Good. I'll get it from you when we drop you off." She glances at me in the mirror.

"No, we won't," he says, glaring at his sister. He turns to me. "I told you . . . my insurance is handling everything."

Toni and I both sigh at the exact same time, equally loudly.

Thibault chuckles. "I'm the meat in a stubborn sandwich."

"Shut up," his sister says. "You're a meat*head*, and that's it."

I look over at the baby, bundled up tight in the cheap hospital blanket the nurses said I could keep. I'm going to get him a new one as soon as we're settled. He deserves better.

"Baby looks good," Thibault says, looking between the front seats. "What's his name?"

"You can call him Tee," I say. "That's what I'm calling him now. It's short for Thibault."

"Poor kid," he says. "I was hoping you'd changed your mind about that for his sake."

"You named your kid after my brother?" Toni glances up at me in the mirror again. "What's that all about?"

I hate the insinuation she's making, like I'm after him or something. "He brought my baby into the world. It was kind of a big deal, but I can see how you wouldn't understand." *Boom. Take that, you prickly witch.*

"You sure you want to do that?" Thibault asks me. "The name is terrible."

"Are you serious?" I can't believe he just insulted my child like that. And himself.

He's laughing. "Yes, I'm serious. You need to give him a decent name. Thibault is seriously bad. Do you know how many times I've been called Thigh-Bolt or T-Bird or T-Bone? Kids are cruel. It's not too late, you know."

"Yes, it is too late." I look out the window. Now I'm even more determined to keep the name. When I finally get around to filling out the birth certificate, I'll make it official.

"I know you didn't fill out those forms that were in your room yet."

It's like he can read my mind. I don't like knowing I'm that transparent. "You don't know me."

"Did you?" Toni asks, glancing at me as we sit at a red light. "Did you fill out the forms?"

I don't want to answer, but I do after a while anyway. "No."

"Busted," Thibault says. He hands something to me—the white mug. "Got this for you." Inside it is a miniature teddy bear and some candies. "Congratulations. It's not a donut with sprinkles, but it was the best I could do in a pinch."

I know it's just a silly gift, but it makes me cry. He remembered the donut, too. Maybe he was looking forward to giving it to me as much as I was looking forward to getting it from him, which is ridiculous because it was just a damn donut. The mug has printing on it—words surrounding a heart: *Best Mom Ever*. I turn to look out the side window so my fellow passengers won't see my overly emotional reaction. "Thanks," I say when I'm sure I can control my voice.

"No problem. So, where're we headed?" He looks at his sister and then at me. Both of us shake our heads.

"Uhhh . . . anyone want to fill me in on what's going on?"

I clear my throat. "Toni was going to drop me off somewhere."

"Your place?" he asks.

"Yeah. My place. Take a right up here." A plan is forming in my head as we roll down the avenue. I'll see what cars are in the parking lot before we go in. If Sonia's and Pavel's cars aren't there, I'll chance it. I could leave Tee with Mrs. Barkley down the hall while I grab some things really quick out of my room and the bathroom. Then I could catch a cab to a bus station and hop a ride out of here. Or I'll take the cab to the police station first, so I can talk to Detective Holloway. Maybe he'll give me a lift to the bus station after that.

"Left up there and then right on Lincoln."

Toni follows my directions as Thibault taps out a rhythm on his leg. "Your roommate home?" he asks.

"No idea." I hope she isn't, because not only will she probably rat me out again, but I'll be way too tempted to smack her for the trouble she's caused.

"You have a key, I hope." Thibault turns around to look at me. "They took your keys with the car, remember? We left your car running when we went into the nail salon."

I open my mouth to respond at the same moment I'm realizing he's right. "Dammit," I hiss. Getting the superintendent to let me in will take forever.

"But if your roommate's there, she'll let you in, right?" Toni's question holds a challenge.

"Yeah. Right."

I take my phone from my purse. My thumb hovers over the keyboard. I want to text Sonia and ask her if she's home, but alarm bells are clanging like crazy in my head telling me not to. Instead of sending the text, I slide my phone into my pocket. "Turn right at that light. The apartment building is two blocks down on the left."

Nervous dread fills me from my toes to my head as I imagine what might be waiting for me at my place. As the apartment building's parking lot comes into view, I recognize three vehicles that tell me getting into my home undetected is going to be impossible: Sonia's, Pavel's, and Sebastian's—a business associate of Pavel's. It's like they're having a party there or something. *Since when does Sebastian hang out at my place?*

"Don't pull in," I say, too loudly and too quickly.

Toni pauses with her foot on the brake and then lets the car roll forward. It's going too slow. Someone is going to notice.

"Hit it," Thibault says, whatever joking tone he was using earlier gone from his voice. "Now."

Toni presses on the accelerator and speeds by the parking lot, leaning over the steering wheel like she's about to try to outrun the cops.

Thibault looks around the side of his seat and smiles at me, looking as though he has no idea that I just freaked out about them stopping at my apartment. "Feel like coming over to my place for a quick bite to eat? Before we bring you to your place, I mean?"

He's saving me again. Against my will . . . *again*. But same as last time, I realize I'm in no position to refuse the help. It burns my butt a little, but a mom's gotta do what a mom's gotta do. I'm going to keep telling myself that as long as I need to.

"Sure," I say, affecting the same tone as he did—clueless and happy. "That would be nice. Thanks."

Toni lets out a long breath, shaking her head. I sink back into the seat, feeling both shame and fear in equal measure. Toni and Thibault exchange glances, but neither of them says anything.

I pretend not to notice their unspoken conversation, focusing most of my attention on the baby. It's the only thing that can keep the burning tears in my eyes from escaping to make salty trails down my cheeks.

After a few miles driven in silence, I glance at the seat next to me and catch sight of the mug Thibault gave me. Best Mom Ever. *Yeah, right*. It's like a cruel joke, mocking me. I grit my teeth at the unfairness of it all. My grandmother would be so disappointed in me. I knew better than to let myself get into this situation. Or I should have. I shake my head, trying to push away the negative thoughts. "Shake it off," my grandmother always used to say. "Whenever those dark spirits try to get in, shake 'em off."

Thinking of her and her wise words gives me a shot of courage. I can do better than this. I know I can. I won't let my life stay this way, and I *am* going to be the best mom ever. Tee didn't ask to be brought into this world; he's the innocent one in all this. I may not have chosen to bring him into the world, either, but that doesn't matter. As his mother, I have a duty to make sure he's safe and well brought up, so he can be a good man, a good husband, and a good father. I believe I can do this. Eventually. Once I'm free.

I just need a plan that'll get me out of here and away from all this craziness. There's only one that makes any sense, even though it scares the living daylights out of me: I have to contact Detective Holloway and let him know I'm ready to deliver the goods and turn state's witness against Pavel and everyone involved in his criminal organization.

CHAPTER TWELVE

So this is where you live, huh?" I look around his living room, taking in the details as I put the car seat with Tee in it down on the floor. I rest my hand on my stomach, wincing at the cramps that keep coming up to spoil my mood even more. Having a period after giving birth seems really unfair. After all I went through, it seems like I should get a several-month break from that nonsense, especially since I never had regular periods to start with.

"Yep." He gestures at the couch. "Please, have a seat."

I bring the baby with me, placing the carrier at my feet as I relax against the cushions. It's not a new couch, but it's very comfortable. I could easily fall asleep on it. I sit up straighter to make sure that doesn't happen. I'm so damn tired and sore.

"This used to be my parents' guest cottage." He points out the window. "Toni lives there in the main house with her husband Lucky and their two kids."

"You grew up in a nice place." There's crown molding ringing the ceilings, built-in bookshelves, a cuckoo clock that looks really old, and some framed prints of bayou country on the beige walls. The bigger house he's pointing to across the lawn is huge, with a grand old porch wrapping around the front and sides of it. There are kids' toys scattered in the grass. If the cottage looks like this inside, I can imagine what the big house is like.

"The house was nice, sure." He grunts, balancing his weight on one leg as he lifts the baby seat up and sets it down next to me on the couch. "The atmosphere, not so much."

I find it hard to believe Thibault didn't get along with his parents. Based on what I've seen of him so far, I picture him as the high school football star, getting straight As and making his parents proud.

"What was wrong with the atmosphere?" It seems like a strange way to describe family life.

"My parents were both big drinkers. They started early in the day, every day. Toni and I didn't spend a lot of time at home. We preferred to be out with friends or at our grandparents' place."

I nod. I can appreciate that. "I was close with my grandma, too."

He leaves the room, headed for the kitchen. "Do you want something to drink? I've got bottled water in here."

"Sure." I feel like we're playing a strange game, where we pretend everything is normal when it's not. Not at all. Toni left the car to go into her house without a word. Thibault's invited me into his without hesitation. I know she didn't approve of it, but he doesn't seem to care. And I don't know what's going to happen now. I have no plan. It's making me really nervous.

"Here you go," he says, coming back into the room with a tall glass of water for me.

"Thanks." I take it and drink half of it immediately. "I'm so thirsty lately."

"Yeah. Toni was like that, too. After the twins were born."

His expression is completely neutral. He's taken a chair next to the couch and is sipping a glass of water.

"What?" he asks, looking down at himself. "Is there something wrong?"

"No. I'm just trying to figure you out."

A ghost of a grin appears. "Any luck?"

I shake my head. "No, not really."

I don't want him to think I'm being flirty, so I change the subject. "Toni's kids are twins, huh?"

He nods. "Yeah. Melanie and Victor."

"You said you're their favorite uncle. I assume that means you have other siblings. Are they as close as you and Toni are?"

"No, we don't have other siblings."

"And her husband?"

"He lost his only sister a few years ago."

"Soooo, you're their *only* uncle."

"Technically, yes, but not-so-technically, no."

I tap the side of my water glass. "Explain."

He leans back in his chair. "We have some really close friends who are here a lot, who are a big part of our lives, and she considers them uncles and aunts to her kids."

A niggle of jealousy sneaks into my heart. I wish I had people like that in my life. "Ah, okay. And who are they?" It's calming me down to learn more about his life rather than worry about my next move—a temporary reprieve from the real-world problems I'm facing.

"People we grew up with and work with. And their spouses."

"Do they have names?" I take a slow sip of my water.

He frowns. "You sure are curious about my life."

I shrug. "Just being friendly."

"How about if I ask you a few questions? Friendly ones."

I'm immediately on edge. I should have known better than to try to be nice. "Sure." If I want more of his help, which I'm afraid I'm going to have to ask for at least to get some clothes, I need to play along.

"What exactly are you running from?"

I put the water glass down on the table and pull the baby seat closer to me, occupying myself with the buckles strapping Tee in. "No one. Nothing."

"Bull." Gone is the smile and the easy charm he was sharing just moments earlier. His mood is now completely cold.

I take the baby from his seat and rest him against my shoulder. "No one you need to worry about."

He looks down into his water glass for about a minute before coming back to the conversation. "I'd like to help you, but I can't do that if I don't really know what's going on."

"I don't need your help."

He sighs, shaking his head at me. "Why are you so bullheaded?"

"Why are you so pushy?" I pat Tee on the back rapidly, trying not to let my frustration show but not being very successful at it. I really want to just get up and walk out of here, but where would I go? I'm in a neighborhood now, not the city. There are no cabs out here, and if I stand on the corner in this getup waiting for one that I call, someone's liable to sic the cops on me. And cops mean social services, which means Tee being taken from me. I'm caught between a rock and a hard place. But that doesn't mean I'm going to kowtow to anyone, either.

"I wouldn't have to be pushy if you weren't being so stubborn," he says with a hint of a smile. He thinks he has me on the ropes.

"Oh, so your bad attitude toward women, thinking you should be allowed to boss them around and push them in whatever direction you want, is their fault?" I snort. "Please. Could you be any more of a misogynist?"

He hisses out a breath and drops his head back onto the seat cushion. "Lord, spare me from belligerent, bullheaded women." He lifts his head and looks at me. "You are exactly like my sister. *Exactly.* Two peas in a pod."

"You're kidding me." I actually found his sister to be incredibly rude, so I'm pretty sure this is an insult.

"No, I'm not." His smile is faint, like he's confused about what he's saying as he says it. "You're both stubborn, outspoken, hard-edged, tough, and walking around with a chip on your shoulder."

My jaw drops open in shock. I didn't think Thibault's opinion of me really mattered, but I guess it does; this hurts more than it should. "Well, excuse me, but I don't recall signing up for a personality review when I accepted your offer of a ride. But now that I know I did, I'll just be saying goodbye." I take Tee from my shoulder and place him as gently as I can into his car seat while my hands are shaking. The buckles and straps are all mangled together, so it takes effort to get them straight. I'm trying really hard not to cry tears of frustration. Nothing is going right for me today. Nothing.

Thibault leans forward, struggling to get his leg to cooperate. "No, wait. Don't do that."

I pause and look up at him, stupid tears filling my eyes. "Don't do what? Stand up for myself? Refuse to accept poor behavior on the part of a man? Leave a place where I'm not wanted?" It feels like there's a shard of glass lodged in my chest. Rejection by this man shouldn't matter one bit to me, but it hurts. I'm not going to lie to myself and say anything different.

He holds out his hands at me in surrender. "No, don't say that. Don't do that." He sighs heavily as he looks away. "I screwed up."

I get the buckles straight finally and click them together. "No, you didn't. You just told the truth."

He shakes his head, his voice low. "No, I didn't."

I take in his slouched shoulders, flared nostrils, and the pulsing of his jaw muscles. He's disappointed and maybe confused. Angry about something. He looks at me all of a sudden, catching me examining him. I drop my eyes to the baby and busy myself with tucking his blanket in around him.

"I'm an asshole."

I wasn't expecting that. I look up at him. Blinking. I can't think of anything to say. I think courtesy would require me to disagree, but I can't do it. He hasn't always been an asshole around me, but he sure did a good impression of one two minutes ago.

He rubs his knee over and over as he stares at the floor. "My knee is really bugging me, and the painkillers aren't working so well, and I'm worried about my job and the people I'm going to let down if I can't do it." He sighs. "I took it out on you, and that wasn't fair."

Guilt assails me. It's partially my fault that this is all happening to him. I haven't just made a mess of my own life; I've dragged him down too. "Listen . . . I'm really sorry I hit you with my car." I'm unable to get my voice up to normal volume. "It sucks that you need surgery. It's really terrible. I'll bet it's ruined a lot of your plans for yourself and your job and stuff."

He shakes his head. "Don't worry about it. Like you said . . . I should have looked in your direction before I stepped off the curb."

The atmosphere is heavy and sad. Being around this man throws me for so many loops, I don't know which way is up anymore. "So what exactly is your job, anyway?" I stop messing with the baby and fold my hands in my lap. I want to move this conversation out of the dark place it was in and get us back on friendly footing. There's nothing to be gained by making this man an enemy, and I've already brought enough negativity into his life.

He sits up straighter in the chair and his shoulders lift, making him seem much bigger. "I work as a security consultant. Mostly my company works for the NOPD, helping them gather evidence for warrants or convictions, but we also work for private companies or individuals who need protection."

"How fortunate," I say before I can stop myself.

He gives me a half smile. "You need protection. I offer protection."

I shake my head. "No, I don't need protection."

He sighs. "I don't mean to be rude . . . or pushy . . . but I have to say this . . ." He presses his hands together. ". . . It sure seems like you need some."

"Why? Because I left the hospital in a robe? As you might recall, I arrived in the hospital in an ambulance and my car was towed. There was no way I could have clothes to change into."

"Unless you had a friend to bring you some."

I shrug. "As you've so kindly pointed out, I'm stubborn sometimes. Maybe I have friends but I don't want to inconvenience them."

"Are you going to punish me for saying that about you forever?" he asks, looking slightly pitiful.

"Maybe."

"Stubborn," he says, smiling.

I try not to smile back, but it's hard not to.

"Do you want to know what I think?" he asks, scooting to the front of his chair and then wincing and rubbing his knee.

"Probably not."

He says nothing and the pressure mounts.

"Fine. Tell me what you think."

He keeps his eyes locked on his knee. "I think that there's a man named Pavel who came to see you and the baby he thinks is his, and that this man is not a very nice man, and that you're trying to stay away from him as best you can." He looks up at me to gauge my reaction.

I open my mouth to hit him with a barrage of questions, but he stops me with a lifted hand.

"Hold on . . . I'm not finished . . . I also think you're a good girl who might have gotten into a bad situation, and maybe just a little help could get you on the right track, because you're tough and self-sufficient and you want to do the right thing by your son."

My emotions are swirling around like they're caught in a tornado. One second I'm offended, then sad, then proud, then confused. I say the first thing that comes to mind. "How in the hell do you know anything about Pavel?"

He presses his hands together and rubs them a little. "I told you. I'm in security. And my company has a great relationship with the NOPD." He pauses, glancing at the floor for a few seconds before looking back at me. "I came to see you this morning, like I said I would. I had a donut with sprinkles on it for a young woman who'd just had a baby and hadn't yet had a visitor other than me." Before I can question him on that, he answers. "I asked the nurses and they were more than happy to give me the information. Turns out they were hoping I could talk some sense into this woman who was refusing to fill out the baby's birth certificate."

"Ha. You want to talk about stubborn women . . . talk to those nurses."

"I know, right?" He smiles. "They sure do love their paperwork over there."

I move the baby's little foot, covered in a sock. He's sleeping so deeply he doesn't even flinch. I can't look at Thibault anymore. He's digging into my fears, but I know efforts to stop him won't work. And I want to know what he knows and how he found out my personal details, because if he can do it, so can Pavel. I need to learn how to guard my privacy better by not making the same mistakes twice.

"There were two police officers outside the maternity ward when I got there. I know them well from work we've done together. They told me about a young mother who had a visit from a known gangbanger named Pavel, who, after refusing to see him, disappeared from the hospital with her baby. She'd somehow figured out a way to short-circuit the security bracelet the baby was wearing."

"I had to go," I say softly. I can still picture the look on that nurse's face when she told me Pavel was outside wanting to get in. She knew he was bad news. Thank goodness she followed her instincts and didn't let him in.

"I have no doubt. His rap sheet is pretty scary."

I nod. The police don't even know the half of it. It makes me sick to think my baby has half his DNA, but I'm going to do everything in my power to make sure he grows up on the right side of the law. I'm more determined than ever to see this through.

"So, it wasn't too complicated to figure out where you'd gone. I asked my sister to find the tow yard that had your car, and she got over there just in time to find you trying to get it. But I guess Pavel beat you to it."

"Yeah. And how in the hell did he find my car before I did? That's what I want to know."

"Your story was all over the news. Still is. They even had shots of your car being towed away, so the tow yard got a bunch of free advertisement and Pavel didn't even have to make a single phone call to find it."

I let out a long sigh, settling back into the cushions and staring at the ceiling. "You're pretty good at your job, I guess."

"I'm damn good at it."

"And humble, too." I have to smile. He's a good guy. Pushy, but good.

He chuckles. "You got me there."

The room goes silent. My head swims with possible futures for myself and Tee. *Where will we go? How will we go there? How much money do I have, and how long will it last?* I haven't checked my mutual fund account lately, so I don't know if the balance has gone up or down. I'm guessing I have enough money to last us six months if I live frugally and find a dirt-cheap apartment somewhere. I wonder how hard it will be to rent a place without giving my true identity.

I look over at Thibault. "At your work . . . do you guys get fake identities for people?"

He frowns at me. "No."

"Oh. Bummer." I go back to staring at the ceiling.

"Wouldn't you rather fix the problems that are making you run rather than change your identity?"

I laugh bitterly. "Sure. And I'd like to own a winning lottery ticket, too, but I don't see that happening in my near future."

"Can't win if you don't play," he says, staring at me.

I look at him again and sigh, tired of the conversation, of the topic, of the entire concept of my life and the horrible direction it's going in. "Is that supposed to mean something to me other than the obvious?"

"It means that running isn't going to get you anywhere but in another place with the same problems. You'll never feel safe. This guy—Pavel—seems to have a lot of resources, from what the police said, anyway. Aren't you worried he'll find you?"

I sit up, angry now. He's doing it again. "You're always pushing, aren't you?"

"No, I'm just—"

"Yes, you are. Pushing, pushing, pushing. Yes! Okay! I get it! I'm screwed! I'll run, he'll find me. I'll run again, and he'll find me again. There's nothing I can do but play this out and see what happens. Maybe I'll get lucky and he won't find me."

"Do you have a plan?" He's completely unaffected by my rude response. It makes me think he's not listening.

"Maybe I do, but it's none of your business."

He nods. "You're right."

"I know I'm right." My nostrils flare with aggravation.

He smiles. "You're arguing with me about something I agree about."

"So?"

"Stubborn. Just like I said."

"Whatever." I stand. "Where's your bathroom?"

He points. "Down the hall, first door on your right."

I stand and grab the car seat handle.

"You can leave him. I'll keep an eye on him. Make sure he doesn't unbuckle himself and crawl away."

I roll my eyes at Thibault as I release the handle. "Thanks." I feel foolish, thinking I needed to take the baby with me. I have no idea what I'm doing. I hate feeling so stupid and helpless.

Thibault stands with great effort. "Wait. Hold on a second."

I pause in the middle of the room. He approaches on crutches and stops a couple feet away. "I'm sorry."

I blink a few times, trying to figure out what he's up to now. "Sorry for what?"

"For being a jerk. I'm just worried about you is all."

I shake my head slowly and give him a pitying look. "Poor Superman. He's got a damsel in distress who doesn't want his help. Whatever will he do?"

He frowns at me. "What is it with you and Toni calling me that? I'm no superhero. I don't think I'm one, and I don't try to act like one."

"Sure seems like you're trying to be one." I walk to the bathroom.

"I don't know how you can call me a superhero with this bum leg I've got!" His voice follows me into the hallway.

I smile. I know I shouldn't, but I can't help it. "I guess we know what this Superman's Kryptonite is."

"Oh, yeah? What's that?"

"Toyota car bumpers!" I close the door to the toilet and giggle to myself as I take care of business. My heart is lighter now than it was a half hour ago. I know the feeling won't last, but I'll enjoy it while I can. By the end of the afternoon, I need to have a plan that includes me being gone from here and out of Thibault's life forever. The thought makes me sadder than it should. He's a nice guy, and someday I'd like to have a guy like him as a friend in my life.

CHAPTER THIRTEEN

After feeding the baby and taking a nap sitting up on Thibault's couch, I find myself alone with Tee asleep beside me in the living room. I don't hear anything other than the cuckoo clock that just woke me up. It's five in the evening and my stomach is growling.

I look around the room, and my eyes land on a photo album. I take it from the coffee table in front of me and start paging through it.

The first thing that strikes me is how happy everyone seems. I think I'm looking at Bourbon Street Boys employees since one of them is wearing a logoed T-shirt with that name on it. They celebrate with a lot of barbecues apparently. I can tell I'm seeing more than one in the various photos because the people are wearing different outfits and the trees are different. Someone has put the shots together with little captions next to them, and whoever that person is, she has a great eye. I'm assuming it's a woman responsible, since I don't know any men who make photo albums like this.

The twins are in some of the pictures, almost all the time with either Thibault holding them or another man. Maybe the father. He's gorgeous, with a thick, long beard that does nothing to hide his handsome face. He's standing next to Thibault in the photo I'm looking at now, and I find this man's appeal dimming when compared to Thibault's.

Thibault looks stronger. More compact. With a darker skin tone and harder angles to his face. He looks very sure of himself, of who he is and where he belongs in the world. I envy him that.

"Ah, you found the famous photo album." Thibault comes limping down the stairs, one arm using a crutch, the other holding on to the banister.

"You guys have a lot of barbecues."

"Every time we close a case, that's how we celebrate. Rain or shine."

I turn the page. "Lots of kids."

"Yeah, everyone but me has at least one now."

I look up at him. "Some of them are very young, so I guess this is a new thing for your company? To have all those kids around?"

"Yep." He joins me on the couch, setting the baby seat off to the side so he can point to the pictures. I focus on the large man in the photo. "That's Ozzie," Thibault says. "He started the company, and he was the first to go down."

"Go down?"

He smiles. "Yeah. Fall under a woman's spell and put a ring on her finger."

I shrug. "Well, if you like it, then you better put a ring on it."

"Ha, ha. Nice one, Beyoncé."

"Who's this?" I ask, pointing to a man who's a couple feet taller than the woman he's standing next to.

"That's Dev and Jenny. He was the second to go down."

I laugh. "And the third?"

"Lucky." He points to the man with the beard. "My sister's husband. Went down with her."

"Poor guy," I say, before I can stop myself.

Thibault barks out a laugh. "Ha! You said it." He leans back on the couch. "Nah, I'm just kidding. But that was funny. I'm going to tell Lucky next time I see him."

"She doesn't drive you crazy?" I can't imagine having a sibling like her. "She must test her husband's patience."

"Sure, she drives me crazy. And the day I get married, it'll be to someone who's her total opposite. But I love her more than anything or anyone in the world." He shrugs. "We've been through a lot together. And she might be a little harsh, but inside she has a heart of gold. I wouldn't change who she is for anything."

"You've been through a lot together when you were young, you mean? With your parents?"

He gets a far-off look in his eye. "Yeah, then. And later in life, too."

I slowly close the photo album. Things are starting to sound interesting, and I can't think of anything that could work better at getting my mind off my problems than hearing about someone else's instead.

"What happened?"

He doesn't answer for the longest time. Then he seems to snap out of whatever trance he was in and sits up suddenly. "Nothing I'd like to rehash." He takes the book from me and sets it down on the table. "Let's talk about you."

"I'd rather not."

"Are you hungry?" he asks.

His abrupt about-face puts me off-kilter. "Uh. Yeah? A little. Maybe." My stomach growls. My face burns with embarrassment. "Definitely. I'm definitely hungry."

He pats me on the knee and then presses on my leg to lever himself up. "How about I cook dinner while we chat in the kitchen? You can help me, since I'm temporarily handicapped."

I stand, grateful for the change of scenery. I've been sitting in this room for hours. "Sure. Can I leave the baby here?"

"Yeah, of course. Feel free to take him out of his seat and put him on the couch. He'll probably be more comfortable."

"But what if he rolls off?"

"He won't. He's too little yet for that. But we can wrap him up really tight and then put that album next to him so he won't be the first two-day-old baby to learn to roll over and land on the carpet."

I feel silly not knowing the most basic things about babies. "Okay." I watch as Thibault wraps Tee up like a pro, until my little man resembles a human burrito. Then he sets him gently down on the cushion and uses the photo album near his middle to box him in.

"We'll come check on him every few minutes to make sure he's okay. And I can go over and borrow Toni's old bassinet, too, in case you want to give him an actual baby bed."

"We'll see." I'm not comfortable with the idea of borrowing anything from Toni, and having a bed here feels like a commitment to something I don't want to make. I follow him into the kitchen, glancing back at my son. He's sound asleep, not moving a muscle.

"Do you like pasta?" he asks, opening up a small door that leads into a pantry.

I go over to help. "Sure."

"Grab that box, please," he says, pointing.

I take down some rigatoni from the shelf along with some sauce he points to next.

"I'm an expert at boiling noodles," he says, pretending to be proud of himself.

I hide my smile, for some reason not wanting him to know that his charm does have some effect on me. I put the items down on the counter next to the stove and then watch him do his expert noodle-making thing.

"My sister has started doing more cooking lately, since she had the kids. I go over there for dinner a lot."

"You guys are really close. You live next door to each other, share meals . . ."

"Yeah. We're real close now, but there was a time when we weren't so much. When she was with this guy. Charlie."

"Really? Why? Did you not like him?"

He shakes his head while he fills a pot with water. "I said I didn't want to rehash it, but here I am bringing it up again."

"Maybe you *do* want to talk about it."

He shrugs, watching the pot as the water inside comes to a boil. "Talking helps sometimes. Some people. Not me, usually."

"Do you do it often? Talk to people about your problems?"

"No. Never."

"Then how do you know if it helps or not?"

He dumps noodles into the water, stirs it a little, and sets the spoon down on the counter before turning to face me. "Maybe I don't." He shrugs and reaches for the salt, turning to add some to the water. "It's a long story."

It's on the tip of my tongue to say, "I've got time," but then I realize I might not have time. *What am I still doing here?*

"What's that look on your face mean?" Thibault asks me, catching me frowning at the floor.

I shake my head. "Nothing."

"Come on, it's not nothing. You look stressed."

I shrug. "It wouldn't be crazy for me to be stressed right now, would it?"

"No, probably not."

"Do you mind if I get myself some water?" I ask.

"Not at all. Help yourself. Glasses are in the cupboard there. Water bottles are in the pantry."

Happy for the distraction, I move around the kitchen, getting water for both of us.

"I have an idea," he says, putting another pot on the stove and adding sauce to it.

"Am I going to like it?"

He chuckles. "Are you always so suspicious?"

"Pretty much."

He mumbles his next words. "God, you remind me so much of her."

"Of who?" I'm afraid I know the answer already.

"My sister."

"So, essentially, I remind you of a person who annoys the hell out of you."

He looks over his shoulder. "Yeah. But I also love her to death, so it's not all bad . . ."

"Yeah, well, no offense taken. Not to be rude or anything, but you're not really my type, either."

"Oh, yeah?" he chuckles. "What's your type, exactly?" He's stirring the sauce, his back to me. It makes it easier to be honest when I answer.

"Kind. Supportive. Lets me do my own thing. Doesn't treat me like I need help all the time, like I'm weak."

He stops stirring. "Offering someone help isn't the same thing as calling them weak." He turns to look at me. "Accepting help doesn't make you weak, either."

I raise a brow at him. "Do you accept help?"

He turns his head to look at the box of pasta. "You got that food down from the shelf for me, didn't you? You didn't hear me complain about it."

I have to smile at that. "That's not the same thing." I get up quickly to check the baby and come back after assuring myself he hasn't moved an inch.

Thibault returns to the sauce, giving me his back. "If you say so."

I chew on my lip as I consider what he's said. *Am I being stubborn?* "I've accepted your help."

He nods. "Yes, you have. Some of it, anyway."

"I'm here at your house. That was a big help to me, you giving me a ride and a place to hang out for a while so I can gather my thoughts and have a nap."

"Any idea where you're going from here?" he asks.

His shoulders are moving with his cooking efforts, and I'm enjoying staring at them without him knowing. He is so solid. His body's almost as hard as his skull. I smile at my thoughts.

He turns around and catches me. "What's so funny?"

I shake my head, the easy humor dropping away. "Nothing." I take a sip of water. "In answer to your question about where I'm going from here, I can honestly say I have no idea."

He bangs the spoon on the side of the saucepan and then sets it down on the counter. Limping in a circle, he leans against the sink and folds his arms across his chest. "You could stay here. For a little while. Until you figure it out."

I shake my head. "No, I don't think that's a good idea."

"How come?"

"Well, as you know, there's a certain guy looking for me, and he's not the nicest guy in the world, either. I need to leave the area—the sooner, the better. Probably tonight would be a good idea. I'll have to check the bus schedule."

"Do you know where you're going?"

City names flash through my head: Baton Rouge, Atlanta, New York, Seattle . . . None of them sounds right. "No."

"Tell me about Pavel," he says. He lifts his chin, like he's challenging me.

"Tell me about Charlie," I counter.

"What's he got to do with anything?"

I shrug. "You want to know all about my life. Maybe I want to know a little bit about yours."

He presses his lips together for a few seconds and then gives me a slight nod. "Deal. I'll tell you about Charlie, and then you can tell me about Pavel."

"Fine." I'm not sure I really expect him to come clean on this. I can tell by the way his eyes are darting around now that he's regretting his decision. "You can back out if you want, though. Anytime, just say the word, and we'll keep our secrets to ourselves."

He pushes off the counter and goes back to his sauce and pasta, stirring both. "No, it's not a problem. I just have to figure out where to start."

"How about at the beginning?"

He smiles at me over his shoulder. "Now, why didn't I think of that?"

I laugh but leave it at that. If I keep playing with words, it'll just delay the story, and this one interests me probably more than it should. I walk over to the living room threshold and check on the baby as Thibault starts talking.

"Toni got caught up in him pretty quick. I didn't know why she fell so fast at the time, but I found out later that she did it to keep our friendship with Lucky and the others tight."

I turn to look at him. "I don't get it."

He sighs. "There's a lot of backstory, but basically, all the guys I work with . . . we've been friends since we were kids. We all hung out on the streets together. When Toni and Lucky were younger, they kind of hooked up—which I didn't find out about until much later—but at the time it happened, Toni was worried something between them would break up our group, and that group was all we had . . . it meant everything to us . . . so she latched onto the first guy she found so she could get away from Lucky. That was Charlie."

"And he wasn't a good guy?"

His voice goes deeper with emotion. "No. He was a really, really bad guy."

"How bad?"

"At the time, I just thought he was kind of an asshole." He looks at me. "Sorry, but there's no nice word for that guy."

"That's okay. I've heard that word before. You're good."

He looks down at his hands, staring at them, twisting them around each other as he flexes his muscles. I don't know who this Charlie guy is, but I'd bet if he were here, he'd be getting a black eye from Mister Delacroix.

"Anyway, she was with him for a few years. And we found out later that he'd been abusing her. A lot."

I feel sick. Now we're entering the kind of world I live in. "You saw it?"

"I saw the bruises, but she always gave us good reasons for them being there that had nothing to do with Charlie. She played sports, she was tough, she picked fights with people . . . She always had an excuse." He shakes his head. "But I should have known better."

"Because you've got that Superman complex."

"No. Because I'm not blind, and I love my sister. But I was very self-absorbed back then." He stops, looking as though he's gathering his thoughts and emotions before finishing, maybe traveling down memory lane a bit. "Anyway, long story short, the abuse got so bad that my sister got a gun. And then one day he came after her, and she defended herself."

"She *shot* him?" I was not expecting this ending. I figured he was going to say there was a big fight and some jail time for someone. I picture the diminutive woman who drove me over here in her SUV, and I suppose I could see her kicking ass and taking names, but shooting someone? That takes a special kind of badassery I don't think I'm capable of. Her life must have been hell with that Charlie guy. A trickle of pity for her drips into my heart. No wonder she's so angry all the time.

Thibault looks tortured as he rubs his chest over his heart, staring blankly at the wall. "She called me on the phone as she kneeled over his dead body. She was screaming and screaming . . ." He pauses for a long while, as if reliving it. He frowns and his eyes get shiny, and when he speaks again, his voice is rough. "I'll never forget that moment. It was like living in a waking nightmare; it follows me everywhere to this day."

He shakes his head and refocuses his gaze on me. "So, yeah . . . She shot him and she killed him. And she served time for it." He turns around and grabs the wooden spoon, jamming it into the saucepan. "And I will never forgive myself for not paying attention to her and what was going on in her life. I could have stopped all of that from happening. She ended up in jail, and she ruined her life . . . Or she nearly did. She's got deep scars that'll probably never go away."

I walk over and tap him on the arm to be sure he's with me in the present and can hear me. "You can't say it's your fault. She's a grown woman. That's not fair to put it all on yourself."

He shrugs. "It's how it is. When you love someone, you have to be there for her. You have to pay attention to the details of her life and not accept lies and excuses as the truth."

Now I understand why Toni said Thibault lives with ghosts. These are pretty powerful memories, and not something anyone could forget easily. Or at all. I know exactly how he feels. "Is that why you're in security?"

"I was in security before that happened, which only makes it worse. I should have seen it. I'm trained to deal with violent people." He takes a long breath and lets it out slowly, as if practicing some sort of relaxation technique. It doesn't appear to be helping. He looks like he's either going to cry or punch a hole in the wall.

I don't fear him in the least, though. He's only mad at himself. Poor guy. He really does have a complex, but at least I can understand why now. I feel bad for him and his sister. What a horrible thing to live through. He and I are really not that different, now that I think about it. We've both been involved with violent crime, both trying to find our way back to peace, struggling, sometimes succeeding, more often failing; at least in my case. It looks like he's doing all right for himself, and his sister appears to have picked up the pieces of her life and carried on.

The ticking of the clock breaks through my thoughts. It's getting late, and I still don't have a plan. The door on the front of the clock opens all of a sudden, and the little wooden bird comes out, making me jump. "Cuck-oo! Cuck-oo! Cuck-oo! Cuck-oo! Cuck-oo! Cuck-oo!"

"That little bird thinks you're crazy," I say, pointing at the clock. "Cuckoo, he called you."

Thibault tries to smile. "Maybe I am."

I go into the adjoining room and pick up the baby, needing to feel his warm body near me and wanting to inhale his sweet smell. This is where I find peace now, as fragile as it is. "I don't know you that well, but I think you're a good guy, Thibault. Too hard on yourself, of course, but I get that." I walk across the carpet and into the kitchen, handing him the baby. I'm not sure if Tee's magic will work on Thibault as well as it works on me, but it's worth a shot. "Could you hold him for me?"

"Sure." Thibault adjusts the bundle to be over his shoulder so he can gently pat the baby's back. He turns sideways and smells the baby's head, closing his eyes, a vague smile appearing to lighten the darkness that surrounded him.

Yep. Works on him, too. I walk out into the hallway where it connects to the kitchen.

"Where are you going?" Thibault calls out.

"I'm going to wash my hands. Take care of business."

"Yeah, okay. I'll just hold this little critter for you until you get back."

I talk to him from inside the small bathroom under the stairs. "Maybe you can show me how to wrap Tee up like you did. He seems to like being trussed up in that blanket like a mummy."

"Sure!" he yells to be heard over the running water I'm using to wash my hands.

When I come out, I find him rubbing Tee's back gently.

"We call that the baby burrito wrap," he says. "Guaranteed to quiet a fussy baby." Tee hiccups and Thibault tips his head down and inhales deeply.

"He smells good, huh?" I come over to get a whiff of that baby magic myself. I lean in, the scents of my boy and Thibault's cologne mingling together. It's a heady thing, to be so near this man when he's holding my child so tenderly. It makes me a little dizzy. It's almost too emotionally charged for me to handle. I pull the baby away from him without a word and turn around so he won't catch the look I'm pretty sure is on my face. I need to put some distance between us. My heart is aching for something it can never have. Not with this man, anyway, and not in this town.

Walking over to the kitchen table, I take a seat. "I guess it's my turn to confess my worst moment." There's no better way to get myself back on solid ground than to remind myself how messy my life is right now.

Thibault walks to the corner of the kitchen, where there's a bedroom dresser against the wall. "Why don't you bring Tee over here, and I'll show you my wrapping technique while you tell me your story."

I join him, hoping the instructions will help distract him from listening too hard. This story represents the most humiliating moments of my life, not something I'm proud to share. But he told me about his past, and now it's my turn. I never back away from a deal once I've agreed to it.

I hand over Baby Tee, and Thibault places him on top of the dresser, where there's a cloth-covered cushion. He unwraps the baby and then starts his lesson. Tee remains asleep. "Fold a corner of the blanket down and put his head on the folded corner." He glances at me, giving me a look that I think is meant to be encouraging. It's time for me to start talking.

I clear my throat. "My parents were both drug addicts. In and out of jail as long as I can remember."

He keeps all of his attention on the baby, which I very much appreciate. "Tuck his arms down at his sides or across his chest. He'll let you know what he prefers."

"So, when I was twelve, and both my parents got arrested together, my grandma took me in. She's the one who raised me after that. She got legal custody and everything."

He nods, letting me know he's listening. "Start with the left part of the blanket and bring it over across his body, tucking it in really tight under him on the opposite side."

"We didn't have much, but we had each other. She helped me with my schoolwork. Helped me see the value of an education. She didn't go beyond junior high herself, and she always regretted it."

"Then do the bottom, bringing it up and folding it down if it's too long."

I'm struck by how gentle Thibault is with those big, muscular hands of his. I've always noticed men's hands for some reason. Maybe because they've often been used against me, so I have to keep an eye on them. But his hands are not the kind that worry me. They do make me think of him in other ways, though. They make me wonder whether he's as gentle with women as he is with babies. Imagining him that way makes me tingle in certain places, and I lose my train of thought.

"Got it?" he asks, jarring me out of my mesmerized state.

"Yeah. Got it." I pause, giving myself a moment to get back on track. *Where was I? Oh, yeah* . . . "I started junior college to get my AA degree, but my grandma passed during my first year."

He looks up at me, pausing his baby-wrapping lesson. "I'm really sorry to hear that. You must have been devastated."

"Thanks. Yeah, I was." I nod and look at the floor to keep my emotions in check. The day I lost my grandmother will go down in my personal history as the worst day of my life. I speak my thoughts aloud by accident. "It was the day I realized what being alone truly meant. She was all I had." A hitch in my chest keeps me from saying anything else, thank goodness.

"Did you finish? School, I mean?"

His question helps me get over the emotional hump. *Yes, let's talk about the aftermath.* "Yeah, I finished. Got my AA degree, but I couldn't keep going to get my four-year degree right away because I had to get a job to pay off the loans I took out to pay for my books and such. I also had to pay for my apartment and food. When my grandma was alive, I lived with her, but after she died I had to move out. I had a little savings that lasted me until the end of my second year, but it all dried up eventually."

He points at the baby. "After you have the bottom of the blanket secured like that, grab that last side over and tuck it under really tight."

I nod, trying to smile. I'm pretty sure he's using this baby-wrapping lesson to distract me from my pain, which I really appreciate. He's a nice man, this Thibault Delacroix. "I tried to get a job as a bookkeeper, but no one would hire me. They said I didn't have enough experience."

He holds up the baby. "*Voilà*: baby burrito." He hands Tee over to me, and I gather him in the crook of my arm, staring down at him as I tell the rest of the story.

"I got desperate. I thought I could just get a job doing *something*, even if it wasn't doing financial stuff, but everywhere I went, all I got were doors closed in my face. I even tried to get a job at a fast-food place, but the economy was so terrible, none of them were hiring. I couldn't even get an interview. I had bills to pay, and I wanted to finish school, too, but I had no money, no family . . . no hope left. It felt like the entire universe was conspiring against me."

"So what did you do?" He reaches up and moves a bit of the baby's blanket away from his face and tucks it under his chin. It's a small gesture, but thoughtful. It warms my heart and makes me feel like I'm in a safe place. I haven't felt this sensation in a long, long time. It gives me the push I need to finish my sad story.

"So, there was this guy in my neighborhood who said he wanted to help me out."

"Uh-oh," Thibault says. "Sounds like bad news."

"It was. He is. But I felt like I didn't have a choice. I'd tried to do the right thing over and over, and it just wasn't working out . . . So I took him up on his offer." I look up at Thibault, angry at my past, fully expecting his judgment to come, swift and sure. What I did was wrong and terrible, and there's no way out of that. I did what I did and I am who I am.

"What happened then?" His words come out soft. I don't yet feel his judgment, but he hasn't heard the worst of it.

I shrug, feeling my walls strengthening around me. They protect me from being hurt. I first erected them on the day I met with Pavel to discuss his proposal, and I haven't let them down since. They're a permanent part of who I am now. "I started working . . . standing on the corner. You know . . . turning tricks." Despite my self-protection, my walls, and the years I've spent telling myself that what other people think of me means nothing, my face burns with embarrassment. I wasn't raised to sell my body; I was raised to use my mind to support myself, but the world had a different plan for me.

His expression slowly shifts. He looks angry. His face takes on a red tinge.

"I know. Disgusting, right?" I look away. I can't stand to see the distaste there.

"No, hey, it's not like that." He takes me by the upper arms, squeezing lightly and then patting me awkwardly, trying to get me to look at him. "I wasn't thinking you're disgusting. I would never do that. I'm not judging you."

I look at him, trying to figure out from his expression if he's serious or just being nice. I don't see any deceit there. Maybe pity or frustration.

"What you did . . . it's not easy. It's not easy to be put in that situation and feel like you don't have any other choice. I just wish I'd known you then . . . so I could have helped you."

I try to smile, but I'm too sad. "Superman to the rescue?"

He steps back, his face twisted up. "No. Just . . . a person. A man who would've been happy to help you out." He runs a hand through his hair.

I reach out and grab his forearm for a second and then let it go. "I'm just giving you a hard time. I'm sorry. I didn't mean to make fun of your need to help people. I get where it's coming from now . . . Now that you've told me about your sister and Charlie. Please don't be mad at me."

He looks up suddenly, surprise in his expression. "I'm not mad at you. Not at all." He pauses, and his facial features smooth out as he attempts to smile. "I'm just mad at that guy. I don't know who he is, but I really want to rearrange his face for him."

I can barely get my words out as the present catches up to me and the reality of my situation comes crashing in. "He was the one who came into the hospital today looking for me. Pavel."

Thibault looks at the ground, his jaw pulsing in and out. "So, he's your pimp?"

"No. He's my *employer*."

He looks up and blinks a few times, obviously confused by my answer.

Thibault's probably going to laugh at me or think I'm a complete idiot, but I can't stop telling my story now. I need to share all of it with him; it feels like some sort of therapy to finally be able to tell someone the entire thing instead of just parts of it like I told Detective Holloway.

"Turns out, I actually suck at being a prostitute." I smile a little, remembering the times Pavel came at me, yelling about how I needed to learn how to be a proper whore.

He smiles cautiously. "Seriously?"

"Yeah. I've come to find out that men don't really like it when you give them shit during the act, if you know what I mean." I hold up a stiff finger and then slowly bend it down until it looks very limp and sad. My frown is exaggerated.

His smile is dangerously charming. "Imagine that," he says.

"But . . ." I lose my smile and become serious again, moving my attention to the baby. This story does not have a happy ending, even though there were some personal triumphs along the way. ". . . It also turns out that I'm good at keeping books, what with my finance degree and all. And Pavel needed someone to keep track of his growing enterprise, so when I got fired from his string of girls, I didn't get to go free; instead, I got recruited into this new job."

"And what's Pavel's story? Where's he from?"

"He's Russian. He came over here when he was nineteen, about seven years ago. People call him The *Vor*. It means thief, but a special kind of thief . . . One his people really respect."

"So you work as his bookkeeper?"

I shrug. "It was either that or end up in a ditch somewhere."

Thibault nods, all traces of humor gone from his face. "I get it." He turns to the changing table and pulls out a diaper, setting it on the top. "Well, at least you were off the streets."

I shake my head, wishing it was as positive as he makes it sound. "I just traded one hell for another." I walk over and place Tee down on the cushion. "Do you mind if I change him?"

"Not at all. That's one of Melanie's diapers from when she was a newborn. I don't know why I kept it, but it should be perfect for Tee. He's pretty tiny. These might fit him better than the ones you have."

"Thanks." I slowly unwrap my baby burrito and go through the motions of changing his diaper as I finish my tale of woe. "I've been doing this work for four years now. Officially, Pavel has a few laundromats, and I keep the books for them . . . a separate set for the government to see, of course. But unofficially he has a whole prostitution ring that has its own set of books, and he pushes most of the money he gets from that through the legit business to clean it up. I know everything about his life, work and personal. He's taking on girls from Europe now, too." I stop and clear my throat in an effort to keep the tears at bay. My life went from bad to horrifically awful in five years. I let it get away from me, and I feel like I'm drowning in a sea of regrets as I stand over my child. "I couldn't just sit there and do nothing anymore . . . Let those girls get used and abused like that. Some of them are really young, and unlike me, none of them signed up for it. When they left their home countries, they thought they were coming to have a better life. I had to do *something*."

"What did you do?" He reaches over and helps me with one of the diaper tapes. My fingers are trembling too much to work right. He doesn't say anything after the job is done; he just rests his big, warm hand on my shoulder as I finish and snap the baby's clothing together.

"I went to the police and became an informant." I place my hand on Tee's tummy and take a few deep breaths. "Part of me still can't believe I did it."

"It takes a lot of courage to do that. To take that risk."

"I didn't know I was pregnant. I don't know if I would have done it if I had known."

Thibault limps around me to help me with the blanket, gently guiding me in the wrapping process as he waits for me to speak again.

"Maybe I would have, I don't know." I sigh. "There's no point in wondering what might have been. I'm here and I've done what I've done. I just have to figure out where to go from here."

"How long have you been informing on him?"

"Three months. But then I wasn't feeling so good health-wise, so I was going to tell the detective I had to stop for a little while so I could get better. I was going to tell him that I needed to go to the doctor and that he had to pay for it because all this sneaking around was giving me indigestion." I sigh with the memory. I was all fired up then, so sure of myself. "I was going to start helping the cops again and do what I could when I was feeling better . . ."

"But all that time you were pregnant." He pauses. "With Pavel's baby?"

I laugh bitterly. "Stupid, right? How could I not know I had a baby growing inside me?" I don't want to go into detail about how I managed to have sex with Pavel when he's the son of the Devil himself and I've known this about him from day one. My story is already sad enough.

"It happens," he says.

"Not to me, or so I *thought*." I pick up the baby and hold him against me. My voice drops to a whisper. "Turns out I'm pretty clueless about a lot of things." Tears rush to my eyes and burn them. It feels like I'm sharing a dark secret with my baby as the fuzz from his head brushes against my lips and the words escape. "And now I don't know what I'm going to do." My chin trembles with the effort of holding back the emotion that threatens to overwhelm me. That hopeless feeling is sneaking in again. I hate feeling so desperate.

He takes me by the upper arms and gently turns me to face him. "Listen . . . I know you say I have a hero complex or whatever, but if you'd just hear me out, maybe I could show you something. If you could just trust me, trust that I'm not in this to get you hurt or to get something for myself."

I sniff, clearing my throat to get the frog out of it. "What are you talking about?" I step away from his touch, not comfortable with his warmth and the feelings his close proximity is starting to create in me. My life is already complicated enough; I don't need to hunt down more trouble for myself.

"I'm talking about the Bourbon Street Boys."

I have to think about that for a second, but it doesn't help to clarify his statement. I think I'm too tired. "I don't understand."

"We could help you. All of us. My team. If you'd let us."

I don't dare hope, but that doesn't stop my curiosity from taking hold. "How are you going to do that?"

"First, you'll need to rest. Three days, minimum. You just had a baby, and your body needs at least that much time just to start to recuperate. To be honest, my knee could probably use some downtime too, so I could keep you company. Then I could introduce you to the team. Explain the situation. Discuss options. And once they're on board, we could go talk to the police, and together we'll all come up with a solution you can live with. And you and Baby Tee will be safe through the entire process. You have my word on that."

I want to believe him so badly it makes my heart ache, but I know better. "I don't think it's going to work."

"Why not? We're trained for this kind of thing. My leg isn't at a hundred percent, but that doesn't mean I'm completely useless." He glances down at his knee, and I once again feel guilty about the part I played in his injury.

"Yeah, but Pavel . . . he's not going to stop looking for me. He came to the hospital, he took my car . . . He'll keep searching until he finds me. I know way too much about his life." I look around the room. "I probably shouldn't even be here. I've stayed too long as it is."

Thibault leans on his crutches and looks me in the eye. "I have a state-of-the-art security system that's monitored at all times by an off-site company. I've been trained to manage dangerous individuals and situations by some of the best experts in the business."

"You don't know Pavel. He's not just bad . . . he's evil."

Thibault stands up straighter and puffs out his chest. "And I'm a good guy, remember?" He pretends to draw the letter *S* on his T-shirt.

I have to laugh. He's so serious and tough one second and then making a joke the next. I can tell he's had a lot of practice dealing with his sister's moods. He seems to know how to manage mine well enough.

"How about if I say that I'll think about it?" A glimmer of hope has lit up my heart, and I want to hang on to it, even though it's crazy and dangerous and probably ten kinds of foolish to entertain the idea of sticking around here. It's like playing hide-and-seek in Pavel's front yard.

"That's a great start," he says. "Why don't you have a seat, and I'll serve up the pasta?"

"Sounds good to me." I sit down, holding my baby close. He opens his eyes at the movement. I don't know if he can even see my face yet, so I lean close and whisper to him. "Mama's going to make sure you're safe. I promise." I kiss him on the forehead and then look up to find Thibault turning away to walk to the stove, an unreadable expression clouding his face.

CHAPTER FOURTEEN

"Can I use the twins' diaper changing station?" I ask as Thibault puts our dirty plates in the dishwasher. Tee has just finished having his own meal and his diaper is already getting heavy. I can feel my hair standing up all over the place and could sure use a washing, but my first concern is for my boy. Maybe after I'm done with him I can sneak a shower in, before we leave for the bus station. As much as I appreciate Thibault offering to help us, I know I can't take him up on it any longer. There's just too much danger involved. My heart is heavy, but my mind is made up.

"Of course. Help yourself."

I unwrap the baby, unsnap his outfit, and peel back the tapes of his diaper. As I reach for another one of the twins' leftover tiny ones, I'm hit in the face with something warm. A nanosecond later, I realize what's happening.

"Oh, help! Ew! Gross! He's a fireman!" I hold my hands out, trying to block the stream of urine flying toward my face. The baby tips sideways and his fire hose moves with him, blazing a trail across the wall. "What the hell! Stop that, Tee-Tee! That's not nice! Oh, God, it's going everywhere!"

Thibault is by my side suddenly, snagging a baby wipe out of the container on the dresser and dropping it over my son's pee cannon.

I have to take a moment to calm myself before I speak. "I am *so* sorry. Jesus, what was that all about?" Baby pee drips down my cheek. I grab a wipe and attack my face with it, scrubbing furiously.

Thibault's voice is strained. "'Help' . . . ? 'He's a fireman'?"

I give him a sheepish grin, tossing the wipe into the nearby trash can. "It just looked like a fire hose or something, the way it was spraying all over the place, out of control. Is that normal?" I glance down at my child. He's staring at the light overhead, mesmerized, his skinny little legs quivering.

I quickly put the blanket over his lower half, feeling guilty that I left him unprotected in the cold air. The blanket is wet on the bottom, which is a big problem because it's the only one I have.

"Completely normal . . . for boys, anyway. Girls, not so much." Thibault uses a tissue to soak up droplets from the cover on top of the dresser.

I move the blanket and maneuver the diaper under the baby. After wiping him down, I try to get the diaper on, but it's not cooperating for some reason.

"Tapes come from the back and go to the front," Thibault says, taking the diaper off and turning it around.

"Oh. Brilliant." I'm starting to think I seriously suck at this mothering thing. I actually feel like crying over a silly diaper.

"Eh, it's no big deal. I did that a lot when Mel and Vic were first born. Bringing the tapes to the front makes it easier to get them on and off." He folds the top of the diaper down after cinching up the sides as much as possible. Listening to him talk and act like it's not the end of the world gives me the moment I need to collect my runaway emotions.

I look up at him, hoping he isn't going to hold this event against me. "I'm sorry my boy peed on your wall."

"Don't be sorry. Be proud." Thibault grins big.

"Proud?"

"Yeah. He's only a newborn and look at the power he's got." He points at the swath of destruction Tee left behind. "Look at that distance."

I roll my eyes. "Great. I guess I'd better invest in some plastic to tape on the walls." I grab a wipe and do my best to clean the mess.

"Nah. Just drop a couple tissues on his business as soon as you take the diaper off and you'll be fine. The problem is the cold air. It makes 'em go." He reaches down and pretends to poke Tee's belly. "Better behave yourself, young man. Your mommy doesn't need any trouble from you." While I finish with the wall, Thibault buttons up the baby's little outfit and takes one of his tiny feet, wiggling it. "Look at those skinny little legs." He gives one of Tee's thighs a squeeze with his thumb and forefinger and leans down to stare into his dark-blue eyes. "Better start bulking up. Momma needs you to grow up big and strong."

"You think he's too skinny? Like, not healthy?" I lean in and check the circumference of Tee's legs by wrapping my fingers around them. They do seem pretty tiny.

"No, he's perfect in every way. Gorgeous." Thibault wraps him up and lifts him off the dresser, handing him over. "Here's your momma." He pauses, not releasing Tee into my hands.

"What's wrong?"

"This blanket is wet in the back."

I cringe. "I think he peed on it. It's the only one I have."

Thibault sets him down on the table. "Not a problem. I'll be right back." He leaves me there with the baby, and I take the moment alone with my boy to undress him down to his diaper and wipe him with a washcloth I find in the dresser's top drawer and some water from the sink. Using the clean part of the blanket, I dry him off and then open my hospital robe so he can eat; he gets plenty warm enough lying against me that I'm not worried about him being mostly naked.

Thibault comes back into the kitchen, quickly averting his eyes when he sees what I'm doing. "You want to do that in the living room? It might be more comfortable."

"No, I'm fine here."

He looks at his watch. "Listen . . . it's getting late. I know you said you wanted to get to the bus station, but are you sure you want to do that in what you're wearing?"

He has a point. I do a better job of covering my chest, pulling the robe over the baby's head a little. "It's probably not ideal. I could go to Target if you'd take me. Or I could get a cab. I know your knee isn't good."

He leans on his crutches. "Don't worry about my knee. That's not an issue. But maybe you could consider waiting until tomorrow?"

I shake my head. "No. I have to go tonight. The longer I stay here, the worse it could get."

He opens his mouth to say something, but someone knocks at the front door. I stiffen up, imagining Pavel there insisting on seeing me and taking me out of here. I should have left sooner. *Why did I take that nap?*

"That'll be Toni," he says.

"Toni?"

His back disappears down the hall as he heads toward the front of the house.

I pull Tee off me and button myself up as best I can. She'll probably think I'm trying to make a move on her brother, exposing myself to him. I didn't even realize until now that I've been nursing in front of him all day without being embarrassed about it. I think it helps that he told me right up front that I'm not his type. I don't have to worry about him checking me out because of that, and besides, he must've seen his sister breastfeed hundreds of times. He's probably immune to mom-boobs by now.

I hear voices, and then Toni comes into the kitchen with a duffel bag over her shoulder.

"Where's Thibault?" I ask.

She drops the duffel on the ground and sits down in the chair next to me, turning it so she can face me. "He's outside bringing a couple things in." She rests the heels of her stiletto boots on the rung of the chair, her legs spread. She's tough and she knows it.

"But his knee . . ."

"His knee can handle it. I wanted to talk to you without him around to hear me."

"Oh." *So it's going to be like that.* "Fine. Say whatever it is you have to say." I lift my chin. I've been judged by women better than her. She can't hurt me.

"Thibault is a good guy," she says. "A really good guy."

"I know that."

"And I told you before he likes to think he's Superman."

"Yeah, I noticed."

"He also carries around a lot of guilt."

"Yeah, he told me about Charlie."

Her face goes slack. "Say what?"

I shrug. I don't want to upset her, but I also want her to know that I'm not here to hurt her. "I get it. He told me that he feels guilty that he didn't take better care of you and he won't ever let that happen again. I know that's why he wants to help me."

"He told you *what?* That he didn't take better care of me?" She stands, pissed.

I reach out and take her by the wrist. "Please don't say anything to him."

She looks down at me, slowly pulling herself from my grip. "He's wrong. He shouldn't have said that to you."

"Why?"

"Because. It's none of your business." She hisses out a breath. "Why would he tell you that? He must be more into you than I realized."

I nearly choke hearing that. "No, he's not, don't be ridiculous. I'm not his type at all."

"Says who?" She barks out a laugh.

"Says him. Thibault. He told me."

"Seriously? He just came out and told you that?"

"Yes." I hate that she thinks I somehow caused him to say that, like I made a move on him or something. "If you must know, he said when he ends up with someone, she'll be the polar opposite of *you*, and since he thinks we're a lot alike . . ." I shrug. *Let her do the math.*

She just stares at me.

"I know you think I'm going to get him in trouble." I shake my head, looking down at my baby. "But you don't need to worry about that. I'm leaving tonight, and you'll never see me again."

Toni slowly sits down. "Oh, yeah? Where're you going?"

I shrug. "I don't know. Away from here."

She studies me for so long I have to look up at her. I cannot read her expression for the life of me. "What?" I finally say, getting annoyed at her silent evaluation.

"I'm just trying to figure you out. Find out what your game is."

I understand that she's being protective of her brother, so I try not to be too angry at her cold approach. "I don't have a game, okay? Thibault and I met under very strange circumstances, and he was a really good guy about all of it. And he wants to help me out even more than he already has, but I've already told him no, okay? I'll be gone tonight, and by tomorrow your lives can go back to the way they were." I feel low. Dirty. Like I'm a bad person who will taint their lives. It's not my worst moment, but it's close, and I think I feel that way because I'm holding my son. He's so perfect, so innocent. I don't want the darkness of my life to bleed into his.

Toni's nose twitches. "What does Thibault say about you leaving?"

"It doesn't matter what he says. He's not my keeper, and I'm not his responsibility."

She smiles, or at least I think the expression on her face is a smile. It looks more like she's in pain than good humor. "Try telling my brother that and see how far it gets you."

My heart softens a little. "He is pretty stubborn."

"I'm guessing you're no slouch in that department." She raises an eyebrow in challenge.

I shrug. "Maybe not."

She leans down all of a sudden and grabs the duffel bag from the floor, unzipping it in one fluid motion. "I brought some stuff over here for you. You can keep all of it." She pulls several things out and drops them on the table. "Baby blankets, onesies, a couple nursing shirts for you, flip-flops, a pair of sweat pants . . ." She looks at my lower half and frowns. "They might be a little tight, but you can shop tomorrow and get something better."

I think she just made a comment about my butt being bigger than hers, but I'm going to let that slide because she just lightened my load about twenty pounds by thinking of my baby and making sure he was provided for.

I reach up and touch the soft blanket she's given me. "I don't know what to say." I put the material against my face, so grateful to have this for my child. He won't have to be wrapped in a urine-soaked, freebie hospital cloth. It's overwhelming me that she would be nice when she obviously doesn't like me. It's so silly . . . just some onesies and a couple blankets . . .

"Hey, what're you doing?" she asks, reaching over and tugging on my wrist. "Don't cry. Jesus, it's just baby clothes."

I look up at her, swallowing the lump in my throat before I talk. "Yeah, sorry. I guess I'm a little hormonal right now or something."

She snorts. "Hormonal and running for your life from a Russian gangster. Not a good combination."

My blood freezes in my veins. *How does she know about Pavel and that I'm running from him?*

There's banging out on the porch, and Thibault lets loose a few choice cuss words.

"What are you talking about?" I ask her, suspicious as hell.

"The team has done some digging."

"What team?"

"My team. Thibault's team. The security company we work for. We looked into this Pavel guy who came to the hospital. We talked to Holloway."

"You did *what*?"

"When my boss, Ozzie, called the NOPD to inquire about Pavel, the chief put him in contact with the detective managing cases involving him. Holloway. We talked to him, and once he learned we had you with us, he let us know you were working with him confidentially. We told him we know where you are and that you're safe."

"Why would you do that?" I stand up, my chair scraping the floor as I glare down at her. "And why would he? Our relationship is supposed to be confidential!"

She gets to her feet and glares at me. We're eye to eye, and if I didn't have a baby in my arms, I'd be ready to throw down. She looks like she's ready to lay me flat herself.

"Because. You got involved in my brother's life for whatever reason—fate, if you want to call it that—and he wants to help you. I don't agree it's the best idea for him, but it's not my call. He tells me he wants to help you, so that's what I'm doing. We work with the cops all the time. They know us and they trust us."

"But Thibault doesn't get to decide that for me."

She shakes her head. "No, he doesn't."

I huff out a breath. "You're not making any sense."

She shrugs. "I think I am."

"You're telling me you're helping me without my permission or blessing and in the same breath saying you don't have the right to do that."

"Yep."

"That's . . . insane."

"Welcome to my world." She walks around me to the hallway, stopping just at the threshold. She turns to look at me. "If you survived as long as you have working with that gangbanger, you've obviously got street smarts. But having that baby changes everything. You know that. And I don't think you have a lot of options, so maybe you should consider accepting some of our help while it's being offered."

"But I thought you said you were against it."

"I am. But I respect the hell out of my brother, and he seems to think you're worth the effort."

"He told me I'm a lot like you."

"Poor you." She walks to the foyer.

"He wants me to spend the night here," I say loud enough for her to hear.

"Do what you gotta do," she says as she opens the front door.

I stare into the open space she's left behind, my thoughts tumbling over themselves. Then I look at the table and the pile of things she brought over for me. I touch the blanket and the clothing, the smell of the freshly laundered items reaching my nose. It reminds me of my grandma. She must have used the same soap as Toni does.

Tears come to my eyes, and Thibault finds me with them dripping down my cheeks.

"Oh, hell. What did she say to you?" He glares down the hallway.

"No, no, nothing." I reach up and take his elbow. "Listen, I'm really tired. I was going to go to the bus station tonight, but I think I could use a good night's rest before I do that. Would you mind if I spent one night here?"

He nods, his face blank. "Sure. No problem. You can take the bedroom at the top of the stairs. Mine is just down the hall."

"I'm fine on the couch."

He shakes his head. "Trust me. You'll want the bed. And you'll want to have Tee close when he wakes up. My sister brought over one of her bassinets for you to use. You can put it right next to you on the floor."

"Is that what you were cussing at out there on the porch?"

His smile is sheepish. "No comment." He looks at the table. "Oh, cool. She brought you some stuff for the baby. I asked her if she had any extra things lying around."

I hold up the sweat pants. "She brought stuff for me too, although she's not sure they'll fit."

"I can go out and get you something from Target now if you want."

I shake my head. "No, that's fine. I'm fine, really. I'm going to go to bed now anyway. I'm sure I'll be up all night, so I might as well make it an early one."

He nods. "Me, too. That medication they gave me at the hospital is kicking my butt." He pulls out his cell phone. "Are you sure you don't want to call anyone?" He holds the cell out toward me. "This one has an untraceable chip in it if you want to use it."

"That's okay," I say. "I have my own phone."

Thibault turns into a statue for a few seconds. "What?" he finally asks.

"I said I have my own phone. Is that a problem?"

He clenches his jaw a few times. "I'm an idiot."

I frown. "Excuse me?"

"Can I see your phone?"

"Sure." I go into the living room, anxiety growing. "I don't see what the issue is, though. If you're worried about my phone being a problem, I don't think you need to."

"Why's that?" he asks, hobbling behind me.

I dig through my purse until I locate the small black cell phone. I put it in his outstretched hand, not bothering to check the texts that are surely there. "It's not a smartphone. It doesn't have GPS or any of those things that make it traceable."

He pulls the back off the phone unit and slaps it on his hand, making the battery pop out. "Any phone with a SIM card is traceable."

My blood runs cold. "What? Are you serious?"

"Yes. If Pavel has the technology, he could at least triangulate your position by pinging signals off the nearby cell towers. It's not generally a technology the public can buy off the shelf, but it's available on the black market."

My heart skips a few beats. "I don't think he does, though. He never said anything about it to me. I never saw him use anything like that with anyone else, either."

"I don't want to risk it. My sister lives right over there." He glances up through the front window. "And she has two little kids."

"Okay. I guess that's fine. Feel free to destroy the SIM card, too, if you want. I have a backup of my phone numbers anyway." Not that there's anyone from my life I'll want to contact after I leave here. Except Alexei, of course, but having his phone number isn't going to help me, since he stopped answering my calls weeks ago. I'll worry about making sure he's okay after I'm safe. I won't let Alexei down. I can't. He has no one but me to watch out for him, because his cousin Pavel doesn't give a hoot about him. It's why he was at my place so often. My heart feels bruised over having to leave the poor guy behind. He won't understand why I left.

Thibault pulls out the SIM card and swings on crutches into the kitchen, where he puts it in the microwave and zaps it until it sparks and melts.

"Damn, you don't mess around." I'm almost mesmerized by the light show. It's like my life is going up in smoke. The melting plastic stinks. *So very appropriate.*

"Better to be safe than sorry." He pulls it out with tongs and drops it into his garbage disposal. Turning on the water, he runs the motor for an extra-long time, grinding the plastic up into bits.

I feel terrible for causing him to worry, although I really, truly don't think Pavel could find me using that stupid flip phone. It's the reason I bought it in the first place. I'd seen him track other girls down with an app he put on their smartphones. He gave me one of those phones too, but I always managed to lose it. He finally told me to buy the flip one because he said I was too scatterbrained to be trusted with something valuable. It was one of the few triumphs I enjoyed under his thumb, so it sucks to know that he could defeat me by using it to find me anyway.

"Sorry for the trouble. Maybe I should go to the bus station now instead of staying the night."

"Don't worry about it," he says as he types something on his phone. "The card is dead now. Staying here for the night isn't going to change anything."

"Are you sure?"

Thibault looks me in the eye, all seriousness. "If he started a search of your signal, it's already done. We'll keep our eyes and ears open, but I really don't think he's going to do anything tonight. It's hard finding a needle in a haystack. He'll need more time to find you than one day."

"Are you sure?"

He nods, all businesslike.

"Will you tell your sister?"

He holds up his phone, which has texts on the screen. "I already did. And her husband." He pauses. "What about a computer? Do you have any other electronics with you?"

I shake my head. "No. Just my purse with my wallet and basic stuff in it. Nothing electronic at all."

"What about the data you're giving to Holloway? Did you bring that?"

"No. I don't have any of it on me."

Thibault rubs his head, leaving his hand in his hair. "Does that mean you need to get back to the place where it is?"

"No."

He's waiting for my explanation, but I'm not ready to give that information to anyone. He's obviously concerned for my welfare, but that doesn't mean I'm going to give him everything he wants just because he thinks he needs it. The less he knows about my situation, the better. I can't believe I've already told him so much. And Holloway is going to get an earful and a half from me for blabbing to Ozzie or whatever his name is about our arrangement. That jerk needs to go back to detective school or something.

"Okay." Thibault starts to say something else, but stops himself. "Uh . . . yeah. So, I'm going to bring these things upstairs for you. If you hear me cussing again, just plug your ears."

The stressful moment has passed, and I let out the breath I didn't realize I was holding. "Okay. Thanks." I move Tee to my shoulder. "We'll be right behind you."

Thibault limps out of the kitchen, and I sit quietly, letting my brain buzz through the events of the last few hours. Banging sounds and frustrated mumbles from the hallway barely break through the activity going on in my head.

My escape from Pavel's clutches is only temporary. Maybe I'm just being overly paranoid, but I'm going to assume he has what he needed to track me down by following my phone, and that, as Thibault surmised, he's going to start looking for me tomorrow. That means he's probably going to have a friend or two at the bus station in town and possibly people paid off at the local cab companies who will contact him if someone looking like me with a baby gets a lift anywhere. That also means I need to find an alternate ride to another town where I can catch some longer-range transportation, like a bus or train.

I hate to admit this to myself, but it seems like Thibault is my only hope of staying safe right now. For tonight, he's offered me his home. Tomorrow he said he'd take me to Target and the bus station. The idea of asking him for a ride to Baton Rouge or Lafayette makes me feel horrible, like I'm taking advantage of him after I've already done him and his family enough harm. But what other choice do I have? Detective Holloway comes to mind, but I worry if I go to him first and he forces me to deliver on our deal, I'll no longer have any leverage to make him help me out. He might even insist I stay nearby to be a witness or whatever. I can't trust that man anymore.

No . . . I need to be far away when I contact Holloway so that everything can happen on my terms. New Orleans feels like a trap now. I need to put this town in my rearview mirror as soon as possible. As soon as I get some sleep. My eyelids feel like they're made of lead. Thibault shows up at my back and startles me with his touch.

"Hey. You sleeping sitting up?" he asks, his hand on my shoulder.

I shake my head to get it back online. "Yeah. Maybe." I yawn. "What time is it?"

"Almost nine. Your room is ready. It's at the top of the stairs. I put a towel on your bed in case you want to take a shower. The bathroom is right next door. And my room's at the end of the hall if you need anything. Just shout if you do."

I nod. "Okay." I stand, shifting the baby to a more comfortable position. My arm is half-asleep. "Thanks, Thibault. For everything. I'm really sorry to be such a pain in the butt."

He backs up on his crutches. "No, don't worry about it. I'm happy to help."

I move off down the hall. When I get to the bottom of the stairs and look up, his voice stops me.

"Mika?"

"Yeah?"

"I'm sorry you're going through this . . . That this is happening to you."

I rest my hand on the banister. "Yeah, well, my grandma always said you make your bed and then you have to lie in it. I've got no one to blame but myself."

I hear his crutches coming down the hallway as I mount the stairs. "You're too hard on yourself."

"Hello, Pot," I say with a sad smile. "Meet Kettle."

"Nice to meet you, Kettle," he says, his voice so soft I almost miss it.

I go into the bedroom and close the door behind me and Baby Tee, a smile battling to come out and remove my frown. Even in my darkest hours the light sometimes slips through. That's what's happening here, today in Thibault's home. I would have been on the street in a hospital gown if it weren't for Thibault and Toni. I imagine my grandmother looking down on me and telling me that I shouldn't run so fast from people who are trying so hard to help me.

CHAPTER FIFTEEN

The doorbell rings, waking me from a fitful sleep. I sit up straight and wonder if I should be worried about a visitor showing up at Thibault's house this early in the morning. The alarm clock next to the bed says it's eight a.m. As the sleep-fog lifts from my brain, I decide it doesn't make sense to freak out; if Pavel were coming for me gangster style, he wouldn't bother with the bell.

I yawn, swinging my legs over the side of the bed to put my feet on the floor. Tee was up four times last night, giving me very little rest between feedings. At least I was able to take a shower before midnight. I feel ten times better than I did yesterday. Toni's sweat pants are too small, but I don't care. I've got a mama-booty now, and I choose to be proud of it. The zippered jacket fits just fine, as does the nursing shirt she gave me to wear underneath.

As I run a brush through my hair and put it up in a ponytail, I hear Thibault making his way down the hall below me. I crack the door when he makes it to the foyer so I can listen in and spy on who's there without exposing myself. Just in case it's Pavel.

Thibault is shirtless, wearing jeans that hang low off his waist. His back is broad and well-muscled. It sends my pulse racing to see him standing there in bare feet with his hair all mussed up. In another life, I could picture him being a pretty good boyfriend. I mean, he's bossy, but who wouldn't want Superman in her bed, right? He looks through the peephole, punches a code into a keypad, and pulls the door open.

"Good morning, Mary Sunshine!" I can't see the person speaking, but I recognize her voice. Her name is . . . May. She was at the hospital visiting Thibault with her sister and Toni. The girl who had the parrot hallucination. She steps into the house as Thibault backs out of her way. Her smile is nothing short of radiant.

"You forgot to put a shirt on," the second woman through the door says, pointing at his bare chest—*Jenny*.

"Nice abs," May adds. She looks at her sister. "Dev's training is really paying off."

He rubs his stomach absently and then scratches at his head. "What?"

"You can say that again," Jenny says, wiggling her eyebrows.

He sighs. "I'm feeling sexually harassed right now." I can tell from his voice he doesn't mean it, but he doesn't sound like he's really enjoying their compliments, either.

"I think a shirt would solve your problem," Jenny says, sighing and smiling. She holds up a plate. "Homemade muffins. Guaranteed to cure your sleepless-night-induced aches and pains."

He looks down at his knee. "Is it guaranteed to fix a torn meniscus by any chance?"

"I'm afraid not. I believe surgery is your only hope."

May tries to see over his shoulder as he slips a T-shirt over his head. "Where's the baby? I need to get my hands on him, stat. I've got baby fever, and if someone doesn't give me an infant to cuddle soon, I'm going to have to make another one of my own."

He holds up his hand like a stop sign. "Not so fast with those grabby hands of yours. We need to keep it down. She's sleeping."

"I'm up now." They all turn as one to look up at me. I'm standing at the top of the stairs with Tee in my arms. Spying on them any more than I already have doesn't seem right.

Thibault sighs. "Mika, this is May and Jenny." He gestures at the women in turn. "May and Jenny, Mika."

"Now *that* is what a motherly glow looks like," May says. She holds out her arms. "You don't know me yet, but you and I are going to be really good friends. Can I hold your baby? I have one of my own, so I know what I'm doing. He's in day care. Oh, and I disinfected my hands and arms before I came in, so you don't have to worry about me giving your little guy any cooties."

I walk slowly down the stairs, hanging on to the railing. When I glance at Thibault, I can see he's chomping at the bit to come up and help me, but he doesn't. I nod at him to let him know I appreciate him giving me my space.

"Thank you," I say, trying to relax, even though May's approach is a little strong. "I'm happy to have somebody else hold him for a change. Last night was really rough."

"You didn't help her?" May turns her ire on Thibault. "What were you doing? Sleeping like a log the whole time?"

"For your information, no . . . I didn't sleep like a log. I was up most of the night too."

"I'm so sorry," I say, losing my smile. "Were we too loud?" Now that I'm closer, I can see Thibault does look a little rough. He needs a shave and more REM time for the bags under his eyes to go away. I should probably find this look unattractive, but I can't. Even rough, he's something to see.

"No, not at all," Thibault assures me. "I was just hearing every little sound because I was on alert or something." He shakes his head like he's still trying to wake up. "I'm a light sleeper."

May takes Tee into her arms and moves the blanket away from his face. "Oh my god, he is *so* adorable." She bends down to sniff his forehead. "And oh my *word*, he smells like a teeny tiny newborn baby . . . Oh my goodness, my goodness, my goodnesssss . . ." She inhales deeply with her eyes closed.

Jenny leans over her sister to see him better. "Easy there, Looney Tunes. We can't have you overdosing on baby scent."

"Better get used to it, sister," May says, winking at her.

Jenny glares at her for a second and then goes back to adoring the baby. They both ooh and ahh over his sleepy little face. I have to agree; he is pretty damn cute with those puffy cheeks he's got.

A slight moment of dizziness hits me. I hold the banister and blink hard a few times. I haven't eaten or drunk anything since nine last night. I think I'm dehydrated.

"Are you okay?" Thibault asks softly.

Jenny looks at me. "Cramping? I had it bad after my last child."

The dizziness passes as quickly as it came. "I'm fine." I yawn. "I have a little of that, but more than anything, I'm just really tired and thirsty."

Thibault rubs my upper arm. "Jenny's got muffins and I've got coffee and juice. Come on."

Jenny and May both notice him touching me and share a quick look filled with meaning, but they say nothing. I want to tell them that it's no big deal, that Thibault and I have let each other know in no uncertain terms that nothing could ever happen between us, but that would be silly. They'd see that as a sign I was just trying to convince myself of something I didn't believe. I'll just let them imagine things that aren't there; when I'm gone they'll realize it was all just Thibault being friendly.

May and Jenny wait for me to go ahead and follow behind with Tee between them. They're baby talking, saying the silliest things. It's kind of cute, actually. I always found that stuff annoying before, but when someone's doing it at my baby, it's different.

Thibault puts a pot of coffee on as we settle around the table. Talk turns to the labor I went through, and he puts his back to us. He's acting like he doesn't care about what I'm saying, but he pauses his motions whenever I answer a question. He's listening to everything.

"So, he literally walked right out in front of your car?" May asks. She's leaning in, eating up every detail of my story. I find myself warming to her and her easy enthusiasm. Jenny carefully takes Tee from her sister's arms, and her expression goes sappy as she stares down at his sleeping face. Pride wells up in me.

"He sure did," I say, pulling myself away from the happy scene of Jenny loving my child. "And then he came around to my window, all hot under the collar. But boy was he surprised to find me trying to breathe through labor pains." At the time it was seriously stressful, but looking back at it now, I can see the humor in it.

"That is in*sane* that you didn't know you were having a baby," May says.

"I've read it happens more than you'd expect," Jenny says.

"Yes, well, I was in denial. I should have known what was going on. There were signs, but I just kept explaining them away. Thibault knew right away what my problem was, though. He pulled me out of the car and carried me into that nail salon."

"He carried you?" May looks over at him, her voice going dreamy. "Aww, how romantic."

I frown. "No, not romantic. It was disgusting, actually. My water had broken and it was everywhere."

May shakes her head, her chin resting on her hand as she leans her elbows on the table. "That just makes it more romantic, if you ask me."

Jenny nudges her. "Nobody's asking you." She gestures at me with her chin. "Continue."

"There's not much more to it. He put me in a massage chair and it happened."

Thibault turns around, putting mugs down for each of us. "Bada bing, bada boom, the baby was born. End of story."

May frowns at him. "Don't ruin it, party pooper. Let her tell it." She turns her attention on me, smiling again. "Was it awesome? Was he, like, all bossy and stuff?"

"May . . ." Jenny frowns at her.

"What?" May looks at Jenny and Thibault. "You all know he's bossy, right? That's not news to anyone at this table, I hope."

I can't help but laugh at that.

Jenny shrugs, a small smile trying to break free.

"Hey. Why do I feel like I'm being ganged up on here?" Thibault asks. He doesn't wait for an answer, turning back to the counter to fetch the sugar and milk.

"So he was the one who delivered the baby?" Jenny asks.

I nod. "Yep."

"Man, he was *all* up in your business," May says.

"Yeah, he sure was." My ears are getting a little hot with the embarrassing memory. "A perfect stranger seeing parts of my body *I* haven't even seen."

They all laugh, even Thibault.

The room goes quiet until May comes up with her next question. "So . . . what's your situation? Are you seeing someone? Or are you married? Or single, maybe? I don't see a ring, but these days that doesn't matter much."

It seems like a strange question to ask, but I don't want to be rude and ignore it. Besides, May is really easy to talk to. She seems completely harmless, which isn't a brand of human I'm used to seeing very often. "I'm single but not looking for any kind of relationship. Not right now, anyway."

"I think you're going to be a little busy for a while," Jenny says, laughing.

"Oh, I don't know," May says, sounding mischievous. "Speaking from experience, I can tell you that it's a lot easier to raise a baby with help."

"True," Jenny says. "I can vouch for that. Even after my husband left, I had May to help me out."

I nod, not wanting to comment and share my private business with them. They're lucky; they have partners, but not everyone has that luxury. Would I rather be doing this with a man who loves me? Sure. The midnight feedings might not change, but the rest of it would. Having someone next to me to support me would be nice . . . and someone to pay the electricity bill until I can find another job . . .

"Oh, but don't worry. You have us now," May says. "We can help you out, can't we, Jenny?"

I open my mouth to protest, to explain that I'm leaving as soon as they walk out the door, but Jenny speaks first.

"Absolutely. And so can Thibault. He's great with kids."

"He seriously is," May says. She looks at Thibault's back as he stands at the sink. "A real softy. Melanie and Victor have him wrapped around their tiny little fingers."

I get the distinct impression that they're trying to sell me on the idea of Thibault as a father figure. Too bad it's not in the cards for us.

"I'm standing right here, you know," he says. "I can hear you."

"Where's that coffee?" May asks. "I can't eat this muffin without liquid refreshment."

"Do you have decaf?" Jenny asks. "Mika should have decaf."

"I'm already on it," Thibault says. "I'm having a cup too. I need to try to catch up on my sleep this afternoon."

"Aw, isn't that sweet?" May says, winking at me. "Sharing a pot of decaf after a sleepless night together."

The room goes silent. Thibault turns around and looks at me, making my face go aflame.

"It wasn't like that," I say. For a moment, I picture Thibault and me losing sleep together. It makes me tremendously sad to know that'll never happen, which is crazy, because I should be really happy that I'll never be in a relationship with a guy like him. Bossy, bullheaded . . . bossy . . .

"You both lost sleep, right?" May looks at her sister. "They did say that, right?"

Jenny nudges her. "You made it sound like they were *together*, together. But they're not. They're just . . ." She looks at us. "Roommates?"

Thibault points at her. "Exactly. Roommates. Very temporary roommates."

I know if I say I'm leaving in an hour, it'll make everything awkward, so I keep my mouth shut. My future will be here fast enough; I don't need to hurry it along by turning it into a conversation killer.

May leans over the baby, who's still in her sister's arms. "Hello there, pudgy wudgkins. Hello there. What's your name, eh? Is it pudgy wudgkins?"

"His nickname is Tee. Short for Thibault."

The sisters share a look and then May sighs. "So perfect . . . You took a wrong turn and ended up almost running over the man who helped you give birth to your baby. Of course you used his name." She pauses for a moment, still staring at the baby. "If I didn't know any better, I'd say the whole thing was destiny. And maybe even a little ro*man*tic."

"But you know better," Thibault says, bringing the pot over and pouring a cup of coffee for me. "Caffeinated version is coming up next."

Jenny points to her mug. "Hit me with the decaf, too."

Thibault stops in midturn and fills her mug.

"You said you don't have any family in the area," Jenny says to me. "How about friends? Is there anyone we can call for you or anything we can pick up for you? Toni mentioned you didn't have any clothes over here." She sips her coffee and removes the top of a muffin as she waits for my answer.

I guess she didn't get the memo about Pavel. I go ahead and play along, hoping the conversation will be over soon. "No, not really. I . . .

recently moved out of my apartment, so Thibault was nice enough to offer me a place to stay before I . . . find a new place." *In another town far, far away.*

"But you must have clothes somewhere," May says. "Where are all your things? Are they in storage?"

I start to answer, but Thibault cuts me off. "Who's got a muffin for me?" He leans over toward the plate. "Keeping these all to yourself, May?" He looks at her, not smiling.

She looks up at him and blinks a few times. Then she takes a muffin from the plate and hands it to him slowly. "Here's a muffin for ya, Thibault."

He takes it from her and bites the whole top off. "Good stuff," he says with his mouth full. He points at her mug. "You ready for some coffee?"

She nods and hands him the mug. Where she was completely talkative before, now she's acting like she's mute. The atmosphere is very tense.

"So how long are you staying here with Thibault?" Jenny asks.

When I don't answer right away and Thibault glares at her, she adds, "Or do you not know yet?"

I shake my head, glad for the easy out. "No, not yet. We're still trying to figure that out. I have some things I need to get and some loose ends I need to tie up before I make any serious plans."

"Yeah," Thibault says. "She's welcome here as long as she likes, but we may need to head out to another location."

"What do you mean?" May says, her mood more subdued.

Thibault pours himself a cup of coffee and sits down at the table. He looks at me, his gaze intense. "Jenny and May are both part of my team. We all work at Bourbon Street Boys security, and we're all trained to deal with . . . situations."

May rubs the crumbs off her hands onto her napkin. "Ooooh, we have a situation? Cool. What is it?"

The fact that she's acting so excited gives me little faith in her ability to handle the problems I'm having. "I wouldn't look that happy about it if I were you," I say, wishing it were the fun adventure she seems to think it is.

Thibault nods. "This is serious."

"Does Ozzie know about this yet?" May asks. "I'm asking because he didn't mention it to me and he normally does." She looks at me. "He's my husband. He owns the company. Bourbon Street Boys security."

"Oh."

"We all own the company," Thibault says. "We're all shareholders. But that's irrelevant. What matters is that Mika needs to stay on the down-low for a little bit while some other things fall into place for her." He looks at me. "Do I have your permission to share what you've told me about your employer?"

My face drops. I can't believe he wants to talk to them about things I shared with him in confidence. "No."

"You can trust them," he says, glancing at the girls before looking at me again. "I know them inside and out, and I can promise you they're good people. They've had my back many times, and they've never let me down."

He's being pushy again. Taking over my life. Thinking he knows better for me than I do for myself. "I understand and I appreciate what you're saying, but no. I prefer to keep my business private." I stand, no longer in the mood for muffins or coffee. "Can I have Tee back, please? I need to go feed him."

Jenny hands him over and I walk out of the kitchen, heading toward the stairs. I hate that I'm being rude to them, but I can't let this man railroad me into doing something I don't want to do. In a few hours he'll be gone from my life, and letting him think he has any say in that is a mistake. I am the captain of this ship. I decide how it runs and where it goes. I don't care how nice he is or how good he looks in the morning, he is not going to push me in a direction I don't want to go in.

I'm halfway up the stairs when I hear May's voice. "What in the heck is going on?" she says, whispering a lot louder than she thinks she is.

"I can't say," Thibault responds. I mount the stairs to the sound of whispers, sadder about my situation than I was before I came downstairs, and I didn't think that was possible.

CHAPTER SIXTEEN

I feed Tee for twenty minutes, trying to empty my head of the sad, angry, and stressed-out thoughts that keep banging around in there. I need to have my brain clear and firing on all cylinders if I'm going to get out of here and on the road with any kind of plan. Right now all I can think about is May and Jenny saying how much easier it is to raise a baby when you have someone to help. For the moment I have Thibault. Tomorrow I'll have no one. For the first time since I hit that man with my car, my problems seem insurmountable.

I get up to go to the bathroom, leaving Tee in his bassinet. I pause after opening the door when I realize that the voices downstairs are coming right up the staircase, easy enough to hear, as if the conversation were going on in front of me. The girls must be in the hallway, getting ready to leave.

"You're not doing so well, are you?" Jenny says.

Thibault hisses out a breath. "I don't know. I think it's my leg. My knee is bothering me."

"I don't think it's your knee," May says.

"No, definitely not the knee," Jenny agrees. They sound like they're sharing a joke.

"Lack of sleep, then."

"Or the sleep," says May.

"No, not the lack of sleep, either," Jenny agrees.

"What, then? Do I want to know?"

"You like her," Jenny says.

"So romantic," May says. "Love at first hit."

"Hit? Don't you mean *sight*?" Thibault asks, surprising the heck out of me by not telling her she's nuts right off the bat. He does sound like he's exercising a lot of patience, though.

"She hit you with her car, so she obviously didn't *see* you. It's like love at first sight, but instead she hit you." She pauses. "Less subtle, but I like it."

"You two . . . You're always looking for trouble."

"I think you're the one looking for trouble this time," Jenny says.

May's voice is lower, but I can still hear it. "You've fallen for a gangster's girlfriend. Are you *insane*? What's gotten into you?"

I'm instantly upset. So much for trust. He told them about Pavel even after I told him not to. If I were sticking around, I'd give him a serious piece of my mind.

"Love at first hit," Jenny says matter-of-factly. "Took him down in one shot. The mighty Thibault has fallen."

"Seriously, you two need to stop. This is not happening. You're dreaming. Fantasizing. Bored with your married lives and trying to stir up trouble."

Jenny gasps loudly. "How dare you." Then she giggles. "As if married life with four kids could ever be boring."

"Or two dogs and one child," May says.

"I already told her she's not my type."

There's a long silence before Jenny speaks. "Why in the heck would you do that?"

His voice sounds funny. Younger. "I don't know. It just came up."

"Oh, baloney," May says, laughing. "You're afraid of her. I can totally see it. You were like, 'Oh, don't get any ideas . . . I'm a bachelor for life,' and she was like, 'Dream on, you wish,' and the whole time you guys are both sweating each other."

"Is she for real?" Thibault asks.

"I'm afraid she is," Jenny says. "Come on, May. Time to go. I have to bring Jacob to therapy in a half hour. I can't be late."

"I haven't fallen for anyone," Thibault says, sounding a little desperate, if my ears aren't mistaken. "I'm just helping her out."

The girls respond in tandem. "Yeah, right."

Footsteps come toward the foyer, so I back farther into the room. But I leave the door cracked because I'm a glutton for punishment and my curiosity is piqued to the max.

Thibault's voice is very low. I have to strain my ears to hear him. "So, if I can convince her to stay a while, would you be willing to help me and Mika out or not?"

"See? He's already referring to him and her as a couple," May says.

"Strange how he doesn't see it, though, isn't it?" Jenny says.

He hisses at them, whispering loudly. "Would you be quiet? I'm standing right here and Mika is just upstairs."

"Yes, but you have man-hearing," May says.

"Yep," Jenny says. "Man-hearing. Otherwise known as *selective* hearing. So we have to speak up."

"I hear everything you say. Doesn't make it right."

"Denial is not just a river in wherever, Thibault," May says.

"Egypt," Jenny says. "The Nile is in Egypt."

"That's what I said. Wherever."

"Dear Self . . . Remind me not to let Auntie May teach my children geography."

"Watch it, lady, or Ozzie and I won't babysit for you and Dev tonight."

Jenny's voice turns into a threatening hiss. "I will seriously kill you if you back out on me. Dev and I have *plans*."

Thibault clears his throat. "Are you in or are you out?"

"As if you even have to ask," Jenny says.

"Just tell us where and when you want us, and we'll be there," May says. "With bells on."

"Excellent," Thibault says. "I'll go see Ozzie later today. If I can convince Mika."

"He's going to be gone all day, but come over to Jenny's place tonight and you can talk to him. Eight thirty, after the kids are in bed. I'll get him warmed up for ya," May says.

"You can do it," Jenny says. "After all you've done so far for her, she has to see that you're a good guy. And I know you couldn't give us details beyond what we already knew from Toni, but it sure seems like she could use a friend right now."

My heart squeezes in my chest at her words. *He didn't tell them anything. He didn't betray my trust.* It makes me feel light-headed, which tells me how important that was to me.

"Yeah, but she doesn't want my help. She says I'm too pushy."

"Well, you can be . . . stubborn about some things, but that's one of your best qualities," May says.

"It doesn't sound like a good quality when Mika talks about it."

"She just needs more time with you, to see that you're not pushy-controlling, you're just super-focused on helping people," Jenny says.

"Like Superman," May adds.

"I really wish you guys would stop saying that about me," he says, sighing. "It's not a compliment."

"Okay, no more Superman comments. Come on, May. I have to go. For real. No more chatting or psychoanalyzing. Jacob is going to be waiting."

It's one thing for them to say I need help; that idea just gets my back up because I've been taking care of myself for so long and it's all I know. I've survived this long, so I don't think I *need* help. But for them to say I need a friend? I honestly can't argue with that. I know Tee and

I could really use one of those, probably more now than I ever have in my life.

"I'll see you at your place tonight," Thibault says. "Wish me luck at convincing her."

"Just flex your muscles a few times. That'll impress her." May giggles.

"Nah, she's not into me. It's not like that."

Jenny sighs. "Whatever you say, Big T. Whatever you say."

The front door opens and footsteps move across the foyer. "She's really not," he says. "She told me."

May's voice fades out as she walks through the door. "Methinks you *both* doth protest a little too much!"

I slowly withdraw into the room until I'm sitting on the bed, the baby on the floor next to my feet in the bassinet. He's sleeping soundly in his new hand-me-down onesie, wrapped in one of Toni's baby blankets. He makes such a pretty picture. And I just shared a muffin and a coffee with two nice women who really like the man who has pledged to help me. It all seems so *normal*. I can't have this life now, but I'd like to someday.

I hear footsteps on the stairs. I quickly lie down on my side on the bed, facing away from the door. I can sense Thibault's presence outside my cracked door, but he doesn't do anything but continue on down the hall to his room. I'm both relieved and sad when he doesn't try to talk to me.

The teasing he endured from the girls makes me feel so conflicted. Do I *want* him to like me? Hope sparks for just a moment as I imagine what that would be like, but then reality settles in. *No, of course not . . .* My world is no place for a man like Thibault; he deserves better than what I can offer.

The revelation makes me very sad.

CHAPTER SEVENTEEN

I didn't mean to fall asleep, but the warm room, the baby sleeping, and the muffin in my belly proved to be too much. When Tee wakes me up, it's almost noon.

The house is completely silent except for the ticking of the clock. I put Tee down in his bassinet and look around the house, but Thibault is gone. I find a note on the counter next to a sandwich on a plate.

I had to go to the store for a few things and I need to see the surgeon about my knee. Lucky's working from home. He said he could drive you to the bus station if you couldn't wait for me to get back. Don't answer the door if you can help it. The alarm is on and it's probably safer if you keep out of sight until we know more. The code is 0220 if you need to leave. I hope you like the sandwich. It's my specialty. Thibault

I lift the top slice of bread and find a piece of bologna slathered in mustard underneath. I can't help the laugh that pops out of me.

I take a bite of the Thibault Special, sure I'm going to hate it, but surprised when I don't. He's hidden pickles underneath the meat. I munch away as I re-read the note a few times, trying to decode the message I know is hidden beneath the words.

He told the girls he wants me to stay, that he's going to try to convince me, but then he arranged for someone else to drive me to the bus station while he's gone? Is he playing games? Most men I've known have been masters at this kind of thing, but something is telling me that Thibault's not doing that. I take another bite of the sandwich, the gears in my brain turning and turning.

If I assume he's not playing games, what does this mean? Is he backing off, letting me have the space I have made it very clear I need? If he is, I know this is a big step for him. Not only have I seen him being pushy and bossy from the moment I met him, but both Jenny and May talked about it enough that I know it's one of his main character traits. *Is he worried I'm falling for him, so he's stepping back?* That doesn't feel right, because I can't think of a single moment that I flirted or encouraged May and Jenny's being silly about us.

The idea that he's so easily rid of me is bothersome. Mostly because I know it shouldn't be bothering me. I take another bite of the sandwich. The food is salty, which makes me notice a bottle of water on the counter. There's a yellow sticky note on it with Thibault's handwriting:

Drink all of this.

I smile. Yeah, he's bossy. I take the top off and down almost half of it before stopping. So this invitation to walk away without him even being involved was definitely a big deal for him. Letting go and letting someone else call the shots is not his strong suit. Is he hoping I'll take him up on it? Wishing I wouldn't? There's no way for me to know.

I walk back upstairs to check on Tee. He's too cute to leave in the bassinet, so I bring him into bed with me. I put him down next to me and stare at his face, my eyes skimming over his fine features: his tiny, almost invisible eyebrows, his itsy-bitsy eyelashes, his little button nose and wrinkly lips. He's perfect, and I so want to give him a safe and happy life. Getting onto a bus going nowhere seems like a really bad idea right now.

I try to imagine our destination and what we'll do when we get there, where we'll live, how we'll survive, and my mind feels too heavy to manage the visions. Slowly, the room goes dark as my lids fall closed . . .

CHAPTER EIGHTEEN

When I wake again, it's almost four thirty. After feeding Tee and changing his diaper, I go downstairs with him in my arms. There's another note on the table and more food. This time it's takeout—ribs, a hamburger, and corn on the cob. I take a bite of the hamburger as I read the note.

Sorry I missed you again. I had to run into work for a little while and then I have to go to Jenny's place. I should be back in time for a late dinner. If you feel like waiting up, I'll have pizza. If not and you're hungry, there's food in the fridge and I'll see you in the morning. Thibault
PS. Thanks for sticking around. But if you need to go, Lucky should be there until 7:30 and I'll be back not long after that.

I battle with myself for less than a minute. I'm not going anywhere tonight. I'm a needle and this whole area is the haystack; Pavel isn't going to find me this quickly. And even if he does find the house, he'll never see me in it, and there's an alarm. I'm too tired, too hungry, and too out of hope about what I can accomplish with a newborn baby in my arms to think of going anywhere right now. I just want to take a time-out from my life and make all the important decisions later. I wish Thibault were here so I could talk to him. At least he gets me fired up; right now I feel totally . . . *blah*.

I watch TV numbly for a few hours before I give up on finding anything worth watching. *Duck Dynasty* reruns really aren't cutting it for me, and the home decorating shows just make my heart hurt. I don't even have a home, so forget about decorating.

I look through Thibault's photo album again. It's both charming and sad. Crazily enough, it makes me jealous. I hate that I can't watch other people enjoying their lives without wishing I could have what they have. I close the cover before I get to the last pages because it's too painful for me right now to see happy people living happy lives. Thibault is alone in every picture, with no woman at his side, but that's how he wants it. He made that perfectly clear.

Tee demands his dinner, so I do the mom thing and then the fire hose thing again—I'm going to have to buy Thibault some paint for his wall.

I look around the living room, Tee dressed in clean clothes and a new diaper, wrapped up like a burrito. *What am I going to do now?* Thibault won't be home for more than an hour. *I need some air.* Thibault gave me the alarm code, so he's obviously okay with me leaving the house. The idea of getting out lifts my spirits. I'm feeling too cooped up. I'll just take a little walk, and hopefully it'll clear my head of all this fog that's settled in.

I don't have a stroller, but I don't need one. Tee weighs six pounds. My purse weighs more than that, and I can carry that thing around all day long. And my cramps have subsided, so I'm actually feeling a little energetic. I reach the bottom of the driveway with my borrowed flip-flops slapping away at my heels and turn right. I seem to recall passing a park or something on the way into the neighborhood.

The walk takes a lot longer than I thought it would. Two blocks turns into three and then four and five before the park comes into view. By the time I finally make it, the sun is starting to set and my body is aching all over.

"What the hell, Tee?" I sit down gently on a bench near a swing set. "What is wrong with this body of mine?" I know I just gave birth a couple days ago, but damn . . . I'm only twenty-seven. I shouldn't feel like I'm fifty.

I take a few deep breaths and look around me. This place has seen better days. Two of the three swings are broken, and there's trash overflowing from multiple bins. There's no one here but Tee and me, though, so I'm not worried. It's not like Pavel is going to come sauntering by or anything. This place is probably safer than Thibault's house if Pavel is hunting me down using my cell phone signal.

Bugs and other creatures start singing. The night deepens. Time slips away from me, and Tee grows ever heavier in my arms. I wonder what Thibault is doing right now. He's probably at Jenny's house, hanging around all of his friends and co-workers. I've never had that experience—being able to spend quality time with my colleagues. Quality time to Pavel's people meant shooting up, or shooting some-*body* up. Not my thing. No, I always went home as soon as I was done doing his work, and I stayed put. It was rare that Sonia or I had visitors at our apartment. Pavel would come by once in a while, but usually only when he was drunk. I always locked my door and pretended to be asleep. Well, almost always. There was the one time I didn't lock my door fast enough . . .

A sound startles me out of my trip down memory lane. Someone's foot kicked a stone or something, and it rattles across the blacktop.

I look around and see a figure approaching from a couple blocks away. He's moving slowly. I can tell it's a man by the shape and width of his shoulders. He pauses, staring at the park, and then continues on.

My heart races as I try to size him up. Is he tall like Pavel or stocky like Thibault? Or neither? He has a peculiar gait, making me think he's drunk or high on something. As he gets closer, I realize how stupid it was for me to come out here to a park I don't know after sundown. *Why did I leave Thibault's house, where I was perfectly safe? Is this what a good mother does? No!* I hold Tee closer to my body, trying to shrink down and become less visible.

CHAPTER NINETEEN

"Mika?"

I've never been so relieved to hear a voice in my life. *Thibault*. It's not Pavel, and I was so sure it was. I could even picture the expression he would have on his face upon discovering me served up on a silver platter here on this park bench: triumph, anger, excitement over what he would soon be doing to me as punishment for refusing his visit and disappearing. I feel like I'm going to vomit.

He slows down, favoring his leg and holding out a hand. "Hey, Mika. It's me, Thibault. Are you okay?"

"Yeah." My voice trembles.

He limps over to the bench and lowers himself onto it gradually, his weight making the wood groan in complaint. I'm grateful for his effort at trying not to jiggle it too much and wake the sleeping baby.

We sit there together and stare out at the swings in front of us, neither of us saying anything for a while. It gives me a chance to calm my heart and my nerves, to chase my tears away. I feel bad that I disappeared on him without leaving a note. Maybe he thought I left for the bus station. I wonder if he was sad about it.

"I thought I would take a little walk," I say. There's regret in my tone. I feel stupid and naïve. I'm worried about my ability to be a good mother.

"I'm sorry I didn't leave you a phone you could use. That was stupid. You probably felt like a prisoner in my house."

I put my hand on his arm, my palm cold and clammy in comparison to his warm, dry skin. "Don't say that. I didn't feel like a prisoner, I promise. Not exactly. I guess I just needed to think, and it was hard to do that in an unbiased way while I was surrounded by all of your stuff." The photo album mocks me, all that happiness inside.

"I get it." He sighs. "Don't worry about it. You have to do what you have to do."

"It's just . . . you can be very overwhelming sometimes."

"What do you mean?" He looks at me like he's trying to study my expression. I can barely see his; it's too dark out.

"You're big, you're strong, you have all your friends and family around you. And you're really sure of yourself. And you're also really sure about what you can do and what I need to do and what's going to happen next. But the problem is *I'm* not so sure."

His voice is soft. Caring. "Which part aren't you sure about? Maybe I can say something to make you feel better."

I sigh heavily, taking my time with responding because everything is a jumble in my head. "I need to leave. But whenever I picture doing that, I can't figure out where I need to go. Where I *can* go. I have money but no contacts. No plan. You've offered to let me stay a little while, but your sister has two kids and she lives right next door. I'm worried about them. What if Pavel . . ." I can't finish. Instead I shiver, and it's not because of the temperature.

He nods. "I hear you. And that's a concern I share with you, and probably my sister does too. But I have a solution to that problem if you're interested in hearing it."

I'm afraid to hope for too much. "Okay," I say, tentatively. "What is it?"

"My family has a cabin out in the bayou. It's not bad, as far as cabins go. I mean, it's not a ramshackle place held together with mud, sticks, and old tires like some of them are, but it's not ultrafancy, either."

I'm picturing the place he says his cabin is not, tires and all; but even so, it seems way better than getting on a bus to nowhere. "Sounds . . . quaint."

"It's outside the city, and nobody knows it's there. It's got a bed-room, a bathroom, and a nice little kitchen. No TV, and hardly any cell signal, but it's private. There's no one else anywhere around."

"So, no one knows about it except everyone on your team."

"Yes, they know about it, but you can trust them. I'd stake my life on it. You have nothing to fear from any of them."

I stare at him and shake my head. "It must be nice." There's that jealousy again. I hate how it keeps rearing its ugly head.

"What?"

"I don't know . . . To have that much faith in somebody, maybe."

He shrugs. "They're my family."

"You sound like Pavel."

"In what way?" His voice has lost the caring touch.

"His people are all very loyal to him and each other. Part of it is because they've bought into the whole brotherhood thing like it's a damn cult, but the other part is that if you screw them over, they kill you. There're no questions asked, either; they just do it—*bam*—it's an execution. That kind of ruthlessness inspires loyalty like I've never seen before. In the hospital, I was worried about what was going to happen to me and the baby, but now I'm also worried about what could happen to you and your family. If Pavel finds out you're helping me, they're all going to be in danger."

He puts his arm over the back of the bench and turns toward me, clearing his throat before speaking. "Okay, I don't want to be pushy, because I know you're already feeling pretty overwhelmed, but I need you to understand something."

I turn a little to face him. "I'm listening."

He places his hand flat over his heart. "I have dedicated my entire adult life to working with the police, helping them solve crimes, and getting bad people off the street. It's who I am. I'm not saying I'm a hero or that I'm perfect or that I don't screw up sometimes, but I *am* saying that I don't know anybody who will work harder than me to keep you and Tee safe. I helped bring him into the world, and I know it's crazy to say, but I feel a responsibility toward him and to you. Can you understand where I'm coming from?"

"But it was all just bad luck!" I say, quickly becoming agitated. This man is a good person, and I know he means well, but I can picture so clearly the regret he'd have if helping me got someone he cared about hurt . . . or worse. "I *hit* you with my *car*! It's not like you *chose* to be around me or involved with me. It's not like you *know* me. I'm just some girl who almost ran you over, and you're just the distracted dummy who got in my way, right? So, what I don't get is how I go from being *that* girl to *this person* you want to protect at all costs. It doesn't make any *sense*! You should be suing my butt off, not protecting it." My head is spinning. I have no idea where all that came from, but I'm glad it's out of me. *Damn.*

He throws his hands up. "Mika, I don't believe in random events just floating through our lives. I believe everything happens for a reason. There's a *reason* I decided to get up that morning and drive all the way over to Lotta Java when I haven't been there in months. And there's a *reason* you took a wrong turn and headed up that particular one-way street, driving like a crazy maniac." He pauses, his volume going down a notch or two. "And I stepped off the curb at exactly the right moment, while I was distracted."

"*Wrong* moment, you mean."

"No, I mean the *right* moment. There's a reason for all of it. You were correct when you yelled at me from inside your car—I should've looked both ways. But I *didn't*. Normally I do, I swear it. All the time, I do. But on that day, at that moment, on that street, when you happened to be driving where you shouldn't have, I didn't. And then you hit me, and the rest is history."

He takes a breath before finishing. "So . . . I have to ask myself, why did all of those little things arrange themselves in just that way, so I would be in the perfect position to see a pregnant lady about to give birth, at the precise moment she was having labor pains that made it impossible for her to continue driving?" He shakes his head, and I can see his smile in the lamplight coming from across the street. "You could have been one block ahead or one block behind where you were and I never would have seen it. You never would have hit me, and our paths would have never crossed. I believe it all happened because I was meant to bump into you—or be bumped into *by* you—so I could help you and the baby. What other explanation is there? Too many events had to roll out just perfectly for this to happen randomly. And if that's true, then it means I have to keep helping you. I can't help you give birth to a healthy boy and then drop you off at a gangster's doorstep. It's not me." He runs his hands through his hair. "It's just not me." He pauses, his voice dropping off to almost nothing. "Not anymore."

Tears come and won't stop. He's talking about fate and destiny and things that were meant to be, as if someone up there in heaven has a plan for me, and it includes putting good men like Thibault in my path to help me out. I don't believe it. I've had too much bad luck in my life to believe I deserve the good kind. It's more likely that the universe has a plan for Thibault, and it ain't pretty. "Maybe both of our times have come, and this is destiny's way of putting us both in the path of a killer."

He shakes his head. "I don't believe that. No way. I'm here to stay. I have more work to do on this earth. And one of my jobs, something I feel deep in my heart, is to make sure that you're safe. That you can move on with your life with your baby and not worry about some Russian mobster sneaking up behind you and slitting your throat." He hisses out a breath. "Jesus, I'm sorry. That was ugly."

A bitter laugh moves past my tears. He's a lot closer to describing my life than he realizes. "No, don't apologize. Thanks for the graphic visual. Did you know that's his preferred method of execution, or was it just a good guess?"

He shakes his head. "No, I didn't know, but I do know lots of guys like him. They're ruthless dirtbags begging to be taken down." He picks up my hand and holds it lightly in his. I should probably pull away, but I don't. It feels too good to have him touching me like this. "You've got the goods on Pavel. My team has agreed to help you out on the condition that I double-check all the facts you've given me and verify that they're true."

I sigh heavily, hurt that they don't trust me, but understanding completely why they don't. "I guess I can't expect them to trust the word of a former prostitute, can I?"

He squeezes my hand gently. "First of all, don't talk about yourself like that. Just because you were forced into doing a job, or you chose to do something to survive, it doesn't make you a bad person. Second of all, I haven't told anybody that part of your story. That's your secret to share or not share, not mine."

I look at him, staring at his profile for several minutes. I want to see into his head and his heart, find out what's in there, learn what makes him tick. He's complicated, stubborn, kind, firm, and sexy . . . all these things rolled into one solid man. His hand is strong. Callused. Safe. I'd be willing to bet every dime I have that he's never used this hand in violence against a woman. It's dangerously alluring. I could get addicted to this person sitting next to me. He's so different from what I've known these last years. My last sexual experience was unpleasant, to say the least. I wonder what Thibault is like in bed. Is he gentle? An alpha male who calls all the shots? Rough? Adventurous? I will never know, but that won't stop me from imagining. Dreaming. Wishing things could have been different. He said I'm not his type and I said he's not mine, but the more time we spend talking, the more I think we could both be a little wrong about that.

"I have a confession," I say. The words spill out of me before I can think to stop them.

"Another one?"

He's trying to sound put out, which makes me smile and keep going when I shouldn't. "Yes. One more."

"Is it going to blow my mind?"

If he took my pulse right now, he'd know how crazy this is for me, to flirt with him. That's what I'm doing. I'm flirting, God help me. "Probably."

"Fine. Go ahead. Lay it on me. I'm ready." He closes his eyes, pretending to be preparing himself.

I can't stop staring at his mouth. Those lips of his . . . full, dark, a mystery. *How would it feel to have them on mine?* "I really want to kiss you right now," I whisper.

He looks at me, shrugging. "So what's stopping you?" He tugs on my hand and leans a little toward me.

I can't believe it. He didn't laugh at me or tell me to keep dreaming. He wants to kiss me too. "Things are already really complicated," I say as I draw nearer. I can't ignore the attraction between us. Not when we're sitting out here in the dark on this bench with the real world a thousand miles away. "This will make it worse."

"But I like complicated."

"I'm beginning to think I do too." We meet in the middle. Our lips touch . . .

And then the baby starts crying because he's hungry and it's way too late for him to be out in a neighborhood park. And I should know better.

Thibault groans a little and pulls away. "Another time," he says. He stands on one leg and holds out his hand. "Are you ready to go home? Back to my place?"

I put my hand in his and lean on his strength so I can get my sore body off the bench. "Yes. It's pretty damn cold out here, actually." I laugh uncomfortably. I also have to pee so badly I can hardly stand it.

We walk together down the sidewalk. "You should always have a diaper bag with you when you leave, just in case Tee decides to have a blowout. My sister has had some real doozies with the twins. You can tuck a jacket in there for yourself, too, for those nights you want to take random walks to the park and the temperature drops." He looks over at me and smiles.

"Whatever you say, Superman."

He pauses. "Don't call me that. I'm no superhero. I'm just a guy."

I stop and look up at him, no longer joking. "I don't know who told you that, but they were wrong. You're definitely not *just* a guy."

The baby squeaks again. "You want to feed him here?" he asks.

"I'd rather do it at your place."

"Well, let's go, then."

He hobbles along next to me, and I find myself enjoying the sounds of the night that rise up around us—crickets and bats and owls calling out with their evening song—despite the fact that whatever we have between us is completely surrounded by a pretty gloomy reality. The idea of getting away from it all holds a strong appeal right now. I can picture being tucked away in a cabin in the bayou where no one could find me. I could be happy there, taking care of my son and figuring out our next steps. The only thing that would be missing would be Thibault. But I couldn't expect him to join us there. His job ends when we're safe.

"So when are you thinking I could go to your cabin?" I ask.

"How about tomorrow morning?"

"Sounds good to me." I can't believe how sad the idea of leaving Thibault behind makes me. That near-kiss has thrown me for a serious loop.

"And I didn't mean that you'd go out there alone. I'll go with you. My knee is shot right now anyway, so Ozzie—my business partner— told me to take a few weeks off until I have my surgery."

"Don't they need you at work, though?"

"We're hiring a new guy who Dev'll get up to speed real quick. They'll be fine without me for a little while. We don't have anything big on the books right now that needs me specifically."

It almost pains me to say this, because I'm so used to being on my own and not depending on anyone, but I can't keep it to myself. It feels too dishonest when he's making such an effort. "I think I'd prefer that. For you to be there with me."

"Good."

I can hear the smile in his voice, and it chases away the chill of the night. I don't need a jacket anymore.

CHAPTER TWENTY

Our first stop on the way out of town is the local warehouse super-store. I've never been inside it before, although I've driven past it plenty of times. Thibault is driving; I guess it was just dumb luck that I hit his left leg and not the right one and that he has an automatic transmission.

"Do I need to get out?" I ask, looking up at the red, white, and blue sign and then at the parking lot jammed with cars and people moving fast with their shopping carts.

"You probably should. I'm going to stock up on food and stuff for the cabin, and I don't know what you like to eat or what you might need."

"You mean we're not going to be eating bologna sandwiches for every meal?" I grin at him.

"Well, we might, if you keep that up."

I bite the inside of my cheeks for a few seconds to make the smile go away. "I'm sorry. You've been taking great care of me, and here I am giving you a hard time about it."

"That's okay," he says as he shuts off the engine and gets out of the car. "I'm getting tired of sandwiches too." He leaves the crutches in the car.

I set the baby seat in the cart and walk next to Thibault as he pushes it toward the entrance. "Do you want me to do that?" I ask, pointing at the cart. "Push that?"

"Nah. If you don't mind, I'm kind of using it as a replacement for my crutches."

"Oh. Yeah, okay. No problem. Push away." I'm actually glad he's taking over that duty; my whole body is sore from that walk to and from the park last night.

"I can't believe I still feel so tired." I rest my hand on the side of the cart, selfishly glad Thibault can't go very fast, then hating myself for celebrating the injury I helped cause.

"I think it's normal to feel tired and out of it. It's only been a few days since this little guy did a number on you." He pauses to poke the baby gently, smiling when he squirms around and squeezes out a bubble of gas. Thibault looks at me as we wait for our turn to enter the store. "If you want to go see a doctor before we leave, I'd be happy to bring you to one."

"No, that's all right. I'm sure this is totally normal. Too much walking around isn't such a great idea, I think, but some is good. The nurses told me that in the hospital. This will be my exercise for the day."

He leans over the cart and looks right at me. "You can wait in the car. Really, I can do this. And I can take Tee with me too, if you want. You can take a quick nap, maybe."

I cuff him lightly on the arm. "I'm not weak, okay? I just . . . had a baby."

He smiles and pushes the cart forward. "Okay, Miss Tough Stuff. Let's go, then. If you get too tired, I'll put you in the cart and push your . . . butt through the store."

He was going to say *big* butt, I know he was. I turn around and look at my rear end. "What's wrong with my butt?"

He pushes the cart past me. "Absolutely nothing." He's grinning like a devil.

"Boy, I'm-a . . ." I shake my head at him, enjoying the banter but pretending like he's getting on my nerves. I like playing innocent flirting games with him. I can't remember the last man I was able to do that with.

He keeps going, flashing his membership card at the entrance and moving into the television and stereo area. I catch up with him when he's staring at the radios that hook into cell phones to play music.

I gaze over the interior of the huge warehouse, amazed at the product selection. I can just make out a huge refrigerated section in the back. I wonder how close the cabin is to a grocery store. "Does your cabin have a big fridge or one of those little dorm-room-size ones?"

"Big one."

"It sounds like a real honest-to-goodness vacation place. And you said it's in the bayou?"

"Yep. Surrounded by big trees with hanging moss. It's beautiful."

"I'm looking forward to seeing it." It sounds like heaven compared to what I've been living in, actually. But I probably shouldn't expect too much. It's only temporary, and Thibault did say it's not that fancy.

"Me, too." He picks up a package of headphones to examine them. "I just realized I haven't had a vacation in a couple years." He glances at me. "Not that this is a vacation, but it is time off work."

"Two years? Wow. Don't you get vacation days at your job?"

"Yeah, sure. It's not that the company doesn't give me time off, I just never take it. I'm always too busy working one case after another after another. Even now, when there's nothing big going on, I still have to handle employee issues, share business decisions with Ozzie, be there for training when my knee is better . . ."

Someone pushes past me and bumps my arm, going so fast he doesn't even stop to apologize. I frown at his back, the stranger whose pants are pulled up way too high. "This place is crazy."

"A madhouse," Thibault says, looking around. "Where's the snack aisle?"

I stop at a set of glass shelves, lifting up a purse displayed under lights. I can't believe what I'm seeing. "This is a Gucci bag. Do you know how much this costs in the Gucci store?" I try to find the price tag. This is the kind of gift Pavel buys a woman to signal his possession of her. I figured out how he operates very early on and never accepted anything from him if I could help it.

"I'll bet it costs more there than it does here," Thibault says.

I finally catch the price on a little ticket stuck to the shelf. *Damn.* "You can say that again." I put it down gently next to the others. Even though it's about half its regular price, it's still too rich for my budget. I couldn't even imagine spending that kind of money for a bag now that I have to buy diapers.

Thibault pushes the cart toward another area of the store, out of the luxury goods and electronics sections. "We have to buy almost everything in bulk here, but I figure with as many diapers as this little guy is going to go through, we're in the right place." He pauses to let someone go by and strokes Tee's cheek. The baby squirms in response but remains sleeping. He scowls like Thibault's bugging him, and it makes us both laugh.

"He's saying, 'Get your hands off me. Can't you see I'm trying to sleep?'" I say, touching his tiny chin.

"I'm sorry. I should leave him alone." Thibault looks apologetic.

"I was just kidding." I tap him on the arm with the back of my hand. "Come on, lighten up. I was just messing around. You can tickle his little face all you want."

His eyebrows go up. "Did you just tell me to lighten up?"

"Yes." I try not to smile.

He presses his pouting lips together. "Okay, then. I'll lighten up." He grins and points the cart down an aisle full of junk food. "Bulk packages of beef jerky, here we come."

When I see him pick up what looks like about a hundred packages of dried beef, I have to ask the question that pops into my mind. "How long do you think we're going to be at the cabin?"

He shrugs. "Maybe just a few days. It depends on what the team figures out after seeing your data."

"What data?" I freeze in place, not sure I understand what he's talking about.

He grabs another bag of dried meat and studies the package as he answers. "Whatever it is you plan to give Holloway." He looks up at me. "Assuming you trust us to see it and pass it on for you." He goes back to his snacks, giving me time to gather my thoughts without the pressure of his gaze.

"I don't remember saying that was part of my plan," I say as he pushes the cart farther down the aisle.

"We haven't had a chance to talk about it. I figured we could discuss it on the way to the cabin. It's an hour drive."

My first reaction is to tell him to stuff it. Giving his team anything was not part of my plan. But then on further reflection, I realize I don't really have a plan. I haven't had one since I went into labor.

I walk over and take hold of the edge of the cart, using it to prop myself up a little. My lower back is bothering me. "So are you saying that you think your team can give Holloway what he wants for me? So I don't have to go meet with him?" I'm liking the idea of never going back to New Orleans again. Not because I don't love the city, but because Pavel is there, and I imagine he has eyes everywhere and they're all looking for me.

"Maybe. I guess it depends on what you have."

I'm seized with the desire to tell him everything. It would be so nice to unload to someone and share the burden. But I can't. Not yet, anyway. Still, he has a right to know some things; he is hiding me and my baby away, after all.

"I have what the detective said he needs. Let's just put it that way."

He glances at me before pushing the cart to the next aisle over. "Once we get settled in, we'll get in contact with them and give them whatever you have. If you want. It's totally up to you." He pauses, lowering his voice and looking me in the eye. "I don't want you to think I'm a pushy jerk all the time."

He's obviously taken the things May and Jenny said to heart. I have to give him credit for that; most men think the advice they get from women is worthless. "Okay. That sounds like a plan."

"I think it's only fair, since you've started to let me help you a little bit."

"What's that supposed to mean?"

He shrugs, pushing the cart off again as he leans heavily on it with both arms bent at the elbows. "Nothing. I'm just saying that before, you were going to get on a bus and disappear, and now you're letting me help. A little. And I'm glad." He pauses to look at me over his shoulder. "We're good, right? This isn't freaking you out too much?"

I shrug. "Yeah, we're good." It is freaking me out, but it's not his fault. He's trying hard; that much is clear. And I am, too. I don't know what's fueling my efforts, though. Is it fear? Jealousy? Desire? Madness? I've been riding an emotional roller coaster for weeks, so any of these could be a viable explanation. But I'm not going to focus on that right now. I'm going to get this shopping done, get to that cabin, breathe calmly for about a day, and then worry about everything else.

"So do you know how to cook anything besides sandwiches and noodles?" I ask.

He points at his chest with his thumb. "Who, me? Are you kidding?"

"No. Why would I be? You're a single guy living on your own. I think it's safe to assume you eat heated-up frozen food or takeout almost every night if you're not at your sister's. That's what Pavel does."

"I mostly do takeout. I'm not a fan of frozen food."

"Oh. So you don't cook, then, aside from pasta."

"A little. I cook a little, but feel free to take over the kitchen duties if you want."

We pass a few more aisles before Thibault speaks up. "So you guys lived together? You and Pavel?"

He stops the cart when we reach the next aisle.

"No." The very idea makes me stress. It was bad enough working with him almost every day.

Thibault puts a big box of gum in the cart. "Pick what you want. Anything at all. Sky's the limit."

I'm happy for the distraction. "Ooo, this is exciting." I put a bag of Oreos in the cart.

He stops rolling along to look at me. "When we drove by your place and you couldn't go in, I figured that meant it was because he was home."

For some reason, it's easier talking to him in the middle of this giant warehouse with strangers around us than it is when we're alone in his home. "No, I wasn't living with him, but I was living with somebody he knows very well. And his car was there, so . . ." I shrug.

"Oh." He pushes forward, eventually reaching a table full of books. He looks through the titles.

I do the same, stopping when I see one with pretty pictures of food on it. "Do you mind if I buy a cookbook?" I hold it up. "I can pay you back once we get to an ATM machine."

"Be my guest." He moves closer and drops his voice. "But I think it's better if we stay away from the ATMs for a little while. They can tell people where we are, and right now I'd rather no one be able to track us."

"Okay." I nod, all the horrible feelings and worries about Pavel rushing back to me.

"So you never told me how Pavel found you in the hospital," he says, acting like his question is casual when it couldn't possibly be. "Did you call him?"

I sigh, dropping the cookbook into the cart. So, so many problems could have been avoided if I'd just listened to my instincts and not called Sonia. "Not exactly." Maybe Pavel would have found out eventually after seeing my car on the news, but it would have given me more time to get away.

I move on to examine bags of refrigerated cheese, glancing back to make sure Thibault is still following with my baby. I trust Thibault not to do anything unsafe, but I still feel really uncomfortable when Tee is more than five feet away. It's like the umbilical cord was cut, but they left an invisible one behind that's still connecting us.

Thibault is staring down at the baby, forcing people to move around them. I walk over and stop at his elbow, looking down at my son. "What are you staring at? Is he okay?"

"He's fine. I think he's dreaming." Thibault points to his face. "Look at him; his eyebrows are all scrunched up like he's mad."

I smile. "He does that all the time. I wonder what he's thinking right now."

The baby starts smiling in his sleep and makes sucking motions with his tiny lips.

"He's dreaming about your boobs, I think."

A laugh bursts out of me. "Excuse me?"

He smiles like a little kid who's been busted. "What? He's a baby. Your boobs are the focus of his entire world."

"Is that so?"

He holds up his hands. "Hey, I'm innocent. I'm just making a comment about a mother and her baby."

"I think you need to keep your mind off my you-know-whats and put it back on your shopping."

"Yes, ma'am." He limps away, hunched over the cart handle. I'd be willing to bet he's still smiling even though I can't see his face.

His hands come up. "I'm innocent," he says, louder.

I shake my head at him as he turns the corner to the next aisle. I don't think he could possibly be more charming.

"Hey, Tamika. What's going on?" The voice comes from behind me. My heart lurches as recognition seizes me. *Sebastian?! In this store?!*

My paranoia tells me Pavel has him out searching for me, and I want to scream over the fact that he's found me—I was supposed to be the needle in a haystack. But then I see Sebastian has his own cart full of items, and the paranoia fades into the background. Now I'm just plain old scared. Sebastian is a warehouse shopper like everyone else around me right now, but he'll be on his phone in no time telling Pavel who he saw here.

Thibault has paused, looking back at me, the cart no longer visible as it's turned the corner around the next aisle. I bug my eyes out at him and give him the slightest of head shakes before turning around and facing the man behind me.

"Hey, Sebastian. How've you been? I haven't seen you in ages." I can't look back at Thibault; there's still a chance Sebastian didn't see me with him and the baby. I feel sick. I have to swallow over and over not to lose control of my stomach.

"I've been good. I've been meaning to get in touch with Pavel. Have you seen him? I went over to his place yesterday, but he wasn't there. I sent him a couple of texts, but he's not answering."

He's totally lying. He was at my apartment with Pavel and Sonia the other night; I saw his car there. He's playing games.

I shrug, sliding my hands into the pockets of Toni's sweat jacket to hide the trembling. "No, I haven't seen him. I've been kinda busy."

"Really? What have you been up to?"

"Oh, nothing much. You know Pavel . . . Always keeping me on one thing or another. He doesn't like me telling people too much." *There.* I'll plant a seed of suspicion in Sebastian's head. It's not tough with Pavel's people to do that; they're uber-paranoid. Maybe he'll believe that Pavel was playing with him the other day, pretending to look for me when he knew exactly where I was all along.

Sebastian frowns. "Yeah, I hear you." Then he visibly cheers up as he delivers his next question. "And how is Alexei? Is he okay?"

More games. I can't freak out right now about why Pavel's sweet disabled cousin stopped coming around my apartment for random meals a few weeks ago. The cops will just have to search for him as part of my deal. I'm not going to abandon the one person who gave me a reason to keep getting up in the morning.

"I haven't seen him. Not for a long time. Weeks." When Alexei stopped showing up at my apartment, I had to pretend it didn't matter. It was the only way to keep Pavel from getting too interested in my life. I try to ignore the fact that Alexei is also the reason I stayed as long as I did and that him disappearing made it easier to trade Pavel's secrets for my freedom, but it's impossible. The guilt over not being a better friend burns my heart.

"I haven't seen him in a while, either." Sebastian looks to his left and right, lowering his voice. "Did he do something wrong? Did he get . . . put down?"

I shrug, drawing my arms in tighter against me. It feels like the warehouse just got ten degrees cooler. "I don't know. You know I don't ask questions like that."

"Yeah, but I would've thought with Alexei it would've been different. You guys were friends, right? You took care of him sometimes?"

I glare at Sebastian. He's messing with me and we both know it. But I'm not going to grab the bait because I need to get the hell out of here before he contacts Pavel and tells him he saw me.

Sebastian straightens up and smiles. "Look at me, bringing everybody down." He reaches up and play-punches me in the arm. I shy away, but he still makes contact. There'll be a bruise there, since he made sure to use a knuckle. "I'm sure Alexei's fine. When you see him, tell him hi for me."

"Yeah, okay, I'll do that."

He puts his hands on his hips. "You take care of yourself, Tamika." There's a message in his statement, but I don't even want to guess what it is.

"Yeah, sure. You, too."

I turn to walk in the opposite direction, back toward the front of the store. I have to get away. Hide. Never let Sebastian see me with my baby. He's exactly the kind of psychotic ass-kisser who would think nothing of grabbing Tee and walking out the door with him, thinking he was doing Pavel a favor by delivering his child to his doorstep. I pray Thibault knows I wouldn't abandon my child. I'm just going to hide until I know Sebastian can't see me anymore.

CHAPTER TWENTY-ONE

I'm standing next to the hot-dog stand that's on the other side of the registers. There are three people ahead of Thibault at the register he's chosen. Baby Tee looks like he's waking up, the way he's squirming around in his blankets. Thibault leans over to talk to him, but I can't hear what he's saying. Knowing my baby is hungry makes my body react. My breasts are suddenly heavy and raring to go. *Dammit.* I look down, hoping this jacket is thick enough to hide wet spots.

A woman standing in the next aisle over walks over to my baby. "How old is he?" she asks in a loud voice. Her top could not be cut any lower or her pants any tighter. I hate her instantly. *Get away from my baby. Get away from my . . . friend.*

Damn. I almost said "man" there. I shake my head, trying to get it back on track and focused. I'm obviously in need of some food. The smell of the hot dogs is killing me.

Thibault answers with something I can't hear. He's focused completely on the baby. It's curious to me that he's not ogling the woman when every other guy nearby is. Even I'm having a hard time tearing my eyes away from her. I see a major wardrobe malfunction on the horizon; her boobs look like they're going to fall out of her top at any second.

"Oh, my goodness, a newborn," she says, jiggling her jugs in Thibault's face. "I can't believe you have him out in public already."

Thibault looks worried when he responds.

She shrugs. "Some people don't like exposing their newborns to the germs for a little while. But I'm sure your doctor knows best." She shrugs and flashes him her veneers.

I feel colossally stupid for not staying in the car. The brochure I read in the hospital said I should limit Tee's exposure to strangers and germs. *What is wrong with me?* I could have avoided a psycho *and* the plague at the same time.

Thibault covers more of the baby with the blanket, giving the woman a perfunctory nod. He pushes the cart forward as one more person finishes their checkout in front of him. He's scanning the crowd, looking for me, probably, but I'm worried if he sees me, he'll wave me over and then Sebastian might lock onto us too. I assume he's still in the store somewhere, because I haven't seen him leave.

Come on, come on. My chest is aching, both from the need to feed my baby and also out of fear. Tee is too far away. Anyone could grab him. The only thing keeping me from totally losing it is knowing Thibault is with him. He wouldn't let anything happen to my baby. I take several calming breaths, trying to slow my racing heart. I'm freezing cold but sweating.

The checkout takes forever. When Thibault's almost done, I walk briskly to the exit, not looking up when an employee waves at me and tells me he needs to check my purchases. Since I have none and I can't afford to waste any time hanging around where Sebastian might see me, I go straight to the back of the parking lot and stand next to some bushes on a high curb, hoping to get an elevated viewpoint from which to spy on Thibault. As soon as he gets to the car, I'll move.

Thibault finally comes limping out of the exit. He stops and looks all over the place, shaking his head when he doesn't see me. I'm relieved because if he can't find me, neither can Sebastian.

When he's at the SUV and puts the lift-gate up, I take off walking as fast as I can, looking left and right, ready to move in another direction if I see Sebastian's face or the bright-red shirt he was wearing. As soon as I'm just one row over, I start running.

"Where have you been?" he hisses at me, slamming the back shut.

I hold out my hands. They're shaking uncontrollably. "Give me the baby. We have to leave."

Thibault's expression changes in an instant. He goes from pissed to taking charge. "I've got him. Get in the truck. The back windows are tinted. No one'll be able to see you."

As soon as I'm inside, he hands me my son and shuts the door. I gather Tee in close, leaning down so I can inhale his scent. "I'm so sorry, baby. I left you. I'll never do that again." I feel like throwing up. I can't believe that just happened.

Tee fusses, so I quickly do what I can to feed him. I'm sweating, shaking, and my head is spinning, but as soon as he latches on, I'm finally able to breathe properly. "Jesus Christ, save me from those evil bastards," I whisper.

Thibault gets into the front seat and looks at me in the rearview mirror. "I won't go anywhere until the baby's all strapped in. You can relax. You're invisible to anyone in the parking lot." He wipes sweat from his temples and upper lip.

"Okay."

He stares out the front windshield, his arm stretched across the top of the steering wheel. The silence grows between us, but as awkward as it is, I can't speak. There's nothing to say. This event was a reminder of the dangerous game I'm playing, informing on Pavel and trying to stay alive in the process. I must be insane to think I can pull it off. I battle tears as I think about what this means for my child.

CHAPTER TWENTY-TWO

The drive to the cabin goes smoothly. I catch a nap between feedings, and Thibault only stops the car when I have to take the baby out of his seat. The more miles that go by, the more relief I feel trickling in. My past is back in New Orleans and my future is somewhere out in the world, but my present is in this car with Superman, and for once I don't mind him suffering a hero complex.

I'm resting with my eyes closed when I feel the car slowing down. A gas station appears up ahead, and Thibault is stopping. I close my eyes again and try to relax.

He pulls up to the pumps and turns off the car, getting out and limping over to the side of the truck. The vehicle sways a little as he starts filling the tank and then settles when he walks a few feet away and pulls out his phone. The windows are closed in the back, but Thibault's front one is open. I can hear every word.

"Hey. It's me. Do you have a minute?" He pauses. "Yeah, listen, I'm with Mika, and we're headed out of town for a little while. Ozzie told me to take a couple weeks off before my surgery, so that's what I'm going to do. At least, for now."

I really want to sit up and look at his expression, but I stay in my fake-sleeping position. I'm shameless. My trust issues make it impossible for me to not take advantage of the situation. What if he has other plans for me? What if he isn't being totally honest? My grandmother always told me people who eavesdrop deserve what they hear about themselves, but I'm not going to let that stop me.

"Yes, as a matter of fact, there is," he says. "Could you do me a favor and call the detective working on her case and talk to him a little bit more about the relationship? He was pretty open to it before; maybe he has more to share now that she's gone missing. Maybe there's some talk he's picked up on the street. And could you ask him about a guy named Sebastian?"

My pulse quickens at the name. *Sebastian.* They won't find anything about him—he works in the background, always keeping his hands clean and letting other people do his dirty work. It doesn't mean he's not dangerous as hell, though.

He goes quiet for a few seconds. "I have no idea. We ran into him today. He recognized her and she was afraid of him, but I don't know anything other than that." He waits and then sighs. "No, she's not holding out on me. Not really. She's just . . . nervous. I don't think she trusts anyone right now, but I don't blame her. I'm just going to keep asking her questions, and hopefully one of these days she'll start answering. Maybe if she sees that all I want to do is help . . ."

He hisses and then kind of laughs. "Would you cut that out? Seriously. Talk with your wife or May if you want to analyze the finer points of the relationship. That's their gig; I'm not your guy for that."

My heart beats faster. It must be Jenny's husband, Dev, and it sounds like he's teasing Thibault about what's going on between us. I know I shouldn't want him to have any feelings toward me, but I can't seem to control my emotions at all these days. That half a kiss we shared only made things worse.

"Anyway, I'm going to try to get her to talk to me about what she's feeding Holloway, so if she does, I'll text you whatever I think might be helpful."

There's a really long pause as he listens before he speaks again. "If this makes you uncomfortable, just let me know. I can do it myself. It's just that my cell signal's not that good out here, and I'd really like to focus on Mika and the baby while I have her undivided attention. She's scared and she's convinced she needs to leave, but she doesn't have a plan. I want to try to help her come up with one, at the very least."

His kindness is both a gift and a curse. Its value is quickly diminished when I know he wouldn't feel the same way if he knew everything there was to know about me.

I hear gravel crunching and his voice grows fainter. "Okay, cool. Thank Ozzie for me, would you? I need to go pay for my gas." He stops all of a sudden. "Yeah, what?" Then he coughs out a laugh. "Are you serious? Holy shit . . . congratulations!"

I sit up and turn around, peeking over the top of the seats. Thibault is resting his hand on his head. "Seriously? That's awesome news. I'm so happy for you guys. Damn. That's going to be a hell of a houseful. When is she due?"

Jenny's pregnant? I turn back around and close my eyes again, resting my head against the seat. I'm happy for her. Her husband seems nice, and they both have good jobs with normal, non-criminal co-workers. I try not to be jealous, but it's really hard. I want that so badly for myself and Tee. As I sit in this man's truck running from a gangster, it seems like an impossible dream.

Thibault told Dev that he wants to help me come up with a plan. I've been trying to resist his offers of assistance as much as possible because I'm not used to depending on other people or trusting them enough to do that—it's all I know. But now that we're on our way out to his cabin and I'll finally feel like I have some time and space to think in a safe place, continuing to block him seems silly. I just listened to him having a private conversation, and he didn't say anything that made me worry about ulterior motives. I haven't regretted him being in my life so far. Maybe I should consider hearing him out. It can't hurt just to get his opinion, right?

CHAPTER TWENTY-THREE

"Everything okay back there?" Thibault asks, settling into his seat.

"Yep. Who were you talking to?" I decide to play innocent to see how much he'll tell me. It's a test. I really, really want to trust him. I hang on to the armrest of my door tightly as I wait for his answer.

"A friend from work. He's going to make some phone calls for me. There's not much of a cell signal out at the cabin."

"Are those phone calls about me by any chance?"

"Yes."

Honesty. Good. Point for Thibault. "Thanks for letting me sleep. I was really exhausted."

"Sure. No problem."

I suddenly notice how brightly the sun is shining. It makes it seem like the hood of Thibault's car is sparkling. "It's a pretty day out today."

"Sure is. Very mild. Nice breeze."

"It looks like you got a lot of stuff at the warehouse place," I say, looking over the seat into the back. Even though I took off on him before we'd put much into the cart, he had the presence of mind to get what we needed. I see two cases of diapers piled on top of tons of food and other baby items. I like his practicality and ability to keep a cool head under pressure.

"Yep. Baby Tee and I handled it together. He's a pretty good shopper."

Shame is making it hard for me to speak, but I have to do it. "I'm sorry I took off on you guys. Thanks for taking care of Tee for me. Being apart from him like that was horrible."

"Yeah . . . What was that all about?"

I shrug, wondering now if I overreacted. "I just didn't want anybody knowing my business."

"I noticed. Can you tell me who Sebastian is?"

Tee starts to cry, so I take him from his seat and settle him in my arms so he can have a quick meal before we get back out on the road. I'm stalling for time so I can come up with my answer. Having my baby close to me helps chase away those bad feelings that were created when we were apart.

"You don't have to tell me if you don't want to," Thibault says.

He's being so nice and patient with me, I feel bad holding out on him. And when I try to imagine the things that could happen to me as a result of him knowing my business, I come up with zilch. I sigh, still battling the fear that comes when I picture letting someone into my private life.

Please, God, don't let me regret this. "Sebastian is one of Pavel's associates. He's not in the family exactly, but he's about as close as you can come and not be blood related."

"Is he Russian too?"

"I don't know. I don't think so. He's from Eastern Europe somewhere, but where exactly? I have no idea. I never asked." I look up at him, really hoping he'll believe me, because I'm being completely honest. "I always tried to just keep my head down and focus on what I was supposed to be doing, which was keeping the books. There was always drama with those guys, but I stayed out of it."

He nods. "I get it. Your life was about survival. It seems like a smart move, to keep all that stuff at a distance."

"Yes. But then when I made this arrangement with Holloway, part of the deal was that I had to get closer to their business. He wanted to know about what Pavel did on a daily basis, where he went, who he spent time with."

"Did you tell him? Holloway, I mean? Did you get the intel for him?"

"I haven't told him anything yet, really. I checked in with him a few times to tell him what I was trying to do, and I did what he asked as much as I could, but I just kept getting sicker. Or that's what I thought it was. I thought me violating my personal rule of not getting involved was giving me an ulcer or irritable bowel syndrome or something. So I went to see him at the district office to tell him that I had to stop with the sneaking around until I was feeling better, but he wasn't there. And then, well . . . I met you."

Thibault has a half smile. "And then you had a baby."

"Yeah. Exactly." I look down at Tee's precious face. "And all my plans went up in smoke. *And* I found out why I was gaining weight and my ankles were so puffy."

Thibault turns more fully, gripping the edge of his seat. "So what *was* your plan, exactly? After you informed on Pavel, I mean."

I look up at him, not exactly excited about his enthusiasm.

He holds up a hand. "If you want to share. Only if you're comfortable."

I have to smile. "You need to relax."

"What? I am relaxed, see?" He holds up his hands and grins. Then he makes a goofy face, something I never thought I'd see him do.

He makes me laugh for a few seconds, but then I have to remind myself that this isn't a game. And he might be as charming and cute as a man can be, but that doesn't mean it's going to change my reality.

"Listen . . . I get that you're trying to help me, okay? I know that stepping back and allowing me to call the shots hasn't been easy for you."

He nods, calming his inner comedian. "I guess I can agree with that assessment."

The baby has fallen asleep on my breast, so I detach him and work on trussing him up like a burrito. "And I hope you realize how hard I'm working to try to trust you."

"I do. And I appreciate that."

I look up at him, pausing what I'm doing. "It's a big deal for me. I still don't really know you, and there's a lot on the line for me. To be honest, I think I'm just desperate at this point, so I'm taking more of a risk than I normally would with a stranger."

He takes hold of the seat again. "How about this . . . How about we spend the next couple days at the cabin getting to know each other? So you can feel more comfortable with me and we won't have to consider each other strangers so much anymore."

I nod. I like the low level of commitment and risk. "Okay. I can agree to that."

"But it has to go both ways," he says. "I work on letting go of my need to control your every movement, and you work on trusting me enough to share whatever you can. Is that a deal?"

"Yes. I agree. Deal."

He holds out his hand. "Shake on it."

I shift the baby into his seat and then take Thibault's hand. It should be nothing, the two of us just forming a casual pact, but touching his skin does something to me. His eyes widen in surprise as we make contact. He feels it too.

"Deal," I say, my voice strained. I pull my hand from his and busy myself with buckling the baby in. There's so much tension between us, but I can't decide if it's being wrapped up in this dangerous situation together or some crazy form of attraction. I know I've never felt anything like it before. Touching his hand should have been no big deal, but it felt intimate.

"You're getting pretty good at that." He's pointing at Tee. "The burrito wrap, the feeding stuff, the car seat. You look like an old pro."

I give him a tired smile. "Well, I feel like I've had a lot of practice at this point. It's only been a few days, but my body is telling me it's been weeks."

"How does it feel?" He looks at the baby and then me. "Being a mom. Are you enjoying it so far?"

It warms me that he's bothering to ask, and I like how it somehow turns him from a tough, deal-making security man into a guy who enjoys being around kids.

"It's good. I like it, but it's not easy. Not by any stretch of the imagination. I guess for me it's just plain *strange* still, because I didn't even realize I was pregnant, and then suddenly there he was." I take Tee's tiny hand, his itty-bitty fingers closing over my thumb. "When it first was happening, all I could think of was what a nightmare it was. But now I realize what a miracle he is. I'm very lucky."

"You are. You really are." He turns around to start the car, shifting into drive so we can continue our journey. "This might sound corny, but I'm glad to be experiencing it with you." He looks up in the rearview mirror at me. "Corny, right?"

I shake my head. "No. Not at all." When he looks away I find the courage to add to my response. "I'm glad you're doing it with me too. I think I would question my sanity if I didn't have someone like you standing there guiding me along. Teaching me how to do things like wrap him up or put a diaper on him."

"I'm here for ya," he says, as he pulls out onto the road.

His words give me such a sense of peace. Sadly, that makes me paranoid and suspicious, peace being such an alien concept, so the sensation only lasts a few seconds. I don't trust destiny to do right by me, so my good humor quickly gives way to a feeling of gloom and sadness. I turn to look out the side window so he won't see it on my face. Just because I have a problem with trusting happiness, it doesn't mean I need to bring him down with me.

"How much farther?" I ask as trees flash by my window, one after the other. The environment has become decidedly woodsier, with nothing but that gas station around.

"Fifteen minutes or so. Once we get there we're probably going to have to do some cleaning up before we can settle in."

"I'll help."

"That's all right. You should probably just relax."

"I think I need to do something other than relax and feed the baby." I sigh. "I'm not used to being so useless."

He taps his steering wheel, following some inner rhythm for a few seconds before he stops and responds. "I know Pavel's enterprise isn't exactly aboveboard—at least not parts of it—but to be a bookkeeper for an operation like that takes a lot of work. I can understand why it might be frustrating for you to be just hanging around feeding a baby all day and night. The same thing happened to Toni. She was climbing the walls about a week after she recovered from the birth of the twins."

I'm so impressed by the fact that he gets all of this. I feel a lot of respect coming from him, which is definitely not something I'm used to receiving from men. "Yeah, you're right. It is a lot of work being his bookkeeper. And it's not like I could call up someone with more experience and ask them how to do this or that. A couple times I emailed an old professor with some questions, but when he started demanding details about why I was asking, I had to cut him off. I learned pretty quickly that I had to stop trying to connect with people outside Pavel's influence. It forced me to do a lot of research and figure things out on my own, but it was okay. I got used to it."

"Maybe it sounds crazy to say this, but you should be proud of yourself." He looks up at me in the mirror.

"Thanks." It shouldn't matter that he admires what I've accomplished, but somehow it does. It makes me feel like it's okay to have some personal pride.

"Did you ever think about saving up your money and then disappearing? Going to another town and reinventing yourself there?"

"Every day," I say, sighing as I watch trees slide by my window. "Every *single* day." I know what he's saying underneath that question: that I should have done this. I shouldn't have stayed as long as I did. That I had the power to leave and never used it to help myself. I don't blame him. It's hard to understand a person sometimes when you can't walk in their shoes.

"And what stopped you?" he asks.

"Circumstances weren't right. Pavel would get suspicious and start watching me too closely. Something would scare me and make me think if I tried, I'd get killed. Alexei . . ." I stop, not wanting to go down that road. *Where is he? What's he doing? Who's feeding him dinner?*

"Alexei? Who is he?"

How can I possibly explain Alexei to him? He'll think I'm crazy. He'll think there's a part of me that wanted to stay there. "Just some guy."

Thibault lets it drop, for which I'm grateful. I feel like I've already overshared.

The exit off the highway is up ahead. He slows down and turns off, sending gravel dust up around the windows. He shuts his. "The road gets a little rough from here. Bumps and potholes. The parish doesn't maintain it much, since it's hardly used. I'll take it slow."

"Thanks." I reach over and take the baby's hand, stroking the back of it with my thumb. He doesn't seem to mind the rocking much, but I sure do. I hold my lower stomach with my free hand, hoping it's going to end soon. *Damn, that hurts.*

"I'm going to ask you for something, but I don't expect you to answer me now about it, okay?" Thibault says.

I'm instantly suspicious. "Okaaayyy . . ."

"If you feel comfortable with it, and feel like you can trust me with it, I'd like you to think about telling me what it is exactly you're planning to give to Holloway."

My temper flares, but I tamp it down. He's being as nice as he knows how to be, and I can tell he's trying not to push, even though he really wants the info. "Why do you think you need it?"

He slows down some more and takes a particularly big bump that rocks the truck hard. "Well, I was thinking that if I know all the parts of the puzzle, I could help you put together a plan of action. Get you headed into the sunset with the best chances of making a go of it."

Thibault sending me into the sunset. I like the image but feel just the tiniest bit sad about who I'll leave behind, both Thibault and Alexei. Life is so damn complicated sometimes. I wish I could just cut all the cords and disappear. Start over. Forget that I care about certain people.

"You don't trust me, do you?" I ask when the car finally stops rocking. I need to get all the cards out on the table. I'm tired of playing games with people. From now on, my life is going to be run at face value. Time for some hard truths.

"I want to. I really do."

"I wouldn't blame you if you didn't. Your job is putting criminals behind bars, and I've been working for one for five years. I guess that makes me a criminal too."

"Technically, it probably does. But I think, based on what you've told me, there are extenuating circumstances. And if that's the case, I'm sure if it came to a legal situation with the state, the prosecutor would be willing to make you some sort of deal. But only if you're able to hand over the information that gets convictions on murderers, drug dealers, and sex traffickers."

The reality of my situation is too depressing. I've avoided thinking about the criminal aspect of what I've done pretty well so far. Thibault bringing it up is a serious downer, and I'm having a hard time not holding it against him. "I'll do whatever I have to do, like always." I stare straight ahead, letting my mind go blank. The car bounces some more, but I hardly notice. I've gotten pretty good at detaching, even when sitting in the midst of chaos.

"Guess what's for lunch," he says a few minutes later, startling me out of my self-induced trance.

I look at him in the mirror. "Sandwich?"

He grins big. "Peanut butter and jelly, baby, with extra-crunchy peanut butter."

I can't help but smile back. "Can't wait."

CHAPTER TWENTY-FOUR

Thibault sets two sandwiches along with big glasses of milk down on the coffee table in the living room, waking me from the nap I caught on the couch.

"Oh, shoot. I'm sorry about that. I fell asleep, I guess." I reach up and touch my hair, trying to smooth down the bumps. I look around the room and see that he's been busy cleaning. All the covers are removed from the furniture, and the air smells like dusting spray.

"No big deal. Your body obviously needs it."

I nod at the transformation in the room. It looked old and smelled musty when we came in, and now it looks warm and fresh . . . inviting. "Wow, you cleaned this place up fast." I look at my wrist, but there's no watch there. "Or I slept like Rip Van Winkle and it's really late."

"Nah. Just a half hour or so." He drops down into a recliner opposite me with a plate in his lap and a glass of milk on the arm of the chair. "I have lots of practice cleaning this place up."

"How's that?" I sit up and place Tee on the couch cushion next to me. He slept in my arms as content as could be while I snoozed away the rest of the morning.

"Every time we came here with our grandparents, it was my and Toni's job to pull all the covers off the furniture and dust everything down. My grandfather would chop wood and my grandmother would clean the kitchen. It was a team effort."

"When was the last time you were out here?" I bite into my sandwich and chew slowly.

"Four years? Five years? I don't remember."

"You and Toni are close, huh?"

"Yeah. We bonded over our mutual shitty childhood."

Not wanting to bring the mood down by digging up too much unhappy history, I choose a different tack. "You said you came here with your grandparents. Does that mean you lived with them all the time?"

He shakes his head. "No. We lived full-time with our parents. They weren't very nice people or very happy. When we were with our grandparents, it was like our sanctuary. No yelling, no fighting, no anger-management issues."

I'm struck by how our lives have somewhat paralleled. Before he said this, I would have thought we had very little in common. "That's how it was for me, too, kind of."

"Really? Tell me about it." He pauses as he grabs his sandwich. "If you want."

"All of my grandparents have passed on. My dad, too. My mom . . . who knows where she is. She's been gone a while. I lost track of her after she went to prison. I knew at that point that she was never going to change and become a real mother to me, and I didn't need that negativity around me all the time. Just going to school was hard enough."

"I'm sorry to hear that."

"Thanks. Yeah, my parents weren't worth much to me. Even when I was real little, I spent a lot of time with my grandmother, but by the time I was twelve years old, my parents were hopeless. Services came and got me out."

"Drugs are terrible on families."

"Yep. Drugs, and my father was also a car thief." My smile is sad. "I got some great DNA running through these veins, let me tell you."

"Sounds like your grandmother was a pretty cool person, so I guess you're right about that."

I nod but say nothing. I appreciate him trying to put a positive spin on things, but I'm afraid whatever I say now will sound too much like self-pity.

Thibault's gaze roams the room. I follow it and take in the details: another one of those cuckoo clocks, only this one is much bigger; antlers from various animals hanging on the wall; family photos on the shelves; old board games stacked on top of one another on a table.

"Yeah, we always liked hanging out with our grandparents here," he says. "They were really cool. They just let us run amok. There's a lake not too far from here that Toni and I used to go to and swim around in for half the day. I remember doing cannonballs, trying to make the biggest splash I could just to piss Toni off." He takes a sip of his milk. "But I wouldn't go there and swim nowadays."

"How come?"

"Gators. There never used to be that many, and they never bothered us, but I imagine that place is totally infested with them now. They don't have any predators out here, and they multiply like rabbits."

Pavel has been known to hide bodies inside the stomachs of gators. It makes me literally shiver to imagine it. "Brrr, no thanks. I don't need to swim in a gator-infested lake. I don't even need to see it."

"Okay. I hope you don't mind snakes, though."

I slowly lower my sandwich from my mouth. "I actually *do* mind snakes. Do you mind telling me why you said that?"

"Well, you know . . . this tends to be a very . . . uh . . . snakey area. They like the trees and the leaves and the sunshine . . ." He's trying really hard not to laugh.

I slowly lift my feet from the floor and tuck them under me, balancing my plate in my lap. "Thanks for the information." I glance over my shoulder toward the bathroom.

"What are you looking for?" he asks.

"I'm trying to figure out how I'm going to get from here to the toilet without actually touching the floor."

He laughs. "You don't need to worry about it. There won't be any in the house."

"Can you guarantee that?"

He shrugs. "Mostly."

I shake my head slowly. "You sure love getting on my last nerve, don't you?"

He grins, taking a big bite of his sandwich. Then he points to his chest. "Me?" he says around the food.

I chuckle. "Yeah, you."

He frowns at me like I'm crazy.

I sigh, looking around the room for something else to talk about. This feels like flirting, which is fun, but a bad idea to encourage, considering our situation.

"So . . . you said there's not much cell phone signal here. And I don't see a computer, and you said there's no TV, either. What are we going to do all day?" I look at him for an answer and watch his eyebrow slowly go up. Too late I realize I've flirted with him again. Talk about a loaded question.

He points with the remainder of his sandwich at the bookshelves. "We have cards and board games." He clears his throat after. It sounds like he has a frog in it all of a sudden.

"The only thing I know how to play is crazy eights."

"Well, then, we can spend some time learning a few basic card games."

"So what you're saying is, we're pretty much going to die of boredom out here."

He chuckles. "We could talk."

I shrug. "I think I'll probably sleep a lot. If this baby keeps eating the way he does, I don't know how I'm going to stay awake long enough to play a whole game of cards, anyway."

"You don't have to do anything if you don't want to. I can keep myself busy. I already plan to work some of my frustrations out on the wood-chopping tree stump out back."

"What frustrations?"

The air between us is charged. I did it again. *Dammit.* He's going to think I'm sweating him or something.

"Oh, just the usual kind." He winks and then chugs down the rest of his milk, standing with his empty dishes in hand.

"You finished fast," I say, pointing to his plate, desperately trying to move past the innuendo I keep serving up.

"My sister, Toni, says I'm capable of eating a sandwich in three bites."

"You took four," I say.

"Watching me pretty closely, I see." He winks again, embarrassing me with that more than with his comment. "Taking care of damsels in distress kicks up my appetite, I guess."

I snort and look away.

He puts his dishes down on the table and holds out his hand toward me. "Come on. Let's go."

I reach up and take his hand, letting him help me up off the couch. "Where're we going?"

He lets me go and leans over to pick up the baby. "For a walk."

"Out there? With all those snakes and gators? No, thank you." I reach up to take the baby from him, but he turns away so I can't reach him.

"You'll be safe, I promise. Any snake tries to get you, I'll grab it and throw it across the woods."

"While you hold my baby? No, I don't think so."

"Okay, I'll kick it."

I look down at his leg. "With that knee of yours? Nope."

"Oh, yeah, that's right. I forgot . . . Some crazy woman hit me with her car."

"Give me that baby." I take Tee from him but gesture toward the door. "Go on, then. Let's take this silly walk. It's going to be the first and only one I'm taking in this place, though. I'm putting my foot down on that. I don't like reptiles of any kind—little ones, big ones, or slithery ones, especially."

He grabs his crutches from the nearby chair and eases his way over to the door. "Okay, Miss Bossy Pants. Let's go take our one and only walk." He holds the door open so I can go out before him.

We're not thirty feet from the back door when it hits me: this place is amazingly beautiful. "Oh, my good lord. This is *so* pretty." Moss hangs down in trailing bits from the huge, gnarled trees whose branches sweep out and dip down before rising to the sky. Everything is dark green, blue-green, or brown. The color palette God used here is so serene. I can't believe there are serpents hiding in it. It just doesn't seem right to have danger lurking in something this picturesque.

"This is my paradise. This is where I go when I need to think."

I stop and look at him. "I thought you said that you haven't come here for five years."

He leans on his crutches and looks out into the forest. "That's true."

"Sooo . . . that means you haven't been doing much thinking for a long time, I guess." I feel like he's revealing something very personal to me. I wait impatiently for him to respond.

He smiles just a little. "You might say that."

"I get it." I kick some sticks out of my way as I shuffle through the soft, rotting leaves. Thibault swings along behind me. "I haven't done much thinking for the past five years, either. I just got up every day, went to work, and did what I was told to do."

"I think a lot of people do that. Me included."

"Like a damn robot. Brainless."

"It's not brainless; it's survival. At least it was for you. From what you've told me. Sometimes you get locked into a routine, and then a change in the routine seems riskier than sticking it out."

"Yeah. I can relate to that. That's definitely me. But it's not you, right? You love your job and your life." I look at him for confirmation.

He's staring off into the trees again, lost in thought, or so it seems. Then he speaks. "About a year and a half or two years ago, my sister got it into her head that she needed to talk to the family of the man she killed."

I'm not sure where he's going with this, but I'm definitely intrigued. His sister is obviously crazy. "What for?"

"I'm not exactly sure. She tried to explain it to me. I just thought she was nuts at the time. She said there were too many loose ends. No closure. She wanted to apologize. I always thought that was just some silly psychobabble, especially since there was no way those people were ever going to forgive her, but it meant a lot to her."

I try to put myself in her shoes. If Pavel came at me with murder in his eyes, and I fought back, killing him, would I have the burning desire to explain myself to his family? Apologize? I think of Pavel's cousin Alexei, the sweet, simple-minded man who ate my horrible cooking and laughed about silly things with me, and the answer is simple: Yes. I would absolutely need to try. He's the only person in that family I could ever care about, and I would feel bad about turning his world upside down, taking away the person who provides for him financially.

"I understand what she means by that. I got a lot of loose ends I'd like to tie up, and I haven't even shot anyone. But if I did, I'd want to tell the family I'm sorry. Not everyone is evil through and through, you know? Even bastards who deserve a bullet for some of the things they do are kind to some people. Even gangbangers have moms and brothers and cousins who love them, who will miss them when they're gone, who need them in their lives to be happy or safe or whatever . . ."

"Are you going to tell me what those loose ends are?" He keeps walking. He sounds like he's challenging me, daring me to do it.

"I don't know. Maybe."

He walks past me, his crutches dragging up rotting organic matter hidden below the upper layer of decaying leaves.

I don't like seeing his back as he walks away from me like this. It feels like he's leaving me behind, and although I know it's all in my head and I also know we're both better off if he actually does do that, I want to stop him. I want him to wait for me and Tee. "I just . . . need some more time."

He pauses, looking down at the ground. "Tell me when you're ready. I'm not going anywhere for now."

"But you're going to go eventually." It's better if we're absolutely clear about this. The flirting we've done is silly and fun, but it's also dangerous. Living in a dream world can cause me to lose focus. "And so am I."

He nods, still not looking back at me. "It is true that a lot of times people go. People walk out, die, disappear." He looks up, locking eyes with me. "And there're lots of reasons why they do that—some of them good, some of them not so good. But sometimes there are people who stick, too. They stay, even when things get really difficult."

I shrug. "Not in my experience."

"I've had the same group of friends since I was in the single digits," he says, taking a couple swinging steps toward me. "And no matter how difficult things got for any one of us, we always remained friends, and we always stuck by each other."

"That's great . . . for you and your friends. I'm not sure how it applies to me, though."

"I'm just saying . . . I'm the kind of guy who sticks around." He stares at me, but I can't tell what's going on behind those eyes of his. It sounds like he's making me a promise of some sort, but there's no way he could be. I'm not asking for one from him, and besides . . . sticking around as a policy is not always the best idea.

"I hope you don't stick around all the time," I say. "Not when it's the wrong thing to do."

"Well, sure. I'm not going to lie to you and tell you that I haven't been close with a woman and then left. Sometimes you start to spend time with somebody and you think you're compatible, and then after some more time goes by, and you get to know them better, you realize you're not. In cases like that, I don't stick around, no. It's not like I just take off and disappear, but I'm also not the type of guy to lead a woman on and let her think there's something between us when there isn't."

I try to smile at him. "Spoken like a true player."

He looks annoyed. "If you say so."

Thibault walks over to a tree and rests his hand on the bark. I join him, feeling bad that I insulted him. When I get close, I see initials carved in the tree: *TCD.*

I trace the letters with my finger. "What's the C stand for?"

"Charles."

I sigh. Apologies aren't easy for me. "I was just messing with you earlier. I don't think you're a player."

"I don't think I am, either, but there might be some women out there who would disagree."

"How many?" I feel bad for those women. I'm starting to get an inkling of what they missed out on.

"There are a couple who come to mind who weren't happy with me when I broke things off. But it was better that way. We weren't good together for the long run."

"For some women, it's easy to get really attached, and then when the guy doesn't get attached too, it feels like he was playing her, even though he was just going along to see if it could work out, if she was the right one for him."

"Have you ever been played?" he asks.

I laugh bitterly, thinking of Sonia, the foolish girl who thought she was in love with Pavel . . . a man who could never *not* play a woman. "I don't know a woman over the age of twenty-five who hasn't been, at least once in her life."

Thibault is nothing like Pavel; I know that much. Even though I'm sure he has his secrets, I don't think for a second they involve purposely hurting women. I look up at him and wait for him to make eye contact. I want him to know that I believe he's a good person, so even when this situation plays out and he goes his way and I go mine, he'll feel good about what he did for me.

"I'll bet there're probably more than a few girls out there who thought they were going to marry you and have all your babies and live happily ever after."

He half-laughs. "Why would you say that?"

"Because . . ." I shrug. "You're a good man. You're the kind of guy that most girls are looking for."

It's so still and warm out. The wind has stopped moving the leaves, and the dust motes around us have all settled. It's just him, Tee, and me, all of us surrounded by the magic of the woods. I want to kiss him more than anything in the world, but I can't do that when my life is about leaving now.

"Come on, we gotta go back." He pushes off the tree and maneuvers around me, moving faster than he was before.

I hate that I opened my big mouth and tried to say something nice, tried to connect. He probably thinks I'm making a move, trying to add myself to that list of women he left because they weren't his type, so he took off to keep me from making a bigger fool of myself. *Ugh,* how embarrassing. As he puts even more distance between us, the idea of snakes coming after me suddenly appears in my mind. I swear I see things moving in the leaves nearby.

I trip trying to keep up with him, holding the baby tight so he won't fall. "Why the rush?" I ask, righting myself with the aid of a nearby tree.

"No rush. My leg is sore. I need to go take a painkiller."

"Yeah, okay." My heart hurts, but I'll get over it. I always do.

We get back to the front porch, and he stops at the door before opening it. "I'd really like you to tell me what you have for Holloway." He looks up at me, waiting for my reply.

"Yeah, I know you would." I adjust the baby's blanket, refusing to make eye contact. He couldn't be clearer with me right now: this isn't about a relationship or compatibility; it's about a man who has a need to help people, who happens to be helping me. "Maybe later."

"There's paper and pen on the counter over there." He points toward the kitchen. "If you don't feel comfortable talking about it, think about writing it down. I could go out later and find a cell signal and send it off in a text to my team. That way, at least, they could get a conversation started with Holloway and see what he'd be willing to do to help you, see what resources would be available to you based on what you can give them."

"Thanks," I say, passing by him and going into the cabin. I take the baby straight into the bedroom and disappear behind the closed door before I let the tears come.

The pressure is killing me. I need to make a decision about whether I can trust him with everything I have, or whether I just need to put my foot down and end this thing—this . . . whatever it is—and ask him to take me to Lafayette and say goodbye for good.

CHAPTER TWENTY-FIVE

I leave Thibault passed out on the couch and Baby Tee in the bedroom and go into the kitchen. After hunting around, I find enough ingredients to make my specialty: pasta Alexei.

I smile with the memory of making this dish for Alexei. He always grinned like a little kid when he was eating it. I miss his uncomplicated presence. I push away the feelings of guilt that rise up when I think about how I'm leaving him behind. If it weren't for Tee, I would have considered taking him with me, but with a newborn baby it would be too much. Pavel would never give up searching if I took his son and his cousin away. I still have to find Alexei, though, and make sure he's okay. I won't let him down entirely. I'll make sure he's safe before I give away the keys to the kingdom.

The sun is setting by the time Thibault wakes up. He sits up and looks around, a little disoriented if the confusion on his face is any clue. I turn away to get some juice out of the fridge and pour him a glass. I think mixing beers and painkillers is probably a bad idea.

"Mika?"

"In the kitchen. Putting together some dinner."

I look over to see him scrub his face and then his hair. "What time is it?" He looks at his watch. "Nine o'clock? Damn, I slept too long."

"That's okay. It gave me time to go through all your stuff."

"What?" He looks toward his duffel bag at the door.

He thinks I meant that I went through his personal things. I try not to be hurt by the mistrust. "You bought a lot of things at that store. I think we can stay here for two months and not run out of anything. Do you really think we needed eight bags of flour?"

"Well, we're pretty far from the nearest convenience store, so I figured I'd use the bread machine and make some fresh bread for us."

"I don't think I've ever had fresh bread before."

"Really?" He takes his crutches from the floor next to the couch and stands, slowly making his way toward the kitchen. "I'm a bread machine expert. I'll show you how it's done."

"I thought bread machines did all the work." I smile. "I must've misunderstood how they operate."

He walks up behind me and leans over the pot on the stove that's filled with red sauce. "Someone's got to put all the stuff in the machine, right?" He inhales deeply, closing his eyes. "Mmm, smells good." He backs away and sits down at the small table in the kitchen. "No wonder you were so sad about my sandwiches. You can cook."

"Just a few things. Spaghetti is easy."

"Mmm, my favorite."

"Well, it's not the same as your recipe. Hopefully you'll still like it."

"I'm sure I will." He stands. "Can I get you something to drink? Some juice or water maybe?"

"I poured you some juice there, but if you want to get me some water, that would be good. I'm really thirsty lately."

"That's the breastfeeding." He helps himself to a sip of the juice and gets me a glass of water. He pauses at the notepad where I've written down the information I decided to trust him with. There's no point in messing around anymore; he's either going to help me or not. And the longer we hang around together, the more I'm probably going to want to be near him in a way I shouldn't, so it's time. Shit or get off the pot, as my grandma used to say.

He doesn't say a word. He just sits back down at the table.

I work to keep it casual. "You know so much about breastfeeding because of your sister?"

"Yep. I am all up in her business." He sounds happy. I think he's glad I trusted him enough to write those things down—the list of general information I can provide to Holloway.

I laugh. "Not as much as you were up in my business, I hope."

"No." He shakes his head slowly, his eyes wide. "No, never have I been that far up in somebody's childbirth moment, and hopefully I never will be again."

"Don't you want to have kids of your own?"

He gets up and limps over to the stove, picking up a spoon to stir my sauce. "I definitely want to have kids. I'm just not going to be the one standing there playing catcher. I'm going to stay up at the top end instead of the bottom end."

"I get it. I don't blame you. It was probably really nasty down there."

He puts his hand on my shoulder. "No, it was a miracle." He shakes me gently before letting me go. "But I won't lie . . . it *was* scary as hell and not something I want to repeat."

I stop buttering the sandwich bread with a garlic spread I found in the fridge and turn to look at him. "I didn't think you were scared. You seemed pretty brave to me. You handled everything like a pro. You were completely cool."

"On the outside, I was cool. On the inside, I was a mess."

"And now? How are you doing now?"

"Right now . . . I feel . . . satisfied." He nods, like he just figured it out and is confirming its truth.

I tilt my head, not sure I understand. "Satisfied?"

"Yeah. I had a walk, I had a nap, I've got painkillers coursing through my veins, and no one's trying to shoot me."

"And that's a regular thing for you?" I lift a brow in disbelief. I think he's either making a joke or trying to sound manly. "Someone taking a shot at you?"

He shrugs. "Not a regular thing, but it's happened a time or two." He lifts his T-shirt and shows me his left side, just below his ribs. "Almost got me once."

I drop the knife on the cutting board and bend down to take a look, squinting at the scar there that definitely looks like it came from a real bullet wound. Pavel and his friends have a few that they like to show off, so they're not unfamiliar to me. "Are you serious?"

"Yep. A bullet got a little too close, but God was watching out for me that night and sent it wide."

"That's the real deal." The skin is puckered and raised a bit. "I wasn't sure I believed you about all your Bourbon Street Boys work with the cops. Up until now, I guess."

"All it takes is a scar to get you to believe me?" He turns and lifts his T-shirt over his back. "Check this one out."

I run my finger along this scar, a few inches above his waist and about three inches long. His skin is warm. My hand lingers. He glances at me, his expression unreadable but suddenly intense.

"That looks like you got stabbed," I say, pulling my hand back, hoping to distract him from the fact that I was just basically stroking his skin.

"I did."

"Who did it? A gangster?"

"Kind of. It was my sister."

"Get out." I stand up and push on his arm. "Stop messing with me. I know she's mean, but she can't be *that* mean."

He holds up his hand like a Boy Scout. "I'm dead serious. Swear to God. My sister is mean as *hell* sometimes."

"Oh, I know your sister's mean." I pick up the knife and finish my buttering job. "She doesn't pull any punches."

"What did she say to you?" He leans against the counter and takes another sip of his juice as he stares at me.

"Oh, you know. She warned me not to mess around. Not to take advantage of you, basically."

He laughs. "As if you could."

I look at him. "What's that supposed to mean?"

"First of all, you're not the type."

"How could you possibly know that about me? I could be taking advantage of you right now."

"You can't take advantage of a person who's offering to help. And my sister knows that I don't offer my help to just anybody who walks across my path."

"Yeah, I know. Just damsels in distress."

He stops me from going back over to my pot of sauce with a hand on my arm. "No, not even them sometimes."

"Oh, right," I say, pulling myself easily from his grasp and picking up the wooden spoon. "Like you'd walk away from a woman in need. I don't think so."

He moves toward me, close enough that I feel his breath on my neck as I stir the pot. "I let things go plenty, believe me."

I stop stirring to look at him. His face is very close. "Oh, yeah? Tell me one time."

"My sister." He shrugs and steps back. "I let her fight her own battles. After the Charlie thing, I had to."

"Why? You told me you regretted not helping her. You said you should have."

"Yes. If I could do it all again, I would have intervened at the beginning to keep it from getting as bad as it eventually did. But after it all went down, she was in a really bad place. She needed to believe in herself again. Whenever I helped her too much, it made that impossible.

190

She took it to mean I didn't think she could, and it made her doubt herself."

"So . . . helping her hurt her?"

He shrugs, his expression going dark. "I guess I never thought about it like that, but yeah . . . Sometimes you have to *not* help to be a help."

I tap the spoon on the side of the pot to knock the extra sauce off. "So what about me? Are you going to stop trying to help me too?"

He shrugs. "I'm going to do whatever you want me to do. I'm done trying to boss you around."

I smile. "Did you give up on me already?"

"No, not at all." He moves in closer, resting his hand lightly on my shoulder. "I know I don't know you really well, but I have learned a thing or two about you."

"Oh, yeah? What's that?"

"You're a survivor and you're smart. So, knowing that, I'm going to keep making you aware that I'm here and that help is available, and you're going to do the right thing by you and Tee and take me up on whatever offer makes sense for you, for whatever help you need. Or none at all. You'll reject whatever you don't want or need, and I'll just have to live with that."

"That sounds very mature and self-aware, Thibault."

He laughs, letting me go and backing off. "Yeah, well, I've had a Vicodin cocktail; talk to me in the morning when I'm completely off my meds."

I laugh. I love that he can be so honest about himself. "The noodles are almost ready. You feel like setting the table?"

"No problem." He does the job and then sits in one of the four chairs.

I dish out two bowls of pasta, mine much smaller than his, and set them down on the table. "I don't have any sprinkle-cheese to put on top." I take a seat and sip my water.

"Not a problem." He digs in immediately, scooping up and swirling a big pile of noodles onto his fork before shoving them into his mouth. He chews fast at first, but then slows. He pauses and looks confused.

"Do you like it?" I ask, watching him closely.

He chews a little more. "Mmm."

I narrow my eyes at him. "Does that mean you like it, or there's something interesting going on in there?"

He chews a few more times and swallows both the food and then the rest of his juice. "What did you make that sauce out of?"

I stab my spaghetti noodles and swirl them around haphazardly. "Ketchup."

He slowly prepares another bite on his fork as he nods. "Interesting choice." He puts his fork down and limps over to the fridge, pulling out a beer.

"That's how a friend of mine likes it. With the ketchup."

"A friend, huh?"

I shrug, feeling silly now. I should have known pasta done Alexei-style wouldn't go over very well. "I guess I never bothered to make it different, since it was his favorite thing."

He takes several more bites in quick succession, gesturing with his fork at his almost empty plate. "I like it. This is perfect." He grins. "What's for dessert?" he asks enthusiastically. "If this was dinner, I can't wait to see what's next."

I try not to smile at his obvious lie. "Popsicles."

"Mmm, popsicles. My favorite. Perfect."

We look up at each other at the same time and share a grin.

"I'm having fun," I say, wanting him to know he hasn't hurt my feelings by not liking the food I put together.

"Me, too."

"Even though you make me crazy sometimes," I add.

He lifts his beer, tilting the bottle toward me. "Right back at ya, babe."

CHAPTER TWENTY-SIX

Thibault leaves after dinner to go find a cell signal, taking with him the note I left on the counter with the information for Holloway on it. I'm sitting at the kitchen table with a deck of cards when he gets back, trying to ignore my nervous stomach. The baby is asleep in the cabin's only bedroom in the bassinet. *Will Thibault expect to sleep in there with us, or will he take the couch? Could I share a bed with Thibault and calm down enough to sleep? Doubtful.*

"Are you ready to play some crazy eights?" I ask as he swings himself into the kitchen on his crutches.

"Yep. I hope you're prepared."

"I am. I've been warming up."

He smiles, sitting down across from me. "How does a girl prepare for a game of crazy eights, exactly?"

I shuffle the cards. "I'm not going to share *all* my secrets with you."

"Well, I hope you're going to share *some* of them." He keeps staring at me until I look up. "What do you think?"

"I think I can do that. I believe I already have, actually."

He nods. "That you have." He takes the first cards I deal him and arranges them in his hand. "So who is it you were living with? Can you tell me that?"

"One person permanently, another from time to time." I give us both more cards.

"Do these people have names?"

"Yes, they have names." I know this is serious, me talking about the details of my carefully guarded life, but he's being so ridiculous . . . trying to pretend he's not being nosy when that's exactly what he is.

"Do I get to know what their names are?"

"Will it make a difference?" I put the deck of remaining cards down on the table and flip the top one over next to it.

"To what?" he asks.

"To whatever it is your team is doing with the information I already gave you."

He shrugs, putting a card down on the discard pile. "Maybe. I won't know until I hear more."

I sigh in defeat. What he's saying makes sense, and I don't see the harm in telling him something minor like who I was living with. "I was living sometimes with Alexei, and all the time with a girl named Sonia." I play my best card and wait for him to take his turn.

"Is Alexei missing or something? Did I hear that guy Sebastian say that?" He puts a card down.

My smile disappears as I glance up at him. He's not looking at me; all his focus is on his cards. "You don't beat around the bush, do you?"

He shakes his head. "I don't see the point in doing that." He moves the cards to different positions in his hand. "We're either going to get to the bottom of this, or you're going to keep holding out on me, and eventually I'm just going to have to decide whether I can continue to function in the dark or if I'll have to step back."

I put a card down, not really paying attention to strategy anymore. "I don't know why you think that me possibly having a few secrets means you're functioning in the dark."

"You never know what one piece of information can mean to the entire picture." He drops his discard on the table. "I'd rather know it all and put the pieces together myself than have you decide what I need to know and what I don't need to know."

I bite my lip as I look at the cards I'm not really seeing. The suits swim before my eyes. He's pushing again, but I told myself I was going to try to trust him. "It just feels like . . . an invasion."

He looks at me over his cards. "Of your privacy?"

"Maybe. Or just my safety." I rearrange my hand, my eyebrows drawing together as I try to figure out what to do. This was supposed to be about a hand of crazy eights, not delving into the details of my life.

"You think telling me these things is somehow going to put you at risk?"

I nod, looking up at him. "I think it could. I think it could also put *you* at risk."

"I'm a big boy. Why don't you let me decide how much risk I'm willing to take?"

"That's the thing . . . You might not know how *much* you're taking by knowing certain things."

He sighs and shakes his head at me. "Did you or did you *not* see my war wounds?"

I can't help but smile. "Yes, I saw your war wounds. They're very impressive."

He loses his smile. "Seriously, though . . . I do this kind of thing for a living. I've been training for years. I've even done things with the police department, gone to their training programs and their conventions, worked in the field with highly qualified personnel in both the police department and the military. I can handle it."

"But if something happened to you or somebody in your family, I would never forgive myself."

"I understand. But I wouldn't do anything that would put those people at risk." His voice softens. "Just talk to me. Pretend I'm a priest and you're in the confessional."

"I don't go to church, but if I did, it wouldn't be to the kind that had a confessional."

"Okay, then pretend I'm a counselor. Like a therapist."

"Do you think I need therapy?"

"Who doesn't?" He puts down a card.

The room goes silent as we work our way through the deck. The cuckoo clock in the other room squawks, alerting us to the top of the tenth hour.

Cuckoo! Cuckoo! My life is crazy. I'm sitting in a cabin in the middle of nowhere, playing cards with Superman. My mouth opens and words tumble out. "Alexei is gone. I don't know where he is." The confession pops out of me like a cork from a Champagne bottle. Crazily enough, I feel a huge release of tension I didn't realize I was carrying.

"Do you think Pavel did something to him?" His calm acceptance makes it easy for me to keep talking.

"I'm pretty sure he did or he knows where he is. He didn't seem upset when Alexei stopped coming around. That tells me he had something to do with it."

"Do you think he . . . killed him?" His tone is compassionate. Concerned.

I'm battling tears now. I hadn't let myself think that far. I wanted to believe that because Alexei was family, it wouldn't happen. "I don't know. It's hard to say with Pavel. He might've just sent him somewhere and told him to stop contacting me."

"Is Alexei your boyfriend?"

I shake my head, almost laughing at the idea. "No, he's definitely *not* my boyfriend. I took care of him. Cooked him some meals. Kept him company. Let him stay over when he seemed like he needed to. He always slept on the couch."

"Oh. So he's a kid?"

"Only in his head. He's twenty-five years old, but he has the mentality of a child."

"And he's the one who likes ketchup-based spaghetti sauce, I'm guessing." He smiles warmly.

I scowl at him. "Excuse me, but *everybody* likes ketchup spaghetti sauce." I calm myself, realizing it's not him I'm angry with. "But yes, he's the one I started making it for."

"I knew it. Well . . . kind of; I thought for sure you had a three-year-old hanging around."

I try to smile but keep my eyes on my cards to help control the tears that are still threatening. "Yeah, he's really young at heart. He smiles a lot. He's fun to be around. A lot less serious than Pavel or anyone else in the family."

"And what about your roommate?"

"Sonia? She was Pavel's girlfriend, on and off. We're not friends." *Bitch sold me out.* I'm not one for revenge, but if I were, I'd get some on her. She almost ruined everything, and all I asked her to do was pick me up and bring me some clothes.

"Why aren't you friends? How did you become roommates?"

"Because she's Russian, and it's hard to be friends with any of them. And she was always worried that I was having an affair with her boyfriend, so there was a lot of jealousy there. Pavel is the one who set us up to live together."

"Did you? Have an affair with him, I mean?"

The thought nauseates me. "No, never. Pavel's dangerous. I work for him, but I would never let him get that deep into my life."

"But I thought . . ." He looks toward the bedroom.

"That he's Tee's father? He is." I sigh. I really don't want to get into this, but I'm already halfway there. "Pavel is not a nice person, obviously. And he likes to drink. One night he came over very drunk looking for Sonia. When she wasn't there, he refused to leave. Then he started drinking more and told me to drink with him. I tried to say no, but he was very insistent. I figured if I nursed a drink long enough, he'd pass out and I could go to my room and let him sleep it off." I shrug. The rest of the story is not pretty enough to share. I numb myself to it so it won't push me off the deep end.

"But he didn't pass out because he probably has a really high tolerance to the alcohol."

"Either that or he wasn't as wasted as I thought he was to begin with." I huff out a breath to keep the tears away. "End of story." I've blocked all the details from my brain, and now that Tee is here there's no point in dredging them up. I choose to believe that the night with Pavel happened for a reason, and that reason is my son. Tee is a silver lining I never saw coming, but I'll take him happily.

"So you never dated or were in a relationship?"

"No. But he was pushing harder in the last few months to change that. It's part of the reason I decided to help the police out. I don't want him in my bed. I had this premonition that it would be the beginning of the end for me. He likes how I keep his books, but that wouldn't keep him from killing me if I made him angry enough." I try to laugh, but it sounds like someone's strangling a bird. "He's the one person in the world I've been able to learn to hold my tongue in front of. Mostly. He's like a walking nightmare; you never know what mood he's going to be in, and it changes so fast, like lightning-quick. You can't trust him from one second to the next."

Thibault nods, his expression dark. "I don't think guys like him are ever respectful of women, even when they're sleeping with them."

"He's definitely not respectful. I've heard stories that would turn your hair white. Like I said, it's why I'm helping put him in prison. Or I was, anyway." I look toward the bedroom. "I don't know what I'm going to do now that I have a baby to take care of." I refuse to think about the fact that it's Pavel's baby. I don't want to imagine what that could mean legally. *Later.* I'll worry about that later, after we're safe.

"Mika . . ." Thibault extends his hand toward me.

I jump to my feet, angry with myself. I've said way too much, and now he thinks I'm begging for his help with my poor-me comments.

I busy myself with getting out a glass and the juice.

"How did you get in touch with the police?" Thibault asks. "Did you just call them up and say, 'Hey, I've got information for you,' or did they find you?"

I sigh. "No, it was me. Pavel got arrested, so I went in to bail him out, and when I was there a detective went up to him and basically told him he was going to bring him down one day. I happened to see his nameplate on his desk, and I never forgot it. So when Pavel was pushing me hard one day, telling me I wasn't allowed to sleep with anyone other than him, talking about how we were going to be together soon, I decided to call the guy."

"What's going to happen, do you think, now that you've been missing for a few days?"

"Well, Pavel knows that I had a baby, and he told the nurse it's his. He probably assumes I'm hiding with a friend or something. He'll keep looking for me. It's not his style to give up." I sit down at the table with my glass of juice. "I don't know what Holloway thinks. I haven't talked to him in a while, so he only knows what your people have told him."

"How did Pavel know you had Tee? Did he see it on the news?"

"No, I called Sonia. I was freaking out, and I was worried that Alexei was going to come back and I wasn't going to be there for him. I don't know, I think I had a moment of insanity. I shouldn't have called her. I shouldn't have said anything to anyone. Like you said . . . I should have just disappeared and started over somewhere."

He shrugs, his eyes filled with what looks like understanding. "You were going through a life-changing event with no one to talk to. Of course you reached out to someone you knew. Don't be so hard on yourself."

"Maybe." I take a sip of my juice. "I'm usually pretty independent, but sitting there in that room with a baby I didn't even know existed two hours before was really freaking me out. Most people have nine months to prepare. I had none."

"And then I showed up in your room." He gives me one of his most charming grins. "The weirdo stalking you, who you probably thought was going to sue your pants off for running him over."

I have to smile at that. "I never considered you a stalker. You were pretty persistent, but I could tell you were just trying to look out for me. I understood that. And besides . . . I didn't run you over. *You* hit *my* car."

"Nothing's changed, you know. I'm still trying to look out for you."

I pick up my cards and then take the top one off the deck, putting it in with my hand. "Yes, something has. You're not acting the same as you were before, but I understand why." I discard and look up at him. If he can ask intense questions, so can I. He was warmer toward me before. He almost kissed me. But now he's being polite and distant. The minute I started sharing my stuff, he closed up. I should be glad, but instead I'm offended.

He puts his cards down and folds his arms on the table, looking right at me. "I like you, Mika. I admire the hell out of you. I've told you that I'm going to help you no matter what. None of that has changed." He pauses, looking down for a second before lifting his head again. "But I realized when I kissed you in the park that I feel other things for you, too. And I'd be cool with that, except for the fact that you're not really being up front with me about everything, and like you said . . . I have family and friends to protect. I don't mind putting myself at risk, but I can't put them at risk in the bargain.

Especially because they have kids, and those kids depend on them, like Tee is depending on you."

It's hard to tell which is the stronger emotion I'm feeling right now: sadness or frustration. I asked for this, probably, with my challenging question, but still . . . what right does he have to expect me to just open up like a damn book for him to read?

"You want me to tell you *everything* about my life? All the people I spend time with? Everything I say? Everything I do, every day, all day long . . . all my secrets?"

"I do. But I know it's hard for you to be open like that, especially with someone you don't know very well."

"I don't have any plan to hurt you or take advantage of you, if that's what you think."

"You can tell me that all day long, but until I know your story, I have no reason to completely trust it or believe it. Maybe I'm too jaded, being in the security business, but I also have instincts, and those instincts are telling me to be careful. I'm sorry to be so blunt, but I think you deserve the honesty." He sits back in his chair, sliding his cards off the edge so he can look at them again.

This is the first time I've seen him be so cold. I go back to staring at my cards to keep myself from crying. He's judging me too harshly for me to bear. "Yeah. Okay. So you feel this way because I'm a criminal. Because you think I'm like Pavel. I get it."

He reaches out and puts his hand on my wrist, holding on to it. I should detach myself from him, but his touch is like a magnet, and I'm not strong enough to resist the pull.

"No, Mika, don't say that. I actually *don't* see you as a criminal or like Pavel. I see you as somebody who's a survivor. And there's one thing I know about survivors, because the woman I love most in the world—my sister—is one: they'll do anything they have to so they'll be around to take their next breath. If something's in their way, something that's threatening them, they'll take it down. And if a lie works better than the truth, so be it—you live to see another day. It's survival. I get it. I don't like it, but I respect it."

I blow out a long breath, slowly pulling my hand from his touch, but not in an angry way. I'm still hurt to be branded a liar, but I appreciate his honesty. "I guess it's fair to say that about me being a person who will do what's necessary to survive. Not that I'm lying to you, because I'm not, but I do know I'll go pretty far to protect myself."

The room goes silent. We've reached an impasse, maybe.

"Come on, Mika . . . ," he cajoles. "What's the deal? Are you going to level with me and tell me what I need to know, what I *want* to know, or are you going to keep hiding things from me to protect yourself?"

I take a big breath in and let it out slowly, trying to make the tension that's built up leave my body. "I don't know. I guess I need to think about it a little bit longer."

He throws down a card, the ace of hearts. He smiles sadly. "My grandfather used to call me Ace."

I'm sad too. "Ace of hearts. How appropriate." Since he's doing a good job of bruising mine.

"What's that mean?" he asks.

The air is charged with tension, with unspoken desires on my part. I asked him for a kiss once. I'll never do that again, even though when I see his hands holding those cards, I wonder what it would be like to feel them on my body.

"Nothing. I just need some time."

He nods. "Fair enough. I have Dev working on the situation, and he's probably going to get back to me tomorrow or the next day. Until then, we can enjoy our spaghetti and card games and see where that takes us."

I feel bad that I let him down, but I have to put Tee and me before his feelings. Like he said . . . I'm a survivor. "Maybe you could teach me to play something other than crazy eights. I'm ready to take a bigger risk on that."

"Is that so?" He holds out his hand. "Okay, then. Let's do it."

I give him my cards and he shuffles the deck, taking a moment to move his chair closer to the table. "I could teach you how to play poker. Then we'll see how good you are at bluffing."

"Sounds good." I pause, smiling devilishly at him. "Not that I want to be good at fooling you or anything."

He shakes his head at me. "You think you've got me on the run, don't you?"

My heart skips a beat at his flirtatious tone. "I don't know. Do I?"

"Maybe," he says, shuffling the cards again. "Maybe you do."

CHAPTER TWENTY-SEVEN

One thing Thibault failed to get at the warehouse store was feminine products. He's kind enough to drive me first thing in the morning to the convenience store and wait in the car with the baby strapped into his seat as I shop for what I need. I have just enough money left in my wallet. I'm pretty sure I'm their first customer of the day.

As I climb back into the SUV with my bag in hand, Thibault's phone rings. He picks it up.

"Thibault." He glances at me in the rearview mirror, giving me a thumbs-up and a questioning look.

I nod. "All good."

Thibault goes back to his phone call. "Yeah, no, it's fine. Perfect timing, actually. You got lucky, because I usually don't have a signal. I thought you were going to email me."

He laughs. "Yeah, yeah, keep bragging about your big hands, man. You're wasting your time, though; I don't play for that team. Just buy a bigger keyboard, why don't you."

A man's voice comes dimly through the phone's earpiece. When it stops, Thibault responds. "You did? Great. What did he say?"

I try really hard to listen in, but the voice is muffled by Thibault's ear.

He lifts the phone away from his face when he catches me staring at him. Then he puts the mouthpiece near his lips. "Hold on a second. I'm going to put you on speaker."

"Are you sure you want to do that?" a male voice says, coming out into the car.

"Yeah. You're on speakerphone. You were about to tell me what you found out."

"Uhhh, okay. Hi, Mika. Are you there?"

"Yes, I am."

"Okay. Cool. Hi. Sooo, what was I saying? Oh, yeah. You wanted to know what I found out after talking to Holloway." He pauses. "A lot, actually. I'm not sure the guy knows the definition of the word *confidential*, but anyway, he was happy to fill me in on the details, which was mighty convenient."

Thibault looks at me apologetically. I shake my head. Turns out I'm working with one of the Keystone Cops. *Great.* Just my luck.

"There was no pushback whatsoever."

"Lay it on us," Thibault says. "You're making me worry."

"Okay, so this guy . . . Pavel Baranovsky? He's a really bad dude."

"Yeah, I got that impression already."

I nod. He'll get no argument from me there.

"No, I mean like notoriously bad. Like, he's kingpin-murdering Russian-mafia asshole bad."

I smile bitterly. *Yep, sounds about right.* Leave it to me to find the very worst Russian of the bunch and then get a job with him. *God, I was so young and naïve.*

"Yep. Got it. Mika was pretty clear about that."

"He's moving drugs, guns, women . . . the works."

"Guns? I didn't hear about that from her."

I shake my head at Thibault when he looks up at me. I have no idea what Dev is talking about.

"Yeah. Guns. If there's something illegal going on in Louisiana, he's got his hand in it."

"Why haven't we heard about him before?" Thibault asks.

"Because he's FBI material. The local PD usually hands those cases off to them and just gets out of their way. Our contract's for work on local stuff only. You know that. He's first-generation Russian mafia, not one of our homegrown gangbangers."

"So why is the district talking to her and not the FBI?"

"From what I could gather, it's some political game-playing. Not that Holloway came out and said that, but he made some comments. I think they're tired of being shoved in a back drawer by the FBI, so they're looking to get some cred for themselves before they hand the evidence over."

"Bastards," I say. *How dare they involve me in their ego-driven politics!*

Thibault nods, agreeing with me.

"Hey, you know how it works over there; they play jurisdictional games all the time. This is nothing new."

Thibault looks right at me when he asks his next question. "What's Mika's reputation over there at the district?"

"Well . . . ah . . . She hasn't given them a whole lot yet. They were trying to get her to give them his movements, but she was playing hard to get. At least that's what he said. He said she was always acting cagey." He pauses. "Sorry, Mika. I'm just repeating what I heard."

"Don't worry about it." I thought I had a friend at the NOPD, but I guess I was wrong about that. I look at Thibault, realizing I need his help now more than ever, or I will seriously be all alone. Me and Tee against the world . . . a world that happens to be owned by Pavel.

"Do they have a theory on why she was doing that?" Thibault asks. He reaches out and taps my knee once. I take it to mean he's being supportive. It eases the pain in my heart just a little.

"They thought maybe she was getting cold feet."

"Did you tell him she was pregnant?"

"No. Was I supposed to?"

"No."

"Cool. Anyway, they heard through the grapevine that she disappeared, and they also talked to Toni before, who told them she knows where Mika is, so they're wondering what's going on and what we know about it."

"None of them realized she was the one on the news with the baby? Did you tell them anything?"

"No, they didn't. I told Holloway that we heard from her, but that was it. He was glad she's still alive. He pushed to get more info from me, but I told him I didn't have any."

"Good. Perfect. So you confirmed that she's definitely a CI and she's on their payroll?"

"Yep. It's all legit. But she's not on the payroll. She's working voluntarily and isn't taking any money from anybody for it."

"Did they tell you what it was she was going to provide to them specifically, besides his movements?"

"Well, they know that she does his finances, so they're hoping she can give them some hard evidence, but they don't have a specific idea about what exactly that will be."

"Did you tell them the stuff on the list I gave you?"

"No. I thought I'd tell you this first and then let you decide our next move."

"Okay, good. Could you hold on a sec?"

"Yeah, no problem."

Thibault looks at me, covering the phone with his hand. "Can we give Holloway that list?"

Panic hits me like a punch to the chest. "I'm not sure what I should do."

Thibault fixes me with a stare. He looks like he's trying to see into my head. "You said you don't have a computer or any other electronics.

How are you going to access all the information on Pavel if you're leaving?"

Can I trust you, Thibault, or are you going to screw me over too? I look down at my son sleeping peacefully in his seat and then back up at the man who's offered me sanctuary. I learned watching him play poker last night that every time he tried to bluff me, he moved his jaw left and right. Right now, it's completely still.

"I put all of the data on a cloud account. It can be accessed from anywhere as long as you have the account number and password."

Thibault nods, chewing his lip as he thinks that through. Then he puts the phone back up between us. "Dev?"

"Yep, I'm here."

"Do me a favor and don't share that stuff outside the team yet. I'll get back to you."

"Okay. I have one more thing to say, though."

"Sure, go ahead." Thibault's expression tells me he's as curious as I am.

"I know we deal with criminals all the time, but they're small-time in comparison to Pavel. This guy is operating in other states, too."

"Mika, did you know this?" Thibault asks.

"I know he does deals with people overseas, but as far as I know his business is concentrated in Louisiana."

"He might keep that stuff separate from what Mika's working on. But the fact is, she knows a lot about his enterprise, and it's a big one, so he's gonna want to find her. And he's got a lot of dough; I'm talking millions."

His words send a shiver through me. I already know this, but to be reminded of it is enough to make me want to run to the farthest reaches of the globe.

"How do you know that? Did Jenny find stuff on him already?"

"No, she's not on it yet. She had a problem with Sammy yesterday that kept her up last night, but she's going to work on it all day today. I heard this from Detective Holloway."

"Oh." Thibault reaches out and takes my hand. I let him because I need the human connection. It's very uncomfortable for me to listen in on two men discussing my life like this. I feel untethered, no longer linked to the world. Thibault's touch brings me back down to earth.

"Also, this guy Pavel doesn't live large like you'd expect him to, so they suspect he's got a *lot* of money hidden away. If he wants to find Mika, he's got the resources for it. And if he's hiding his money somewhere, she probably knows where, and he's not going to want her telling anyone about it. You need to be *real* careful."

My ears are burning. Dev is clearly doing his job, but he basically just told my knight in shining armor that he's holding a ticking time bomb. Me being the bomb, of course.

"Remind Toni and Lucky to be sharp," Thibault says. "I destroyed her phone but not soon enough, probably. He could have started a trace that'll get him close to my neighborhood."

"Will do. But I think they're already on it. Jenny said something about them having their house tented for termites or something? I think they're moving in with May and Ozzie until the fumigation is done, anyway."

"Cool. Thanks, man. I gotta go." Thibault hangs up and lets go of my hand. He doesn't turn around, though. He keeps looking at me.

"Pretty ugly, huh?" I ask. "Welcome to my life." I reach over and pull Tee's blanket up higher.

"I'm not going anywhere," he says.

"Not yet, you're not," I say.

He turns around and starts the truck. We leave the parking lot and drive all the way back to the cabin without exchanging another word.

CHAPTER TWENTY-EIGHT

When we get back to the cabin, Tee needs to be fed, changed, and bathed, and so do I. It takes up most of my morning and thoughts, but when I'm finally done and the two of us smell and look clean again, I settle down on the couch with a book. Problem is, I can't concentrate on the words.

"What's that you've got there?" Thibault asks, dropping down into the chair across from me.

I flip it over. "*Me Before You.*"

"No, don't read that one," he says, frowning.

"Why? I heard it's good."

"Yeah, but do you have enough tissues? Because it's going to make you cry your eyes out."

I laugh. "Did you read it?"

"Hell, no. Do I look like a man who would read romances?"

The banter is silly, but it lightens the mood. "I don't know. You seem pretty sensitive."

"Well, I'm not *that* sensitive." He pauses. "May read it. She was a mess. It was when she and Ozzie were living at the warehouse, before they bought their house together, so she finished it before we came in for work. She'd stayed up all night, and damn, she looked like hell.

Her eyes, even her nose, were swollen. I thought she got in a fight with Ozzie or something."

I put the book on the table. "Okay, that's all I need to know. My life is already sad enough; I don't need to read about someone else's misery."

"It's not all bad," he says.

I pick Tee up from the couch next to me where he's sleeping. Staring down into his face, I have to agree. "I do have this little guy going for me, at least."

"He's getting big already," Thibault says.

"Well, he should with how much he eats." I reach down and squeeze his tiny thigh through his blanket. It is bigger. It makes me proud. At least I'm doing something right.

"How about we play some more poker? I'll teach you some different variations."

"Nah, cards are boring."

"How about if I up the ante . . . We can play for money."

I laugh. "What money? I just spent my last dime on sanitary pads."

He stands and gestures at me. "Come on. I'll show you." He takes the baby's car seat and sets it down near the kitchen table. I follow him and place the baby inside. Tee doesn't even twitch an eyelid, he's so sound asleep.

Thibault deals the cards. "Okay, so here's our money." He reaches around to the shelf behind him and grabs a bag of Cheetos, opening them and spilling them out. He divides them between us. "Big ones are worth ten, little ones five."

I'm trying really hard not to laugh. He's acting so serious, but now he's got Cheetos dust on his nose. I'm not saying a word.

He deals the cards. "We're going to play seven-card draw. Aces wild. Small Cheeto ante."

I play along, all the while trying to decide if I should go all in with Thibault, share the username and password to the cloud account so his team can get the information they need and give it to the police. I could finally leave and start my new life out in the world while Pavel starts his in prison, assuming no one screwed me over along the way.

"That's the fifth time you've grinned at me like that in the last two minutes," he says during our sixth hand. "Stop trying to psych me out."

I'm tired of playing and anxious to move on. With everything. I've overheard his phone conversations, one of which he let me listen in on, and I've yet to hear him try to double-cross me. In fact, he's withholding information the cops want, people he works with, in an effort to help me out. If I'm going to trust anyone right now, it has to be him.

I move my cards up to hide my mouth. "Don't try to make excuses so you can get out of the game. I'm about to take *all* your money."

He looks down at the table. There are thousands of Cheeto bucks at stake. "Please . . . ," he scoffs. "I'm gonna be snacking *all* day on my winnings. How many cards do you want?" He gestures at me with his chin, trying to look like a badass Vegas dealer.

"Give me two," I say. "Two good ones. Don't be givin' me any more of that junk, either." I slide two cards over, and he gives me two in return.

"I'm not going to take any," he says, his jaw moving back and forth. "I'm satisfied with what I have in my hand here. Your bet."

I smirk. It's almost too easy. "I bet you *thirty* Cheeto bucks I'm going to win." I slide three large Cheetos over to the pot, grinning like the Cheshire Cat.

"How about this . . . I'm all in." He pushes the rest of his Cheetos into the center of the table to join the others.

"Fine. I can handle it." I slide my few remaining snacks into the center of the table too. "I call. I'm good for the rest." I gesture at the uneven pot balance.

"What do you have?" he asks.

"Let's put them down at the same time." I smile really big. My triumph is near and I've decided: I'm going to tell him everything.

"Fine. Show me what you got."

We both put our cards down.

"Full house," I say, shimmying my shoulders and snapping my fingers. Then I point at his crap cards on the table in front of him. "And all you have is a pair of twos. Poor Thibault, you lost to a girl." I give him a giant fake pout for a few seconds before going back to my shimmy dance.

He folds his arms. "Damn, girl. You've been holding out on me."

I reach out and put my arms around the pile of Cheetos so I can drag them over to my side of the table. I take one off the top and crunch down on it. "I'm a pretty lucky person most of the time, actually."

"Oh really? Do tell. I can't wait to hear the evidence you're going to try to use to back this claim up."

I sit back and fold my arms over my chest to mimic his posture. "I ran you over, didn't I? Wrong turn, right direction."

He laughs so hard it makes the veins stick out in his neck. "Damn," he finally says when he can speak again. "If that's good luck, I'd hate to see your bad luck."

I know he meant it as a joke, but he's right. My bad luck is pretty bad. "No, you don't want to see that." I stand and stretch, my shirt coming up to expose my skin. I catch him looking. I stand straight and pull my shirt down. "Stop staring at my fat belly."

"Your belly is not fat. And I wasn't staring."

I look down at myself. "I used to have a totally cute stomach. I guess that's over now." It seems silly to worry about my body at this point, but I'm sitting across from a gorgeous man who at any other moment in my life I'd be drooling over and wishing I could date. I have more than a few regrets about the way things rolled out.

"You'll go back to the way you were before. But I think you look just fine now. Better than fine."

I gather the cards together. "Stop flirting with me. You're not supposed to do that. I'm pretty sure it's against the rules."

"Whose rules?"

"Your rules."

"Screw the rules."

I pause, looking at him to see how drunk he got with those beers he drank during lunch. "Are you sure you're allowed to say that, Superman?"

He grabs me without preamble, pulling me over toward his good leg. I lose my balance and fall onto his knee as the cards go flying everywhere. "Eeek! What're you doing?"

He grins lazily at me. "Just messing around."

I feel awkward and unsettled. Happy and sad. "You have Cheeto dust on your face. Hold still." I wipe his nose and chin. He sits very still for my ministrations. When he's all cleaned off, I sigh, looking at him, so frustrated that we're in the situation we're in. "Has anyone ever told you what a pretty face you have?"

"Nope. I don't think anyone has ever described me as pretty. Toni's called me pretty ugly, maybe."

I pretend to look closer. "No, you aren't ugly. Not really."

He smiles. "Thanks. I think." He smacks me on the side of my butt.

"What was that for?" I ask, pretending to be mad.

"For bluffing me. You stole all my Cheetos." He pauses, staring at me just long enough for me to wish we could start kissing.

"I won them fair and square." I get up off his leg to find a bowl in the cupboard, effectively putting an end to the flirtation between us. I'm both relieved and bummed. There's no point in encouraging something that can go exactly nowhere, regardless of how fun it is. I need to get real and move toward the plan that will get me started on my new life, not keep wishing for one that can never be.

As I brush all the food and orange dust off the table and into the bowl, I talk. "Listen, I've thought about what Dev said and what you said . . . and some of what Toni said to me before . . . and I've decided to give you some information."

He looks hopeful, so I have to cut him off before his brain goes too far.

"Not all the information, okay? Just some of it."

He loses his smile. "I don't understand."

I put the bowl on the counter and sit down across from Thibault. "I will give you the account number and login information. You'll be able to access all the books I kept. But there's one more thing you'll need for it to all make sense, and that's the piece I'm keeping to myself for now."

"For it to make sense? Like a code?"

"Yes. For my protection."

He taps the table with his fingertip. "And what do you hope to accomplish by doing that?"

I raise an eyebrow at him.

He holds up his hand. "I'm not pushing. I'm just trying to understand your motivations, that's all. I promise." He looks so sincere.

"I don't trust Holloway. He's playing games, and he doesn't seem to appreciate that my life is in the balance. And Tee's life is too. He sounds like a bumbling fool, and I wish I'd contacted someone else, but that's neither here nor there. I have to just make sure that we're good and gone before all the shit hits the fan, do you know what I mean?"

He nods. "I do. But would you consider giving me the code now, and then we can decide as a team when to reveal that part of it?"

It's so tempting to turn everything over to him and let him take over. But I can't. I have to look out for Tee and me. "No. Sorry. I can't do that."

"Can't or won't?"

"Does it matter?"

"To me it does."

I hate that he's backed me into this corner. "Won't."

He nods, saying nothing. Then he gathers his crutches and puts them under his arms. "You can write it down there on the paper. I'll be back in a few minutes." He goes out the door and down the front porch stairs. I see him through the window heading out back, to the pretty forest he showed me yesterday where he said he does his best thinking. It'll probably be there that he decides he's better off without me and Tee in his life.

And who could blame him?

CHAPTER TWENTY-NINE

Thibault is cooking. I can't believe how long Tee and I slept. The sun is going down already. My dreams were full of self-doubt. I was on the outside of life looking in. It left me feeling melancholy.

"I smell something delicious." I come around the corner of the kitchen, holding Tee over my shoulder and rubbing his back. He's fussing, but no matter what I do, he won't burp.

"How did you sleep?" Thibault turns from the sink and reaches for the baby. I gladly hand him over.

It feels like Thibault's calling a truce. I gave him the data I promised, and he left with it to call his team, but I stuck to my guns and didn't hand over the key to the code. I just can't do that. I have to be so careful now that I have Tee. He's all I've got that's worth a damn.

"I slept pretty good until this little booger woke me up." I take a glass of water from the counter and drink the entire thing without stopping.

"Would you like a glass of water?" He winks at me.

I try to smile. "Don't mind if I do." I refill the glass and hand it to Thibault. "Here you go."

"I was thinking about making some coffee. Are you interested?"

"No, thanks. I'm not really into that decaffeinated stuff, and I guess I'm not supposed to have the real deal."

"I'm going to make myself a cup of the real deal. How about I make you a cup of chamomile tea?"

I slide into one of the chairs at the table. "No, thanks. I'll just stick to the water."

He tips the baby back, supporting his head so he can look at his face. Tee's eyes are open. "This is the first time I've seen you awake all day, Baby Tee. Look at you with those big blue eyes and chubby cheeks."

"Do you think he's okay?" I ask. "He sleeps a *lot*."

"He's fine. Little babies sleep almost the entire day. I remember trying for weeks to get Melanie and Victor to play with me, and all they ever wanted to do was close their eyes. I was starting to get a complex . . . I thought I was going to be the boring uncle." He reaches up and strokes Tee's fat little cheek. "He sure is getting chunky."

"Hey, watch it. That's my baby you're insulting."

"It's not an insult. Chunky babies are healthy babies." He squeezes Tee's two cheeks together and laughs at the funny face he makes.

"So, what's for dinner?" I look toward the oven, trying to make the fluttery feelings in my stomach go away. Seeing Thibault being tender with my child is both endearing and painful. He's such a good guy. I'm not just saying goodbye to my life—which really isn't such an awful thing—I'm also saying goodbye to him. My hero. And I'm pretty sure it *is* an awful thing to be doing that.

"Chicken casserole. One of my specialties."

"Sounds good. I'm starving." I rub my stomach.

"While you were sleeping, I talked to my team." He puts the baby up on his shoulder and pats his back, giving me a thumbs-up when Tee burps.

"And? Are you happy with whatever they told you?"

"Yes and no." He turns in a slow circle, mindful of his knee, heading over to the cupboard that holds the drinking glasses. He pulls one down and grabs the juice out of the refrigerator. "I know you said you wanted water, but you should also have some of this stuff. It's got some good vitamins in it."

"Whatever you say, boss."

He looks over his shoulder at me. "I like that. Keep it up."

"You wish." I can't help smiling.

He pours the juice and hands the glass to me. Sitting down in the chair opposite me, he puts Tee on his shoulder and rubs his back in small circles with his hand, so big in comparison. "You know, I really don't want to push you on this, but now that I've talked to my team members, I'm afraid I'm going to have to insist on a couple things."

My eyebrows go up. "Is that so?"

He shakes his head. "Please don't get angry at me. I don't want this to be a battle of wills between us."

"I'm not fighting anybody." I take a sip of juice while watching him over my glass.

"Okay, well, Jenny has been on your cloud account and she's found your files. She says that they're in really good shape, except for one thing."

"What's that?"

"Except for the fact that they're completely coded and there's no way to connect any of it to Pavel until we get the key to unencrypt them. Jenny said that the entries are impossible to identify, and the books could just as well be for a company that sells clown noses as anything else."

"That would be an awful lot of clown noses."

"Clown noses, widgets, guns . . . You get my point. We can't identify a single thing without the code."

"I know. I told you." I shrug. I don't know why he's acting like this is news to anybody.

He looks at me for a long time and then turns his attention to Tee. He speaks softly. "My sister and her husband have moved their family out of their house for their own safety. I'm here at the cabin indefinitely until you're safe. My entire team is working to help you out, and I'm paying for it out of my own pocket."

His gaze shifts to me. "If you can't trust me now, if you can't believe me when I tell you that I'm on your side at this point, I don't know what else to tell you. Should I just walk away? Tell you I'll see you later, have fun talking to Holloway at the district, and good luck? Leave you to fend for yourself with Baby Tee on your shoulder?" He gestures at my baby's tiny body.

"Why can't you trust *me*, though?" I ask. My heart feels like it's breaking. "Why does it have to be me doing all the trusting?"

"I do trust you. I know you're telling the truth."

"Yeah, you know that because you double- and triple-checked everything I said to you. You have a whole team of people making sure everything I say is true. But why can't you trust me when I say that everyone will have the code once I'm safe? Once Tee and I are free of Pavel's influence?"

Thibault turns to me, cradling the baby in his arm. "You are safe. That's why we're here."

I shake my head. "No. This is just a temporary reprieve, and you know it. A rest stop. I need to move on. To find another home. To get a job and eventually be able to enroll my child in school without worrying that he'll be kidnapped by his father."

"If you give us the code so we can pass it on to the police, that can all happen."

"Or they could screw me over."

"Why would they do that?"

My voice goes up. "I don't know! Why *wouldn't* they?"

"Because they need you to testify about the data."

"Bull. They could depose me and then cut me loose. If I died, oh well. They have what they need. I know how the law works, believe me . . . I checked."

He stares at me for the longest time. "You don't trust anyone, do you?" He says it like I'm somehow a bad person for being that way. But that's not my problem.

I lift my chin. "No. I don't."

He shakes his head, disappointed. "I am doing everything I can to help you, but it's not enough. You need to help me too. You need to help *yourself*, and the only way you can do that is to recognize that you can't do this alone. You need me . . . or someone like me." He stands, coming over to place the baby in my arms.

"I've been doing just fine alone up until now."

"Up until the moment you gave birth to this beautiful baby right here." He points at Tee. "The game has changed. It's not just you running away from this criminal; it's you and a newborn baby. What are you going to do when he gets sick?"

Sick? I panic, pulling back to look at Tee's face. "Is he?" I don't even know what a sick baby looks like.

"No, he's not. But babies *get* sick all the time. You can't just wander into a doctor's office with a random baby who has no records and expect to be treated with no questions asked. Did you even fill out that birth certificate in the hospital?" He doesn't bother waiting for my answer. "That's not how it works in this day and age. You need to be able to prove who he is, who you are . . . you need your insurance information . . ."

"I have access to cash."

"I'm sure you do. According to Jenny you've got a pretty sophisticated setup. I wouldn't doubt it if you told me you've been skimming money from Pavel this entire time. Maybe you have a million bucks in the bank somewhere."

"I wouldn't do that . . . take his money just to give myself another paycheck." I'm offended he'd think of me like that.

He looks at me like I'm crazy. "What? Take money from a criminal? Why not?"

"Because it's wrong to steal, first of all, and he's dangerous. If he thought I even took a single dollar for myself, he'd slit my throat."

He throws his arms out. "Exactly! This guy is evil . . . the Devil himself, if the stories the cops are sharing with my team are true. You cannot handle this on your own. I know you're strong, and I know you're independent, and I *know* you're used to doing everything on your own, but you can't do it that way anymore. Let me help you, dammit." He glares at me.

I glare back, my chin trembling. He's making sense, but at the same time, he's asking too much from me. I've been burned too many times to just put my life in his hands. "I really hate you right now."

His tone drops real low. "Well, I don't hate you. But I do hate what you're doing."

"And what is that, exactly?" Stupid tears escape, and I brush them away angrily.

"Being foolish. Taking needless risks."

"I thought I was being a good person."

"How are you being a good person by putting your baby at risk the way you are?"

My face falls. Talk about a low blow. "What?"

"You heard me. Before it was just your life that you were risking. If you made a mistake, if Pavel caught you informing on him to the police, well, you'd be gone. That's it. No more Mika. Now if he finds out what you've been doing, it's not just you who'll pay the price. How do you think you're going to feel when he finds you and takes your baby away from you? How are you going to feel when your baby disappears like Alexei did?"

Without thinking, I grab my glass and throw its contents into his face, standing and throwing my chair out behind me with my legs. "How *dare* you! Don't *say* that!"

He stands there blinking the juice from his eyes.

"You're just as rude as your sister is, you know that?! Ruder! Not just rude, but mean!"

He shrugs his shoulders as he leans over to grab a paper towel from the nearby roll. "Call me mean, but at least I'm on your team." He wipes the sticky juice from his face.

"You're not on my team!" I'm breathing like an angry bull, tears still trickling out. I can't keep up with them; more come than I can wipe away with one hand. This is breaking my heart. I wanted him to be on my team. Hell, I wanted to be on *his* team. It's only now that I'm realizing how much—and yet how impossible it would be.

"Oh, yes, I am, whether you like it or not." He stares me down.

"Maybe you should just drive me into the city and drop me off." I grit my teeth together hard, making my jaw ache.

"I don't think so. I think we're going to sit down right here at this table and work this out."

I glance at the chair I recently abandoned. "There's nothing to work out."

He softens his voice, making my heart ache even more. "Yes, there is. Come on, don't play me like that. Even though I think you're being stubborn right now, and even though you're trying like hell to push me away, I'm still on your side. Look at me . . ." He holds his arms out. "I'm not going anywhere." He huffs out a sigh. "Please, Mika . . . Give me that code so I can send it to Jenny. And then we can talk about our plan."

"And what are you going to do for me?" I ask, lifting my chin.

"What do you mean?"

I shrug. "You want me to trust you with everything I have, with my one and only bargaining chip. What are you going to trust me with?"

He looks around. "I've given you my team, my home, my word. What else is left?"

"How about just your trust? How about you trust me that when I am safe, when I am in my new home, I will give you that code? Can you do that?"

He stares at me, his jaw muscles twitching like mad. "You're asking me to keep helping you on blind faith."

"That's what trust is, right?"

"I guess."

"Have I lied to you yet?"

"Technically, no. But you haven't been exactly forthcoming, either."

"Ask me about anything and I'll tell you. Anything but the damn code."

He stares at me. "Have you taken any of Pavel's money and put it away for yourself?"

"No."

"You said you have access to money. Where did you get it?"

"I saved it. And I invested it. I have a finance degree, and what they didn't teach me in school I learned on my own."

"Do you love him?"

I frown. "Love who? Tee?" I look down at my baby.

"No, not him. Pavel."

I laugh until I realize he's not joking. "Pavel? No! God, no! Don't even . . . God, that's disgusting. How could I love a man who murders people?" I feel sick to my stomach.

He shrugs, but all he can do is look at Tee.

My lips are trembling. He has to hear it to believe it. And if I want him to trust me, I have to stop running from his questions. "Fine, you want to hear me say it? I'll say it. Pavel raped me. Does that make you happy?" I cough, which jump-starts the sobs. I try to cover my face with my hand.

Suddenly Thibault is there next to me. He holds me around my waist, leaning into me, touching his head to mine. "Oh, shit, that's terrible. Mika, please don't cry. I'm sorry I pushed. Jesus, what a dick I can be sometimes." He sighs and he holds me tight. "God, I want to fucking *kill* that guy. Please don't be mad at me. Please don't cry. I'm just trying to understand."

"What do you expect from me? My life is completely falling apart right now, and I have a baby to look after . . . I have no clue what I'm doing, and now you're standing there looking at my baby and judging me!"

"I wasn't judging. I wasn't, I promise." He strokes my hair. "And it's not just you, okay? I'm here, and I'm not going anywhere. I've already said that ten times, but I'll keep saying it until you believe me, okay?"

"You should leave. You should go far and fast away from me. Just get away."

"No. I wouldn't do that. You're too important to me."

I pull back out of his embrace. "Why? You don't even really know me, and what you do know is a total nightmare."

"Of course I do." He reaches up and slides my hair out of my face. "I know where you grew up, I know who raised you . . . I know you're good with money and could teach me a few things about payroll, a task I hate doing with all my heart . . . I know you make horrible spaghetti, and I know you stink at poker. Oh . . . and I know you're a great mom. I know you love your baby and you're going to do everything in your power to keep him safe. What else do I need to know?"

I can't respond. The tears won't stop long enough for me to speak. The person he's describing doesn't sound all bad.

"And I know that you want to believe me. I know that you don't want to do this on your own."

"How do you know that?" My voice comes out like a frog's croak.

"Because you're biting your lip again."

"What?"

He reaches up and strokes my mouth with his thumb. "Every time you bluffed when we were playing poker, you bit your lip. And you're doing it now, too, so I know you're lying when you say you want me to go far and fast away from you."

I immediately leave my lip alone. Then I laugh once. I think he let me win at poker. "You are such a bastard."

He shrugs. "I can live with that."

I sigh, letting a lot of the tension in my body leave with the hot air from my lungs. "I don't want you to think that I don't hear everything you're saying or that I don't appreciate what it means. I do. But if I give you the code and you share it with your team, I'm going to have to live with the fact that I could be signing their death warrants. Pavel will come after anyone he thinks has unauthorized access to his business."

"No . . . Once you share it, you're going to have to live with the fact that you just became a part of my team . . . my family. We're all going to take care of you. It's not going to be just me anymore."

I try to smile, but my lips tremble too much so I stop. "I really want to believe you. I really want to believe that's possible." I pause to take another breath and calm myself. "But the only way it's going to happen is if you can trust me enough to keep going without the code."

We stare into each other's eyes for the longest time. Tee goes completely silent. Then Thibault sighs long and loud and pulls me into his arms, careful not to squish the baby. "I'm not going to let you down. *Nobody* on my team is going to let you down. You can absolutely count on the Bourbon Street Boys to have your back, code or not."

CHAPTER THIRTY

After I've cried all the tears I can squeeze out, the three of us limp and struggle into the bedroom. The timer goes off on the stove as I lower myself to the bed.

"I'll be right back," Thibault says. "Don't go anywhere."

My laugh is really weak. "I don't know where I'd go."

He leans down and gives me a quick kiss on the lips before heading out of the room, hopping on one leg. "To be continued," he says over his shoulder. My heart flutters at this newfound intimacy between us.

I slowly sit up and get the baby situated so he can eat. He hasn't asked for his next meal yet, but if I'm going to relax in this bedroom and have any chance at further conversation or *whatever* with Thibault, Baby Tee needs to have a full belly and be sleeping.

I'm not going to try to imagine what that *whatever* might be. I just had a baby, so my body isn't ready for much, and messing around with Thibault is only going to complicate an already impossible situation. And yet, I don't bother covering Tee or me with the blanket, enjoying the freedom of just doing what needs to be done without worrying who will see something they don't want to see. *This is me, Thibault, like it or not. Natural and in the flesh.*

Thibault gets back when I'm sitting up at the headboard. As soon as he sees I'm nursing, he turns his back to give me some privacy. "Oh, sorry."

"You don't have to do that anymore."

He twists around to look at me. "Are you sure? I don't want to make you feel uncomfortable."

"As if that's possible." I shake my head. "Just a few days ago you were looking at my lady-v when it was in the worst state possible. If there's anyone in the entire world who can watch me breastfeed, it's you."

He gives me a big grin and turns completely around. "Hallelujah. Because I love watching you."

I frown. "What . . . ? Are you some kind of pervert?"

He limps over bringing a bowl of food, leaving a second one behind on the dresser. "No, I'm not a pervert. But I am kind of fascinated with the way you've just picked up this whole motherhood thing and are doing so well at it."

My smile is awkward. His compliment makes me feel shy for some reason. "Now you're just buttering me up."

"Nope, just calling it like I see it. You ready to eat some dinner?"

I look down at the baby. "I'm a little busy right now."

"You want me to feed you?" He holds up a fork with what looks like some steaming-hot chicken on it.

"Are you serious?"

"Hundred percent. I've been feeding those babies of my sister's for months now. I'm a pro."

I shrug. "Seems a little weird, but okay."

"Open the hatch." He blows on the fork a few times to cool the food off before moving it toward my mouth.

I giggle as I part my lips. This is ridiculous. Silly. But it warms my heart toward him. He really is a good guy. I don't think anyone seeing him on the street would imagine he could be this tender and considerate. He looks too tough. Serious. Hot.

The taste of the food in my mouth registers and breaks through my wandering thoughts. "Mmm, that's good. You made that?"

"Sure did." He takes a bite from the same bowl. "I'm not just a one-trick sandwich pony."

I nod my head. "Sandwiches and chicken casserole. I think I could survive on that."

"Not just survive . . . thrive, baby. You're gonna thrive."

"I like your positive attitude, as misplaced as it might be."

"No, see . . . it's not misplaced. I've got it all figured out."

"A plan, hmm? Does this plan include me and Tee moving to a private island in the middle of nowhere, where no one can ever find us?"

"No, not exactly." His smile disappears. "Although, from what I understand, it might be possible that the feds are going to want to put you into some sort of witness protection program."

"Forever?" Two days ago that sounded like a great plan. Tonight . . . not so much. Because I know that means I'll never see this man again, and the more time I spend with him, the harder that is to bear.

He gives me another bite of chicken. "I don't think so. Not forever. I mean, I'm not the authority on this kind of thing, but for sure we can talk to them about it."

I talk around my mouthful of food. "Talk to who? I don't know how it works. Is it the NOPD who decides things? The FBI? The prosecutor?"

"The FBI." He takes a bite too, chewing thoroughly before he answers. "I think they're going to be the ones handling this case. This is way out of bounds for the NOPD."

"But if I go into witness protection, doesn't that mean that I can never contact anybody from my past and they can never contact me?" There's only one person I'd like to talk to again. Two, if I count Alexei.

"I don't know." He gathers more chicken up onto the fork for me. "I don't know the details, and I don't think we need to worry about that right now. The most important thing is to get the information to the police as quickly as possible so we can put a stop to whatever is happening. We'll figure out the rest after that."

It's burning me up inside, this idea of disappearing so thoroughly from Thibault's life. I'm not sure, but I think it bothers him too. The only way I'm going to know for sure, though, is to say something. "But . . . if I go to witness protection, that means I'm not going to see you anymore." I break out in a cold sweat as I wait for him to respond.

He gives me another bite of dinner, his eyebrows furrowed and his nostrils flared. "I really don't think we need to worry about that stuff at this point."

I can't believe how much his response hurts. I've assumed too much. I guess I'm going to be one of the girls he's let go because they weren't compatible. I might as well make it easy for him to say what he needs to say. "So, what you're telling me is not to get too attached."

"I'm *not* saying that." He drops the fork into the bowl and stares into my eyes. His dark expression changes to one that looks . . . anguished. "Listen, I know this is nuts . . . I just met you, and we came together in the weirdest way possible."

"You ran into my car."

He gives me a somewhat sad grin. "No. I got hit by you driving your car, and then I stood between your legs, cut your panties off your body, and watched you give birth to a miracle baby."

I don't want to get too excited about what he's saying. He still hasn't shown me any reason to think he feels a connection to me like I'm starting to feel for him. "So *that's* what happened to my panties? You cut them off?" I pretend to be offended, to keep the mood lighter.

He tries to smile. "What did you expect me to do? There was a baby coming any second. They were in the way."

I look down at the boy who brought this man into my life and stroke his cheek. "Those were my favorite ones. You owe me a pair of panties."

Thibault reaches up and tucks some strands of hair behind my ear. "I'll buy you as many panties as you want when we get out of here, but I need you to do something for me first."

"What's that?" I flutter my eyelashes at him, embarrassed about how intimate this feels when I know he's just being kind to me.

"Kiss me."

My heart leaps and my expression softens as stress leaves my body and heart. He does care about me, at least a little bit. "Oh, that's easy. I can do that, no problem."

His smile is so sexy as he moves in closer. I can tell he's trying to be tender and gentle, cognizant of the fact that I'm feeding the baby right now. I hang on to his shirt as our lips touch, and then his tongue comes out and touches mine ever so softly.

"I don't want to hurt you," he whispers against my mouth.

"I won't let you." I put my free hand in his hair and pull the strands into my fist. He moans and kisses me some more before he breaks off contact to look down at the baby.

Tee has fallen asleep on my breast. I slowly ease him off, wrapping him up in his blanket.

"Want me to put him in his bassinet?" Thibault asks.

I nod, handing him over.

Thibault gets off the bed and takes the baby gently in his arms, lowering him into the tiny bed next to us on the floor, making sure he's bundled up with warm blankets all around him so he can't roll over. Then he sits on the edge of the mattress and takes my hand in his. He looks at me, his expression unreadable. The paranoid part of me says he's regretting starting something. The hopeful part of me says he's being respectful.

"What are we doing?" I ask.

"I'm not really sure, but I'll stop if it's making you uncomfortable."

"It's not making me uncomfortable at all. It's making me . . . anxious. Not in a bad way, though." I sigh. "I'm not making any sense, I'm sorry." I smile at him. "I'm going to blame my confusion on that kiss."

He smiles back. "I know that we can't . . . do certain things right now, because you just had the baby and everything, but if I could just kiss you a little and hold you, that would be really cool."

My heart soars up into the clouds. "We could do that." I pause, not sure how it works. I've never just cuddled with a man before. "Are we going to do this with our clothes on or off?"

"How about we start with them on and see where that gets us?"

"Okay." I giggle. I feel like a virgin must when she meets a nice boy who takes things slow. "That's different."

"I know, right?"

"You're not normally into rated-PG cuddling?" I ask.

"To be honest, not really. But for some reason with you it sounds like fun."

"I'm going to try to take that as a compliment." I smile so he knows I'm not being mean.

He takes my hand and kisses the back of it. "It is a compliment. Big-time." He looks toward the door. "I'm going to turn the light off, if that's okay with you."

"Sure. Better move the food over first, though."

He takes the bowl of chicken casserole and puts it on the dresser.

"Just be careful of this left knee of mine," he says, hobbling across the room. "This crazy lady hit me with her car the other day, so it's pretty sore."

"You'd better stop talking about it like that. You know you walked right out into traffic like a blind fool. I'm innocent. No jury will convict me."

He comes back to the bed and lies down very slowly. He moves in close and slides his arm under my neck, pulling me toward him. My breasts are pressed against his chest. He props himself up on his elbow partway and leans over me, putting his nose in my neck. He inhales deeply. "You smell so nice."

"I need a shower."

"No, you don't. Then you'd just smell like boring old soap and not you."

I giggle at his foolishness. "I think there's something wrong with you. Or at least there's something wrong with your nose."

"There's nothing wrong with me except for the fact that I've got this woman living in my house who's driving me insane." He kisses my neck, tickling my skin with his tongue when he's done.

I rest my hand on his hip, sighing with the pleasure of being next to him and knowing that I make him as nuts as he makes me. "Maybe you're feeling a little crazy because you're sexually frustrated."

"That could be it, but I'm not sure. I think it could be this girl's attitude that drives me wild." He kisses me on the mouth, playing with my tongue for a few seconds and making my heart race before he stops to look at me.

"Her attitude?" I look at him with my head slightly tilted, my tone playful. "What are you talking about?"

He pulls me closer and kisses my neck again. My body goes limp as relaxation and warmth settle into my bones.

"I think you deliberately bait me to try and make me nuts," he says.

"You're crazy."

He pauses and pulls back a little so he can look down at me. "No, actually, I'm pretty intuitive. I think you're a little bit of a rebel and you enjoy getting a rise out of me just because you can."

I love the idea of having that kind of power over this man. "Huh. I think you're right . . . I think I *will* enjoy getting a rise out of you." I reach down and rest my hand against the front of his jeans. He's rock hard underneath. "Yeah, you're right. I'm enjoying this, all right." I can't stop grinning.

He moans. "You'd better watch it, girl. I'm going to catch fire down there if you keep that up."

I stroke him up and down. "You want me to stop?"

"Yes and no." He sighs, pulling away a little.

My hand stills. His voice is saying yes, but his body language is saying no.

"It's going to be really hard for me to stop once we get going, so maybe we should just hold off," he says.

He's being so kind, so generous here in this bed with me when I know he wants release. His body has to be aching for it. "I really don't mind doing things for you, even though I'm not physically ready for you to do anything for me."

He kisses me gently and then pulls back again. "I appreciate that, but I think for our first time, it'll be more fun if we can do something together."

Until he responds that way, I hadn't realized how much of a test I was giving him. He's proven to me that he does really care about me and isn't just in this for his own satisfaction. He truly is gentle and kind. I let out a long sigh and move in closer to him. I feel genuinely safe when I'm in his arms.

"Are you okay?" He tries to see my face, but I leave it tucked into his chest.

"Yeah, I'm fine. I'm just wondering why fate is so mean to me sometimes."

He plays with my hair. "What are you talking about?"

It's crazy to say these things out loud, but time is so short for us. I know Thibault is right; I'm going to be put in some sort of witness protection program, which means I'll need to be cut off from him and everybody else in my life. If I don't say these things now, they'll never get said.

"All these years I've been looking for a guy like you who would be kind and gentle and understanding . . . watch my back . . . and here you are."

He kisses the top of my head. "So, what's the problem? I'm right here, and I told you I'm not going anywhere."

"I don't mean to be morbid, but I feel like I'm standing at the threshold of either death or oblivion."

He laughs a little. "Well, that is pretty morbid. I don't know why you feel that way, though. I thought things were getting better for you. Was I wrong about that?"

"Either Pavel is going to come for me and there'll be nothing I can do about it but say, 'Goodbye, cruel world,' or I'll get put into a witness protection program that forces me to cut off all ties with everything and everyone. Goodbye, New Orleans, and goodbye, *you*. Like I said . . . fate is mean."

"No, you've got it wrong. If Pavel comes for you, I'm going to be standing right next to you, so you don't have anything to worry about."

"I want to believe you. I really do." It's intoxicating to imagine Thibault being by my side and keeping Tee and me safe, like a guardian angel or a real-life superhero. But it's just not realistic.

He pulls me in tighter and wraps his good leg around mine, drawing me into him. Our bodies are completely entwined. "Believe me . . . I can be twice as stubborn as you ever dreamed of being."

I giggle. "I actually believe you when you say that."

"Good." He reaches around and smacks me on the butt. "Now maybe you'll listen to me more often, since you know I speak the truth."

I squeeze him tight, imagining for a split second what our future could look like. "Boy, you're gonna be in so much trouble when I'm back to a hundred percent."

"I'm looking forward to it."

No more words need to be exchanged. We know how we feel about each other, and we both know the chances of it working out aren't great. But I hold him and he holds me, and I'm able to drift off to sleep feeling like I'm floating in a cloud, high above the earth and all my troubles.

CHAPTER THIRTY-ONE

I wake up in the pitch-dark. It takes me a few moments to realize where I am and what I was doing before I fell asleep. When I feel heavy limbs and smell the scent of Thibault filling my head, I remember what happened earlier: I'm in bed with a man who I have very strong feelings for after only knowing him for a few days. Then it hits me that the sound that woke me up was the baby whining in his bassinet nearby.

I nudge Thibault on the shoulder with my chin. "Baby's awake."

"No, he's not," he mumbles. "I'm still sleeping."

"Just stay where you are." I struggle to get out of his embrace and then untangled from the covers, careful not to bump his knee. I'm stiff, but I make my way over to the bassinet and reach down to pull the baby out. He's kicked off most of his blankets, so I hold him next to me and warm him up before bringing him back to bed. "No need to cry, baby boy, Mommy's right here."

I sit up against the headboard and let out a big yawn after he latches on.

"Do you want me to turn on the light?" Thibault mumbles.

I stroke Thibault's thick, curly hair, whispering my response. "No, then he'll wake up too much and I'll never get to go back to sleep."

"You're already a pro at this." He sits up and drags himself back to be next to me. He reaches over and takes the baby's hand. "Can I get you something to drink?" he whispers.

"Yes, a glass of water would be nice."

"Coming right up." He moves to leave but I grab his hand.

He looks back at me. "What's up?"

"I want to give you that code." I have a hard time swallowing. My throat feels swollen. Breathing becomes difficult.

"Are you sure?" he says softly. He reaches up and rests his hand gently on my cheek. "I don't want you to think you owe it to me or anything like that. You need to be totally okay with it. I understand why you want to hold things back, and I won't be mad if you're not ready."

I nod. As soon as the words leave my mouth, I know . . . "I trust you."

He turns more fully, wincing at his knee. Then he focuses on me. "This is a really big deal for you. I want you to know that I get that. And I don't want you to think you have to do this in order for me to trust you. I already do."

"I know." I'm getting choked up over his sincerity. It means so much to me.

"And I'm going to help you regardless."

"I know that, too." I start to cry.

"Why the tears?" he asks tenderly, leaning forward to wipe them away.

"I'm afraid. And happy. And sad." I laugh at how ridiculous I'm being.

He smiles. "I get it. I'm those things too."

"So where are your tears?" I ask, trying to be funny.

"Superman never cries." What sounds like a cough comes out, and then he tips his head down, pressing his fingers into the bridge of his nose.

"What's wrong?"

He looks up and swipes at his face. His voice trembles. "I told you I'm no Superman."

I hold out my arm and he moves in, holding me while I hold him, the baby nestled between us. Thibault's voice is muffled in my shoulder. "I won't let you down. I promise."

"I know you won't. You haven't let me down yet, right?" I hold on to his head, taking his thick hair in my hand and squeezing it. "We're going to be all right. I know we are. God is not cruel. God is good."

"Yes. God is good." Thibault pulls away. "I'm going to go get you that water."

"Grab me some tissues too, please. And that paper and pen."

"Yes, ma'am."

He hobbles into the kitchen and comes back with everything.

"Could you turn on the light?" I ask.

"I thought you said it would wake the baby up."

"Yeah, it probably will, but I need to see so I can write that stuff down."

"How about this instead?" he asks, using a flashlight app on his phone to dimly light the small area where I need to see.

"Perfect. Much better."

"Are you left- or right-handed?"

"Right-handed. If you could just get me a book or something hard to put the pad on . . ."

He turns around and grabs a hardcover off the nearby bookshelf and brings it over to the bed, positioning it under the pad of paper. I pick up the pen and start writing while he holds the light above.

"What's this?" he asks.

"This is the name of the file where Jenny or whoever is looking at the cloud account is going to find a software application."

"Okay."

"When they're inside that file, they need to click on the application to open it up."

"Okay . . . That seems simple enough."

"And then the software application is going to ask for a password, and this is what they need to enter. It's case-sensitive, so make sure they put it in correctly. If they put it in incorrectly even *one* time, it will shut down and stop working, and will need to be reset."

"How do you reset it?"

"You need my thumbprint inputted into the system using a print scanner, which is a little piece of hardware that's connected to the computer. It'll be a big mess, so it's just better if they don't make any mistakes."

"Okay." He pauses. "Wow, this is complicated."

"Yes. I wanted to be sure it couldn't be hacked. So once you put in the password, the executable file is going to go into all the other files in the other folders and reveal the data you're looking for."

"We don't have to go in and decipher all of the data with the code by hand? It's going to do it automatically?"

"Yes, that's exactly what I mean."

"That seems pretty sophisticated."

"It is." My smile is sad. Bitter. "I used some of Pavel's money to pay for it, so maybe when I said I didn't steal from him I wasn't being entirely honest."

"This code keeps his numbers from being read by anyone who's not authorized, so I'd say you used his money to do him a favor."

"It's only a favor if he has the code, though."

Thibault shrugs. "Details. I'm not worried about it; I don't think it means you're a dishonest person."

"I'm not going to lose sleep over it." It was this or die. For me it was an easy decision, because Thibault is very right about me: I am a survivor. And now that I've seen through his eyes what it means to be a survivor, I'm proud to be called that.

"Where did you buy it?" he asks.

"I hired a software engineer to make it. He lives in India. It's not a problem; no one can trace him back to me."

"Okay. That's cool. If you don't mind, though, I'll mention that to Jenny."

"Sure, no problem. I've got nothing to hide from you or her." I hand him the paper and he looks it over.

He points at the first line. "So this is the file where Jenny will find that software, and then she needs to open the software and put in this password?" He points to the second line, a string of letters, numbers, and symbols I committed to memory over a period of several days.

"Yes. Tell her to make sure not to change any of the files in the cloud. They need to be named the same way they were when I put them up there, and positioned the way they were initially, for it to work. If she moves anything around or renames any files, it might not work right."

"Okay, I'll tell her." He folds the paper up and sticks it in his pocket. Then he looks down at the baby as his jaw twitches.

"You want to go talk to her right now, don't you?" I smile at him. He's not saying a word, but his posture couldn't be any more tense.

"Am I that easy to read?"

"Yeah . . . like an open book with large-print letters."

He reaches over to pinch my cheek lightly. "Sassy. Do you mind if I drive down the road a little bit until I have a signal and give Ozzie a call?"

"No, I don't mind. Just give me that bottle of water and leave me here." I look down at the baby. "The milk bar is open and he's really hungry, apparently." I poke his cheek gently. "Little piggy."

"Okay. I won't be long. I'm just going to drive up the road like five minutes and have a quick conversation. I'll come right back when I'm done."

"No problem. If Tee finishes before you get here, I'm going back to sleep."

He pauses on his way out the door, disabling the flashlight app. "When I get back, do you want me to sleep on the couch?"

"Are you crazy?"

"That's what I was hoping you'd say." He swings out of the room on his crutches and heads for the front door.

CHAPTER THIRTY-TWO

After giving up on falling back to sleep, I get cleaned up, dressed, and sit on the couch, waiting for Thibault to get back from his early-morning phone call. I'm paging through a random magazine when I hear his truck sliding to a stop out front. The sound of rapid footfalls, running up the gravel drive faster than I would have thought possible with the injury he has, comes to my ears. The engine of his SUV is still running.

I stand, my heart rate picking up. He sounds . . . panicked.

"Mika!" he yells as he mounts the porch steps.

"I'm in here!" I run to the door, worried he's injured himself. I pull it open to find him standing there in the still-dark morning, breathing like an Olympic sprinter. The living room lamp throws its light on his face, and I can see sweat rolling down his temples.

"I'm sorry to have to say this, but we need to go. Like, *now*."

My eyes go wide. I can't process why he's saying this to me. Everything was so cool just twenty minutes ago. "Is there something wrong?"

"Maybe not, but I saw a car up on the road, and I think it might be coming in this direction. It's definitely not anyone from my team."

I dash from the living room to the bedroom, grabbing the baby from his bassinet to put him in his car seat and yanking the diaper bag off the dresser.

Thibault is right behind me.

"Grab our clothes," I say, pointing at the drawers. I get busy stuffing diapers and wipes into the bag. It's almost empty from me plundering it yesterday over and over. Tee is slumped over in his seat, sleeping off his last meal. I pause to straighten him out and buckle him in.

Thibault takes an armload of clothing and limps out of the room with it. When I'm done collecting as much as I can, I look around the room, my head swiveling left to right. "What else should I bring?!"

"You don't need to bring anything except your purse. Let's go!"

I come out of the bedroom with Tee's seat over my arm and my purse on my shoulder. Thibault's standing at the door with a gun in his waistband and his duffel bag over his back. Some of Tee's clothes are sticking out of the top of it.

I rush across the living room toward the front door but pause at the coffee table to grab the bottle of water sitting there. Thibault gestures at me as he mumbles aloud, almost to himself. "The car went past me a couple minutes ago. I got here in three minutes, max. The driver has eight minutes, give or take, before he gets to the next driveway, and if he's going as slow as he was going before, it could take him as much as ten minutes. It's just a couple minutes down the winding path before he's here at the front door, assuming that's where he's headed . . ."

His furious calculations are freaking me out. I stare at him, trying to figure out what he's doing.

"Come on, we have to go," he says gesturing wildly. *"Run."*

"You're really scaring me," I say as I race out the front door.

He comes limping behind me, his crutches hanging uselessly from his left hand.

"I'm sorry," he says, opening the door next to the car seat's base. "I don't mean to, but I just want to be safe."

"Okay, okay. Let's go." I click the car seat into its base while Thibault throws our bags onto the front passenger seat.

"Get in the back seat!" he yells, hopping on one leg to the driver's side.

I don't hesitate. I use the running board to jump in and climb over the baby, pulling the door closed behind me.

He gets in and throws the SUV into reverse, peeling out and whipping the car around. I fall back into my seat and scramble to get my seat belt on.

"Where are they?" I ask, fear tainting my voice. I grip the back of Thibault's seat to pull myself forward. I look through the front windshield, but all I see is the driveway and trees.

He focuses on the road ahead, flipping a switch on his dashboard that turns his headlights and dashboard lights off. "I have two driveways to my place," he says. "They're looking for the other one off to your right. They passed by the one we're using now. It's too well hidden from the road when it's dark out for them to see it."

"Won't they see us when they come in?"

"No. I had a special device installed in my vehicle last year for black ops purposes. There'll be no lights coming from my vehicle at all, not even running lights or brake lights."

"Who is it?" I stare through the side window, searching for signs of an intruder. I see nothing but the dark shapes of trees and bushes flying past. "Do you think it's Pavel?"

"I don't know. Maybe it's nobody. I was talking to Ozzie on the phone when the car went by, and something felt off. There's usually no traffic on this road, and this driver looked like he was searching for a driveway, slowing down at every break in the trees. I might just be paranoid, though, so don't panic."

"I don't think so." I'm twisted almost all the way around in my seat, and I'm pretty sure I see something there now. "I think I see somebody coming through the woods," I say, my voice high with panic.

"They're not going to see us, I promise."

"I definitely see someone," I say as the beams of someone's head-lights cut through the trees. "They're really far over there, though. I can barely see them."

"That's somebody coming down the other driveway." He presses on the accelerator.

"Where are we going?" I ask. I feel like my head is going to explode with the stress.

"As far away from here as we can get."

"Do you have any idea where, though?" I desperately need a plan. I hate knowing we're running blind, at the mercy of whoever this is. *Pavel.*

"Not yet. But when we get onto the main road and out a few miles, I'm going to call Ozzie. I'm sure he'll have a plan for us by then."

"I sure hope so," I say in a small voice. "Did you give him the code?"

"Yes, I did."

I sit back in my seat as the SUV bounces over bumps and into potholes. Reaching out, I take Tee's tiny hand, gripping the door's arm-rest to steady myself. I feel like I'm in a nightmare, racing as fast as we can to get away from it, all the while knowing it won't be quite fast enough. This car showing up here at Thibault's place has proven to me that I'll never be safe from Pavel . . . not even in a cabin in the middle of nowhere.

I've never felt so helpless in my entire life. My one consolation is knowing that I gave Thibault the code and he shared it with his team before anyone was able to kill me.

I just wish I hadn't put him in danger too.

CHAPTER THIRTY-THREE

He drives until he puts enough miles between us and the cabin to feel comfortable pulling out his phone. "You okay back there?" he asks as he uses his thumb to navigate to a phone number.

My heart rate has calmed a bit, but my mood has gone very dark. It feels like no matter what I do, I'm screwed. "Not exactly. Scared more than anything."

"How's the baby?"

"Sleeping. Fine." At least Tee's able to relax.

"I need to call Ozzie while I drive. Are you okay with that?"

"Yes, I'm fine with it. I trust you."

"I'll be careful, I promise. I've got precious cargo on board."

I can hear Ozzie's voice even though he's not on speakerphone. "Talk to me," he says.

"We're on the road. Somebody was definitely coming to the cabin."

"Somebody came to your house, too. We caught it on the surveillance cameras."

I grip Thibault's seat and pull myself forward so I can be sure to hear everything.

"Is everything okay over there?" Thibault asks.

"Yeah." Ozzie sighs. "Listen, man . . . I'm sorry I didn't jump on this when you first talked to me about it. Maybe we could have avoided this."

Thibault shakes his head. "Stop right there. You did exactly what you should've done. I was out of line."

I had no idea that helping me had caused Thibault problems with his partner. Now I'm even more touched by the choices he's made. It's one thing to make a decision to help someone when everyone you trust is backing you up, but when you do it on your own without that, it says something. He's proving all over again how much this—Tee and I, our safety—means to him.

"Doesn't matter now. We're all in. Where're you headed?"

"I was hoping you could tell me where to go. I'm just driving."

"What direction? Should I put on the locator?"

"No. I'm going to switch over to a black phone in a minute anyway; the locator won't have time to work."

"Good idea. We're going to shift into all-black protocol over here just as a precaution."

Thibault nods. "I'll call you back."

He hangs up the phone and puts it in his lap, using his leg as a support to push down on it so he can remove the battery.

"What are you doing?" I ask, peering over his shoulder.

He rolls down his window. "Just making sure nobody can trace us." Ten seconds later he tosses the phone out, and another ten seconds later the SIM card joins it, scattered on the side of the road. He throws the battery on the seat next to him.

"But how are you going to talk to your team?"

"I have a burner phone." He hands me his duffel bag through the space between the front seats. "Do you mind pulling it out of here? It's in a black case that looks like a shaving kit."

I dig around until I find it, handing it up to him. "Here you go."

He powers it up and waits for the welcome screen. When it's ready to go, he scrolls down to the first number, pressing the button and putting the phone to his head. I lean forward and get my ear as close to his as my seat belt will allow.

"Good. Your phone is operational," Ozzie says without preamble.

"Yep. All charged and ready to go. Looks like I've got all the team's numbers loaded into it, too."

"Remind me to hug my wife for that when this is all over," Ozzie says.

"Give her one for me too."

"Okay, so you left your cabin. What direction you heading?"

"West."

"Okay. Let me take a look on my screen here." Several seconds go by before he speaks again. "All right, you're going to get off the highway at Exit 28, and then you'll go about fifteen miles before you hop onto Highway 10. Go another twenty miles and you'll see a Motel 6. My guess is they'll have a big billboard you can see from the road if it's not right there at an exit."

"Okay. That sounds good."

"I'm going to pay for it with one of our black cards."

"Great. When I get there, I'll give you a call."

"You got it. And we're going to come and set up nearby, so just hold tight."

"Are you sure that's a good idea?"

"Would you rather do this out there by yourself?"

He shakes his head. "Definitely not."

"Okay. I don't know who it will be yet, but at least one of us will be there before sunrise."

He breathes out a sigh of relief. "You have no idea how much better that makes me feel."

"I can imagine. I'm sorry you were stuck on this by yourself for so long. Your knee must feel like shit."

I want to hug Thibault and both thank him and apologize. I had no idea how broad his shoulders were until now. Here's a man used to working as part of a team who had to fly solo because he'd made a promise to me.

"I'll live, but I've definitely felt better. It was my own fault things went the way they did. I'm real sorry."

"Stop. I'm not going to play the blame game anymore, and neither are you. We all make mistakes. Nobody's perfect. Now we know to handle things differently next time."

I should have trusted him sooner, told him the things he asked me about so his team could do their investigation. Maybe we could have avoided this situation. I've caused him so much grief, first with his knee and then with his team . . .

"Hopefully there won't be another next time that goes down like this," Thibault says. "I'm going to settle in with Mika, but we left with almost nothing from the cabin. We've got a few diapers and basic stuff for the baby, but we don't have any food or much in the way of clothing for her."

"Or sanitary pads," I say weakly from the back. I feel like such a burden.

"Or . . . uh . . . feminine products," he adds.

"All right, we'll bring stuff with us. Not a problem. Anything else special for Mika or the baby?"

"If Toni could give us more of her clothes, that would be awesome. And lots of water. Bottled water."

"You got it."

"Talk to you soon."

"Yeah, stay safe. Remain vigilant. I don't see any way they could possibly find you now, but you never know."

"How do you think they found us at the cabin?"

Ozzie sighs. "Well, if I were looking for you, I'd find your house either from the phone you had there or I'd get your name from the news reports and use it to search property records online. I'd find both your house and the cabin in less than thirty seconds. It wouldn't be difficult. If you weren't so close to this case, you'd know that, though."

Thibault hisses out a sigh. "We need to petition the court to have our addresses made confidential like they are for police officers and DAs."

"Agreed. It's first on my agenda with the chief when this is over."

"You said they came to my house, too?"

"Yeah. Your place and Toni's place. I'm glad she wasn't there."

Guilt hits me hard. I reach up and grip Thibault's shoulder to apologize.

"Me, too." Thibault pulls the phone away to rub his chest for two seconds before going back to the conversation. "Holy shit. I feel like I'm having a heart attack."

"Well, we've had it happen before, with May. That's why we've got protocols in place for this. We just need to stick to the plan and shore up any problems that appear."

"I can do that."

"We can too. See you soon."

"I'm counting on it."

Thibault hangs up the phone and drops it onto the seat next to him.

My heart feels bruised. "Thibault, I am so sorry."

He glances at me before going back to watching the road. "Don't apologize." He takes my hand at his shoulder and kisses it really quick, making my heart flutter. "This is not your fault. This is on Pavel, and he's not going to win."

"I wish I had your faith," I say.

"Just put your faith in me, and I'll take care of the rest."

I nod. "I can do that." And I'm not just saying that. I believe in Thibault. I trust that he will do whatever he can to keep Tee and me safe, and I can't ask for more than that.

CHAPTER THIRTY-FOUR

The Motel 6 is easy enough to find with Ozzie's basic directions and a little help from Thibault's Google Maps app. I expect the front desk clerk to give Thibault some trouble because the credit card Ozzie used to pay for the room is in a name Thibault doesn't know, but the clerk must've been briefed enough to satisfy his curiosity and the motel's rules. Thibault comes walking out of the reception office and gets into the SUV, driving Tee and me over to the door and dropping us off with a key.

"Go inside and lock up behind you. I'm just going to park behind the building and I'll be right back. I have a key."

I leave the truck with the car seat hooked over my arm and the diaper bag on my shoulder. After entering the room, I don't stop; I go right into the bathroom and lock that door behind me too.

Five or so minutes later, there's a light knock. "Are you okay in there?" Thibault asks.

I wipe the sweat from my upper lip and temples. "I'm fine. Is it okay to come out?"

"Yeah. It's just me in here."

"What's the secret code?" I'm mad we didn't come up with one before.

"Uhhh, what code?"

"We have to have a secret code we can use to let the other person know everything's okay. I've seen lots of movies where all the dying could have been avoided if they'd just had a secret code word." I feel a little light-headed. That's my excuse for being ridiculous.

"You do like your codes," he mumbles.

"What?"

"I said, how about *Popcorn*? Is that a good code?"

"Yeah, that works. I can't think of a time I'd use that in normal conversation."

Time ticks by.

"Are you coming out or what?" Thibault asks.

I'm afraid to open the door. This bathroom feels really, really safe; it has no windows, the door's a couple inches thick, and there's a big, fat lock on it. "You haven't used the secret code yet."

"Popcorn," he says. "It's raining popcorn out here."

"I'm coming out." I stand, getting up from my seat on the edge of the tub. I take Baby Tee's car seat off the closed toilet lid.

"I have all the lights off, so be careful not to trip," he says. "I don't want anyone outside the motel to see that this room is occupied."

"Good." I love that plan. I open the door and step outside the bathroom. Seeing him standing there in the dim light of the room's exit sign brings a wave of relief. "I'm so freaking scared."

"You're scared? Little Miss Bossy Pants? I don't believe it."

I step into his arms and place my head on his chest. "Shut up. You're not funny. Only I'm funny."

He rubs my back and kisses the top of my head. "It's going to be okay. Somebody from my team is going to be here by morning, and they're going to bring us what we need. I think you're safe drinking water from the faucet until they arrive."

"I couldn't eat anything right now no matter how good it looked." I sniff, willing the tears to stay away, but only getting partial buy-in from my emotions. "Not even that delicious chicken casserole you made."

"I don't blame you. This is scary stuff. But it's all going to be over soon."

"I don't know why you think you can say that." I look up at him. "This is just the beginning."

"No, it's not. You gave us the code. In the morning Jenny will start the ball rolling. The sooner Pavel is behind bars, the better."

Panic seizes me. "Please tell Jenny not to give it to anybody yet." I can see Alexei so clearly in my mind. His face, his smile, the conversations we'd have. He was always hanging around, never doing anyone any harm. He doesn't deserve to be left behind or left for dead.

He pulls back to look at me. "Why?"

It's time for another confession. I wish I'd said something sooner, but I'm not going to beat myself up for being cautious. Their ability and willingness to track us down prove how determined these people are to get what they want and how dangerously resourceful they can be.

"What's going on, Mika? Please tell me."

I look down at the floor, ashamed that I'm about to unload a whole other bunch of garbage on Thibault and his team, as if keeping me and Tee safe wasn't enough. "If we give the cops everything they want, they're not going to try to find Alexei. And I need to find him. It's important."

He puts his hands on my shoulders. "What do you mean? What does Alexei have to do with this?"

I look up at Thibault, pleading with my eyes for him to believe me, to hear what I'm saying. "Nothing . . . He's got nothing to do with this, other than the fact that he's a nice boy . . . a nice *man*, and when everything else was shit around me, when every*one* was shit, he wasn't, okay? He was kind to me. He listened to me. He never did anything rude or cruel or mean to me, unlike everyone else in my life. He's innocent in all this. He's never done anything wrong to anybody."

I'm feeling desperate, like Thibault is going to blow this off because Alexei's well-being doesn't relate to my personal safety. But it does relate to me as a *person*. The more I think about it, the more I realize how important it is to be sure Alexei is okay. I could never feel free of my past knowing I left his gentle soul behind to be destroyed by those evil people. It would haunt me forever. I need to convince Thibault.

"I don't know why Pavel is hiding him or if he got rid of him, but I need to know he's okay, or at least what happened to him. It's torturing me, imagining what . . ." I have to pause for a breath, trying to calm myself. "Alexei needs me. I can't just abandon him completely. If he's still alive, he needs me to find him, and if he's dead . . ." I stop again to manage my tears. ". . . If he's dead, I need to bury him the right way. Pavel never does it the right way."

Thibault talks to me in a soothing tone. "If the police go through the process of arresting Pavel and the DA starts working on his prosecution, Alexei's going to turn up."

I'm angry that he's not taking this as seriously as I think he should. "Why do you say that? If Pavel killed him, there's going to be no motivation for him at all to tell us what happened, and the police won't do anything about it. Alexei means nothing to them compared to Pavel. And if Pavel's hidden Alexei away, we'll never find out where. Pavel could pay somebody to watch him for the rest of his life."

"Would that be so bad? If somebody's taking care of him?"

I want to scream. "The people Pavel hires to watch over other people are not nice, okay? It's not like Alexei's got a loving foster family providing three meals a day and presents on Christmas. For all we know, he could be being abused right now. He's very simple in his mind. He's easy to manipulate and hurt. Do you understand what that means?"

"Do you think Pavel would involve him in the sex trade?"

"Why not? Pavel has zero morals, and he's evil. Alexei might be his cousin, but he's basically useless to Pavel unless he's making him money somehow."

"Has he done that with him before?"

"No, but he threatened it enough times that I believed him."

"Was he using him as leverage against you?" Thibault's expression turns dark.

"No. I never let Pavel know how much I cared about Alexei. That was way too dangerous."

"And you think he never noticed?"

I shrug. "I hope not. I was always too afraid to even ask him where Alexei was. I hinted around once, saying that I hadn't seen him lately, but Pavel told me not to worry about it." I reach up and touch his face, hoping I can break through that stony countenance. "Don't you see? If we give the police that code, they won't listen to me when I tell them they have to find Alexei. But if I hold back, they'll do everything they can to find out where he is. I can make sure he's okay, that Pavel hasn't hurt him. Then they can have their damn code." I drop my hand and adjust the baby's blanket. "I'm not going to let them call all the shots. That code is my leverage."

Thibault walks away, stopping at the little desk in the room. He opens the drawer and pulls out a pen and paper, dropping them down on the desk. "Write down everything you know about him: first name, last name, any middle names, birthday, any identifying tattoos or markings on his body, places he frequented, the church he went to, people he spends time with . . . Everything."

I walk over slowly, placing the baby on the bed before picking up the pen. "Are we going to report him missing to the police?"

"Not right away. I want to see what my team can find out first."

"Okay." I write down what I know on the paper and slide the pad over to him. "I really appreciate this."

"Don't mention it." He starts to walk away, but I stop him with a hand on his arm. He looks at me.

"I have to mention it. After what happened tonight, I keep thinking that fate is going to steal you away from me any second, when I least expect it. I don't want things to go unsaid between us."

He comes back over and puts his hand on the side of my face, leaning down to give me a slow kiss on the lips. He presses his forehead to mine. "Fate went to a lot of trouble to put us together. It's not going to tear us apart for nothing. I promise."

"You can't promise things you have no control over."

"Watch me."

He goes over to the bed with the pad of paper and sits down, pulling his phone out. His fingers fly over the keyboard as he looks at the information I wrote down.

"What are you doing?" I fear he's put my concerns aside and is doing what he wants instead of what I asked him to do. For a moment, I remember what betrayal feels like.

"I'm detailing all the information you've given me in an email so I can shoot it off to everybody on the team. It's an open invitation for anyone who's awake and available to start doing some digging."

I sigh with relief. He's not telling the cops. Not yet, anyway. I'm so grateful to him for listening to me.

Less than a minute later, his phone beeps, and he looks at the message waiting. "Toni's on it."

I walk over and look at the text.

T: *I'm on it. Stay safe. Stay black. Out.*

"What does that mean, 'stay black'?"

"She's telling me not to send any more messages unless they're absolutely necessary." Thibault stands and looks down at me. He studies my face and then stares into my eyes for a long time.

"What are you thinking right now?" I ask, not sure I want to hear the answer but absolutely certain I don't want any more secrets between us.

"I'm thinking that I've never felt as close to the precipice of death as I do right now. It's bringing a lot of things into absolute clarity for me: like this girl right here . . ."

He takes me by the hand, making my heart skip a beat.

"She's delicate and fierce and angry and funny and silly and serious and smart. And she's got a beautiful body and a beautiful baby, and even though she makes terrible spaghetti, she's definitely somebody I want to get to know better."

"Flattery will get you nowhere with me." I'm trying not to let my emotions run amok, but *damn*, it's hard when he's being so raw and kind at the same time.

He squeezes my hand. "You sure about that?"

A smile sneaks out. "No. Maybe not. Try giving me some more of it and we'll see." No man has ever said these things about me, ever. It's intoxicating to be showered with such kindness. I don't want it to end.

"I could spend a lifetime trying to figure you out, and I don't think I'd ever get bored in the process." He shakes his head. "Nope. My life could never be boring with you in it."

I roll my eyes. "I think boring would be nice for a change, actually."

He puts his arms around me. "Nah. Boring is boring." He glances over at the bed. "Interested in trying to catch some Z's? We probably have a couple hours before anyone gets here."

"Only if you'll lie next to me."

"Deal."

"I'm just going to move the baby over to the other bed," I say, separating myself from him.

"Good idea. Then when you hog all the covers you won't accidentally knock him off."

I smile but keep my comments to myself. I love his teasing, but we still have the undercurrent of danger keeping me from being able to play along with him. I pull the bedding down to make room for us under the covers and donate two of the four pillows to the bed that will serve as a giant crib for the baby. I make sure he's completely boxed in, even though he's still too tiny to move much on his own.

"I'm worried he's going to roll over and suffocate," I say, staring down at him.

"He's too little to move around too much, but I can put my shoes on either side of him to keep him from rolling over if it'll make you feel better."

I raise a brow at him. "You want to put your funky shoes next to my baby?"

"What? My shoes don't stink. My feet smell like cotton candy."

I laugh. "Boy, you're crazy. Nobody's feet smell like cotton candy."

"Mine do."

"Whatever. Just give me those funky shoes." I hold my hand out.

He goes into the bathroom and comes out with two towels, wrapping his shoes up tightly. He positions them on either side of the baby's blankets.

"Are you happy?" he asks, lying back on the bed, patting the spot next to him.

"Yes. And for your information, your shoes do *not* smell like cotton candy."

"Whaaaat?"

"Unless the cotton candy sugar manufacturers came out with a new flavor called dirty gym-sock funk, and I just didn't get the memo."

"Get over here so I can give you a spanking," he says, pointing at the bed.

I smile and walk over, moving my hips suggestively from side to side. "You'd better watch out. I've got a Toyota and I ain't afraid to use it."

He tries to grab me, making me shriek. I dance out of the way just in time.

"Shush!" he says, reaching for me more gently. "You're going to wake the baby."

I lie down next to him, placing my face on his chest. I run my hand over his tight ab muscles.

"Aw, damn," he says, reaching down to rub his leg.

"What's wrong?" I look up at his face.

"My knee. It's killing me."

"Poor baby. You were running pretty fast earlier. It was impressive, actually."

"Yeah, I'm a stud, what can I say."

I nudge him and smile.

"Adrenaline makes it easier, though, I have to admit. Now I'm paying for it."

"You're going to be really sorry tomorrow." I lift my head to look at him. "Do you have any pills I can get for you?" I wish there was something I could do. His injury is worse because he put taking care of me ahead of his own health and comfort.

"I already took what I can for now."

I put my head back down, snuggling into his side. "When are you going to get surgery?"

"I don't know. When this is all over."

"Are you going to last that long?"

"Trust me. I've got stamina." He squeezes me suggestively.

"That sounds like fun. *Stamina.*"

He strokes my side and pulls my butt in toward him. "I'll show you one day, if you behave yourself."

I sigh. "I've never been very good at behaving myself."

"That's all right. I don't want you to behave too much."

For a long time, we remain silent and I think he's fallen asleep. "Thibault?" I whisper.

"Yes?" he whispers back.

"I'm worried about something." Knowing we might not have long together and that my days might be numbered makes it easier for me to share one of my deepest fears with him.

"About what, other than the obvious?"

"I'm worried about Tee. About who his father is."

"Are you worried about him getting custody? Because I don't think you need to. No judge in the world would give the baby to a criminal like him."

"No, that's not what I mean. I mean . . . he's got Pavel's DNA. What if he . . . I don't know . . . has criminal tendencies?" I let out a long sigh. "I love my baby so much, and I hate having these thoughts in my head. It's so not fair to him."

Thibault pulls my head in and kisses it. "Not every baby is created out of a loving union. And who knows what turned Pavel into who he is? Maybe he was treated like an animal, and if someone had been nicer, he wouldn't have turned out to be such a bad guy. Whatever. We don't need to worry about him. Baby Tee came about as a result of a violent act, but that doesn't mean there's anything wrong with him or that his future isn't one hundred percent bright. He was born a perfect, innocent angel, and he's going to be raised by an amazing woman. He's going to be a great kid; I can already see it in him."

I'm tempted to cry over his kindness, because until I met him I didn't have much of that in my life, but instead I laugh. The joy I'm feeling won't let the tears come. "You're crazy. He's only opened his eyes two times in front of you."

"Yeah, but I was there when he was born, and I've spent five solid days with his mom, and I can tell you that he's got a really tough lady looking out for him, and she's going to teach him the difference between right and wrong, between love and hate, between respect and disrespect. He's going to be fine. Just like you."

I want so badly for Thibault to be right. "You have a lot of faith in me."

"You have a lot of faith in you too. I've seen it in action. No one can break your spirit; it's too strong."

"Sometimes I have faith in me and sometimes I don't."

"Well, whenever you don't, you can just ask me for a pep talk."

I almost don't say what I'm thinking, and then I just figure—what the hell—why not go for broke? "Should I call you or just nudge you?" I ask.

"You can nudge me."

I put my arms around him and hug him tight, tilting my head so I can see his face. We just took a step closer to what feels like a cliff together—a ledge so high up I can't see what's below it—and all he's doing is smiling at me. "You're crazy."

"We're both crazy."

"I love crazy," I whisper.

"Me too."

CHAPTER THIRTY-FIVE

Thibault wakes up as the sun is rising, sliding his arm out from under my neck, trying not to wake me. I was up twice with the baby during the night, and I can barely keep my eyes open, but I'm too scared to sleep. I watch him go to the window and flick the curtain back.

Headlights swing into the parking lot.

"Who's that?" I ask, sitting up.

"I recognize the car. It's someone from my team." He drops the curtain back into place and strides over to the bathroom. I can hear him running water and rinsing his mouth. I hurry and fix my clothing, smoothing down my hair with the comb I put in the diaper bag.

Thibault walks over to the door and waits for a very slight tap that comes just a minute later. He taps once so lightly in response it could be mistaken for a sound in the night.

A man's deep voice comes through the door. "It's me."

Thibault looks at me. "Ozzie." He opens the door, revealing not just Ozzie, but Jenny, too. She's carrying a laptop.

"Surprised to see me?" She comes in first, stopping to kiss Thibault on the cheek and patting him on the shoulder before she continues into the room. She puts her computer down on the little table and opens it up, taking a seat immediately. She glances across the room and waves her fingers at me. "Hi," she whispers, glancing at the sleeping baby.

"Hey." Ozzie holds out his hand and Thibault shakes it. Then he gets pulled into a half embrace. They smack each other on the back a few times before Ozzie comes into the room the rest of the way so Thibault can shut the door. He locks it behind him.

"All good in here?" Ozzie whispers.

"Yeah. We had a rough night with the baby, but we're good."

The four of us look at the bed where the little stinker is sleeping peacefully. You'd never know how effectively somebody that tiny can rule your world until you experience it in person. I'm still a little shocked at how awful sleep deprivation can be.

"I've got some things in the trunk for you, but I don't think you're going to be here for very long so I left them there," Ozzie says.

Jenny says, "I'm just logging on to that cloud account real quick using a VPN so nobody can trace it back to us over here."

"Did anybody happen to bring a toothbrush?" I ask, smacking my lips. My mouth tastes terrible.

Jenny pulls her purse off the back of the chair and holds it out at me. "Everything you should need is in here."

"Thanks." Thibault starts to hobble over to get the bag, but Ozzie cuts him off. He grabs the bag and brings it over to me. "You doing okay?"

I look up at him, taking in his height and breadth. It's impressive. "I feel better now, to be honest." I look at Thibault quickly, hoping he doesn't take offense at that. "Not that I didn't feel good with Thibault here to take care of me, but the more the merrier, right?"

"Absolutely." Ozzie tips his head toward the bathroom. "Feel free to go do your thing. We've got about a half hour."

"Half hour before what?" I pause at the bathroom door, waiting for his answer.

"I had a long conversation with the chief last night after midnight. NOPD. And then he got on the horn with some of his contacts at the FBI. Apparently there's a team working on it now, with Holloway acting as point at the NOPD, and they want to talk to you."

"What did you tell them?" Thibault asks.

"Not much. I wanted to talk to you guys first. But I did agree to a tentative meeting." Ozzie looks at his watch. "It's supposed to take place at oh-eight-hundred hours at a diner down off Highway 10."

"How far away?" Thibault asks.

"Twenty miles, give or take."

"Okay," I say. "I can be ready by then." I walk into the bathroom, but I leave the door open partway.

"So what's up?" Thibault asks.

"Let's wait for Mika. She needs to weigh in," Ozzie says.

"Okay. But I think she's ready to dive into this thing and get it done."

"Yeah!" I say around my toothbrush. "I'm ready!" *As ready as I'll ever be.*

"Oh, yeah?" Ozzie's voice carries a challenge. I pause with my brushing. *Is he talking to me?*

"Did I miss something?" Jenny asks.

"Maybe," Thibault says. He sounds unsure of himself. I slow down my teeth-brushing so I can be sure to hear.

"What's going on, Thibault?" Jenny asks. "You look like you've got a lot on your mind."

"I do, but now is not really the time to talk about it. We have other priorities." There's silence, and then Thibault speaks again. "What?" He sounds defensive.

"You got involved, didn't you?" Ozzie asks.

I nearly choke on my toothpaste foam. *They know I can hear them, right?* I step to the side a little so they'll see me more clearly as I lean over and spit into the sink. Maybe they didn't realize I left the door open, but surely with the water running that was obvious . . .

"Of course I got involved. Look where I am."

"That's not what I'm talking about, and you know it."

"Wait a minute. Are you mad at him?" Jenny asks. "I don't get it. What happened?"

"He got involved with a client. That's not something we encourage at Bourbon Street Boys."

I quickly rinse my mouth out. I need to defend Thibault. To explain . . .

"It's not like I had a choice," he says. "That stuff just happens sometimes." He sighs. "I was minding my own business, and then out of the blue there she was, and suddenly I was delivering her baby. You don't come away from that without having some sort of emotional attachment."

I dry my mouth and turn off the water. It feels like time has slowed. *What are they thinking? Do they hate me for bringing him into my problems, for making him have feelings for me? Do they think I somehow tricked him? Made this happen? Have ulterior motives?*

Jenny's voice is kind. "Aww, that's so sweet. Honestly, I didn't know you had it in you, Thibault."

Her easy acceptance dissolves some of the tension in my chest. I step out of the bathroom and clear my throat to make sure they know I'm there.

"What's that supposed to mean?" Thibault asks.

None of them acknowledges my presence. I have the weirdest sensation of being a fly on the wall.

"Come on, you know . . . ," Jenny says, finally glancing over at me before she continues. "You're always such a tough guy about everything. I just figured you were going to be a confirmed bachelor . . . Single for the rest of your life."

"Do you hear her?" Thibault says to Ozzie, sounding incredulous.

"Yeah, I heard her. And I felt the same way."

"What? You guys think I have a heart of stone? That I'm some kind of player or something?" He turns and looks at me as if I have an explanation for their behavior. All I can do is shrug.

"No, no, nooo," Jenny says. She gets up and moves closer to him. "I didn't mean that at all. Don't be mad. You just seemed so focused on work, and then the only other people you had time for in your life were Melanie and Victor. You don't even like coming to the pizza parties."

"What are you talking about? I like the pizza parties." He sounds almost hurt by her accusation.

Ozzie snorts. "Be honest."

"What? Come on, I *like* the pizza parties." His voice downshifts. "Okay, so they're a little loud and there're a lot of kids running around . . . But I like kids."

There's a long pause while they all look at one other and then down at Tee watching from the bed. For once his eyes are open.

"Jesus, you guys *know* I like kids. I'm Melanie's and Victor's favorite uncle."

"That's true," Jenny says, looking at Ozzie and then me. "He is their favorite uncle."

"He's their *only* uncle," Ozzie says dryly.

"Yeah, but even if there were ten guys lining up with uncle status, I'd still be number one." He sounds very proud of himself.

"You're right," Jenny says. "You're absolutely right. I'm sorry I judged you the way I did. That was unfair of me."

"I've known you for a long time," Ozzie says after a long pause.

"Yeah. So?" Thibault is on the defensive.

"I've never seen you go soft on anybody like you are with this girl." He looks at me. "No offense."

I raise my hands. "None taken." Not really. I can appreciate their protective feelings toward him. If he were my best friend, I wouldn't

267

want him hanging around with me, either. I'd want to keep him far, far away from any and all bad influences, because he's a pretty special guy.

"I'm not going soft." Thibault comes over and takes me by the hand, pulling me farther into the room. My heart is racing. I can't believe he's standing up for me. "I just care about Mika and Tee. I worry about them, and I want to make sure they're okay. Is there something wrong with that?"

"And then what?" Ozzie asks. "Are you gonna walk away?" He looks at me. "Are you?"

I open my mouth to respond, to assure them that I'm not going to hurt this man who's being so kind to me, but Thibault beats me to it.

"I don't know." He sounds uncomfortable. He lets go of my hand and crosses his arms over his chest. "I guess we'll see when that happens."

I feel terrible that he's being forced into this conversation that he clearly doesn't want to have. My stress level is rocketing upward. Tee starts to wiggle around, a prelude to fussing.

"I don't think it's going to be that simple," Ozzie says. "Not this time. Not in this situation."

"What do you mean?" Thibault sounds suspicious.

"This is an FBI case. They need her to testify."

"So? She'll testify."

"Her life is going to be in danger for the foreseeable future. She's going to have to go into protective custody."

My ears are burning. I already know all this, but hearing him say it and putting Thibault on the spot with it is making me feel sick to my stomach and in my heart.

"Fine. I'll just . . . I don't know." He sounds disgusted. "Maybe I'll go with her. I'll take a leave of absence and help her get settled in. Or maybe I'll stay. I don't know."

I have to work to keep my mouth shut and the tears away. First I hit him with my car, and now I've forced him into a corner: walk away from a promise to me or a lifetime of friendship. For another man, it might be an easy decision, but not for this one. I hate that I've put him in this position.

"For how long?" Ozzie asks. "These cases can go on for years."

"Do you really think you could leave Bourbon Street Boys for a couple years?" Jenny asks, sounding shocked.

"I don't know." He's flustered.

I've heard enough. He's feeling pressured and stressed and it isn't fair. He and I both know that he's not going to come into a witness protection program with me. We've only known each other for a few days. It wouldn't be right of me to expect that of him, even though I think what we've started between us is something pretty damn special.

I walk over and pick up the baby. "Hello there, little angel. Are you hungry?" I sit down on the edge of the bed and start unzipping my jacket. This situation has gotten out of hand. I need to rein it in, and the only way I know how to do that right now is to pull out a boob.

"Let's talk about this later," Thibault says, stepping to the side and blocking Ozzie's view of what I'm doing.

"I'll be ready in five minutes," I say, lacing my voice with as much false cheer as I can muster.

"We'll be waiting in the car," Ozzie says, turning toward the door and heading across the room. Part of me wants to hate that man, but I can't. He's being a great friend and a smart business partner. I would be doing the same thing if it were me.

I try to pack up the diaper bag while also holding Tee.

Thibault comes over. "Let me help you," he says.

I put my hand on his arm to stop him. "I got it," I say. "Just go. I'll be right there."

"We'll catch up," Jenny says, nodding at me.

"Can we talk about this?" he asks gently.

The baby won't latch on. He's too tired. I shake my head and stand up. "Let's just go."

I zip myself up and walk out the door ahead of him with Jenny as he gathers our things. I feel like I'm leaving my best possible future behind in that motel room.

CHAPTER THIRTY-SIX

We park behind the back door of the diner and split up into two groups, Thibault with me and the baby, and Ozzie and Jenny together. Ozzie and Jenny enter the restaurant first, sending Thibault a text to let us know it's all clear, and then we follow. I'm beyond nervous, droplets of sweat gathering at my temples. I feel sick.

"Don't worry, Mika," Thibault says as we walk slowly around the side of the restaurant. He doesn't have his crutches, so he's limping pretty badly. "You've got us here with you. You're not alone."

"Yeah, but this is the FBI. This is way more than I bargained for." When someone works with the FBI in the movies, it never ends well.

"They're nothing special. Just federal-level cops. The only difference between them and the NOPD cops you see every day on the street is the feds wear suits. That's it."

"I'm feeling really out of my element."

"Your element is with me, and I'm right here." He opens the door and waits for me to go inside, taking the baby seat from my hand as I walk by.

I really wish that were true. I want to be with him, in his element, starting a new and exciting life by his side. Too bad it's not in the cards for us.

"Are you ready for this?" he asks.

I nod, even though I'm not. "Let's do it."

We make our way over to a round table in the corner of the diner where Ozzie and Jenny are sitting with two men—only one of them is wearing a suit. There are two empty chairs.

When we arrive at the edge of the table, the two FBI agents stand. Ozzie and the agents have their backs to the wall. Thibault gestures for me to take the seat next to Jenny, which I'm happy to do because it means that Jenny and Thibault are on either side of me, sheltering me from direct contact with the agents. It gives me a mental boost to have them there. Jenny cares very much for Thibault, and he respects the heck out of her, so I feel like I can trust her too. I put the baby seat on the floor right next to my chair, well out of the way of floor traffic.

The agent in the suit holds out his hand. "Ms. Cleary, I assume?"

I shake his hand. "That's me."

"Nice to meet you. I'm Special Agent Vanderwahl. Thanks for coming so early in the morning."

I nod and shake the other guy's hand. "Special Agent Booker," he says.

Agent Vanderwahl smiles and holds his tie against his stomach as he sits. "We're working a case that involves someone I think you know." He gestures at my chair. "Go ahead and sit down. And feel free to order breakfast, too. Our treat."

"Thanks," I say, taking my seat, "but I'm not really hungry."

Thibault leans in close to me and talks softly in my ear. "Can I get you some juice? You really need to put something in your stomach."

I nod. "Thanks." I reach under the table and squeeze his hand, letting him know I appreciate his thoughtfulness. I may be entering into a deal with the FBI to turn in a murderer, but he's going to make sure I still get my vitamins. He's such a sweet guy; it breaks my heart that I'm going to have to leave him behind.

Thibault signals for the waitress and takes care of ordering himself some coffee, me some juice, and both of us some toast. He also throws in an order of fruit and cottage cheese, which I'm guessing is for me too. I might even try to eat some of it just to make him feel better, although I don't know how I'm even going to swallow anything, since I feel like I'm going to vomit at any moment.

Once everybody has their orders in, most of it beverages, the agents put their forearms on the table and lean in. Agent Vanderwahl's jacket bunches up at his shoulders.

"I'm going to cut right to the chase," he says. "You've got some information about an individual we've been trying to nail down for a long time. We'd like to know what it is you have exactly, and then once we know whether it's something we can use, perhaps we can make you an offer that will make this easier for you."

I'm instantly suspicious. "Make *what* easier for me?"

Thibault slides his foot over and slowly taps mine with it. I do the same back. It feels so good to have his support.

"Let me start over." Vanderwahl gives me a cheesy smile and continues. "The individual we're looking at is Pavel Baranovsky. He's originally from Moscow and moved here as a teenager. He began participating in the local drug trade at the age of nineteen and then quickly graduated to managing large swathes of several downtown districts in New Orleans and also certain areas of Baton Rouge. We now believe his operations extend into forty states and six foreign countries."

I press my lips together but say nothing. I worry that I don't have everything they want, because as far as I know, he's entirely based in Louisiana.

"All we have are rumors, though. We have no hard data. It came to our attention not long ago, however, that he was using a local girl to do his books for him."

The two agents look at each other and smile. The second one, Booker, joins in. "Imagine that. A Russian guy, whose entire network is made up of other Russian guys, hires a girl from New Orleans to keep track of all his money." They both keep smiling and shrugging their shoulders at each other.

Vanderwahl looks back at me. "Can you explain that?"

I feel like I'm being accused of something, but I have no idea what. "No, I can't explain that."

Thibault puts his hand on mine. "Are you guys trying to say something about Mika or Pavel? Because it sounds like you're accusing her of something."

He heard the insinuation, too. I wasn't imagining it. Relief floods through me, knowing he has my back.

Booker tries to look innocent, shrugging his shoulders. "No, not at all. We're just wondering how something like that happens."

They stare intently at me, and they don't exactly look friendly.

Thibault turns to look at me, speaking softly directly into my ear so no one else will hear him. "Can you tell them how you ended up in that position?"

I shake my head. How I got there is none of their damn business. And I don't want to have the conversation in front of Thibault's friends, either.

"I want them to be on your side," he whispers. "You need to say something."

I look at him, my eyes filling up with tears. I feel like I'm being stripped down and exposed to everyone in the restaurant. I speak from behind closed teeth. "I don't want to."

"It's up to you," he says.

I see such kindness in his eyes. And zero judgment. Thibault doesn't hold it against me that I sold my body to survive. So why should I care? None of these other people matter to me. I look down at my baby's innocent face, and my life becomes very clear to me all of a sudden. I only care about three people at this table: my baby, myself, and the man who's sworn to protect me, Thibault. No one else matters.

"I wasn't always keeping his books," I say, looking up at the agents. "In the beginning, I was one of the girls who was working for him in another capacity."

The two men are trying to figure out what I'm saying. Then the lightbulb seems to go on above the suit.

"Are you saying you're a prostitute?"

The word hits me like a slap. Thibault puts his hand on top of mine.

"No. I'm saying I *was* a prostitute."

"Oh." The two agents share a look.

"Is that a problem?"

Vanderwahl answers. "No, I wouldn't say it's a *problem*, but we do need to make a determination as to how reliable your information is."

"So, what . . . You're saying that because I used to sell my body for sex, I'm now an unreliable person, and you can't believe anything I say? You think all prostitutes are liars?"

Thibault squeezes my hand. Jenny glares at the agent. Ozzie's face is impassive, no emotion or thoughts readable there.

"Nobody said that. Not exactly." Vanderwahl looks to Booker, but Booker just shrugs.

"You sell yourself every day, but you don't admit it. At least I'm honest about it."

Booker's chin backs up into his neck. "What? That doesn't make any sense."

"Sure it does." I give him a lazy smile. "What did you have to do to get that job you got?"

"I went to school." He's looking at me with a very judgmental expression on his face.

"Oh really? So you never sucked up to anybody? You never put your values or your judgments to the side and substituted somebody else's for your own?" I pause and wait for him to think about that for a little while. His expression isn't quite as cocky as it was in the beginning. "You never made a decision to get that job that hurt your wife or your kids . . . Or you never sacrificed the happiness of somebody in your family for your own goals, your own ego, your own need to feel important?"

I look at Thibault. "Cops . . . they're all the same. They think they're better than those girls out on the streets, but they're prostitutes too." I look at Booker. "Everybody sells a piece of themselves sometime. Even you."

"I heard that," Jenny says under her breath.

Ozzie gives me the very slightest of nods.

I feel for just a moment as if I'm on their team. It's pretty heady stuff, knowing they're the good guys.

Vanderwahl clears his throat. "I think we're getting a little off track here. And I apologize if either one of us gave the impression that we didn't respect you for the choices you've made in your life."

Thibault's smiling. Out of the corner of my eye, I can see his white teeth glowing. But I keep my gaze locked on Booker. He's my problem. He's the one that'll cause something bad to happen to me. If he doesn't get with the program and get on my team, I'm done with these guys. I don't ask for a whole lot, but I at least deserve some respect. I'm sacrificing *everything* to be here. They're sacrificing *nothing*.

"So why are we here?" Ozzie asks. "How about we start there."

"That's easy," I say, looking at everyone around the table. "I have information, and these guys want it. But then what happens to me when I hand it over? Because I can promise you the minute Pavel finds out I gave you information that's going to hurt him, he's going to come after me. And believe me, he will find me, and then I'll be dead." My blood turns to ice in my veins. This is not an idle threat; it's fact.

Vanderwahl responds. "If the information you give us is deemed valuable enough by a prosecutor, and will result in the prosecution of Pavel and his associates, we'll be willing to offer you a place in our witness protection program."

Ozzie shakes his head. "No. It's Pavel *or* his associates, not *and*."

I'm glad he spoke up, because I missed that little detail.

Booker scowls at Ozzie. "Who are you? Her lawyer?"

"I'm a friend. That's all you need to know."

The two agents exchange a look I can't read.

"We can negotiate those points later," Vanderwahl says. "The question now remains: What is it exactly that you have?"

"How about if we start with me telling you what I want?" I sit up straight and put my hands on the table in front of me, folding them together.

"If that's what you prefer." Vanderwahl sits back, resting his hands on the arms of his chair. "Go ahead. We're listening."

"First of all, I need protection. I need to know that my baby and I are safe." Before Booker can interrupt, I hold up a finger. "And . . . I need you to find somebody for me."

The two agents exchange a look and then turn to face me. "Find someone?" Vanderwahl asks.

"Yes. I have a friend who's a relative of Pavel's. He disappeared, and I need you to find him. He's innocent in all this garbage. He's not a criminal."

"If we can find him, we will, but we can't guarantee anything," Booker says.

I shrug and sit back. "As soon as you find him, I'll give you what you want . . . whatever you need to put Pavel in prison. But until then, I've got nothing to say."

Jenny holds up a finger. "I think I can help you out on this."

Everybody switches their focus to her. Jenny looks up and gives us a nervous smile before pulling out her laptop computer from a case by her chair and opening it up. "I just have some notes right here . . . give me a minute."

Our group goes silent. The sounds of the cooks in the kitchen banging pots and pans around and silverware hitting plates mingle with the murmur of other diners' voices, but everyone sitting at our table just stares at Jenny.

She's totally focused on her screen as she talks. "We got some information about Alexei earlier, so I did some searching and found a few things."

I sit up straight and lean toward Jenny, my pulse picking up. "Did you find him?"

"I might have." She glances up at us and shares a little smile before going back to her computer.

"Alexei Baranovsky, born July 8, 1995. Last known location: New Orleans, Louisiana."

I reach under the table and take Thibault's hand in mine. My palms are clammy, but he doesn't seem to mind. He holds me, stroking my wrist slowly. It helps to calm me.

"He has a bank account funded by deposits that come in once a month from an offshore account in the Cayman Islands. This appears to be his main source of financial support. There have been several ATM transactions on this account, two as recently as yesterday."

"How are you accessing that information?" Booker asks.

Jenny glances up at him but then goes back to her computer screen. "All the withdrawals were taken from the same machine, which is located at Chase Bank on Jefferson Highway."

I frown at her. "That's over by the west side of town. That's nowhere near my apartment or where he stays with Pavel."

"What else do you have?" Thibault asks.

She looks up and closes the lid on her computer. "That's it. I don't have access to the surveillance at that ATM. I could probably get it eventually, but I didn't have time."

"Are you conducting illegal searches and accessing servers without permission or warrants?" Booker asks.

She points delicately at her chest. "Who, me? No." She shakes her head. "I would never do that."

Hope strikes me like a lightning bolt right in my heart. She can find Alexei. If she can do this in such a short period of time, and tap into the things she shouldn't have access to like I know she did, I have no doubt. I feel almost dizzy. She just needs more time.

Ozzie breaks in. "Point is, I think we can find Alexei or at least the person who's accessing his accounts." He looks over at me. "Is that enough for now?"

Everybody is staring at me. The table goes quiet again.

The waitress comes over just at that moment to deliver the food, coffee, and juices, effectively breaking the tension. Booker turns to Vanderwahl and says, "I thought that woman, Son—"

Vanderwahl cuts him off, glaring. "Later. We'll look into it later."

My body goes stiff. *Booker almost said Sonia!* I *know* he did. I dig my nails into Thibault's hand hard enough to make him flinch. If Sonia is talking to the FBI, what the hell does that mean? Only one thing as far as I can see: she's still trying to sell me out. And why would she be doing that with these two guys unless they were *against* me? Sonia told Pavel where I was so he could come get me and the baby. If she'd succeeded, I'd probably be dead now, and my baby would be all alone with that monster. *No* . . . Sonia working with Booker and Vanderwahl can't mean anything good. I don't like this at all. I don't trust them.

"Do they have any popcorn on the menu here?" I blurt out.

Jenny looks at me and frowns. "Popcorn? I don't know. I didn't see any." She looks at Ozzie. "Did you?"

Ozzie looks over at me with exaggerated patience. "Popcorn?"

I nod my head vigorously. "It's a craving. I get them from time to time." I look down at Tee and then at everyone else. "I think it's a post-pregnancy thing, maybe?"

Thibault detaches his arm from my clawed hand and stands, pulling his chair out while balancing on one leg. "I think we need to go change the baby's diaper. He stinks. We can order popcorn later."

I'm so relieved I feel dizzy. I half-expected him to look at me like I was crazy, or try to convince me to calm down. But he's standing up and abandoning a meeting with the FBI just because I said the word *popcorn*. I want to cry with happiness.

Everybody looks down at the car seat, where Baby Tee is sound asleep. Poor little guy, taking the fall for our escape plan with a poopy diaper—a tiny superhero in his own right.

I join Thibault, pushing my chair out. "I know." I wave my hand in front of my face, really trying to sell them on the stinky diaper plan. "Phew! I thought I was the only one who smelled it. I'm so sorry." I look up at Thibault. "I don't want to spoil everybody's breakfast. Can you help me? You know I'm terrible at the diaper-changing thing, still." I look at the agents, trying to seem like an airhead. "I'm a new mom. I still don't know what I'm doing." Hopefully they can't do the math and realize I've already changed about fifty of the damn things.

Thibault gestures toward the bathrooms. "After you."

"You grab the diaper bag, and I'll get the baby," I say.

Thibault gives Ozzie and Jenny a quick lift of his chin. "I'll be right back. Don't talk about *anything important* while we're gone, okay?"

"Nothing important," Ozzie says. "We got it." He nods at Jenny and she nods back. He's way cooler about it than she is. I'm no Bourbon Street Boy, but I'm pretty sure they just passed a code between them.

We go toward the bathroom as casually as we can. I glance over my shoulder a few times, and up until the moment we get to the ladies' room door, Vanderwahl and Booker are watching us, but then Jenny knocks over her glass of juice, throwing the liquid across the table.

Everyone jumps up to avoid getting splashed, and Thibault nudges me toward the kitchen door during the confusion. I run inside without questioning him. He follows behind and looks through the little portal window as the door is shutting.

"Did they see?" I ask.

"Nobody saw a thing; they're still mopping up juice, and now the waitress is in the way of anyone watching the doors."

"What are we doing?" I ask as he hustles me to the back door, past two bored-looking cooks and several racks of pots and pans.

"We're leaving. You wanted to leave, right?"

"Hell, yes. They know Sonia. Booker almost said her name. There's something going on. Maybe they're not agents. Maybe they're moles. Maybe they're on Pavel's payroll. Maybe Sonia is double-crossing someone. I don't know and I don't care. I don't trust them."

We get to the back door and I stop, putting my hand on his arm. "You trust me." I want to cry with the knowledge, with the emotions rushing through me.

"Of course I do."

"You just got up and did what I asked without questioning me." I can't believe this is real.

"That's what we do when we trust each other, right?"

I grab him into a one-armed hug. "Thank you."

He pats me on the back and then steps sideways to open the door. "We can talk more about it when we're out of here. Just get to the car as fast as you can. I'm right behind you."

CHAPTER THIRTY-SEVEN

W"e're not going back to the motel?" I ask.

"No," Thibault says, driving out onto the highway going in the opposite direction I expected him to. "The FBI has way too many resources to risk it, and on the off chance that one of those agents is dirty, I'd rather be inconvenienced than killed." He reaches over to the far side of the dashboard and flicks a switch.

"What was that for?"

"I just disabled the navigation system in my car so it can't be used against us by someone really good with computers. The blocker doesn't come standard with these cars, but we've customized ours quite a bit."

"Oh. Where are we going now?" I look back to check on Tee. He's sound asleep.

"We're going to find another hotel and settle in. Toni can hook us up with a credit card." He glances over at me. "Don't worry. We've got this."

I half-smile. "I can't believe we just ran out of there."

"Me neither."

"I swear he was going to say the name Sonia. That's my other roommate. The one who doesn't like me, who dates Pavel. But why would they be talking to her? And if they are, why would she sell me out?"

"I have no idea. And maybe he wasn't going to say Sonia. Maybe he was going to say Sonny or Sony television."

I laugh. "Are you serious?"

He smiles weakly. "No, not really. But it doesn't matter. You weren't comfortable, and they weren't exactly being respectful, so that's it. We can try again another time if you want."

"Do you think they're working together?" I ask. I can't just let it go like he wants me to. It's bugging me that her name came up when we were talking about Alexei.

He shrugs as we drive along a secondary road not as convenient as the highway but probably less likely to be used by federal agents. "It's hard to say. It could have just been an innocent comment. Maybe their supervisor is named Sonia. Or maybe they were talking about somebody else with a similar name. It doesn't matter; I'd rather be safe than sorry, and I trust your instincts. I trust *you*."

We share a smile. It feels like I just passed a milemarker in my life at the same time we're passing them on the road.

"Me, too. And I trust you too. Completely."

He reaches back, and we hold hands for a few seconds.

His phone rings, so he lets go of me to answer it. "It's Ozzie." He presses the green button and puts it to his ear. "Hey there. Sorry we had to take off."

Ozzie says something I can't hear now. The sound of the road on the tires is too loud, and the baby starts to fuss. I occupy myself with calming Tee down while listening in on Thibault's half of the conversation. "No, not cold feet. One of those guys said something about Sonia, maybe. He only got half the name out. That spooked her. Sonia is the name of her roommate—a girlfriend or former girlfriend of Pavel's. If she's involved in their investigation somehow, it can't possibly be good for Mika . . . We're going to find someplace to lie low."

He hangs up the phone and looks at me in the mirror. "Ozzie's cool. He understands."

"What are they going to do?"

"They're going to talk to the team and come up with a plan B."

Ten minutes go by before I can get Tee to go back to sleep and focus on Thibault again.

"You know, I don't mind talking to the FBI, as long as I know it's not somebody working with Pavel's group."

"I get it, I really do." He reaches back and pats my leg. "We'll figure this out. My team is good."

"I can't believe Jenny already found Alexei or somebody using his account. She's really good, isn't she?"

"Yes, she is."

"They're not mad we took off?"

"That's what we do, we back each other up. Always. And of course they're not mad. Why would they be? They trust me and I trust you. Shit happens. You can't be good at security if don't know how to roll with the punches."

The baby starts fussing again. "His cheeks look really pink to me. Do they look pink to you?"

He adjusts the rearview mirror to look at him. "I can't see his face with the car seat facing the back."

I place my hand on Tee's forehead. "He feels warm to me. I think he has a fever."

"Great, just what we needed," he says, hissing out a breath and shaking his head.

"Don't be mad." I feel terrible. I've been nothing but a burden to him since the moment our paths crossed.

Thibault looks at me in the mirror. "I'm not mad. I'm just worried about him. And I'm worried about you too."

I put my hand on his shoulder, appreciating the fact that he cares. "I'm really glad you're with me. I'm sad that I brought you into this, but I'm happy to not be alone anymore."

"You don't need to be sad about anything. I'm here voluntarily."

"I hope you don't live to regret it."

"The only thing I'd live to regret is walking away from you and Tee. That would be the biggest mistake of my life, I'm sure of it."

I don't say anything else. I'm too choked up over his dedication to me and my child—who I'm pretty sure is sick. And Thibault was right . . . I didn't fill out Tee's birth certificate, and I have no proof he's mine. How will we find a doctor to take care of him? What if social services gets called and they take him away from me? Pavel will come and then everything will be lost.

CHAPTER THIRTY-EIGHT

An hour later, after taking several side roads and rural routes, we find a run-down little hotel that accepts cash. Thibault calls Ozzie as soon as we're settled into the room. I try to feed the baby, but he's not having it. He's very upset and he's burning up.

"I hate to be the bearer of more bad news, because I think I've brought my fair share lately, but the baby is sick," Thibault says over his phone. "We need to find a doctor who makes house calls."

He pauses.

"I know. Tell me about it."

Ozzie says something I can't hear.

"I don't know. He's got a fever and he's real fussy."

Thibault paces on his bad leg, limping from the bathroom to the front door.

"I know. And on top of that, Mika hasn't filled out a birth certificate on the baby yet, so if there's any kind of problem at all, she has no proof whatsoever that he's hers until somebody runs a DNA test. It could turn into a real nightmare." He pauses. "Is there any chance that your friend Teddy is available? Your old wingman?" Thibault looks out the window. "We're out here in the middle of nowhere. I'm sure I could find a field somewhere. We could come to him."

Thibault nods at whatever Ozzie says. "I'll be waiting for your call."

I'm too worried about the baby to question anything being said or planned. But I trust that Thibault is going to take care of us, so I focus on trying to get Tee to eat while Thibault manages things in the background.

CHAPTER THIRTY-NINE

"You want me to *what*?" I ask, upon hearing his plan.

Thibault laughs. "You're looking at me like I just sprouted a second head and asked you to run away and join the circus with me." He pauses and takes me by the hands. "It's the only way. That Motrin isn't working." We both glance down at the baby in my arms. His face is bright red and his eyes are swollen from crying. Cold rags on his forehead aren't doing a damn thing, either. "We've got to get to the doctor fast, and if we drive, it's going to take hours. You know we can't just walk into the hospital. It's too risky. We have to go see our guy. He'll take care of Tee and get him all fixed up in no time."

"Yeah, but . . ."

"Do you trust me?" He drops the smile and waits for my answer.

I glare at him. "No fair playing dirty."

"Hey, it's just a question. Do you trust me or not?"

I whine. "Yes, I trust you . . . But a *helicopter*?"

"It's really easy. We just drive out a little ways until we find an empty field, send Ozzie and Teddy the GPS coordinates, and they'll be there in a half hour. Easy peasy, lemon squeezy."

"Who's Teddy?"

"Teddy's the pilot. He's great. You'll love him when you meet him. He served in the military with Ozzie overseas. He's the best."

"Yeah, but then you're gonna want me to get *in* the helicopter. That's the part I'm having a problem with . . . Easy peasy, I get queasy."

"You've never been in a helicopter before?"

"I've never even been on an *airplane* before, and those have, like, really big seating areas in them and really big wings and lots of gas and engines and stuff . . ."

"So you're worried about it crashing? Is that the problem?"

"Yeah. Isn't that what everybody's worried about when they get in something that flies?"

"I guess. But this isn't going to crash."

"Because you can guarantee that. You just know. It's a fact in your world." I look at him like he's crazy, because he obviously is.

"Yes. I can guarantee it. Because even if the engine goes out, the propellers are still going to turn and the pilot can do a nice controlled landing."

"You're nuts."

He puts his arms around me and pulls me and Tee into him, touching his forehead to mine. "I am nuts. You *make* me nuts. Now would you please, for once in your life, just listen to me and do what I say without arguing?"

"That's probably never going to happen."

He kisses me gently on the lips. "I know. But you need to get on that helicopter."

"Fine," I say, sighing. "But if it crashes, I'm going to haunt you and my baby's going to haunt you too."

"Okay. I accept your terms." He pulls away from me to take his cell out of his pocket. "It's a go," he says. No hello or anything else. He hangs up the phone and slides it into his pocket.

"Ozzie's a man of few words, isn't he?"

"You could say that."

"You're different when you're around him than when you're around me."

"I sure hope so." He holds both sides of my face and kisses me again.

"What do you mean by that?" I gaze up at him.

"Because Ozzie's my friend, not the woman I care about in a romantic way, so of course I'm going to act differently when I'm with him than when I'm with you."

I want to talk more about this liking me "in a romantic way" thing, but the baby is fussing again, so I start pacing the room, trying to get him to latch on. He begins to and then pulls away, crying. It's stressing me out worse than anything I've ever felt before. "He's not doing well. He's not even eating now."

"Don't worry. We've got this." Thibault checks his watch. "We need to go find ourselves a field so they know where to pick us up."

I wander toward the door, all my attention on the baby. "I'm going to trust you on this one."

He grabs the diaper bag and his duffel and limps to the door. His crutches are waiting for him at the entrance. He grabs them too, using them after he slings both bags over his shoulders.

"Stay right here and let me make sure everything's okay." He opens the door and sticks his head out. Then he pops it back in and smiles. "Nothing out here but cicadas and dust."

I follow him quickly to the SUV and get in the back with Tee. We drive until Thibault finds a field that he deems suitable—big enough to host the landing of a small helicopter. He sends a text to Ozzie with the GPS coordinates.

"What do we do now?" I look at the dirt field all around us. I'm sad. Scared. Worried that everything I've put us through is going to amount to nothing when Pavel finds me and takes Tee away. *What if there's something seriously wrong with Tee? What if this doctor can't fix it?*

"We wait. And hope that nobody's tapped into Ozzie's phone." He drags his duffel bag over and pulls out his holster and gun, strapping them onto his body.

Seeing him with the weapon really brings things home. "You're starting to scare me."

He looks at me over the front seat. "Don't be scared. I'm here and I'm one of the good guys."

I try to smile. "It's probably naïve of me, but that does make me feel better."

He smiles back at me. "Not naïve. Hopeful."

"Yeah. You make me hopeful."

"Ditto." He turns to watch through the windshield for the approach of a tiny black speck on the horizon. I stare at his profile, wondering how I got so lucky to make that wrong turn.

CHAPTER FORTY

The helicopter ride is nothing to Thibault, but it's a huge freak-out moment for me. The round windows give me too much of a view and make me think we're suspended over the earth by a string. Everything is buzzing by way too fast—buildings, farms, tractors, animals, cars . . . It's like watching a movie in fast-forward, and I'm worried about the ending. *Will we crash? Will we die in a fiery inferno?*

I don't die, but the landing is the worst part. I glare at Thibault as we make our way across the big, mostly empty hangar after it's over. "I am never, *ever* going to do that again. Do you hear me? You told me that when the engine cuts off, they do a nice, smooth landing."

Thibault is trying not to smile. "The engine didn't cut off. It was running just fine."

"If I hadn't had my seat belt on, I would've been thrown right out of the thing onto the tarmac."

"But you did have your seat belt on."

I refuse to argue with him about it anymore, but he'd better have another way for me to get wherever we're going, because I am *not* getting back in that machine. The pilot looks like a crazy person with a big, scraggly beard. His hat is made out of animal fur with the tail and legs still attached. It looks like a raccoon is taking a nap on his head.

Ozzie is waiting in the darkness of the hangar, and there's a guy wearing a golf shirt standing next to him.

"That's Dr. Rainer," Thibault says quietly as we approach. "He's a pediatrician. He's seen Melanie and Victor before at Toni's place."

"A doctor who makes house calls? How did you manage that?"

"Ozzie has connections."

They're ready for me and the baby in the manager's office. It's not the cleanest place in the world, but the visit is quick.

"He has an ear infection," the doctor says, putting his equipment into a black leather bag. "This is completely normal in babies of this age. He's going to cry a lot, along with having a fever. He'll need antibiotics to kill the bug and more Motrin to bring the fever down. I brought several things with me just in case." He looks up at me. "Do you know if he has any allergies?"

"No, I don't. He's just a few days old. But I don't have any."

"Okay, I want you to start with this one." He holds up a bottle. "It's amoxicillin. You fill the bottle up to this line with water, shake it real good, and feed it to him with the dropper. Keep it refrigerated. If this doesn't work, or if you see him with a rash or having any trouble breathing, you give him some of this antihistamine and try this other one here. Same directions. Add water, et cetera."

I take both bottles from him and look at them closely. "What if he gets a rash with the second one?"

"Then you need to go to the hospital. I know you've got some kind of situation going on here, and I don't really want to know what it is, but if he breaks out in a rash after both of these different medications and he's having difficulty with his respiration, that's an emergency. You'll need to go somewhere that has all of the medications and equipment that a baby suffering an allergic reaction might need immediately."

"You're scaring me right now."

"I don't mean to do that. I know you're a new mom, and you're sensitive to this stuff. My professional opinion is that your son is going to be just fine. Like I said, this is normal. This happens to almost *all* babies. Just follow the instructions that I'm going to write down for you on this paper, give him the antibiotics for the full ten days, and he should be fine. I'll give you my cell phone number so you can call me anytime, night or day, if you have any questions."

"I will call you, you know. I'm not one of those polite people who won't call because I'm worried about bothering somebody."

He smiles. "That's fine. I wouldn't give you my number if I didn't want you to use it."

I look out the office door at Ozzie, who's standing by himself and staring at the flight line. "Thank you, Ozzie."

He looks over at me. "No problem."

Thibault leaves the office to talk to Ozzie. His voice carries right into the space where the doctor and I are sitting. I get up and walk out into the main part of the hangar so they'll know I'm there and that their conversation isn't private. Baby Tee isn't happy, so I busy myself with soothing him and trying to interest him in eating. Ozzie and Thibault's conversation filters into my brain like a television running in the background.

"So what am I supposed to do now?" Thibault asks.

"I think you need to talk to the NOPD. I've spoken with the chief. They're ready to take her in and keep her safe. I don't know what was going on with those guys at the diner. I don't know if they're legit or not, and I'm in no position to figure that out right now."

"We have connections over there."

"I know we do. But I thought these guys were good, and who knows if they are, so now I'm not sure I can trust anything that's happening over there right now. This guy Pavel . . . He's got his fingers in a lot of pies."

"Yeah. It's not worth the risk."

Ozzie looks at his friend. "This girl means something to you." He glances at me.

I think I'm supposed to hear this. I try not to stare at them, but I'm hanging on every word.

He nods. "Yes, she does." I can't see his expression, but I can hear the truth in his voice and in his face. "She's special. I'm not going to let her walk away. I can't."

It feels like a lightning bolt has hit my heart when I hear him say that. I turn away slightly so he won't see my face. Tears well up, but I'm smiling. I think it's wrong to be so happy that he feels this way about me, because it's only going to bring him more trouble, but I can't help it; the feelings between us are mutual. Fate has dealt us a mighty blow, causing us to meet when we can't possibly be together for long, but I can't work up the emotion to regret that.

Ozzie slaps him on the back. "I'm happy for you, man. Just do me a favor . . ."

"What's that?"

"Make sure you fall for the right reasons."

"What's that supposed to mean?"

He faces Thibault fully, and I have to pretend to be busy with the baby's blanket so he won't see that I'm eavesdropping like the desperate fool I am.

"You've been put in the extraordinary situation of helping a woman give birth to a baby. And she's not just any woman . . . She is the quintessential damsel in distress, running from the Russian mafia and all that comes with that. You've had a Superman complex since you were seven years old. I'm just sayin' . . ."

So his friend knows him that well. What a lucky man Thibault is, to have people like that in his life. It makes me care about him even more. I have not only my own experiences with him but confirmation from all these people of how special he is, people who the police trust and work with. It's confirmed: he's one of the good guys.

"Come on, man, give me a break. Enough . . . That joke has been played out." Thibault sounds mad.

"What costume did you wear for Halloween for five years running?"

I look up to see Thibault shrugging. "I don't know . . . Spider-Man?"

Ozzie shakes his head. "Nope."

"Batman?"

Ozzie starts to smile. "Nope."

"Aw, come on. I was *seven* years old."

"You were Superman when you were seven, eight, nine, ten, *and* eleven years old. And the only reason why you weren't Superman when you were twelve is because we stopped trick-or-treating at eleven."

"Lucky didn't. Dev didn't."

"Yeah, but *you* did. Because you were too cool to trick-or-treat, remember?" He shakes his head, staring out at the flight line again. "You were always so serious, so dedicated. You always knew exactly what you were doing and how you were doing it."

"I didn't always."

"Yeah, when your grandparents died. I remember."

"But then you came back from your tours in Iraq and straightened me out."

"You were already on your way to straightening out. You just needed to get your shit figured out first."

"Did I ever thank you for what you did for me? For giving me a job and something to get up for in the morning?"

"Many times. Have I ever thanked you back?"

"For what?"

Ozzie puts his hand on Thibault's shoulder. "For always being my best friend. For always standing by my side. For being the best partner and co-worker a guy could have."

I am so happy for Thibault and Ozzie. I've never had a friend like that. Thibault deserves it, though. It makes me want to hug Ozzie for being there for him. If he hadn't, maybe Thibault wouldn't have been at that coffee shop that day, and he wouldn't have stepped off that curb without looking, and I wouldn't have hit him . . .

Thibault puts his hands on his hips, drops his head, and shakes it slowly. "You've been married too long, my friend. May is really rubbing off on you."

"You got a problem with that?"

Thibault looks up. "Hell, no, I don't have a problem with that. You were way too mean before you met her. And besides . . . she was right, that beard *was* ugly as shit."

Ozzie tips his head back and laughs. "I keep telling her I'm going to grow it back. Every time she tries to make me wear a pink shirt, I tell her I'm putting my razor away for good."

"If I ever see you in a pink shirt, I'm going to shoot you, so you don't need to worry about the beard."

Ozzie puts Thibault in a friendly headlock. "Please do. I'll make myself a nice big target."

The doctor picks up his bag and stops in the doorway, hesitating as he sees the men wrestling. I walk up to the guys. "I don't mean to break up the lovefest, but I think the doctor wants to go now."

Ozzie and Thibault separate, and Ozzie comes over to me.

"Mika, how would you feel about going to talk to Detective Holloway and giving him that code?" He looks at me and Thibault. "I don't know what's going on with the FBI. We can look into that. But the chief of police at the NOPD has given me his assurances that Holloway is a good guy."

"I don't know." I look at Thibault. "What do you think I should do?"

"I think you should trust my best friend and go talk to the detective, but I don't want you to do anything you're not comfortable doing. I trust whatever decision you make, and I'll support it."

"Okay, then." I stand there looking at these big men. I remember Jenny hunched over her computer telling me things about my friend Alexei and the assurances they gave me that they'd look for him. I realize that I trust the Bourbon Street Boys more than anyone else. And I believe Thibault when he says Tee and I will be safe.

"That's what I'll do. Give the code to Holloway if you think it'll help me."

Ozzie claps his hands together and rubs them. "Let's go. We'll take my car."

"What about your SUV?" I ask Thibault.

"We'll get it later."

The three of us get into Ozzie's car and wave to the doctor as he drives away in his own vehicle. Thibault rides in the front seat next to Ozzie while I take a seat in the back next to the baby. I curl up next to him, resting my head on the seat and closing my eyes. I'm drifting off to sleep when Ozzie's whisper weaves its way into my brain.

"She's tough. Brave," he says so softly I almost don't hear it over the radio that's playing.

"She sure is."

"I always hoped she'd come along eventually."

"She?"

"The girl who could crack your shell and get into the soft inside you hide so well."

Thibault laughs. "I *know* that didn't come from you."

"Yeah, so what. It came from May, but I don't disagree."

"You are so whipped."

"Yeah, well, welcome to the club."

CHAPTER FORTY-ONE

The next two days pass by like a whirlwind. The Bourbon Street Boys have a lot of pull at the NOPD and with the local office of the FBI. They arrange everything while I hang out with Thibault in their warehouse apartment, nursing my baby back to health and finding out even more reasons to fall for this man who still wants to be my superhero.

Thibault and I spend half the days and most of the nights lying in each other's arms, talking about our pasts, mostly. We don't discuss the future much because it's so unclear. I don't think either of us wants to risk tempting fate.

I finally feel safe and secure, though. I know it's probably temporary, but I allow myself to enjoy it while I have it. The Bourbon Street Boys' office warehouse is as close to a fortress as I could hope for. While we stay upstairs in Ozzie's apartment, Dev and Lucky take turns on guard duty, stationed on the ground floor, monitoring the security cameras that watch the entire building and the area surrounding it.

Although Tee is still sick, at least his fever is finally gone and he's eating again. I've actually gotten a few hours of sleep too, and with Ozzie cooking for us, we've been eating like royalty. I'm as ready as I'll ever be for my joint interview with the NOPD and the FBI.

I'm allowed to bring one person into the interrogation room for my deposition. Now that they have the data and the codes to decrypt everything, all they need is me on camera saying that it's all real—that I'm the person who created the data, saved it, encrypted it, and then presented it to them. I wanted Thibault to come with me, but he's insisting I bring my attorney.

"You have to, babe. I don't want them to try to mess you up. This lady knows the law, and I don't."

"Are you going to be here when I'm done? They said it'll take hours."

He's holding Tee in his arms as we stand in the hallway at the police station. He lifts him up higher. "Baby Tee and Big Tee are going to be right here. We're not leaving this spot." He points at the conference room. "I'm just going to be on the other side of the wall from you. As soon as you walk out the door, you'll have a hungry baby here who can't wait to see you."

"Have you thought any more about what you want to do?" I ask, glancing over my shoulder at the room. The door opens, revealing six people inside waiting for me. Ozzie warned us: they're going to offer me witness protection, and it's possible I can negotiate bringing someone with me. Thibault and I both heard him say it this morning on the way over, but I haven't had the guts to actually ask him if he wants to come with me. His entire life is here. I don't want to put him in the position of having to choose, but I'm going in there with all those people who want to rake me over the coals, and I desperately need to know if I'm going to leave here alone and have to start my life over without him.

He nods, his brows drawn together and his mouth turned down. "I have. But let's talk about it when you get out of there. I don't want you to stress out about it. Everything is going to be fine." He's anxious, like me.

"If you can't . . . you know . . . come with me, I understand. I want you to, don't get me wrong, but asking you to leave your family and your friends and your job . . . It's too much." My eyes are bright with tears. "I can't do that."

"Stop worrying about it . . . please? Just go in there and talk to them. One thing at a time."

"Ms. Cleary? Could you step inside, please?" Detective Holloway has what looks like his best suit on. He's gesturing to an empty chair on the opposite side of the table.

"I'll be right here."

Thibault leans over and kisses me. "Hurry up. This baby's gonna wake up soon, and I won't have what he's looking for."

I kiss Tee on the head and turn around to leave. As I reach the door I look over my shoulder at Thibault. "Thanks. For everything."

"Love you." He blinks a few times after he says it, looking a little shell-shocked. I think the words came out a lot louder than he planned. Or maybe he wasn't planning on saying them at all.

His declaration is like a ray of light bursting through black clouds to brighten my life. I'm smiling when I walk into the room, which is a hell of a lot better than what I was doing a split second before Thibault opened his mouth and let his heart fall out on the floor—namely, freaking out. Now I'm just having some heart palpitations, but that's okay. I'm getting used to this roller coaster of emotions that I've been riding since we met.

As the door shuts, I look out at him from the tiny square window and mouth the words: "You are so crazy." I love him too . . . so much. But I'm not going to say it now and influence him into doing something he shouldn't. Whatever happens next between us has to be his decision, without guilt, without expectation, and without illusions.

CHAPTER FORTY-TWO

The baby is finally asleep, and Thibault and I are in bed together. We're in my favorite spot: tangled in each other's arms, breathing in each other's scent. I could never get tired of this. I'm going to miss it so much it hurts.

"Are you happy with how it turned out?" he asks. He sounds so friendly. So cool. We're both pretending it's no big deal that Tee and I are going away.

"Yes." I can't tell him how sad it makes me to leave him behind. I have to pretend I got everything I wanted.

"Did they say how long you'll be gone?"

"They just said they don't know. It could be years. It could be forever. It totally depends on what happens with the trial and how many of Pavel's people they can pull in with their sting operation."

"We should know in the next couple weeks," Thibault says. "They have the data. They have all his contacts and the connections, thanks to you. Now it's just a matter of the FBI and NOPD working together with their manpower to tie it all up."

"Yep." I don't want to talk about it anymore. I just want to forget any of this is happening. I can't keep up the charade that it's not killing me to leave him behind.

"I told you I loved you today," he says softly.

My face grows warm and my heart beats stronger. "Yes, you did."

"And you called me crazy."

"Yes, I did." He is crazy. And so am I, unfortunately.

"Is that nuts? To fall in love with someone after knowing her for only a week?"

"I don't think so." I slide my hand across his chest. "Plenty of people do. Lots of people believe in love at first sight."

"Do you?"

"Maybe."

He lifts my chin with his finger. "You are making me crazy, you know that?"

My hand stills. "Do you want me to stop touching you?"

"You know that's not what I'm talking about."

I roll away and sit up, my back to him. I'm trying to make this easier on him, but he's making it impossible.

"What's wrong?" he asks.

I shake my head. "Nothing."

He rubs my back. "Please talk to me."

Tears are burning my eyes, and my throat is instantly sore from the effort of holding them back. "I can't. It's too hard."

He sits up and slides over to be next to me. We're both facing the wall at the edge of the bed. He holds my hand and rests it on his thigh. "You haven't told me whether you negotiated a third seat on that plane out of here."

My heart is aching so badly, it has to be getting a crack in it. "I don't think it's a good idea."

"Why?" he asks.

I'm surprised by the pain I hear in his voice. I look up to find his expression anguished.

"Because!" I throw my hand up. "Look at this place! This is *your* place. These are *your* people. This is what you were born to do!"

"But I can do what I do from anywhere in the world."

"But what about your friends? Your family?"

His face crumples and his eyes fill with tears. "I'll miss them."

I shake my head at him. "You would walk away from the best friends you've had for your whole life and your family . . . for me?"

He drops his face into his hand. He sits there for a really long time. I don't dare move. Everything hangs in the balance. I'm either going to walk out of here tomorrow to start everything on my own, or do it as part of a team. It's a lose-lose proposition; both options will bring great pain to this man I've grown to love. The choices I made five years ago are wreaking absolute havoc today, and there's nothing I can do about it but watch it happen.

He lifts his head and looks at me, his eyes no longer shiny with tears. "I meant what I said. I love you. I love Little Thibault. But I love my family and my friends, too."

I nod. "I understand." I pull my hand away as my heart caves in on itself.

"No, I don't think you do." He takes my hand back. "I've spent a lot of years not thinking. Going through the motions. Doing what I had to do to get the job done. Doing what everyone expected of me."

"We all do that."

"Maybe. And I thought I was going to be this guy who sat on the sidelines of his family. Watching everyone else get married, have kids. I was happy to be the favorite uncle."

"You're great with kids." I'm crying. I can't help it.

"But I've started thinking again. I stopped for a while. My sister's troubles really shook my world. More than I realized."

"Understandable."

"And I've realized something about myself."

"What's that?"

He looks at me. "I don't want to be the guy who watches everyone else have a family."

"You don't have to be. I'm sure there are hundreds of girls in N'Orleans who'd happily give you as many babies as you want." It kills me to say that, but I have to be fair to him.

"But I don't want any of those girls."

"You don't?" My heart feels like it's on fire.

"No. I want the one who drives up one-way streets going the wrong direction. Who makes spaghetti sauce with ketchup. Who worries about everyone else before she worries about herself."

I point at myself, my chin trembling. He's fighting for me. He's saving me. "This girl?"

He takes my finger and kisses it. "Yes, you nut. You. It's you I want."

I shake my head, not daring to believe this is real. He sure looks like he's telling the truth, though. "Your family is going to hate me."

"No, they won't. They'll understand."

"Toni is going to strangle me with her bare hands."

"Toni is going to be happy for me. You'll see." He moves back onto the bed and lies down. "Come over here and cuddle me, woman."

I look at him, taking in his kind eyes, his broad chest, his smile . . . and I don't hesitate. The entire world could be against us, and I'd still be willing to take the risk to be with him.

"Trust me," he says as I settle in and he strokes my back. "Everything is going to work out for the best."

"I trust you. I do." I close my eyes and let myself imagine a life with this man and my child, the baby he helped bring into the world. It fills me with such warmth and love, it almost scares me.

CHAPTER FORTY-THREE

T his is crazy," Toni says. She's pissed. "I can't believe nobody could come up with a better solution than witness protection for an indeterminate length of time."

We're sitting around the conference table at Bourbon Street Boys, Thibault and I holding hands while his family and friends stare at us. Baby Tee is in his car seat on the floor nearby, ready to go.

Lucky has his arm around his wife's shoulders. "Babe, you don't need to make it more difficult than it already is. They have to go. They don't have a choice."

She shrugs his arm off. "I'm not making anything more difficult. I'm just saying what everybody else is thinking. Of course they have a *choice*."

Jenny looks at Toni and shakes her head. "Honey . . . don't."

Toni glares at her friend. "Don't *honey* me." She reaches up and swipes angrily at her eyes, her tears the only sign I have that she's got any kind of softness to her.

"I'm sorry," I say. I really mean it, with all my heart.

Thibault puts his hand on my arm. "Don't apologize." He looks at his sister. "I wish we could do this some other way, but we can't."

May comes over and bends to hug him and then me. "We get it. Toni is sad and upset, but she understands."

"No, I *don't* understand. Don't speak for me, May. This doesn't make any *sense*." She glares at her brother. "You've only known this girl for a week. How is it that I've known you your entire *life* . . ." She gestures at the people standing around the table. ". . . And these people have all known you since you were a *kid*, and yet you choose to be with her over us? How is that possible?"

"I'm not choosing between you like that. Don't think that." He runs his hands through his hair. I can tell he's stressed to the max. I feel like a monster for putting him in this position.

"Then explain it to me again, because I don't get it."

"I've already told you five times; I can't control how I feel. And there's no way in hell that I'm going to let Mika and her baby disappear into thin air where I'll never see them again. I can't do that."

"But you're going to let the rest of us disappear into thin air? You're going to make yourself disappear into thin air so we can never speak to you again? What about my kids? What about Melanie and Vic . . . ?" Her voice breaks and she can't continue. Lucky folds her into his arms.

Tears rush to my eyes, and I get up and turn around so nobody will see them. This is the most awful thing I've ever done in my life—worse than selling my body, worse than working for a criminal. I hate that circumstances have forced Thibault into making this choice—me, a girl he just met, or them, his family and friends. How can I possibly be worth that? My shoulders slump in defeat.

"Maybe we shouldn't," I say, turning to him. "It's going to kill them. It's not fair to your family."

Thibault stands quickly, wincing at the pain it brings his knee. "Bullshit, Mika. I'm going with you. You're not going to be a martyr for them." He turns and glares at his sister. "This is happening. I

307

know you don't like it, Toni. I know this hurts you. And if I could take that hurt away, I would."

"You could, you just won't." She folds her arms across her chest.

"That's enough," Lucky says, surprising everyone with his volume.

The entire room goes silent and watches Toni turn to her husband.

"You know I love you, Toni. More than anything in this world. But you're being really selfish right now, and you need to cut it out."

Her jaw drops open. "What?"

He takes her by the head, his strong hands on either side of her jaw. "I love you. Look at me."

She closes her eyes, tears coming out.

"Look at me," he says more softly.

She opens her eyes at his command. They're bloodshot and watery. More tears fall.

"I love you. You love me. We stand by Thibault no matter what. He's a smart and loving man, and he doesn't do anything without thinking it all the way through."

"You act like I don't know this about my own brother."

"Then you also know that he needs to live his own life. And right now, that life isn't here. It's somewhere else. But one day, he'll be back. Your love . . . our love will bring him back."

Toni holds on to his hands. "You can't guarantee me that."

He nods. "Yes, I can. I just did. Believe in me like I believe in you."

The only consolation I take in separating Thibault from his sister is knowing she has this great guy next to her. Lucky's words make me wish once again that I could redo my life so I wouldn't be here making them all say goodbye today.

Toni looks like she's going to resist, and then she nods once. He pulls her into his chest and rests his chin on her head for a few moments. Then they slowly turn away, getting up and walking over to a far corner of the room. My heart aches for them.

Thibault clears his throat. "I love all of you with all my heart, and I've loved working with you for too many years to count. I've known most of you since I was a kid and one of you since the moment she was born."

He looks over at Toni. I think she's listening. I hope she is.

"And for a lot of years this place was my second home. I woke up every single day happy and excited to be with each one of you, standing side by side with you doing this work that we do for New Orleans."

He looks at the big man to my right. "Ozzie, you and I don't have the same mother, but you're my brother just the same." He looks at Dev and Lucky, who has turned around. "You guys, too. That's not going to change. I don't care how far away I go, what my name ends up being, what happens to me in my new life, that is *not* going to change." He pauses. "I will come back to you if I can. I promise you that."

"We know you will," May says. She looks at her sister. "Not that anybody can hide from us if we want to find him anyway."

Ozzie shakes his head at her, telling her to be quiet. She puts her head down, pretending to obey, but I think I know her better than that.

"I know you all think I'm crazy. And I know you love me and that's why you're worried about me. But I want you to look at the person that *you* fell in love with right now and ask yourself . . . if the world came to you and told you to choose between the Bourbon Street Boys or that person standing next to you, which one would you choose?"

Until he said that, I hadn't truly appreciated what this meant to him, the question he'd asked himself before making his decision to come with Tee and me. When I look around the room at what and who he's walking away from—for me and my son—it blows my mind. I know I should only look inside myself to determine my own worth, but it means something special when a man like Thibault chooses me over a beautiful life filled with wonderful, good people. The only thing I can do is try to be worthy of that love, to work every day to be the kind of woman who deserves it.

The room goes completely silent. He lets his words sink in before he continues. "I know you guys love me as much as I love you, and I know you love this job as much as I do, and I know you love *Ozzie* as much as I do . . . but I don't believe for a second that any one of you would choose *this* over the person you fell in love with. So I hope you can understand why I have to go."

Before anybody can say anything, the bell downstairs rings, signaling that somebody is standing outside the warehouse wanting to come in.

Ozzie goes over to the intercom and turns on the video screen. Detective Holloway is standing downstairs. I can see him from across the room as he looks up at the camera.

"Can I come up? There's been a development."

My heart stops beating for what seems like a really long time. I massage my chest. It feels like I'm having a heart attack. This can't be good.

"A development?" May speaks up. "What's that mean?" She looks at her sister. "Is that good news or bad news?"

Jenny flaps her hand at May. "We're about to find out. Shush."

Ozzie gestures at the door. "Dev, would you handle that?"

"You got it." He slaps Thibault on the shoulder as he runs by, winking at us as he moves to the door. Within a minute, the giant warehouse doors open and Dev can be seen on the screen escorting the detective into the building.

"Do you want something to drink?" Thibault asks me, touching my arm lightly.

I shake my head no. I'm too sick to drink. My stomach is doing flips and my heart feels like it's going to explode.

He limps over to the kitchen to pour himself a cup of coffee. He takes his first sip and winces. He comes back over and sits down, gesturing for me to join him at the table. I do, holding his hand on the arm of his chair.

Holloway appears in the doorway and doesn't waste any time. He doesn't even take a seat. "Have you guys turned on the news?"

CHAPTER FORTY-FOUR

We all look at one another, shaking our heads.

"All right then, let me be the first one to fill you in." He doesn't look happy. "The FBI and the NOPD put together a joint task force to move in on Pavel Baranovsky's assets. The time of execution was oh-seven-hundred this morning. The intent was to catch most of them sleeping so we could maximize our arrests. Unfortunately, someone beat us to the punch."

"What?" Ozzie moves in closer.

"Yeah. Somebody managed to get in there and pop him. He was already cold by the time we entered the residence."

"Pop him?" May looks at Ozzie. "Like they punched him? Or with a gun?"

Holloway looks at her like she's kidding. "Yeah, with a gun. Fifteen times, last I heard. They're still counting the holes."

My hands go ice-cold and I feel dizzy. *Pavel is dead? Really dead?* "Who killed him?" I ask. My voice echoes in my head. *Who killed him? Who killed him? Who killed him?*

"We don't know. But we had a feeling something big was going down when we first started talking about this case. That's why we wanted to get in there with Mika." He points at me. "She was on our source list, but we were talking with other people on the inside, too."

"Sonia," I say.

"Yeah. Sonia. Your roommate."

"But she turned me in to Pavel. She told him where I was."

He shakes his head. "No, she didn't. Not like that. He checked her phone and forced her to tell him where you were."

"Oh." Now I feel terrible. She didn't rat me out.

He nods. "Yeah, well, didn't help her. She was killed too."

I wish I hadn't doubted her. "But who?" I ask. "Who would do that?" I look at the people standing around me. "He had lots of enemies, but he was well protected. No one would dare . . ."

"Do you have any leads?" Thibault asks.

"Not exactly. But I've got some other good news/bad news for ya." He frowns at me.

"What's that?" Ozzie asks.

"You know that code you gave us for that software program?"

"Yes." I lean toward Thibault, wanting to be closer to him and the safety he offers.

"It's not working anymore. We used it exactly like you told us to, but now it doesn't work."

"But surely you printed out all the evidence the first time you got in, so why do you need to get in another time?" Jenny asks.

"Yeah, we printed everything out. But now that everybody's digging into it to verify stuff, we're finding accounts closed, businesses shut down, names that don't exist anymore. It's like it never happened." He looks at all of us. "We're completely stumped. The only thing we're absolutely sure of is that Mika has nothing to do with it."

Relief floods through me so deeply it makes me dizzy.

"What makes you say that?" Toni asks. "What makes you so sure?"

"She showed us everything. She was completely transparent. We dug, believe me, we dug. Everything checked out. And we talked to the software developer she used. He confirmed what she said." He drops his head, shaking it. "We're screwed."

"Maybe we can help," Jenny says.

Everyone in the room turns to look at her. She smiles tentatively. "We know the way the organization is set up. I mean, it's not like these arms dealers or sex traffickers are going to disappear off the face of the earth. They're just going to use other names. But you know, everybody leaves footprints behind. Even when they're online."

"Footprints?" Holloway asks. "What do you mean?"

"People who know how to maneuver online . . . they all have an individual style. After a while you start to notice that style, after you've spent a little time looking at their work. It's kind of like a footprint they leave behind wherever they go, so you can see where they've been. When you see that footprint again and again, it gets easier and easier to recognize it." She shrugs. "I think we could probably track these people down if we had enough time and resources."

"What kind of resources?" Holloway asks.

Jenny looks at Ozzie. "We could probably figure something out."

Ozzie nods. "Yeah, we could do that. I'll send you an estimate if you want."

"Yeah. Why don't you do that? Send it right to the chief."

"So are we a go for our departure at sixteen-hundred?" Thibault glances at his watch, waiting for Holloway to respond.

Holloway shakes his head. "Nope."

"Why not?" Thibault and I ask at the same time.

"Because. Like I said, the whole thing is kaput. Dissolved. *Nada comida.* There's no more need for witness protection because there's not gonna be a trial."

His words make my heart temporarily stop beating. I put my hand to my chest as it thumps back to life.

"But . . . Mika could still be in danger." Thibault puts his arm around me.

"From who?" He looks around the room. "Everything she knew about the organization doesn't exist anymore. Whoever is behind this is a fucking genius." He turns around and heads toward the door. "I gotta get back to the district. You'll be given a more formal briefing by the chief. He just asked me to come over here and give you the basics."

My ears are burning. *Who? Who is responsible for this?* The face that pops into my head is Sebastian's. He's the most hooked in, the most trusted associate, the smartest and most capable. But it could have been someone I don't know, too. Pavel was running arms, and I didn't know about that.

Dev walks over to escort him out of the building. The detective stops at the door that leads out into the room beyond the kitchen and turns to face us. "In all my years of working on the force, I have *never* gotten this close to a case this big and then had it pulled so completely out from under me . . . I gotta retire. I can't handle this shit anymore."

He leaves the room, and we sit there looking at one another. Thibault and I stand, both of us a little shell-shocked, I think.

"Well, I guess that solves that problem," Toni says. She looks exhausted.

Lucky comes over and puts his arms around Thibault, slapping him on the back pretty hard several times. "Glad to have you back, man."

"Glad to be back." Thibault finally smiles, and it looks as though a huge weight has been lifted from his shoulders.

Lucky comes to me next, giving me a hug too.

"I don't know what to say." I'm afraid to believe it's real. I want to yell and cry and sing, but I'm too stunned to do anything.

He pulls back and looks at me. "Don't say anything. There's no need." He gives me a charming smile and then moves on, making room for everyone else to hug Thibault.

Toni is the last one in line. She holds her brother for a really long time. I start to think it would be better if I just left, but she grabs my arm as I begin to walk away.

"Not so fast," she says.

I pull my arm from her hand but stand my ground. I lift my chin, waiting for the hateful words that are sure to come.

"You'd better be good to him."

"Of course I will be."

"Toni, ease up," Thibault says.

I hold up my hand at him, never breaking eye contact with Toni. "No, I got this." I pause, taking in her attitude, her stance, her expression. She's tough, yeah, but she has her vulnerabilities. I saw one today, but I'm not going to take advantage of it. "I respect your relationship with your brother and the love you all have for each other. I won't do anything to interfere with that."

She nods once. "See that you don't."

"But don't think you can disrespect me just because I'm a nice person. I love your brother, but that does not give you a free pass. Are we clear?"

The corner of her mouth twitches. "Yeah, we're clear."

"Okay!" Thibault claps his hands together once. "Well, that was fun. Anybody want to celebrate with a beer?"

"We can't. We're pregnant," says a chorus of voices.

All the men in the room stop moving and stare at the three women who just spoke up: Jenny, May, and Toni.

I hold up a finger. "And I'm breastfeeding, so . . ."

"Holy shit, that's a lot of estrogen," Dev says, fear in his eyes.

CHAPTER FORTY-FIVE

Thibault holds me and Tee together in his arms, right there in the conference room, swaying to some inner rhythm that's flowing between us. My eyes are closed as I soak up the feelings and try to deal with the storm of emotions raging inside me. He was ready to walk away from everything for me, but now he doesn't have to. We get to have it all. It's overwhelming. Too much.

Somebody clears her throat, and whoever she is, she's standing very close. I open my eyes to find May just behind Thibault wearing a big grin.

"Can we help you with something?" Thibault asks, twisting around to see her.

"You guys are invited to the pizza party that's about to start in about a half hour."

"Pizza party?" Thibault sounds like she just invited him to have surgery on his knee without anesthetic.

"I love pizza parties," I say enthusiastically. I pull away from Thibault and smile at her. My heart is soaring into the heavens. For the first time in my life, I'm thinking fate doesn't hate me.

May gets in close and tickles the baby's neck. "Yay! I get to soak up all the baby love."

"Not so fast," Jenny says from behind her. "You have to share."

May glares at her sister. "You're going to have one of your own soon. This one's mine. Go away."

"So are you."

"Yeah, but yours is due first." She goes back to tickling Tee.

I look up at Thibault, smiling. I can't believe he's not being forced to choose between us anymore. And I'm actually participating in one of those parties I saw in his photo album. It feels like a dream. "You like pizza parties, don't you?"

He winces. "Love 'em. Love all the noise, and the kids yelling, and the dogs barking . . ."

I reach up on tiptoes to kiss him gently on the lips. "Yeah, you do."

He sighs and puts his arms around me. "I do now."

CHAPTER FORTY-SIX

The men are enjoying a few beers in the backyard together, and we girls are in the kitchen laughing about the goofy things our men do when they're tired and too scatterbrained from getting up in the night with kids to think straight. All the children are upstairs, including Tee, who's sound asleep next to a baby monitor. The receiver is on the kitchen counter, and it's completely silent. *Bliss.*

The sound of the front door opening and closing comes down the hall, and then May's tiny dog, Felix, starts barking his head off. The bigger dog is outside in the backyard, and she rushes over to press her face against the sliding glass door, leaving a big drool mark.

"Who's that?" May asks, looking around. "Everyone's already here."

Toni is the first one to move. She walks quickly from the kitchen, Jenny and May right behind her.

By the time I get there, Toni is shouting and furniture is flying. A small side table that was in the front entrance hall lands in the living room, and Toni comes right behind it. She falls onto the floor, curled in a ball.

"Felix, no!" May yells at her dog as he barks and growls like a deranged, bloodthirsty beast. She and Jenny are holding each other, slowly backing down the hallway toward me. I stand there frozen in place, taking in the vision before me.

The tiny Chihuahua is busy yapping at a man's ankles, biting his pant leg and shaking it for all he's worth. And I know the man.

"Let Tamika go with me, and we will leave. No one will be hurt." The distinct Russian accent brings back so many memories. Not all of them are bad, either. I'm so confused.

"Alexei?" I take a couple steps forward, my heart filling with irrational joy at seeing him. "Where have you been, sweetie? Oh my god, I thought you were gone!" I move faster, anxious to hug him, to convince myself that he's really there and to help him understand that I'm okay and there's no need for him to be upset on my behalf. The poor guy thinks I need a rescue, apparently.

"Don't go," Jenny says, taking my arm, holding me back.

"Felix, come *here!*" May screams.

The dog stops barking and slinks away into the living room.

I pull myself from Jenny's grasp. "It's okay. He's not going to hurt anyone. He's just confused." I walk past the women as Toni gets to her feet. She looks like she wants to murder him as she wipes blood from the corner of her mouth with the back of her hand.

It's when I see that bright-red blood that it hits me . . . he's already hurt someone. I stop and glance at Toni again; a bruise is already coloring her cheek. She didn't just trip, she was punched. I look at Alexei and find an expression on his face that's never been there before. It chills my blood to see how much he looks like Pavel.

"What's going on here?" I ask him. "What did you do? How did you know I was here?" Suspicion rises up and overtakes the relief I was experiencing at seeing him alive.

"You are coming with me," he says, glaring.

I've never heard him talk like this before. He was always so happy when he was with me. Sometimes he got confused, but never angry. My mind desperately tries to come up with an explanation that makes sense. I've spent years getting to know this man. He can't be here to hurt anyone. *Whoever took over Pavel's operation told him what happened with me. He found out where I was staying from Pavel before Pavel was killed. He's lost his family and is looking for someone to help take care of him.* This has to be it. Alexei isn't like Pavel.

"Why don't we all just calm down and take a breath?" I say, holding out my hands.

The sound of pounding feet comes from above our heads. I look up, panicked the kids will get involved. Alexei is already confused enough; he doesn't need that chaos making things worse.

Jenny's voice rings out with a hysterical edge to it. "Kids! Stay upstairs! Nobody's allowed to come downstairs. Anyone who comes downstairs does *not* get dessert!"

"Okay, Mom!" comes a chorus of voices. A couple of them giggle.

The sound of running feet going in the opposite direction is like a drug, making me feel high with relief. The whirring of Jacob's wheelchair mixes in with their footsteps.

I take another step toward him. "Alexei, what is going on? What *happened* to you? Where did you go? I missed you."

Toni slowly moves out of the living room around the back side of it, disappearing from view.

"You do not have to worry about me, Tamika. You need to worry about you. You have information for me." His expression and voice turn downright sinister. "We will discuss in private."

This doesn't sound like Alexei *at all*. It's like another man has taken over his body. "Alexei, I don't know anything about anything. Whatever I knew is gone now." I stare at him, trying to piece this puzzle together. *Did someone put him up to this?* That has to be it. He's memorized a script. He loves repeating things he's heard.

"That is lie." He laughs. The sound reminds me of an evil clown in a funhouse. There's no real emotion to it. "You have good memory," he says. "You will tell me everything."

I keep talking, hoping this situation will start making sense soon. "Alexei, we're friends. I'll tell you whatever you want to know. I have nothing to hide."

"We are *not* friends," he says. "We are going now. You are coming with me." He holds out his hand. "Come."

He moves toward me, but I back away, pushing the women into the kitchen. I don't want to go with him. He looks crazed. Something terrible has happened to him; maybe he snapped when he lost his cousin. I need to stall him.

"But I don't want to leave the party." I try to sound cheerful, hoping to turn his mood around. "It's a pizza party. You like pizza. We can put some ketchup on it for you."

"No more *ketchup*!" He yells so loudly, it makes my ears hurt. "Your ketchup makes me sick! All you cook is with ketchup." He sneers, his bottom lip turning down almost to his chin.

"But I thought you liked the ketchup." I feel like I'm trapped in a seriously weird nightmare with no way out. Nothing is how it should be.

"'I thought you liked the ketchup,'" he mimics. "And you thought I was stupid, too. I guess you are not as smart as you think."

My heart lurches as an idea starts worming its way into my brain. *Could I really be that clueless?*

"All that time, I watch you," he says. "I see you. I hear you. Pavel was right. You are not *sem'ya*. We cannot trust you." He smiles, obviously proud of himself. "I am the *shpion* living on your couch."

I go dizzy as the blood leaves my head. *Oh, sweet Jesus.* Apparently I *am* that clueless. Alexei was spying on me the whole time.

The disappointment crashes over me, making me think I'm going to suffocate from it. This man I cared about, who I was willing to risk my child's and my own safety for, was playing me all along. He was Pavel's eyes and ears, and I never saw it. Not even a glimmer of his treachery came through the façade he'd created.

Bitterness rises up and takes over my mouth. "I never wanted to be in your horrible *sem'ya*, Alexei, but I guess you already knew that." I mumbled plenty of negative things about his family over the years when he was hanging around. I shudder at how much he was probably able to reveal to Pavel. I'm lucky to be alive.

"Yes. And when Pavel sees you are pregnant, he send me away. He knows all your secrets, even the ones you don't share with me. Then he doesn't care about you anymore. Only baby. Too bad you have baby and get away from hospital before he take him away. Lucky for you, maybe, because you would be dead and baby would be with him." He sneers. "But I don't care about baby. Too much trouble, babies. Baby stays here, you go with me."

My ears are ringing. I can't believe what I'm hearing. "Pavel knew I was pregnant? How?"

He shrugs his massive shoulders. "You are fat and you are sick. It is not hard to see."

"But . . . he never said anything." A heartless Russian gangster knew I was pregnant, and I didn't. My mind is officially blown.

Out of the corner of my eye, I see a figure standing in the kitchen to my right. *Thibault.* He's got something in his hand, above his shoulder. *His crutch.* I back up another step. If I can just draw Alexei in, Thibault could crack him over the head with it. I grit my teeth and make the decision: We're a team, Thibault and I. We can take Alexei down together, that sonofabitch.

"We can talk about Pavel outside," he says. "Come." He holds out his hand.

"Um, no, thanks. I think I'll stay here." I back up another step.

"All these people in here," Alexei says, looking at whoever is standing behind me, "they invite you to pizza party? Did you tell them you are not loyal person?"

"What are you talking about? I was loyal." I pause. "Until I wasn't." Yeah, if Pavel were still alive, he probably wouldn't consider me loyal at all.

"You helped foreigner take my cousin's business. You thought nothing of *me*." He jabs his finger into his chest.

Now I'm back to being confused. "What? I have no idea what you're talking about."

"Sebastian! He took business from Pavel and from me. He is not *sem'ya*, he is foreigner. You let him in."

"I didn't let anyone do anything! Pavel was his contact, not me!"

"But what about *me*?!" he yells, pointing at his chest again. "You forgot about *me*!"

Everyone disappears from view. I have the strangest sensation that I'm alone in this house with a madman. "Alexei, how can you blame me? You always acted like the most important thing in the world to you were your Legos. I had no idea you wanted to run the business. I didn't even think you *could*." None of this makes sense. *How could he even imagine being able to run a business like Pavel's?*

He sneers again. "I was doing my job. Pavel told me, 'Watch Tamika,' and it was a good way. You are always so paranoid. You never say anything to anybody, you never do anything with anybody, you always stay on outside. But to a man who is a child, you say everything. So stupid."

I shake my head at both his naïveté and mine. "For five years, you acted like you had a developmental disability so you could spy on me, and yet somehow that was supposed to make me think you were someone who could take over a multimillion-dollar business?" I snort in disbelief. "I'm pretty sure I'm not the stupid one in the room."

He pounds his chest with his fist. "It is a *big* job. It is a *big* job for a *big* man."

I feel almost intoxicated as what he's saying finally comes together and makes some kind of twisted sense: Alexei was trying to prove his worth and loyalty to Pavel, and when Pavel saw that Alexei wasn't the sharpest knife in the drawer but could still be useful, he gave him a simple job he knew he could handle, all the while leading the poor sap on by telling him one day he'd earn a place at the head table for his sacrifices. Alexei got played as badly as I did.

"You were doing all that so Pavel would trust you and bring you into the business."

"We all do what we have to do. It is for *sem'ya*. Family and loyalty. You know nothing of this. You are not *sem'ya*."

I almost feel sorry for this poor delusional bastard. "But he was never going to do that, Alexei. He was always going to keep everything for himself."

"You do not know this! Shut up!" He lunges at me, pulling a gun from behind his back.

Time seems to move in slow motion as I stumble away and look over at Thibault standing to my right, hidden from Alexei's view.

The gun rises and points at my face.

Alexei's finger is on the trigger, and then . . .

Thibault's crutch comes down in a large arc from above, just as I pass by on my way down to the floor. I'm falling . . .

The aluminum crutch makes contact with the barrel of the gun and smacks it out of Alexei's hand.

The heavy weapon tumbles to the floor and discharges, a loud bang sending the gun skittering sideways into the edge of the stairs.

Several screams follow, one of them mine.

Something stings my leg like the fires of hell.

I fall onto my back and reach down to touch my leg. I feel something warm and wet there.

I roll onto my side as someone grabs my hand, pulling me across the floor. It's May, and she's dragging me away from the two men grappling in the hallway—Thibault and Alexei.

"Oh shit, you've been shot," Jenny says. She grabs a dish towel off the counter and wads it up. "Get me a belt," she shouts.

Toni whips hers off, dropping to her knees next to me.

Other bodies come flying through the kitchen, followed by a galloping dog that looks like a hound from hell, and then there's a lot of growling, grunting, and crashing.

"Knife!" Ozzie roars.

Then more crashing and deep barking.

Alexei's voice comes out in a higher pitch. "He is biting! Take him off!"

I look down at my leg, the sounds of the fight fading out as I realize how bad things are for me. "Am I going to die?" I feel weak at the sight of quickly reddening dish towels. "God, that's a lot of blood."

"Nope. You're not allowed to die," Toni says.

"Why not?" I ask, because apparently *now* is the perfect time for more stupid conversations.

She glares at me. "Because my brother loves you, idiot." She yanks her belt tight over the dishrag covering the hole in my leg. "If you die, I will never forgive you."

I laugh and cry at the same time.

May puts her hand on my cheek. "Are you okay, honey?"

"I think she likes me," I say, still crying.

"She's going into shock," May says. "Somebody call 9-1-1!" She stands and leaves me there with Jenny and Toni.

I take Toni by the arm and make her look at me. "If I die, please make sure to put Thibault's name on the birth certificate."

"I'm sure it's already on there," she says.

"No, I mean your brother's name. Put him as the father."

"Isn't it too late for that?" she asks, frowning at me.

I shake my head. "No. I refused to fill out the form in the hospital."

She shakes her head. "No. I'm not doing that. Do it yourself."

My mouth drops open as she stands up and walks away. I look at Jenny, stricken. "She is so cruel."

Jenny smiles as she wipes the floor. "It means she likes you. Consider it a compliment." She pats me on the shoulder. "Cheer up . . . She could be your sister-in-law someday if you play your cards right."

I lie back on the floor and stare at the ceiling. "Oh, Jesus, help me."

CHAPTER FORTY-SEVEN

I'm exhausted." I look over my shoulder into the back seat. "So's the baby." Tee's been sleeping for three solid hours, poor little nugget.

"Me, too." Thibault lets out a loud yawn. "I could sleep for a week."

"Can you believe everything that's happened in the last twenty-four hours?" I ask.

"Nope."

I sigh, reaching down gingerly to touch my bandaged leg. "Alexei showing up and getting his ass kicked at the barbecue, a five-hour hospital visit for a bullet through my leg, our second trip to the police station in less than a week . . ."

"Unbelievable," Thibault says.

"If you had tried to tell me in any of the five years I knew Alexei that he was not mentally disabled, I would've slapped you. I mean, his act was flawless."

Thibault shakes his head. "Well, he didn't strike me as a particularly brilliant guy, but I get what you're saying. Pavel was some kind of crazy evil genius to have thought that game up."

"I know. I guess if you're not part of the family, their stupid *sem'ya*, you're not to be trusted."

"It depends on the family . . ." He looks over at me.

I try to smile. "Do you think yours will ever accept me?"

"They already have."

"But your sister's mad about me being with you." Even though she said what Jenny considered to be nice things to me on the kitchen floor, I still don't know that I believe it.

"My sister's always mad about something. She likes to be cranky. It's her favorite mood. Don't take it personally."

"You told me I remind you of her."

"Only in some ways. My sister's really loyal, really tough, really smart . . . Those are the things that remind me of her when I'm with you. But I think in general you're a happier and more positive person than she is."

"I'm not feeling very positive right now."

"Well, you should."

"Are you crazy? I just found out that I've been spied on for five solid years by somebody I thought had the mental capacity of a ten-year-old. I think it's pretty safe to say I am entirely clueless."

"No, I think it's safe to say you are a pawn in the middle of a very complicated scheme run by several different parties who all wanted control of a lot of bad-news business." He shrugs. "Who knows if the cops will ever be able to unwind it all?"

"Alexei was blaming Sebastian for everything, but the police and the FBI agents all said that Sebastian has disappeared. Do you think he's dead too?"

"I have no idea, but I'm sure we'll be looking into it. The important thing now is that he's gone and Alexei is too. He won't be getting out of prison, now that they think they can link him to all those murders by his DNA. And Pavel is dead. Whatever business he put together has been dismantled and regrouped, and there's nothing you can do to hurt them, so they couldn't give a flying hoot about you. Going after you will just bring them heat and attention they don't want. You're safe."

"I wish I could still do something. There're all those girls . . ."

329

Thibault looks at me and pats my arm. "We're not out of the game yet. Jenny was right; we can start looking at those digital footprints and tracking down the traffickers' movements. Those girls are going to get the help they need one way or another. But at least you're not in the middle of it anymore. At least you don't have a target on your back."

I rest my head on the seat, sighing and smiling. "This is the first time in years and years that I've felt safe." I tilt my head sideways and look at him. "And it's all because of you."

"I can't take all the credit. You've got to give yourself some of it, and my team was critical, too."

"Yeah. Your team is amazing. You are so lucky. I can't believe you were going to walk away from all of that and the people you love for *me*." It still makes my heart flutter to think of it.

He shrugs. "That's what you do when you love somebody."

"You love me?"

"I think I've already said that." He frowns playfully at me.

"You said it in the hallway of the police station. You didn't really *say* it, like, officially."

"Maybe I'll say it later." He's trying not to smile.

"Well, if you ever want to see me naked, you'd better."

He looks over at me and grins. "I love you, I love you, I love you, I love you."

"I love you too, Thibault."

He reaches across the seats to hold my hand, and I let myself drift off to sleep as he drives us home. Before I'm completely off in la-la land, his voice penetrates my cloudy brain.

"When exactly will I get to see you naked, do you think?"

I smile lazily. "Pretty soon, I think . . ."

CHAPTER FORTY-EIGHT

I find a note on the counter after dropping Baby Tee off at Toni and Lucky's place. They have him just for tonight. Now that my baby's officially four weeks old and sleeping through the night, Thibault and I can finally have an evening alone. I slip my shoes off as I read the handwriting that I know to be Thibault's:

> *Meet me upstairs. If you dare . . . (Remember that stamina thing? Yeah. You're in trouble.)*

My heart skips a beat, and then my body gets flushed all over. I take a few deep breaths to try to calm my racing pulse, but it does no good. I could not possibly be more nervous than I am now. We're finally going to consummate our relationship.

I make an about-face and head for the stairs. From the moment I saw him standing in front of my car, freshly tapped by my bumper, I thought he was hot. And as soon as he saw I was a woman in need that day, he lost that angry look on his face and went into superhero mode and started saving my life. One step at a time, one day at a time, he proved to me that he was the man for the job. Now, thanks to him and his team, I get to start my life over again, and I'm doing it right this time.

I'm still a numbers girl, but now I keep books for the good guys and not the bad guys. Thibault still thanks me daily for taking over the payroll duties at Bourbon Street Boys. And working from our new place with the baby by my side has made my life almost easy. Almost. Like all newborns, Tee can be a lot of work, but his happy little personality and all the help I get from the girls on the team makes it seem like a breeze compared to what it would have been like if I'd left New Orleans without looking back.

I slowly mount the stairs, wondering what Thibault has in store for me. He's proven to be very romantic and caring when he puts his mind to it. The house always has fresh flowers somewhere with a love note tucked inside. He even cooks for me sometimes when we're not eating over at Toni's place or ordering in. I don't care about that stuff, though. I live for our moments alone in bed, tangled in each other's arms, talking endlessly about our future.

I hear music playing softly behind our bedroom door. I push it open and see the room is lit with candles. Rose petals are on the floor and the bed. Thibault is nowhere in sight.

I slip inside and take off my clothing, no longer embarrassed by my body, which is strangely altered by pregnancy in ways I never imagined it could be. My belly is wider and no longer taut, my backside larger and softer, my breasts heavy and pendulous. Thibault says I'm perfect, and I tend to believe him, since we've both had a hard time keeping our hands off each other. Four solid weeks of nothing but heavy petting would be enough to test anyone's patience. I am so ready for this . . .

"There you are," he says, coming out of the bathroom. He's naked. Stunning. His manhood hangs down his leg, thick and dark.

I wait for him to approach, suddenly nervous. We've talked about this moment a lot, but talking and doing are totally different things.

He takes me in his arms and looks down at me. "Nervous?"

I nod. "A lot." A shiver moves through me.

"We'll go slow."

"Okay," I whisper as his lips come down to meet mine.

We kiss, slowly, deeply. My arms go up to rest at the back of his neck. His hands drift to my waist and then to my backside. He squeezes me gently toward him. I feel him going hard as we press into each other.

Little shocks of pleasure rocket through me as his hands roam my body and he moves his mouth to my neck. His hot breath on my recently kissed skin gives me shivers. My nipples are hard and he pauses to tweak them.

"You better ignore the girls tonight," I say, worried the mothering part of me will wake up and force me to put on a bra.

He moves his hand to my backside again. "No problem. I love your ass." He squeezes it and pushes into me again.

I reach down and take his hard length in hand, stroking it, reveling in its size and heat. "I can't wait to feel you inside me," I whisper against his neck.

He groans. "I'm trying so hard to go slow, but it's really tough."

I pull back and look up at him. "Don't go slow on my account."

He grins devilishly and leans down, picking me up in his arms in one big motion.

I scream in surprise and then laugh. "Be careful of your leg, fool!"

He limps over to the bed. "My leg is fine. I'll have my surgery next week and fix whatever we break tonight."

He places me on top of the rose petals and looks down at me. His glorious hard-on stands straight out from his body, his muscles flexed and cut, and his eyes dark and full of sexy promises.

I put my arms above my head and tilt my hips. "What are you looking at, hmm?"

He shakes his head. "The sexiest woman alive."

I try not to smile. "Oh, yeah? Why don't you come down here and say that? See what happens?"

He moves to the bottom of the bed.

I follow him with my eyes.

He lifts his chin at me. "Open your legs."

I shift my hips so I'm lying flat on my back. My knees come slightly apart. "Like this?"

"More."

I open them a little wider. "How about now?"

"More. Spread your legs all the way for me."

I let them drop open, a tiny bit of vulnerability sneaking in past my confidence. "Like this?"

He nods. "Just let me look at you for a couple seconds."

Those seconds tick by with agonizing slowness. I could worry about what's going on in his head, but I won't. Because this is Thibault, and I trust him more than any other human being on this earth.

"You are so beautiful," he says.

My body turns to liquid heat. I put my hand between my legs and touch myself. "You'd better get over here soon, or I'm going to get started without you."

He puts his hand on his dick as he moves closer to the bed. He gets on the mattress on his good knee and comes toward me. When he's between my legs he stops and licks his lips. "You ready for me?" The tip of his dick slides against my folds. It meets with no resistance. I've been ready for him since before I came up those stairs.

I nod.

"Oh yeah, you're ready." He positions himself. "You might want to hang on to something."

I grab the headboard behind me as he slides his hard length into me, inch by excruciating inch. My eyes fall closed and I moan. Then tears come. It feels amazing . . . beautiful . . . hot . . . meant to be.

His body presses against mine as he settles over me. "Oh my god, that feels so fucking good," he whispers.

I look up to see his face twisted in what could easily be pain, but I know it's pleasure.

"Is your knee okay?" I ask.

"Don't worry about my knee. I can't even feel that. All I can feel is you." He pulls out and pushes into me again, this time faster. Harder. His neck muscles bulge, the veins standing out. He looks fierce and sexy as hell.

I moan and let go of the headboard, grabbing on to him instead. He's killing me with what he's doing to me, pressing into me, stretching me, making me want more.

"Do it again," I beg.

And so he does. I hang on with my arms and then my legs too, as he pushes in and pulls out, setting up a rhythm that is first torturously slow but then so fast I feel like it's going to leave me behind. I grip him with my nails, the sweat of his skin making them slide and leave marks behind.

A flutter starts down between my legs and moves up into my core. Heat builds there. There's almost a tickling sensation and then a sense of leaving my body entirely as the warmth between us builds higher and higher.

"Thibault!" I scream, desperate to understand what's happening to me.

"Hang on, babe!" he grunts in my ear.

Sweat falls from his chest to pool with my own. I start to cry and whimper. Unable to hold back. "I think I'm having . . ."

A scream is torn from me as my body explodes with light. My insides are pulsing with need being satisfied. He moves against me, pulling this sensation from me, ripping it out of me, demanding it and taking it. He yells too, arching his back, driving into me with all his force. I'm dizzy. I feel like I'm falling. I hang on to him as I weep.

Eventually, when I feel like I can't take another moment of it, his movements slow, and I have to let him go. My muscles are aching and I have no strength left.

"Are you okay?" he asks, kissing me gently on the forehead. He stops and waits for me to answer.

"Yes." I reach up to wipe my eyes. "Just lost my mind a little bit there." I feel as though I've run a mile at top speed. I'm euphoric and a little dizzy.

He smiles. "I made you cry happy tears."

I can't help but grin back at him. "Yes, you did."

"Maybe we *should* call me Superman."

I grab him and kiss him hard on the mouth. "Maybe we should." I glance down. "Calling you the Man of Steel isn't that far off, I don't think."

He chuckles and nuzzles my neck. "You love me."

I smack him gently on the butt. "Yes, I do."

Cold air brushes across my skin as he separates himself and falls to the side.

"Oh shit," he says, sighing, his hand on his stomach as he looks at the ceiling.

I take a moment to get control of my emotions before rolling to my side so I can look at him. "What's up?" I ask. *God, I love this man so much.* He's so damn handsome it should be illegal.

He turns his head to look at me. "You make me really happy." He frowns.

"Then why do you look so sad?"

He grimaces and looks down for a moment at his leg. "My knee is killing me." He looks up at me, an apology in his eyes. "I don't think I can do that again until I have my surgery and recover."

I get up on hands and knees, moving toward him. "You mean it hurts your knee if I do this?" I straddle him, carefully positioning myself over his already responding dick.

A smile slowly takes over his face. "Mmm, I think I can manage this." He pulses his hips up a couple times, encouraging his hard-on to hurry up and get there. "Oh, yeah, I definitely can." His jaw bulges out as he grits his teeth and takes my waist in either hand. I love how he goes from sweet boyfriend to sexy lover in such a short space of time.

I smile too. "Well, all right then. Show me some of that stamina you were talking about."

"Yes, ma'am."

He slides into me and then spends the next several hours proving in several different ways that he really is Superman, not just outside the bedroom but inside it, too.

ABOUT THE AUTHOR

 Elle Casey, a former attorney and teacher, is a *New York Times*, *USA Today*, and Amazon bestselling American author who lives in France with her husband, three kids, and a number of horses, dogs, and cats. She has written more than forty novels in less than five years and likes to say she offers fiction in several flavors. These flavors include romance, science fiction, urban fantasy, action adventure, suspense, and paranormal.